FALLING THROUGH TIME

MISTS OF FATE BOOK 4

NANCY SCANLON

Cover photo and design: Kim Killion, The Killion Group

www.nancyscanlonbooks.com
Sign up for Nancy's newsletter:
https://www.nancyscanlonbooks.com/contact

For all those who love a happy ending.
And, of course, to Sean.

PROLOGUE

*S*hrimp.

No matter what the bride called it (coral, for the record), Gwendolyn Allen's bridesmaid dress was the color of cooked shrimp. With her mass of flaming red hair, Gwen thought she rather looked like a crustacean on fire.

Looking at the nine (nine!) other bridesmaids, Gwen felt a flash of camaraderie. Shrimp wasn't *anyone's* color.

The wedding reception was one of the biggest parties to hit Boston in years. *People* magazine won exclusive photography rights for the event, but the entertainment shows had reporters there, too.

Gwen's cousin, Kristen Bouchemont, was kind of a big deal. The most famous socialite on the East Coast was finally getting married, and Gwen herself was still surprised. Looking at the bride and groom, there wasn't any doubt in her mind that the union was a true one; for the first time in her life, Kristen looked really happy.

"Gwendolyn, stand up a bit taller. Look at all the potential husbands here!" her mother whispered urgently.

"Mom—" Gwen warned. She always wondered how her mother managed to sneak up on her like a matchmaking ninja. Was it something that happened when one became a mother? Or was it a special talent possessed only by Bev Allen?

"Oh, stop," Bev whispered. She gave a blinding smile to a passing guest wearing a Rolex on each wrist.

Only through years of training did Gwen manage not to roll her eyes.

"Look at Kristen's glow!" Bev continued. She smiled fondly at her only child. "I want that for you. Just pinch some color into those cheeks"—she helpfully did it for Gwen, despite Gwen's attempt to wave her off—"and smile a little. You have the prettiest smile, sweetheart. Your father and I want to introduce you to some of the politicians in attendance."

"I'm twenty-one, Mom. I have zero interest in marriage." *Or in any senator at all, thanks,* she added silently.

"Don't count these men out just yet, dear. There are some future presidential prospects here tonight."

"Seriously, Mom, please don't. I have so much on my plate at college right now…" Gwen looked around in a panic. Her mom was desperate to see her married to the "most promising" candidate she could find, and in a room full of almost five hundred guests, most with major political ties, Gwen was beginning to feel faint. And not in the romantic, heart-fluttering, swept-off-her-feet way.

Her mother was a matchmaking force of the worst kind, and Gwen's usual defense was to escape her presence. But for the moment, she was stuck. Good manners rooted her to the spot; so many people were always watching them. Everyone expected Gwen, as the heiress to the Allen fortune, to marry well, and soon. And her parents expected to decide her future for her.

As her best friend Eleanor always said, it was like a living nightmare from those Regency romance books they both loved.

Bev gave a derisive snort. "I am thrilled you're taking your education seriously, Gwendolyn, I am. That is important. But marriage is more so. Making the right connections is a good place to start, and this event is the perfect opportunity for you to—oh, hello, Edward!"

With her mother's attention now locked on one of the congressmen in attendance, Gwen slipped out of the ballroom. She glanced down a long hallway and saw an exit sign; she hurried toward it and pulled the door open.

Perfect. A cool, empty, hotel staircase. She let the heavy door close behind her, and with it came a welcome silence.

She sighed, but nearly jumped out of her skin when a man peered up the stairs at her from the landing below. "You followed me. I knew you would."

She tried to remember the man, but she couldn't. He was in his mid-twenties, and typical of the wedding crowd. More money than sense, if the expensive suit and strong smell of alcohol indicated anything.

"I don't think we've met," she hedged, inching backward toward the door.

"Not yet. You're Gwendolyn Allen, and I'm Max Drysdale." He tripped up the steps and gave her a lopsided smile. "Our parents have been trying to get us together for weeks, but you've been holding out."

She wracked her brain, but the name wasn't familiar. Of course, she wouldn't put it past her parents to try to set her up with this guy. For all she knew, his was one of the dozen or so names flashed at her weekly.

"Well, school and all that. Come on, let's get back to the party." Damn it, the door was locked behind her. She rattled the safety bar, the sound echoing against the cold concrete walls around her.

He was almost beside her, and she felt a frisson of alarm.

His eyes were unfocused, and he swayed a little. She caught him by the lapels before he fell back down the stairs, and he grinned at her. "I knew you wanted me."

"Uh, sorry, pal. I'm not interested. What I am interested in is getting back to the party, though." She turned her back to him and tested the door one more time.

He reached around her waist and jerked her against him. The tulle overlay of her horrid dress crinkled and swished and he crushed her against him and reached for her breasts.

She slapped his hands away and twisted, coming face-to-face with his lips, which he pushed on her in a sloppy mess of a kiss. She shoved him back, hard, and he stumbled against the small railing. He smiled slowly.

"So you like it rough?"

"Oh my God," she muttered, annoyed. "No, I don't 'like it rough.' Back off, Drysdale."

The dimwit decided instead to lunge at her. She stepped to the side, but he was either not as drunk as she thought, or it was dumb luck that he shifted with her and pinned her against the wall. In one move, he had her wrists above her head and his body flush against her, grinding his hips into hers.

"Get off!" she shouted, turning her head away from his foul breath. "Stop it!"

He merely nuzzled into her neck, making odd slurping sounds that made her stomach sour.

"I will hurt you," she grunted, struggling against his unfortunately strong grip.

"I look forward to it," he murmured, dragging his tongue up her neck.

She clenched her jaw, then brought her knee up as swiftly as she could, jamming it between his legs, hitting exactly the spot she wanted to. She watched his eyes cross, heard the shriek of pain, then watched, satisfied, as he crumpled to the floor in a moaning heap.

The door swung open.

"Don't let it close," she said quickly, her adrenaline still in overdrive as she slipped under someone's arm, back into the hallway. "It locks behind you."

"Aye," a man replied in a thick, melodic accent, "then perhaps we ought to leave it a bit propped for your friend here?"

Gwen looked in the oversized mirror on the wall and attempted to fix her hair. Not too much damage. It had taken the hairstylist almost an hour to wrangle it into the complicated half-up, half-down do. "Ugh. He's no friend of mine. Thanks for opening that." She turned back to the man and froze.

Holy. Hell.

Her first thought was: *enormous*. His shoulders were so broad, she couldn't see the entire (still slightly ajar) door behind him. He wore a black leather jacket, opened to reveal a dark, button-down shirt. Perfectly-formed jeans encased his strong, powerful legs, and he wore scuffed black work boots, one of which still propped open the stairway door.

Then she registered his face, and her entire world shifted. It was perfectly sculpted, all hard planes and smooth skin. Lips made for kissing. Intense hazel eyes, with striking rays of gold and blue, focused on her own muted, soft green ones, and the look he was giving her stole her breath. His face held just the right amount of five o'clock shadow to separate the men from the boys.

His eyes on the heap of moaning man on the ground, the man let out a low whistle. "Well done, lass." Slowly, deliberately, he pulled his foot from the bottom of the door. It closed with a resounding thud. A muffled call of "Hey!" from the other side rang out, but they both ignored it.

"I heard what sounded like a lady in distress." The timbre of his voice resonated in her chest, the words cascading together in a fascinating lilt. Her ears strained for more, the

5

sounds of the letters at once familiar yet unlike anything she'd known.

She grasped for something clever to say, but then the actual words he spoke registered, and she blinked. "Well, it wasn't me. *I* don't need to be saved."

"Clearly," he replied, a small smile playing at his lips as he glanced at the closed door. They both listened to the continued, pathetic cries of pain for a moment more before he added, "Quite the well-placed kick, I daresay."

"I'm...I'm Gwendolyn. Gwen. Thanks for the almost-rescue."

"Reilly. And 'twas almost my pleasure."

She blushed, feeling exposed by his intense gaze. "When I went in there, I didn't know he was there. I just wanted to get away from the noise for a while."

The mysterious Reilly grimaced with a glance down the long hallway to the open doorway of the ballroom that showed people milling about. "I believe you."

His accent was unfamiliar to her, and his voice was so deep, she felt the reverberations in her chest. He was all virile male, and never before had she met anyone like him.

Gwen's normal confidence slipped a notch. She was way out of her comfort zone.

"Friend of the bride or groom?" she asked, unsure how to keep their conversation going. *Dumb.* He wasn't dressed for the wedding, not in those jeans.

Her eyes, of their own accord, strayed back to his legs. Each thigh was thicker than both her legs together.

He chuckled. "Neither. I'm simply here for the entertainment."

She tilted her head, enchanted by the sound of his laugh. "Ah. A knight *and* a wedding crasher."

"A man of many trades, for certain."

"Can I offer you a ride somewhere?"

Gwen wondered if he was hitting on her. Her heart beat

triple time with the thought, but Reilly remained expressionless yet friendly. No overtures of anything, really.

Disappointment flooded her.

She managed to smile at him. "Thanks, but I have to stay until at least the cake cutting. Bridal party," she muttered.

"That explains the horrid dress."

Her mouth dropped open. "Excuse me?"

Reilly reached over and lifted the tulle overlay, and the scent of him filled her senses. Fresh, outdoorsy, clean. No cologne.

Gwen would never forget that smell.

They both watched the scratchy material float back down to its chiffon counterpart.

Reilly spoke again. "Can you honestly tell me that is a dress you'd choose for yourself?"

"Kristen had a designer make these especially for today."

"No insult meant," he returned smoothly. "And that wasn't an answer to my question."

She glanced back at his face, unnerved to see he was still watching her, his eyes still concentrated on hers. She shook her head, unable to form any coherent words.

"I thought not. That dress does nothing for your beauty, yet there you stand, somehow still resplendent."

Gwen blinked. "Th-thank you."

As though he hadn't just dropped the most wonderful compliment Gwen had ever heard, he continued, "That color should be outlawed."

"I was thinking the same thing earlier," she admitted sheepishly. She glanced down and wrinkled her nose. "Ugh. You're right, it really is horrid. And with the amount of money I had to drop on this thing...I just think of all the good it could've done going somewhere else."

"Like where?" Reilly asked.

Gwen blushed again, cursing her pale skin, which no doubt now matched her hair. "Oh, you know...families who don't have anything. It could be a mortgage payment." At his surprised look, she shrugged and fluffed the skirt self-consciously. "Designer isn't cheap. And neither is anything about this wedding."

"That seems like a lot of pressure."

"It is. Kristen—the bride—thrives on it. I'd rather be... well, anywhere else."

"If you could be anywhere right this moment, where would that be?" He seemed genuinely curious as to her answer.

Right here with you, came the immediate thought. Gwen swallowed hard. Her reaction was visceral and overwhelming; she had to get control of herself before she did something embarrassing, such as throw herself against him and beg him to take her with him.

Wherever he went.

He smiled, a mysterious half-lifting of his lips that made her worry that he'd read her thoughts.

He tried another question, as she seemed unable to answer the first. "What do you want to do with yourself, if not be like those people in there?"

"I want to work with people," she replied without hesitation. "Really work with them, create homes and communities."

His eyes crinkled at the sides, the only outward sign she could see of his surprise. She wondered how old he was; he seemed older than the twenty-somethings she hung around.

"Fascinating." It was said honestly, without any derision or mockery. "Though those people in there do good, aye?"

"I guess," she replied, not quite convinced.

"I've learned not to judge until I've gathered all the facts. Though they may not be out on the front lines, so to speak, perhaps their money funds those who are."

Gwen furrowed her brow. "I never thought of that."

"You would have eventually. Perspective comes with

8

time."

A heartbeat passed before she blurted out, "Where are you from?"

If Reilly was surprised by her sudden change of subject, he didn't show it. "Most recently, right outside Dublin."

Max banged his fist on the other side of the door, apparently recovered enough to get to it. "Anyone out there?"

"Nay," Reilly growled, turning his head toward the closed door. His expression went cold, making Gwen's eyes widen. She took a quick step back. He glanced at her and softened his gaze. "Never a need to fear me, lass."

"You're one of the good guys?" she asked, her voice barely above a whisper.

He smirked, and her insides tightened. "Depends on whose side you're on."

She swallowed hard. "I think I'd want to be on your side."

His smile grew. "Then aye. I'm one of the good guys."

"Ry!"

Gwen recognized the matchmaker who had orchestrated the meeting between the bride and groom. The matchmaker —Gwen couldn't remember her name—waved to him from the other end of the hallway. He waved back and held up a finger.

"I'm her ride home," he explained to Gwen.

"Oh, your girlfriend?" Gwen asked, disappointment clouding her tone. *Ridiculous. He's way too old for me*, she tried to reason with herself.

Reilly fished a folded bar napkin from his pocket. "Nay. Cousin." He produced a pen, too, and scribbled something on it. "I'm in town for a few days. Feel free to call me if you want to have a drink or two. Of course, if you're ever in Ireland, you can look me up there, too, Gwendolyn." He glowered at the door, where Max was making pathetic pleading noises. "I'm a good friend to have around, even if you can take care of yourself well enough."

"Are there bad guys in Ireland?" she asked, unwilling for him to leave.

"If there are, be reassured that my armor, though dusty, is always ready when needed."

"What exactly is it that you do, Reilly?"

He flashed her a grin. "I'm just a simple furniture maker. Nothing more, nothing less."

She narrowed her eyes at him. "I don't believe that for a moment."

He gave her a wink, then gently grasped her wrist and opened her hand. Numb with shock from the sensations skittering across her skin, Gwen watched, breathless, as he slid the napkin into her palm.

"What's this?" she whispered.

He lifted an eyebrow. "My number. It comes with the offer of friendship, mayhap a chair or table, and a rescue."

"How many rescues do I get?"

"As many as you need."

She gave him a cheeky grin. "I might need a chair. But I don't think I'll ever need a rescue."

"Perhaps not. Call me."

He headed down the hallway, and Gwen stared after him, a different person than she had been just ten minutes earlier. Something in her had changed in those moments, though she couldn't pinpoint exactly what.

He turned and gave her one last, long look, then disappeared around the corner. She glanced at the napkin in her hand.

Reilly O'Malley, Knight Extraordinaire

A faraway smile graced her lips. *Not just something*, she mused, tracing his bold script with her finger. *Everything*.

• • •

Three interminable hours later, Gwen sat alone in the hotel bar. Kristen and Justin were on their way to the airport, and most of the guests had departed. She'd declined the ride home from her parents and she'd turned down the limo service. She got herself a room. With everything her parents had put her through that day (six attempted setups, thirteen introductions to men old enough to be her father, and handing her number out to all of them), she'd gone ahead and used her dad's credit card to purchase herself some new clothes from some boutique on Newbury Street, which would be delivered by the morning.

There was no way in hell she was leaving the hotel dressed as an aquatic arthropod.

But she also didn't want to stay at her parents' home in Connecticut. They were moving to California soon, which was a blessing, for she needed some distance from them. They expected her to follow them to L.A. once she graduated, but she wanted to be done with the lifestyle. The insincerity, the constant round of parties with the same faces, always being known as "the Allen heiress"—it was overwhelming, and she hated it.

She *hated* it.

She wanted to be someone else, but she wasn't sure how.

"Is this seat taken?"

Her breath caught in her chest, and she slowly turned. She looked up, high enough that her neck felt funny, and blinked at the man standing next to her.

Mutely, she shook her head and quickly looked forward again. Reilly O'Malley slid into the seat, and the bartender—who had barely glanced at Gwen the entire time she'd been there—hurried over to take his order.

"What are you having?" he asked Reilly.

He glanced in her tumbler, then picked it up and gave it a sniff. His eyebrows nearly disappeared into his hairline, but he was smiling when he said, "I'll have what the lady's having. Make it a double."

Embarrassed, she hesitated. She'd been taught that ladies drink wine, and sometimes trendy spirits. Jameson whiskey on the rocks did not qualify as a ladylike drink. Yet, it was her favorite, and since no one was around...

She fiddled with her napkin. "You like whiskey?"

He chortled. "Lass, I'm Irish. Not liking *uisce beatha* isn't an option." She gave him a questioning look, and his explained, "*Uisce beatha*. Gaelic for *water of life*. Or, as you call it, whiskey."

"I like your accent," she blurted out.

"I like you," he returned.

A delicious feeling started to unfurl throughout her skin, and she was pretty sure it wasn't the whiskey. "Are you picking me up in a bar?" She liked this. She liked *him*. He was different than the men she'd dated; he was older, of course. But there was something almost uncivilized about him. She couldn't put her finger on it, but there was an edge to him that thrilled her.

"Do you *want* me to pick you up in a bar?" he asked, his voice, like the whiskey, was smooth and strong.

She chewed her lip for a moment. "I think I do."

He leaned in closer, his lips inches from hers. "Full disclosure: I give but one night."

She sized him up. "So, should I save mine for a special occasion?"

He blinked at her, thrown, and suddenly, he laughed. The rich, warm sound invaded her soul, letting loose a thousand butterflies in her stomach.

He took his double and drained it. "By the saints, I really do like you, Gwendolyn."

She gave him a small smile, a real one. "I like you too, Reilly."

He mock-banged his head against the bar. "You know what this means, though, don't you?"

She hoped it meant he was going to take her upstairs to her room and show her what was inside those soft jeans of his, but she refrained from saying so. She merely remained silent, watching him with what she hoped was a sexy expression on her face.

"It means that I can't take you to bed."

Her mouth dropped open. "What?"

He downed his drink, then signaled to the bartender for another. "You're something special, Gwendolyn Allen."

"I never told you my last name."

He truly smiled at her then, and she was left witless from the wattage.

"You're worth more than a single night, and I'm not capable of giving that. So let's agree to carry on as friends, aye?"

"You're a strange man."

His eyes glinted with humor. "You've no idea, lass. But like I said before, I'm one of the good guys."

"Apparently too good," she muttered.

He chuckled, then tossed some cash on the bar. When she rifled through her purse for her wallet, he frowned at her. "Nay. This is on me. It'll always be on me."

"Always?" she scoffed. The man had just turned down sex, and he was talking as if they were going to be best buds and hang out for all time? He must've been drinking prior to joining her.

He nodded, then glanced in her open purse. "Still have my number, or did you chuck it in the nearest rubbish bin?"

She colored. The napkin was clearly visible in the tiny satchel that held her credit card, a small roll of cash, and her lipstick.

He chuckled, then gently drew her hand to his lips. He kissed each knuckle, weakening her knees to the point of jelly. "Aye, it's always on me." His eyes turned serious. "Please call me, Gwendolyn."

She knew she would. And somehow, she knew *he* knew she would.

CHAPTER 1

Present Day

he hammer came down fast, but Gwendolyn Allen was faster. She pulled her thumb out of the way just as it missed the nail head. She leaned back a little and studied the new indentation on the stair she was attempting to build.

Installation of the risers was not going well.

In fact, this entire trip wasn't going well. Just last night their bodyguards had exchanged gunfire with a couple of men intent on robbing the small group of volunteers as they made camp for the night. In the four months that Gwen had been out in the wilds of Venezuela, she'd been thankful for the guards every single day.

After they completed work on the orphanage, her team was asked to help create some housing for a remote village. She wanted to go home, but the rest of the team agreed to stay on for the additional month, and she knew she couldn't leave them.

Since their arrival to their current area a few weeks ago, however, Gwen wondered if they were there for purposes other than what was written on paper. Sure, they framed out some houses and even gotten some limited electrical and plumbing done. But she hadn't seen any villagers. Or any signs of humanity, other than their team of forty, the ten bodyguards, and some government officials who looked more like members of an army than anything else.

Gwen knew her boss wanted them out of there. Despite his easy manners and teasing words on the job site, there were tension lines around his eyes and a tightness in his shoulders that hadn't been there when they were working on the orphanage. He negotiated their stop-work date by bringing in local Venezuelans to complete the houses, and Gwen suspected people at the top of their charitable organization also did some negotiating to get them out of there faster.

She certainly didn't like living in a makeshift camp in the Venezuelan jungle, surrounded by armed guards and being watched over by armed government men.

"Need any help?"

Gwen gathered the strands of her fiery red hair and secured them with a hair tie. "No thanks, Anth. I can do this."

The project manager, Anthony Ferraro, gave her an understanding smile. "I have no doubt. But stairs are a tricky thing, and they need to pass code. Whatever code they have here…still can't quite figure that out."

Gwen frowned at the stair in front of her. "I know. I think I need a lighter hammer. That'll make it easier for me to control where I drop it. Hopefully next time, it'll be closer to its intended target."

Anthony's good looks and easy charm had most of the women on the volunteer team swooning. He was young, only a couple of years older than Gwen. He was also dedicated to each charitable project he worked. He had infinite patience with everyone, taught the volunteers new skills, and involved everyone in everything that happened around the worksite.

Of all the charity project managers Gwen worked for in the past five years, he was her best boss. They'd been dating for the better part of four months, though most of their together time was on a job site.

In fact, very little of their time together was offsite. It was weird when she thought too much about it, but Gwen preferred not to dwell on it. After all, once she returned to the States, she planned to take an extended hiatus from volunteer work, at least the home-building kind. She needed a personal and mental reset.

"I'll make you a deal. I'll find you a lighter hammer, and you go out to dinner with me when we get back to the States in a couple days." He gave her a mock-thoughtful look. "Hmm. That actually seems to be a good deal all around."

She laughed. "It does, but I can't. I have plans."

He reached around to the back of his tool belt and pulled a smaller hammer from it. He waved it a little. "You seeing someone, Red?"

She smiled easily. "Yep."

"Is it serious?"

"Serious enough for me to say no to a very charming project manager."

He dramatically staggered back, his hand holding the hammer over his heart. "Aw, what a rejection!"

Gwen rolled her eyes even as she grinned at him. "Sorry to break your heart. But I'm sure you'll be just fine."

He winked at her and handed her the hammer. "Not as fine as your serious-but-not-serious boyfriend, but I'll recover nonetheless."

Seeing as he was her serious-but-not-serious boyfriend, she had no doubt. She smiled up at him, and he pointed to a piece of framing under the stair, then handed her the hammer. "Don't nail the step into the riser. Nail the riser into the stringer."

She squinted at the wood, then nodded firmly. "Makes

sense. It's a good thing that nail didn't go into the stair. Getting it out would've been impossible."

"Things tend to happen—or not—for a reason," he agreed, then gave her a smart salute and headed over to the workers struggling to turn on the cement mixer.

"Maybe," she murmured, watching him go, then realigned the nail and hammered it perfectly into place.

She knew what Anthony was referring to, and it wasn't a nail in a stair. Last night, he proposed to her. He got the whole crew involved. They sang some pop song that had been all over the radio a few weeks ago, each taking turns holding up signs and making crazy faces. Then, after the last one dropped her sign to the ground and stepped to the side, Anthony stood there, looking adorably nervous yet determined, holding up the final sign that read *Marry Me*.

She said yes, because really, what *else* was she supposed to say after everyone went to all that trouble, and she did like him a lot. Maybe even loved him. And if she didn't love him yet, she knew she could grow to love him.

And, she reminded herself firmly, she decided months ago to move on with her life. She would marry a perfectly nice man who loved her enough to want to spend his life with her. She could be content enough with that.

Suddenly, a loud bang sounded in the not-so-distant jungle, quickly followed by a series of pops.

"Is it a holiday?" one of her coworkers, Jan, asked, brushing her hands on her jeans.

Gwen shrugged. "Maybe. It sounds like fireworks."

More pops sounded, this time louder, and suddenly the bodyguards were pulling guns from their holsters and yelling at everyone to move out. The hammer fell from Gwen's hand, and she leaped down to the ground, fear clogging her throat when she heard the words.

Pipe bomb. Gunfire. Guerrilla war.

Everyone was running, panicked, toward the five vehicles

parked on the perimeter of their worksite. She ran to the van in the middle of the line, but one of the bodyguards pointed to the Jeep in front of it, indicating that the van was full already. She shoved herself into the all-terrain vehicle and quickly scooted over to make room. Others piled in behind her, and then they were moving, not over the well-packed dirt road, but down a less-worn jungle path, over bumps and tree roots. Her teeth clacked against each other, and she hung onto the strap hanging from the clear plastic above her head, her hands sweating, her stomach in tight, painful knots.

Without warning, the Jeep swerved to the left, the wheels lifting slightly from the ground. Gwen screamed, and as the vehicle righted itself, she watched in horror as a small, round object passed right over them and landed on the windshield of the van behind them. The longest second passed, and the grenade detonated, engulfing the vehicle in a ball of flames.

Gwen's driver lurched them forward, and they were moving so fast through the jungle, it was all she could do to remain in her seat. All around her people were sobbing and screaming.

She closed her eyes and began to pray.

"IF I HAVE TO HEAR ONE MORE WORD ABOUT BOWS OR FLOWERS, I'm kidnapping her and we're going to elope," Colin O'Rourke announced, frisbee-ing his beer cap into the recycle bin of his kitchen.

Reilly O'Malley popped the top from his own beer and shuddered. "Don't see why you didn't just do that in the first place."

"Two words," Colin muttered. "Winifred Emsworth."

Winifred Emsworth—the United Kingdom's most notorious and influential gossip columnist—just happened to be Colin's future aunt-in-law. Colin—rather, Eleanor, his fiancée—was neck-deep in wedding plans with her aunt, and Reilly still wasn't sure if all the fuss was worth it. Not that he'd been to many weddings, or seen any of the black-tie affairs like the one that was currently besieging Colin.

Reilly seated himself at one of the bar stools in Colin's lavishly appointed kitchen. "Sorry, mate. Seems like a headache and a half."

"It is." They clinked bottles and Colin added, "Thanks for agreeing to be in it."

Reilly choked. "What?"

Colin shrugged. "I gave your name to Winifred, so it's a done deal. You're an usher."

He groaned. "Do I have to plan anything?"

"Nope. James is the best man—he'll take care of it. All you have to do is show up, dance with a bridesmaid or two, and enjoy the open bar."

Reilly took a slow pull of his drink. That didn't sound so bad.

"And wear a tux," Colin added with a snicker.

Reilly swore. "Anything else you want to drop on me?"

"Actually, there is." He cleared his throat, then leveled Reilly with a direct stare. "Gwen's the maid of honor."

Reilly's heart jumped in his chest, though he showed no outward signs of distress.

Gwendolyn Allen. The only woman he'd ever met who scared the daylights out of him.

She was, coincidentally, his best friend.

And that's the kind of friendship that you don't mess up with a relationship, he told himself frequently.

Almost a year ago, Gwen and Ellie became lost. And not just a run-of-the-mill lost; they tripped through the time gate in the forest behind Reilly's cottage and ended up in medieval Ireland. In Reilly's opinion, it took them much too long to return home, but Colin needed to figure things out before the Fates let him travel through time. Reilly wasn't about to leave

Colin, Gwen, and Ellie in the past while Colin came to the conclusion that needed Ellie more than he needed air, so he remained with them until Ellie asked him directly to take her home.

During their time in the past, Reilly made such a massive misstep with Gwen that he feared he would lose her forever. He groveled, apologized, and begged her forgiveness, and Gwen being Gwen, readily gave it to him. But she also hightailed it out of Ireland and back to the States almost the moment they returned home.

Gwen had always been direct with him. There was never any beating around the bush, never any word games or mind tricks. She said what she felt and he could always count on her for her forthrightness. Sometimes it made him want to bang his head against the nearest hard surface, but at least with her, he always knew where he stood.

Until that day she left for the States.

She barely spoke to him for the last year. Every time he sent her a message, he received a quick reply such as, "In Rwanda this month. Let's talk when I get back!" or "China is crazy right now. Sorry I missed you last week. Let's talk soon!"

They never did, until she unexpectedly video-called him from Venezuela. He knew then that something was wrong, but she wouldn't say. But he knew her.

To Colin, he shrugged indifferently. "Makes sense Gwen would be maid of honor. She and Ellie are best friends, after all."

Colin idly swirled his own beer, then walked around the kitchen island and sat next to Reilly. "You sure you're okay with seeing her again?"

"Why wouldn't I be?"

"Oh, I don't know. Just the fact that after more than a decade of friendship, she cut you out of her life?"

"She didn't cut me out of her life," Reilly replied mildly,

though his chest tightened with Colin's words. "She's a busy woman. She's got an entire world to save, you know."

Colin grabbed the bowl of tortilla chips and jerked his head toward the bowl of salsa. Reilly grabbed it and followed him into the living room, where Colin pushed a button to make his fancy television appear from behind a piece of art. They arranged the snack and their beers to their liking, then Colin flipped to a rugby match.

About three minutes in, Colin, who apparently couldn't seem to keep quiet, noted in an off-hand sort of way, "Rumor has it she was in South Africa on a safari."

Reilly grunted in response. Gwen had been known to tell her parents one thing, then hop a plane and do something completely different. Gwen's parents were a little high-handed, though he knew they worried about their only daughter. She was a free spirit and fiercely independent. They'd never quite known what to do with her.

Neither, he admitted, had he. But he kept tabs on her anyway; he never stepped in unless asked, but he felt better knowing that at least someone in the world knew where she was.

A text sounded on Colin's phone, and he idly checked it. However, he tossed the remote aside and bolted upright. "Holy—"

Reilly tensed, but waited for Colin to speak.

"It's Gwen."

His eyes scanned the message, then he hit a number and put it on speakerphone.

"Her humanitarian group was attacked." Ellie's voice came through clearly, and it was shaken.

Reilly went into full warrior mode. He was up, his entire body tense, ready for battle. But before he could do anything, Ellie continued in a rush, "She's alive and unharmed. Rebels ambushed them and killed thirteen people by throwing a grenade on one of the cars."

Reilly's heart, which was in overdrive, suddenly felt as though it stopped. "I have to get to her."

"Reilly! I'm so glad you're there."

"Did you speak with her?" he asked, hating the desperation in his voice. Colin put a hand on his shoulder, and Reilly nodded, grateful for the unspoken show of support.

"No. She left me a message."

"How long ago did this happen?" Reilly demanded, needing to move, needing to do something. To get to her.

Even though she was safe, he needed to see for himself.

Colin pulled a laptop out from under the coffee table and handed it to him as Ellie continued speaking.

"I don't know. The message just came through a few minutes ago, but it must not have come through quickly. I have her flight details. She's flying into Boston tonight," Ellie said quickly. "Her plane will land in another hour or so. I already scheduled a driver to pick her up."

"Cancel the driver."

Reilly sat onto the couch, the computer in his lap and his heart slamming against his ribs. The thought of Gwen in one of the most dangerous places in the world terrified him, though he would bite off his right hand before admitting it aloud. He searched for incoming flights to Boston.

"Okay. Hug her for me, please."

Colin and Ellie continued speaking off speakerphone, but once he got her flight details, he stopped paying attention and instead looked up her details.

Colin hung up with Ellie and whistled low. "Wow."

"I need your keys."

Colin nodded. "Yep. But you're not leaving just yet. You need to calm down."

Reilly shot him A Look, and Colin rolled his eyes. "I know, you're a warrior, you do well under stress, blah blah blah. But your hands are shaking, old man, and you've yet to take a full breath."

Reilly clenched his hands into fists and remained silent.

"She'll have to go through customs and get her bags. She'll stay here tonight. I figure I have the room, and it'd give me extra brownie points with Ellie."

Reilly rolled his eyes, allowing Colin to distract him with talk of his lady love. "You're marrying the chit. I don't think you need any extra points right now. When do you see your almost-wife again?"

"This weekend. My frequent flyer miles are adding up."

"Any decisions as to where you'll live after the wedding?"

Ellie owned a bookshop in London and Colin was the CEO of Celtic Connections, a Boston-based elite matchmaking service; they'd been trying to work out how to split their time between Europe and America, with limited success.

"Not yet. When are you going to make your move?"

Reilly didn't look up. "I've no plans to move anywhere. Ireland is my home."

"I meant on Gwen."

Reilly slowly turned his head and pinned Colin with a stare. "I'm certain I've no idea what you speak of."

Colin interlaced his fingers and crossed his ankle over his knee. "Of course you do. At some point, you'll have to admit it, just like we all have."

"We?"

"Yes, we. First Nick, then Aidan, now me. You're next."

"What about your brother?" Reilly returned evenly. "Surely James is next."

"He just divorced. He needs some time before he gets all twisted up over a woman again."

"Well, I'm most certainly not on your short list. Concentrate on your own love life and leave mine alone."

"You haven't been out with a woman in how long now?" Colin asked, ignoring his protests.

"You're bothering me."

"Great, you can take it out on me in the lists tomorrow morning. So, if not Gwen, who's going to warm your bed?"

"Enough with the matchmaking," Reilly growled.

"It's in my blood," he said with a shrug. Thankfully, his phone rang, and Colin held it up. "Work this time."

"Praise the saints," Reilly muttered.

"Hey, Candice. What's up?" A moment passed, then Colin rolled his eyes. He dug in his pocket and tossed his car keys to Reilly. "Okay, define *disaster...*"

Left alone in the living room, Reilly picked up his beer, then carefully placed it back down again, remembering that he was going to be driving shortly. He could hold his alcohol better than anyone, but he took no chances when it came to Gwen, despite the excellence of the brew.

He knew it would be flat by the time he returned, but by then, he would most likely need something a bit stronger.

Gwendolyn Allen did that to him.

ONCE THEY COLLECTED THEIR LUGGAGE, ANTHONY CARRIED Gwen's bag as far as the escalators, but he had to catch the express bus to where his ride was waiting for him. Though he lived in Vermont, his parents lived in Massachusetts, so he was heading there to visit them and meet the niece who was born while they were in Venezuela.

And, perhaps, try to come to grips with losing so many of his team.

He'd been in the first vehicle and hadn't seen the grenade. But he heard it, as had they all. His eyes were as haunted as hers.

He kissed her briefly, and Gwen smiled sadly at him. "I'll see you next Friday."

"I'll pick you up early, around five."

"I can meet you at the yacht club," she protested. "It's ridiculous for you to have to drive an hour and a half north, just to drive an hour south again."

"Ah, you're forgetting that the hour drive south is spent in your company, so it's very much something I want to do."

She smiled a little. After another kiss goodbye, she shooed him toward the bus pickup area.

Yes. Marriage to him would be a good thing. Gwen needed some normalcy in her world, especially now.

She readjusted her bag (she swore again that she'd invest in some real luggage before her next trip) and searched for her ride as she rode the escalator to the floor above. She also searched for unattended baggage and men holding guns, but thankfully, neither were present. Her nerves were still on edge.

Gwen didn't see a driver holding a sign with her name on it as she stepped off the escalator, nor did she see him as she headed cautiously toward the glass double doors. Ellie's text said she would have one waiting; perhaps he was waiting at a different terminal, even though all international flights arrived in this one.

She froze as she felt awareness wash over her body.

Glancing over her shoulder, a surprised smile of relief broke out as she caught sight of the brooding man standing about fifty paces from her.

It had been so long since she'd seen him in person, yet she'd recognize him anywhere, any time.

Dark, almost-black hair that fell just so over the most handsome—and familiar—face she'd ever seen. The deceptively relaxed pose—his leaning against a supporting pole, arms folded and legs splayed. The expressionless face, half-hidden behind dark glasses. An incredible physique, not hidden at all underneath jeans and leather...

Her salvation.

"Reilly?"

He lifted an eyebrow, visible over the rim of his sunglasses, and she rolled her eyes with a laugh, her nerves scattering to the wind. She dropped her bag and ran to him. She leapt into his arms, and for the first time in a very long time, she felt free. Safe.

Home.

She pulled back and grinned at him. "Not even a welcome home smile?"

He gave a half shrug and put her down, though she sensed his reluctance in letting her go. "Never in public," he replied, his Irish brogue sending the words into a melodic dance. "And you should never leave your bags unattended. They frown on that."

She quickly reached under his jacket and pinched his side.

The corners of his lips turned up. "Pain in the arse," he muttered affectionately, before trotting over to grab her bag.

It was almost like it used to be, before their almost-mistake. He would try to keep up his tough-guy image, and she would tease him out of it, despite himself.

But this time, Gwen admitted, it took a little more effort than normal.

This time, she had to put on a smile not because she wanted to, but because she had to. She hadn't seen him in a year, despite the video call to him awhile back, which she wished she never made. It was a moment of weakness, and seeing his face over a grainy camera connection did more harm than good.

It reminded her of all she was giving up.

And, to make things even more complicated, this time, she had a boyfriend. A fiancé, actually…though it still didn't feel quite like an engagement. But Anthony was someone she was ready to introduce to her parents, include in her life, and make a life with.

It wasn't perfect, but it was darn close. After years of

27

waiting and hoping and dreaming for something real, she had it.

It wasn't from the man she always wanted, but then life rarely went according to plan. Settling for the next-best-thing-to-perfect was enough for her. And Anthony was exactly that. She just hadn't told him about Reilly yet.

How could she explain to her boyfriend—no, her *fiancé*—that her best friend was a six-foot-five alpha Irishman? She wasn't naive enough to believe Anth would be perfectly fine with her and Ry's relationship. She and Reilly were close—at least, they used to be, and she hoped to be again. They used to visit each other every few months; she had her own room at his cottage, he ate off her plate, they finished each other's sentences.

They'd be perfect together...except Reilly O'Malley didn't do love. He didn't do relationships, and he didn't do messy emotions.

And so she had to let him go.

"Ellie cancelled your driver. And I find it interesting that there weren't any flights from South Africa in the last few hours," Reilly noted dryly. "The poor man would've been waiting in the wrong spot."

She rolled her eyes. "You know I can't let anyone know where I go," she replied.

"Do you know how dangerous Venezuela is, Gwen?"

More than you want to know. But she managed a sweet smile for him, unintimidated by his large frame, and didn't bother wondering how he'd found out her location. He somehow always knew, and instead of finding it annoying, Gwen actually found it a bit relieving. "Do you know how old I am, Ry?"

"Thirty going on twelve?"

"The correct answer is *old enough to make my own decisions.*" She hated the edge in her voice, but she couldn't help it.

"Even if they're poor ones?"

Gwen ignored him, because in this case, he was right. She was lucky to be out of there, and she knew it. Many innocent lives had been lost. Thirteen of them. She hoped it wasn't on the news over here. She stepped into the cool air and shivered. "Hold on a second. Let me grab my sweater out of the bag."

"Take this," he replied, shaking out of his leather jacket and handing it to her. "You're in a tee shirt; a jumper won't do anything for you."

She didn't bother to protest; she knew him well enough not to insist. Plus, she needed it.

Reilly was her rock, and wearing his clothing always made her feel more grounded, more...safe.

There's that word again. She felt a flash of guilt at how she didn't feel that way about Anthony. *Yet,* she reminded herself. *I don't feel that way about him* yet.

Gwen thanked Reilly and snuggled into the much-too-big jacket, reveling in the warmth and scent of home. She didn't just like it; she *loved* wearing his clothing, especially if it was straight off his body. There was something about the softness of his shirts, and the scent of him, that filled her with...

Warmth. Only warmth. That's all, she told herself. She had Anth now. He was her source of happiness. And he did make her happy. He also made her laugh and feel special.

Why, why, *why* did she have to remind herself of all Anthony's good qualities after being in Ry's presence for a mere five minutes?

They made it to the car without any more speech. She waited for him to drop her bag into the trunk; another battle she had long since conceded was his desire to open the door for her. Chivalry was so deeply ingrained in his chemical makeup that he became insulted when she didn't wait, so she always did.

When he came around to her side, instead of opening the

door, he gathered her into an uncharacteristically sudden hug. Gwen, never one to not show affection, melted into him without hesitation.

"You missed me," she mumbled into the bottom of his sternum.

He pulled his sunglasses off his head, his own hazel eyes softening as he looked down at her. "More than you know."

She hoped her face remained playful, but his eyes searched hers.

Damn. He knows something's wrong.

But, true to form, he didn't call her out on it. Instead, he half-smiled at her. He placed his large hand against her cheek and pressed her head back against his chest. "Why can't you go to St. Croix, like every other trust fund baby?"

Gwen smiled into him and realized that she missed this, their friendship. After a year away from him, she was ready to let go of what happened and be a part of his life. A friend, like he always demanded they be.

She gave him the same answer she'd been giving for years. "Because I'm not *like* every other trust fund baby."

When she came of age to access the trust fund her parents insisted upon, Gwen partnered with a college friend and began investing in various travel and airline companies. As time went on, she showed a knack for understanding which companies would succeed, and which would tank. Her parents were, predictably, shocked and saddened at her mercantile dealings.

"Gwen!"

Reilly glanced back over his shoulder, and Gwen looked around in surprise. "Anthony?"

He jogged over, a suspicious expression on his face. He was holding her makeup bag, of all things, in his hand. "I almost forgot to give this to you." He sized up Reilly, then added, "Remember, we packed it in my bag when it didn't fit into yours?"

"Oh!" she exclaimed, caught off guard. "Right, of course. Thanks."

She disentangled herself from Reilly's arms and took the bag, but Anth didn't release it. Instead, he pulled her into him and kissed her.

Flustered, she let him, then pulled back.

Oh, boy. That was a "she's with me" move if she'd ever seen one.

"Are you going to introduce me to your friend here?" Anth asked pointedly.

"Oh!" Gwen replied, her tongue twisted into a knot. "Right. Reilly O'Malley, this is Anthony Ferraro."

"Her fiancé," he supplied, sticking out his hand.

Reilly raised an eyebrow, but he didn't so much as blink. "Fiancé? Can't say Gwendolyn's mentioned you before."

"I, um, wanted to tell you in person..." Gwen explained, though even to her own ears, it was a weak excuse. But also, when would she have told Reilly? During their single five-minute call a few weeks ago?

Why she hadn't wanted to tell Reilly about Anth was easy enough to explain to herself. But to give an actual voice to that reason?

She'd rather jump off the Cliffs of Moher.

"Oh, aye, of course," Reilly replied without inflection. He gripped Anthony's hand, and the two of them looked as though they were going to crush each other's bones. "I'm the best friend."

"I thought her best friend's name was Ellie." Anth released Reilly's hand—or maybe it was the other way around, Gwen wasn't sure—and looked at her, his eyes accusing.

"Ellie is also my best friend," Gwen tried to explain.

"Really? So that's why you're wearing *her* jacket?"

Reilly slung an arm around Gwen's shoulders. "We've known each other for a few years. And she was chilled." He opened the car door and motioned her inside. "Come on, lass. Last time you caught a cold you were a miserable mess for a week."

Gwen bit her lip. "Right." She turned to Anthony and gave him a genuine smile. "See you in a few days. Thanks for remembering my bag."

"I'll pick you up for the gala," Anth promised.

She nodded with a smile before Reilly slammed the door with more force than was strictly necessary before rounding the car and getting in on the driver's seat.

"I was going to tell—"

"There's no need for an explanation, Gwendolyn," he ground out, his accent thicker than she'd heard it in a long time.

She closed her mouth, hurt by the cold tone, and glanced in the side mirror as they drove away. She caught sight of Anth, his arms crossed, and his expression less than pleased.

She sunk lower into the seat and closed her eyes against the conflicting emotions swirling around her brain. "No, really, I wanted—" she started.

"Like I said, no need to explain." Reilly's cold tone continued, and she frowned when he added, "I'll be glad to not wear the tux at this year's gala."

"I don't recall asking you to go with me," she fired back, a bubble of defiance creeping into her words.

"Nay," he returned evenly. Easily. "Your parents, however, did. And that's on me, of course. I assumed, if you bothered to take time out of your altruistic endeavors—"

"Hey!" she exclaimed.

"—that it would be like all the other times," he continued without stopping, "where we sip subpar champagne, enjoy the good people there, then go out for a beer afterward. But being your wingman at those things is not my job anymore, and to be honest, I'm relieved for it."

She blinked, the hurt like a stab to her heart. *Ouch. I guess not even close to as almost like it used to be.*

"Oh," she replied in a small voice. And, as she did for the last year, she said nothing else for the rest of the ride.

COLIN O'ROURKE HAD A MAGNIFICENT LIBRARY.

Granted, Gwen wasn't the biggest reader, but she could certainly appreciate the lush carpet, peaceful ambiance, and shelves of books. Jumping onto, then gliding across the room on, the book ladder wasn't exactly a hardship, either.

Her best friend (and Colin's fiancée) Ellie Carberry often claimed that this library was part relaxation, part imagination, and part "magication."

Gwen acknowledged that Ellie was far superior to her in words and literary references (being as Ellie's life was books, as she was a lifelong reader and longtime bookshop owner in London), so if Ellie said it was part "magication," Gwen went with it.

Looking around, she had to agree.

The curtains on both sides of the room were drawn, and the only light was from the floor lamps that anchored each wall of windows. The room spanned the entire length of Colin's historic Boston brownstone; the square footage in the room alone probably rivaled Gwen's entire house in New Hampshire.

She wished she was there right now.

When Colin (and Ellie, by phone) insisted she stay at Colin's house, due to the late hour of her arrival, Gwen acquiesced because she really didn't care to drive for another hour and a half after the two days of travel she had behind her. Getting out of Venezuela had been difficult; all the survivors of her group needed new passports expedited to them. It was one of the few times she'd used her name to get what she needed; she hadn't hesitated in calling in favors from a couple of discreet contacts in Washington, D.C.

Within twenty-four hours, she had enough documentation to get them all back to the States. But it took them another day to get on flights.

She dragged her fingers over the spines of books that looked very old, her mind now trying to process just the last few hours.

Reilly was silent on the short drive to Colin's house, and then after plying her with food (during which Colin joked and Reilly remained silent), the two men stiffened and started some strange man-conversation using just their eyes. She watched as they somehow came to a decision, and, amused, watched them try to pretend like it didn't happen.

Colin declared himself ready for bed and left pretty quickly. He wasn't the best of liars, but Gwen wasn't really up for a visit anyway, so she bid him goodnight.

Then it was just her and Reilly.

They looked at each other for a long minute before he asked, "Will you be all right if I leave for a bit?"

She frowned. "I don't need watching over, you know."

He didn't respond verbally, but his lips hardened into a straight line and he gave her a jerky nod before leaving her sitting in the kitchen, alone with her mostly untouched plate of food.

After she went up to the bedroom, she heard a small commotion from somewhere in the house. Already on the second floor, she decided to investigate, so, after changing into her pajamas, she checked Reilly's room, but he wasn't there. She went back downstairs; all was quiet there, so she headed through the magnificent kitchen toward the side stairway. She climbed up past the second floor, and up to the third, which held the library. Finding it empty, too, she figured the noise must've come from Colin's bedroom, which was on the floor above the library.

Instead of invading his privacy, she decided to linger with the books and sense of peace in that room.

Her hand paused, by its own volition, on a thick, leather bound book. A shiver went through her, and she peered at the title: *The O'Rourkes: A Complete History from AD 800 to AD 2000.*

She felt a strange, intense need to leaf through it, but her common sense prevailed again. She had no need to snoop through genealogy of a family that wasn't her own; instead, she grabbed the title directly above it and plopped down in one of the exceedingly comfortable armchairs.

If her gaze continually drifted back over to the genealogy book, that couldn't be helped.

She focused on the book in her hand—*Sense and Sensibility* by Jane Austen—and took it as a sign. She was going to use exactly those virtues to not open that genealogy book, just like she didn't go up to Colin's bedroom. The poor man was probably sleeping, anyway.

And who knows where Reilly had gone.

Not that she was wondering about that, she reassured herself. She determinedly opened the book, which Ellie had been trying to get her to read for years, and soon became lost in the story of the Dashwood sisters.

She hadn't any idea how much time had passed when a loud bang shocked her. Her throat closed up, her ears began to ring, and a panic bloomed forcefully in her chest. Frozen to the chair, her body wouldn't move, though her mind was screaming to get to safety.

Another boom had her up and running toward the stairs, anxious to get out, get away. She ran bodily into a solid wall of muscle, and a scream lodged in her throat.

Reilly, dressed in a tunic and léine, caught her as she fell, concern etching his face.

"Gwendolyn? Why are you still up?"

"Go! Out!" she choked, pushing him blindly.

His expression turned to one of alarm. "Has something happened?"

Her words came out in a strangled sob. They needed to move, to get out of there, before the next explosion hit.

His arms came around her immediately, but she continued to fight him. Didn't he hear it? "The blast," she gasped. "Go, Ry, go!"

He tightened his hold on her. "We're safe, Gwen. I've got you."

The fight began to leave her, but her heart raced on. She tried to slow her breathing. "I can't…"

He gently held her away from him for a moment and studied her face. "I'll never let anything happen to you."

She nodded quickly, drawing in deep breaths. "Okay. I know."

"The noise you heard was me. I accidentally slammed the door when I came in."

She nodded, accepting the explanation. "Okay." She couldn't seem to come up with much more than that.

He studied her face for another moment, then gently pulled her against him. She clung to his chest, her head tucked protectively against his neck, and shook.

"You're safe here," he murmured, giving her a small squeeze.

She let the words settle her before releasing a shaky breath. "I know," she whispered. "I'm okay."

But she didn't let go.

• • •

After he finished his shower and finally climbed wearily into bed, he heard his bedroom door open on nearly silent hinges. He cracked his eyes just enough to gauge the time and the threat.

The time was a simple thing. It'd been less than a half hour since he'd managed to get Gwen back to her room, so he estimated it to be about two thirty in the morning. As he and

Colin agreed to meet in the lists at 7:00 a.m., he had plenty of time yet for sleep.

The threat was rather less of a threat and more of a mystery. He watched as Gwen closed the door, then stealthily crept toward the bed. Her eyes were so round, her face drawn, and she had the look of a frightened child about her.

He immediately held up the blanket, and she dove in next to him, curling her body around his in ways that made him think less-than-chaste thoughts.

He always thought less-than-chaste thoughts about Gwen. Ensuring she never knew about those thoughts was how he got through them.

A mess, for certain.

"You okay?" he murmured.

"Am now," she whispered, then burrowed further into him.

He nodded, understanding that she didn't want to talk, and rubbed her back until her breaths were deep and even. He tucked her body closer to him, determined to give her the safety she suddenly craved, selfishly enjoying her even though she wasn't his to enjoy.

She'd never accepted help in any form from him. In fact, she made it a point not to require his help with anything. He figured it was their game—she would get herself into a situation, he would attempt a rescue, and she would breeze out of it without any aid. She challenged him.

But this...He glanced down at the sleeping figure. Clad in a thin shirt and pajama pants, her hair stuck out every way 'til Sunday, and her sleep was fitful, making him readjust her slightly to keep his manhood intact. Her face was relaxed, though, giving her the appearance of a peaceful, if slightly crazed, woodland sprite.

She started, and he resumed rubbing circles on her back. Even though they quarreled in the car...even though she was engaged to another man, she sought *his* comfort.

Though if she had the choice between him and the fiancé, Reilly had a hollowness in his chest to think who she would choose.

She whimpered, and he wrapped his arm around her, then pressed a kiss to her hair. She settled, and he simply breathed her in.

He needed to make things right with her. She needed him, though he knew she wouldn't admit it aloud, at least not right now, not when they were barely speaking. He wouldn't force her to face her demons.

Not yet, anyway. He tucked her even closer to him, and closed his eyes.

～

SEVEN A.M. CAME FAST, BUT REILLY SLIPPED OUT OF THE WARM bed, leaving Gwen to her slumber, and donned his workout gear—shorts, tee shirt, and a sword. He met Colin outside, the uncharacteristically cool air slapping him fully awake.

"This is so much better than the humidity we were training in last week," Colin muttered, wiping the sleep from his eyes.

Reilly bounced on the balls of his feet. "Aye. Let's make the most of it."

"How are you so bushy-tailed this morning?" Colin asked, stifling a yawn. "I swear you went to bed later than I did."

"Sometimes a person is blessed with many admirable qualities. I am one of those people. Are we done with morning pleasantries yet?"

Colin rolled his eyes, but readied himself. With the first clash of steel, he remarked, "So it has nothing to do with the woman asleep upstairs?"

Reilly shouldered his blade. "You cannot believe that I'm a spritely type in the wee hours?"

Colin snorted. "Since when is any time after sunrise 'the wee hours' to you?"

"Fair point."

"What was going on with her last night?"

"Exactly what you'd expect," Reilly said grimly. He flicked his wrist and his sword swiped toward Colin.

"Ellie's going to ask how she is," Colin replied, jumping backward from the tip of Reilly's sword as it sliced through the air. His own blade clashed with Reilly's, and he shook off the reverberations in his arm after quickly switching hands. "I've no idea what to tell her."

"Tell her that she's safe now."

"Her door was open this morning and the bed was empty."

Reilly raised an eyebrow, daring him to continue. When Colin wisely remained silent, Reilly repeated, "Tell her that Gwen is safe now."

"All right. Next question: Do you have any indications that we might be sent somewhere before the wedding?"

Reilly dropped his sword point-down in the dirt. "I haven't had anything that would say otherwise. But you are free from traveling until well after the wedding. I've lads aplenty who will help if necessary."

"Claire trusts very few," Colin noted. "If she decides to get herself into trouble, you should consider bringing James."

Reilly agreed silently. Claire MacWilliam, daughter of Brianagh O'Rourke and Nioclas MacWilliam, was a troublesome, clever lass who was forever getting herself into scrapes. Reilly wondered if she did so simply to have a visit with him; he did always bring her marvels from the future. The lass had a sweet tooth that seemed only satiated by Nutella.

"I'll take it into consideration. And do let me know when our gossip session is over. I've become bored with your speech and look forward to the moment you decide to attempt to best me—" Reilly grunted as Colin's sword caught his sleeve, then glanced down at his bicep. No blood. He swung again, forcing Colin backward. A particularly satisfying clash between the swords produced sparks, and Reilly couldn't help the smile that curved his lips.

He *loved* hacking at worthy swordsmen. Colin was at the top of that list.

Colin lowered his sword again, and Reilly's smile disappeared. "By the saints, O'Rourke, if you've no stomach for training—"

His words died a swift death when Colin jerked his head toward Gwen, who stood against the house, dressed in her pajamas, her arms wrapped around herself, and her gaze unfocused.

"I think," Colin murmured as he quickly sheathed his weapon, "that she has suffered a shock. That's the look of a woman who's seen violent death up close."

Reilly agreed; he'd seen it on the faces of many souls before her, and suspected he would see it on the faces of many more. But none of those had him tied in knots quite like she did.

He sheathed his sword and reached her in two strides. "Gwen, are you unwell?"

She blinked up at him, taking a moment longer than necessary to reply. "Um…no, I'm okay. I heard your swords, and I didn't know what they were. I'm okay now though."

Meaning you weren't okay when you first heard them, he thought. Gwen wasn't unused to the sounds of swords; she'd been to his sword fighting school many times, and had her own trip to the past where she saw them in action in the lists.

Gently, he drew her to his side and led her back inside. "Care you for some breakfast? I can make something, or Colin would be glad for a run to the bakery."

"You bet," Colin said from behind them. "In fact, I've been looking for an excuse to check out a new place that opened up near Quincy Market. I'll pop over there and grab some stuff after I change."

Gwen was focusing on Reilly's shirt. "Your shirt has a tear in it."

He kept his tone light. "'Twas headed for the rag pile anyway. Colin merely sped the process."

She nodded, slowly coming back into herself. He watched as her eyes refocused and her face cleared.

Colin disappeared, and Reilly turned Gwen toward him. "What's going on, Gwendolyn?"

She swallowed, not meeting his gaze, and replied lamely, "Jet lag."

"Look at me," he commanded, and was gratified when she immediately raised her forest green eyes to his. They were, as he suspected, haunted, despite her expressionless features. "I know what happened, Gwendolyn. Do you wish to talk?"

She shook her head—a short, sharp movement. "No. I really don't."

"Then tell me what you need."

She reached up and placed her hands on his cheeks. His breath hitched. She slowly pulled his head down to hers until they were eye level, then leaned forward and closed her eyes. Gently, she placed a soft kiss on his cheek, and let out a shuddering breath. "Thank you for last night. We'll be okay, right, Ry?"

He nodded, closing his own eyes, as a sweet feeling enveloped him. She held his cheek against hers, simply breathing, and Reilly held onto his rapidly fraying self-control by dredging up every fiber of willpower in his being. Just as he almost gave into his need to cover her mouth with his, she whispered, "I need to go home."

CHAPTER 2

*R*eilly blew the sawdust off his latest creation, then gave it the once-over.

Almost perfect.

The headboard for the bedroom was the final piece in a full set he'd created. The rich mahogany wood was a pleasure to work with, and the four-poster bed, chest, armoire, and armchair were complete. The final piece, this headboard, had been the trickiest. He'd been working on it for months, taking his time to get it just right to pull all the pieces together; the intricate Celtic knot work was carved into almost every available surface on the board.

It was his best work to date.

Woodworking soothed his weary soul. As the leader of all the O'Rourke Protectors, a select group of time travelers tasked with protecting the O'Rourke family line and the secrets the family held, Reilly realized early on in his life that creating something from nature was his best way to remain connected to his roots.

His mobile rang, shattering the peaceful silence, and he frowned when he read the screen. He contemplated for a moment, then hit *answer*.

He didn't bother with niceties. "A bit busy here."

Gwen laughed, the sound, as ever, the best balm for his soul—though the sound this time was definitely forced. "Then why did you pick up?"

Because I will always answer your call, he thought. But he said, "Hit the wrong button. Damn phone's too small for my hand."

"Oh."

He flinched. Too harsh. Why was he so prickly? He was *never* prickly.

He rubbed his forehead, grateful she couldn't see him. If he was being honest with himself, he knew why.

The entire flight back home, he argued with himself; for years, he hadn't allowed himself to think of Gwen as anything but a friend. It took more restraint than he cared to admit, but he'd done it. He spent countless hours—nay, years —cultivating her belief that they were nothing more than that.

But in that moment before she told him she wanted to leave, he almost gave in.

Almost.

But now…now he could finally claim success. Gwen was getting married. She promised herself, body and soul, to another man.

No matter that his world just about dropped from under his feet when that jackass staked a claim on her. Gwen was fully off-limits, just the way she needed to be.

And wasn't that for the best? After she saw him—all of him, and all that he was—she turned tail the first chance she got. Gwen claimed she was heading off on a series of humanitarian projects, bid him adieu just outside the airport, then flew mostly out of his life.

But now she was back.

Over their years of knowing each other, and more than ten years of close friendship, Reilly long ago gave up on lecturing

Gwen about her need to save the world. As such, he was usually the only one who ever knew exactly where she was… though there were many times when he almost wished he didn't. He knew where her last project was because she video called him. It hadn't taken much on his end to track her IP address.

If he now found it strange that she looked lonely while on an extended trip with her boyfriend—*fiancé*, he corrected himself with a growl—he didn't dare question it.

She cleared her throat. "Well, I won't take up too much of your time. I just wanted to say thank you for, um, everything. It was really kind of you. You left in kind of a hurry."

"I had to catch a commercial flight." He forcibly unclenched his jaw and resolved to bring them back to even footing. He had to; their friendship was special. Even if she hadn't told him about her engagement prior to the airport, he couldn't hold it against her, as he certainly kept secrets of his own. And his reaction to her wasn't her fault, either. "I'll always be there to get you, Gwendolyn. Are you looking forward to the gala?"

"Not particularly. It's for my cousin, Rob Bouchement. He's exploring the presidency."

"Sounds like it'll be riveting."

She snickered. "Oh, I'm sure. I can't wait, obviously."

"You'll have to tell everyone about your safari."

"I'm sure I'll tell them how amazing it was."

Reilly began to clean up his sanding supplies. "More amazing than the Venezuelan jungle, I would imagine."

"I also would imagine."

Reilly smiled, but only because she couldn't see him. Gwen tested his patience on every level; she was a completely unmanageable kind of woman who was on a mission to prove that she was more than her trust fund.

Of course, she would never admit that aloud, and Reilly would never dream of pointing it out to her. Doing so would guarantee him a blistering set down, and he'd had enough of those from his mother and sister to last many lifetimes.

"Well, over here in Ireland, we've got this crazy event happening soon."

She made a humming sound. "You don't say. Would it be a wedding between my bestie and your bestie?"

Reilly dumped his tools into the shiny silver tool chest and leaned against it, the phone held against his ear. "Did you just say *bestie*?"

"I did!"

"I beg you, never do that again. My tux fitting is in a couple of weeks."

She giggled. "You men have it so easy. I've got my dress fitting in a couple of weeks too, so I'll be heading out that way soon. Then we have the hen party and all that."

"Eleanor is having a hen party?" Surprised, Reilly couldn't picture quiet, introverted Ellie Carberry—soon to be O'Rourke—partying it up on the town. Gwen, he could see. She loved to go out and have a good time.

Gwen snorted. "In a way, I suppose. We're going to do dinner."

"That sounds more like the Ellie we all know. You want to stay here?"

As soon as the words were out of his mouth he regretted them. Of course she couldn't stay with him. She was seeing someone. Hell, she was marrying someone.

Someone else.

But it wasn't his bed she crawled into when her nightmares became too much, his traitorous mind reminded him.

Just because he wasn't there.

Unlike you, who is always there.

She cleared her throat, interrupting the argument he was having in his head. "Thanks, but I got a hotel room. Anthony will be meeting me out there, so…"

His breathing wasn't quite right, but he managed to sound normal when he replied, "Of course. Figured I'd ask."

"Yeah, and with all the wedding stuff I have going on with El, I'll be crazy busy with her, so, you know, it works out. Thanks, though."

"Sure."

Gwen rambled on, a sure sign she was nervous, and Reilly again vowed to be more civil to her. He wanted them to be as they always were again.

Gwen continued, "I'll be out there for a few weeks. You know, before the wedding. Do you, um, have any travel plans?"

"Do you perhaps mean a weekend away in France, or something a little further?"

She coughed. "Something a little further."

Inexplicably, Reilly felt the tension ease out of him. If she was talking about their last trip together (which was really her and Ellie ending up in medieval Ireland, and him, Colin, and James coming to rescue them), they might be able to find some common ground, and he could smooth out this conversation.

"Not at the moment I don't."

"Oh."

The disappointment in her voice was unmistakable. He ran his hands over the woodwork of his dresser and asked, "Did you *want* me to be gone?"

"Oh, no! I wanted to go with you."

Reilly froze, those six words wreaking absolute havoc on his heart. She wanted to travel with him? *Time* travel?

His pulse suddenly kicked into high gear, and he strove to maintain his even voice. "I don't think your fiancé would appreciate you traveling with me. Especially out of cell range."

"You might be right, but really, he's not like that. He's not the jealous type."

Reilly would beg to differ, as he was the one staring him down in an airport parking lot, but as that was an argument he didn't care to get into, he refrained from replying. Instead, he queried, "How'd the meeting with the parents go?"

Gwen let out a frustrated sigh. "They haven't met him yet, but they seem thrilled. They've been pestering me about finding a man for years."

"I know."

"They love me and want me to—" she started.

"Find a respectable husband with loads of money, become a trophy wife, and bear two-point-five perfect children?"

"I was going to say be a part of their world, but as usual, you're probably right. Maybe not the point-five part, though. A whole child seems like a better deal, if I'm to go through pregnancy a third time."

"Aye, I'd agree. Are you home now?"

"Walking into my house at this very moment. I wish I was walking into yours, though. God, I miss Ireland in the fall."

His heart stuttered a little, and he cursed himself thoroughly. He strove for a light tone. "Perhaps you should look into it for your honeymoon."

She hesitated a moment, and Reilly mentally slapped himself. *Why* could he not just leave well enough alone?

"I should've told you I was seeing someone," she said softly. Apologetically.

"Why didn't you?"

He could almost hear the wheels spinning in her head, but finally, she went with the truth. He could tell from her tone.

"I really did want to tell you in person. Anthony and I have been together for a while."

Reilly's chest tightened. "Define *a while*."

"Four months."

The world again dropped out from Reilly's feet, and he struggled to catch his breath. Four months...meaning she'd been seeing Anthony when she video called him, but she didn't say a thing about it. That bothered him. She shared everything with him—her happiness and her sadness. He lived for those moments, though he doubted she knew that. He *hoped* she didn't know that.

She made it abundantly clear in their early years of friendship that she was interested in being more than friends. But she was too important to him to bring into his world of constantly-changing locations and times. Add to that, she didn't know he was a time traveler until recently, and Reilly couldn't bring himself to ruin what was the best relationship of his life with sex and all those messy emotions that tended to go with it.

Not that he hadn't imagined it. With her fiery, copper-red hair, luminous, forest-green eyes, soft, freckled skin, and feisty mouth, he'd have to be dead not to.

And he was as far from dead as any human had a right to be.

Reilly admitted to himself more times than he could remember that he needed Gwen like he needed air. Her spirit always lifted his own, and her laugh soothed his troubled soul. She knew when to sit in silence and when to tease him out of a mood. She could read him better than anyone of his acquaintance, not that it was hard; he simply allowed her to get to know the real him.

And now she even knew about the time-traveling side of him, not that he'd had much say about that after she and Eleanor ended up on the wrong side of a time gate.

"Are you very angry with me?" she asked in a small voice.

He shook his head, though she couldn't see him. "Never, Gwendolyn. Just surprised. And a bit hurt."

Hurt that she hadn't told him about Venezuela, hurt that she'd been in a relationship long enough to decide that man was the one for her. He could hear her swallow hard, and he felt a rock land in his stomach. She replied quietly, "I'm sorry, Reilly."

"Forgiven." And he did forgive her, because it wasn't her fault. He messed up; he should've confessed his feelings when she gave him the chance. Instead, he shut her down again, and she moved on. He had to accept that.

"So you're okay with it?"

He cleared his throat. "Don't waste another moment worrying, lass. I'm happy for you and your new beau."

"Really?"

"Aye. If you're happy, I'm happy."

They chatted easily for a few more minutes—well, easily on Gwen's part, Reilly had to force a lightness to his tone, lest she think he was still upset—and when they hung up, Reilly sat down heavily on his couch.

Gwen was truly getting married.

He absently rubbed the hollow spot in his chest and stared out his window.

Did he really think she'd wait forever for him to figure out what he wanted?

He dropped his head in his hands. In his heart, he supposed he *did* believe she would. And that, he laughed miserably to himself, is what made him the most arrogant, short-sighted fool of all time.

ALMOST A WEEK LATER, GWEN PACED NERVOUSLY IN THE LIVING room of her quaint Cape Cod house. She loved her little beach home, tucked alongside New Hampshire's small coastline, but in the summer, her tiny coastal town was a tourist attraction, due to the art galleries and homemade candy shops that lined Main Street. The quintessential, sleepy New England fishing community had quite the boom a few years back, and now artisans and politicians alike flocked there during the summer months.

Gwen tried to stay away until autumn came.

She was all dressed up for the big political event at the yacht club in the city. Her mom, Bev, and her dad, Rick, were flying in from their home in California, to support their highly politicized side of the family. This wasn't their first song-and-dance; these kinds of parties were what her parents lived for. They loved to mingle and mix with the wealthy elite; as the only child, Gwen had always simply gone along. It was fun to get dressed up and drink really expensive champagne (which to her, she admitted only to Reilly, tasted the same as inexpensive champagne). Usually.

It was always a good time because Reilly was there. They made games of the various things they were sure to hear, such as whenever someone mentioned their summer home, each of them would tuck a cocktail napkin into Ry's suit pocket. At the end of the night, they counted the napkins, and that's the number of whiskey shots they would split.

A heaviness settled into the pit of Gwen's stomach at the thought. She didn't want to put on a smile tonight. She didn't want to walk around in the high heels, or make up stories about South Africa. She wanted to crawl into bed, pull the covers over her head, and pretend that the last couple weeks of her life were just a really bad dream.

Gwen checked her appearance in the mirror again. It was what it was. She agreed to go to the fundraiser, and go she would. Tonight would be fun. It would just be a different kind of fun, and that would be something to take her mind off her troubles. And her parents were meeting her future husband.

She felt, rather than heard, Anthony's bike pull into her driveway. A moment later, he walked into her house and swept into a bow.

"You look gorgeous. And you're not even holding a wrench."

She laughed. "I can't believe you rode your motorcycle while wearing a tux!"

"I didn't feel like taking the truck," he shrugged, then winked.

He really was charming, and a genuinely nice person. Her parents were going to adore him, for he was definitely a chameleon, and would fit in with the political crowd just as easily as he did with the guys at a bar.

"Good thing I have a car," she replied dryly. "I don't think I can comfortably get onto the back of your bike wearing this." She tugged at the tight bodice, then twisted around. "Would you mind finishing up the zipper?"

"I'd like to *un*finish it," he murmured, but he zipped it and spun her around. "Did I tell you how stunning you are?"

She smiled at him, wishing for the millionth time that she was as in love with him as he was with her.

Do not think of that right now.

She leaned up on her toes to kiss him. "Well, let's go. We wouldn't want to be late to the party."

"Red, there is no party until you arrive."

She smiled at him again. She appreciated the compliment. Reilly usually grunted at her.

Before he left for Ireland, Reilly insisted on driving her all the way to her house, even though she could've grabbed a ride share. The ride wasn't tense, but it wasn't their easy silence, either. As soon as he'd checked every room and assured himself that she was good, he left in a hurry.

She hated that they were at odds. And though he said he forgave her, she still felt like she did something wrong. Which, rationally, she realized wasn't true, but she hated arguing with Reilly.

Do not think about Reilly.

She brought herself back into the present. "Well, we have at least an hour of driving ahead of us, so if you're ready, I am, too."

Anth swiped the keys from her front table. "I'll fill your tank. The reality is that my car battery died and I didn't want to make us late, so I took the bike. If it's okay with you, I'll drive. Those shoes look killer."

She glanced down at the stilettos. "I could drive barefoot."

"Or you could allow me to be a gentleman and drive us."

She capitulated, and after they were well on their way, he flicked a glance to her.

"So. That guy. The Irish one."

Gwen sighed. "Reilly, yes. He's been my friend for years, and my driver was cancelled, so Reilly came to pick me up."

"Does he live here in New England?"

"No, he lives in Ireland."

Anthony's shoulders relaxed a fraction. "Ah. Why was he in town?"

To go to the gala, she thought, a pang of guilt hitting her.

"He was visiting his family, as a few of them live in the city," she replied. "But he's gone back to Ireland now."

He didn't even say goodbye. She got a text from Colin.

That *may* have been about the time when she started feeling panicky. She still wasn't sure why she felt so anxious, but she wished it would stop already.

"Did you two have a thing, ever?"

Gwen blinked. "Wow, you're not mincing words, Anth."

"Well, I come out to see you wrapped up in his arms, wearing his jacket, and it makes a guy a little bit unsure, you know? So I think it's a fair question."

She shook her head decisively. "We did not have a thing. We do not currently have a thing. We are very good friends, but that's it."

Anthony reached over and laced his fingers with hers. "Good. Because it about killed me to see you in someone else's arms. You're with me."

She squeezed his hand. "Willingly."

He brought her hand to his lips and kissed it gently. "Excellent. Now, remind me about your parents and tell me all about the fun I'm going to pretend to have."

"Lots. Remember that they know nothing of Venezuela. However, my parents are thrilled at our engagement, and I'm sure we'll be passed around more than the appetizers."

"Sounds painful."

"It will be."

"And what's your speech about?"

Gwen blew out a gusty breath. "I'm going to be talking about the devastating effects of the opioid crisis in New England, and by extension, the entire country. And I'll be asking for people to consider donating to this cause."

"Well, whatever you do, don't beg. You're better than that."

Gwen frowned. "I'm not sure what you mean by that?"

He patted her knee. "Don't worry about it. Do you want to practice the speech?"

Perhaps it was misplaced humor that fell flat, so she let it go. "Nah, I'm good, thanks. It's important to me—really important—but I just can't practice it anymore."

"Understood."

As they talked and the miles dragged by, Gwen could appreciate that she was content. She wasn't jumping up and down overjoyed, and her belly wasn't fluttering with butterflies, but content was enough for her.

She accepted long ago that security and contentment was more than enough, as it was leaps and bounds ahead of loneliness and heartbreak.

"Where's Mr. O'Malley this evening?"

Gwen smiled politely at the couple across from her and Anthony. "He had other engagements."

"It isn't as though she keeps track of his whereabouts," Anthony added sharply.

Gwen dipped her head at the couple slightly, and placed

her hand on her fiancé's arm. "Excuse us." She ushered him away from the taken aback couple and dragged him into an adjoining room. "What is wrong with you?" she hissed.

"Does anyone see me standing there?" he huffed in reply. He mocked, "Where's Mr. O'Malley? Does he plan to join us this evening? What a wonderful man, that Reilly of yours!"

Gwen frowned. "Stop it. They know him as my friend; he's been to almost every one of these events and has made an effort to get to know these people. They're meeting you as my fiancé, and you're not exactly making the best impression!"

Anthony rolled his eyes. "And are these people the kind of people you care to make an impression on, Gwendolyn?" He glanced back at the throng of well-dressed people, sipping champagne while talking and laughing. "I bet they've never done a day's work in their life! Do they even know what a hammer is?"

Gwen's jaw set. "You don't know them, Anthony—"

He barked out a laugh. "No, I don't. And I don't care to, either."

"They are part of my life," she exclaimed in a low voice. She glanced up at an elderly couple passing by. "Those are the Hendricks. They've donated more than six million dollars to fund research into Alzheimer's. And over there, the man in the dark gray suit? That's Mark Torrey. Two years ago, he lost his daughter to drug overdose and has donated his entire yearly paycheck to—"

"Oh, please," Anthony cut her off with a wave of his hand. "Money doesn't equate with hard work. What *we* do is important. What we do actually *helps* people."

Gwen blinked at him, words failing her. "I'm—I'm sorry, what?"

He looked over the assorted people of her extended family, business associates, and longtime family friends with disdain.

"You joined us to get away from the falsity of all this. I don't understand why we're here. We could be doing so much more with our time. They could be doing so much more. Give them a hammer or bring them to a third world country. Let them see who really needs help. It's those kids without a school building in Nairobi. Not," he sniffed with a glance to Mr. Torrey, "overprivileged rich brats who spent their daddy's money on some drugs and had to pay the piper."

Gwen's heart constricted tightly, cutting off her breath. Jennifer Torrey was one of the nicest women Gwen had ever known, and watching her fall victim to the opioid crisis was something she would always struggle with. Anthony's careless remarks about her friend sliced deeply.

"I live by the creed that you need to gather all the facts before making a judgement," she replied stiffly.

"That's idealistic of you, but hardly relevant. I was in that room with you. Those are hours I'll never get back; those people are so self-important, it makes me sick."

Gwen's mouth worked for a few seconds before she just shook her head in disgusted shock. "I think you need to leave."

His head snapped back. "Excuse me?"

She swallowed, her throat painfully dry, her breath still short. "You need to go. I don't want you here."

"We came together," he pointed out.

"You can take a car service back to my place to get your bike or I can have the bike sent to you tomorrow," she said, her voice stronger. "But I want you gone right now."

"I'm not made of money like everyone else here," he shot back.

She fumbled in her purse and withdrew her wallet. She shoved a couple hundred-dollar bills at him. "Go away."

He took the money and shook his head in disgust. "We need to have a long talk about this, Gwendolyn."

She gritted her teeth, but instead of responding, she spun on her heel and left him behind her.

"Dear, where's your fiancé going?" her mother asked, gliding up next to her with a fresh glass of champagne as she watched Anthony head toward the coat room.

"Away," she muttered, swiping the glass and downing it.

Bev shook her head. "It seems as though you two had a disagreement."

"We've been disagreeing all night," Gwen admitted.

Her mother nodded. "I know. People are worried about you. Said they haven't seen a true smile from you yet. Even with the wonderful news that your cousin is considering a run for the presidency! You know, the press will arrive soon. They've been invited for the second half of the gala. They'll hear your speech."

"I know. And I'll try harder to relax," Gwen murmured. And she would, because despite the pompousness of some people in the room, as she'd grown older, she saw what good they really tried to do. Anthony was right in that some of them had never worked a day the same way he did; however, their strengths were in other areas, and they were using those strengths to make impacts where they could. In fact, Mr. Torrey was working with the governor to go after pharmaceutical companies for their role in his daughter's death.

That could prevent so many future deaths and heartache, and Gwen could only see the good in his intentions. And most of the people at the gala had similar impacts on the charities they supported, too.

And...they were her family, both by blood and by water. For Anthony to not understand that, above all else, made her doubts grow even stronger.

Half an hour later, the doors opened to the press, and Gwen stood as far back as possible. She didn't care to have her picture in the papers or magazines, and she had just about reached her limit of "Where did your young man go off to?" questions. She quietly slipped out the main ballroom doors, but drew up short.

There, in front of her, stood Reilly, in a crisp black tuxedo. He tilted his head at her. "You clean up nice, Ms. Allen."

She blinked, then blinked again. "Wha—how—why are you here?" she blurted out.

He clasped a hand over his heart. "You wound me with your lack of compliments to my person." He leaned forward and dropped his voice to a conspiratorial whisper. "I even brushed my hair for the occasion."

She broke out into a grin and held her hand out to him. "My apologies, Mr. O'Malley. You look…"

"Go on," he encouraged, taking her hand and dropping a kiss to her knuckles.

She could barely string two thoughts together, never mind words. How was Reilly standing here, in Boston, and not in Ireland, where he was when they last spoke a week ago? She took a long look at him and assessed.

He stood, gorgeous, smiling, happy to see her.

In a tux.

Wearing his little-boy, charming, disarming, impish smile.

"Dashing," she finally said, when she caught her breath.

He shook his head. "Weak. Give it another go, and make it count this time."

"Fishing for compliments?" she teased, tugging her hand.

Instead of letting go, he gently pulled her closer and tucked her hand into his elbow. He gave a blinding smile to a passing server, who nearly tripped over herself from the force of it, and took a glass of champagne from the tray. After thanking her, he offered the glass to Gwen, who refused it. He shrugged, then tossed it back. "No need to fish for them, really. Just trying to expand your terribly lacking vocabulary."

"You are an arrogant ass, you know," she replied loftily.

"Still not a compliment," he replied in a singsong voice.

She looked at him seriously for a moment. "Be straight with me, Ry. Why are you here, and not at home?"

He placed the now-empty glass on another passing server's tray and looked into her eyes. His hazel gaze turned serious. "Because your parents invited me. Because when I thought about it, I know that this is a big night for you. You have a speech to give, on a very personal subject. Because even though I might not be your date this evening, I do have an open invitation to these things, courtesy of your dad." He gave her a small smile. "No matter how much we fight, I'll always be there to support you."

Her mouth hung open a little, her heart bursting into flowers and her stomach erupting into beautiful, terrifying butterflies. "*Are* we fighting?" she finally managed to ask.

He laughed. "No, Gwendolyn. We never really fight, because I can never stay angry with you."

"Were you angry with me?" she asked quietly.

He leaned down and kissed her cheek. "Nay, lass. 'Twas only myself with whom I was angry. Forgive an old man for his grouchiness. Let us find your date."

Gwen pursed her lips. "Well, he had to leave, so…"

Ry slid her a look that spoke volumes, but he wisely held his tongue. "'Tis a shame. Will you allow me the honor of clinging to your dress in there? I know so few people, you see."

This, she thought happily. Their banter, the games they always played, the feeling of security on his arm—this is what had been missing the entire evening. Her shoulders relaxed, her chest loosened, and even her cheek muscles slackened slightly. She felt the familiar sense of peace wash over her. Gwen couldn't help her wide smile, and played along. "Of course. Come, come, I'll introduce you."

"My thanks," he replied, leading her back into the room.

"I warn you, they are a little boring," she whispered conspiratorially.

"Ah," he whispered back. "Lucky for you, I'm not."

She chuckled, but the sound was lost when a burst of cheers went up at the sight of Reilly.

As they were instantly surrounded by her family and friends, Gwen understood their happiness at seeing him. It was easy to love Reilly O'Malley.

Not as easy, perhaps, to earn his love in return.

Not that she wanted to anymore. No, that ship had sailed, and she moved on. Reilly was the best of men, and she was grateful to have him in her life. But she knew a reckoning was coming.

She was too much of a realist to know she couldn't have her cake and eat it, too.

"You didn't come home last night."

"Anthony?" Gwen blinked blearily at the phone screen, trying to hit the speaker button so she wouldn't have to expend the effort of actually holding the phone to her ear. She shouldn't have stayed out so late, but really, she was having too good of a time to go home early. Lucky for her, Colin's house was a quick trip from the gala last night.

"I waited at your house like a fool until three in the morning. And then, when I check the local news, guess whose picture is splashed all over the website?"

Gwen rubbed her eyes and looked around Colin's guest room, her eyes landing on an alarm clock a few feet away. "Anthony, it's seven in the morning. Can this wait until I've at least opened my eyes?"

"Are you sleeping with him?"

At that, Gwen sat up quickly, a flash of anger slicing

through her sleep fog. "Excuse me? Absolutely not. I'm not a cheater."

"Well," Anthony replied, scorn in his tone, "in the pictures I'm seeing, you're looking at him like a lovesick teenager."

"Jealousy is not necessary," she snapped. If there was one thing she hated beyond all else, it was the feeling of being caged. She knew from past experiences that jealous boyfriends most definitely wanted her caged; she hadn't thought Anthony had a jealous bone in his body.

Apparently, she'd been wrong.

"I want you to stop hanging around him."

Gwen groaned. "Reilly is my best friend. I'm not going to give up a friendship just because you demand it. That's not how adulting works, Anthony."

"It's how relationships work, Gwendolyn."

"I'm not discussing this. I've barely opened my eyes, much less had any coffee. I'll call you later."

The annoyance in his voice when he began to respond had her hitting the End button, then flipping the switch to silence the phone.

"You really want to marry that bloke?" Reilly asked, appearing at her bed with a steaming mug in his hand.

She greedily reached for it. "Is that for me?"

He held it out of reach with a raised eyebrow. "Yours is brewing downstairs. I figured if I could get you to smell it, I could lure you from your slumber. Alas, it looks like you were woken up in another, much less pleasurable, way."

She flopped back against the pillow as Reilly sat on the edge of the bed. "He thinks I'm sleeping with you."

Reilly's eyes darkened. In another life, whenever she told Reilly of her boyfriend believing she was sleeping with him, she liked to think that his eyes darkened with desire at the thought of it. Now, she knew it was only concern.

He made a non-committal sound, but she knew he wanted to say something. She narrowed her eyes. "What?"

"You know what I'm thinking, so why say it? We both know it'll merely inflame your temper."

"It's too early for your logical nonsense," she replied, pulling the covers over her head.

He flipped them back. "Wake up, Sleeping Beauty. I've a flight to catch in but a few hours' time, and you're driving me."

"Why do I have to wake up now?" she grumbled. "And you still haven't said what's on your mind."

"Lass, move your fetching self out of this bed. I've plans for us yet, and you're putting me behind schedule."

"It's schedule, with a K sound."

"You Yanks have butchered the English language long enough. Halt your attempts to slay it further. It's shhhhed-joo-wel, as you well know. Move, wench, before I make you."

She squeezed her eyes shut. "I'm going back to sleep."

She squeaked as he swiftly lifted her from the bed. "Hey!"

He paused for a moment, looking first at her as she glared at him from his arms, then the coffee cup which he'd obviously just placed on the nightstand. He quickly tossed her over one shoulder and reached for the cup.

"I will breathe my morning breath all over you if you don't put me down," she warned, her face against his back.

"Ah, lass. A bit o' morning breath has yet to ever put any man off from a beautiful woman." He readjusted her so her stomach wasn't crushed against him, and made his way downstairs.

"You know I have no pants on, right?" she grumbled.

"Aye. But the tunic you lifted from my room last night covers the important bits," he replied.

"You should be more out of breath," she added, propping her elbow against his back and resting her face in her hand.

"As should you. Stop talking, wench, or else you'll make your own coffee." He gently deposited her into one of the barstools, placed her coffee in front of her, and as he went to the mammoth built-in coffee bar to make his own, she couldn't help her smile.

And, as always, her happiness was accompanied by that all-too-familiar, all-too-real sharp pain of unrequited love.

Damn him for being so wonderful.

And damn her messy emotions that were nearly—but not totally—impossible to repress.

~

"GWEN, I'M NOT A JEALOUS GUY. I'M REALLY NOT. BUT YOU'RE dropping what, four grand? For a plane ticket to go see another man three thousand miles away?"

Gwen pinched the bridge of her nose. In the back of her mind, when she agreed to marry Anthony, she recognized she'd have to let some of her closeness with Reilly lapse. But did it have to be so soon? She thought she'd have time to wean herself from the unmovable friendship. "It's not like that, Anth. He's my friend. And I told you, I'm going early to help Ellie."

He ran a hand through his hair, his eyes blazing. "Oh, sure. Because your friend needs you for three weeks before her wedding?"

"She asked me to come."

"And I'm your fiancé, asking you not to go."

"You're being insecure."

"I'm not, Gwen. I'm being honest. I don't want you to go for so long. This guy…Reilly. You didn't see his expression when I walked up to you at the airport. He had possession written all over his face."

"Don't be ridiculous! Reilly is protective, not possessive, of me. Like a brother," Gwen explained, though she knew it fell on deaf ears.

"A brother who wants in your pants."

"That's not even funny, Anth."

He grabbed her hand. "Don't go, Gwen. Please. Come to Atlanta with me instead."

"My best friend is getting *married*. I'm her maid of honor. You know this."

His mouth settled into a thin line. "You want to know what I know? Instead of taking a vacation with me, my fiancée is hopping an international flight to go see her friend on the flimsy excuse that she needs to be there three weeks before an hour-long ceremony."

Gwen shook her head forcefully. "That isn't how it is!" She unclenched her jaw and lowered her voice. "You're acting like a child. I do not want to go on yet another charity trip right now, Anthony. I saw too much on the last one. I'm burnt out, and this is the perfect break for me. *And my best friend since childhood is getting married*. Relationships are built on trust, and you're not trusting me."

"It isn't you I don't trust!" he finally shouted. "But it doesn't look good from that angle, either. You are choosing this guy, and your friends, over me! I offer you me, and you pass to go running to your so-called best friend, to whom you didn't so much as drop a letter while we were in Venezuela!"

Gwen's mouth dropped open. "You have no idea what I did or did not do!" She hadn't written any letters, of course. She didn't want the postmark to show her true location, but aside from that, email was significantly easier. And she'd been emailing with Ellie weekly, not that she planned to share that information with Anthony. Not while he was angry, anyway.

"Here's the issue, Gwen. Your buddy, the 'brother-like' guy, has a thing for you. You don't think he's going to make a play for you now that you're taken, Gwen? You don't think he's going to want what he can't have?"

"Reilly has no feelings like that for me!" she shouted back, fully exasperated. "You're being unreasonable!"

Anthony's mouth was hard. "Not if you look at it from my

perspective, Gwen. I know what I saw. And while I trust you, I definitely don't trust that guy."

She gritted her teeth. "Oh, yes, you definitely trust that in the highly unlikely event that Reilly O'Malley, whom I've been friends with for years, makes a pass at me, I won't be able to help myself?"

She pushed down the teeny flutter of excitement that thought brought.

She reined in her temper. "Anthony, I've stayed at his house more times than I can count. He's just not into me the way you think he is. I've known him my entire adult life. He's not going to make a pass at me."

Anth glowered. "So you're going, no matter what?"

"Yes, I'm going to help one of my best friends plan the final details of her wedding, and I'm going to see my other best friend, who loves me like a sister."

Anthony's eyes narrowed. "You know, you say an awful lot about how he feels about you, but not once have you said how you feel about him. Not a single, 'I think of him like a brother,' or an, 'I don't have any romantic feelings for him.'"

"Are you kidding me right now?"

He shrugged. "I don't think I am."

"I'm *marrying* you, Anthony. What other reassurance do you need?"

"The kind that comes from you by my side, instead of on the other side of the ocean."

She held the door open, unwilling to face that truth. *Baby steps.* "I think you better leave."

"That's it, then? Everything we've been working toward, every feeling we've had for each other, and I get shown the door because I don't want you to spend the better part of a month with another man?"

Gwen's shoulders dropped. "I'm not ending the engagement, for crying out loud. But you clearly don't trust me enough to know me. I'm not a cheater. I wouldn't cheat on you. On anyone."

"I believe you."

"Great. Then I'll see you in Ireland for the wedding."

"Gwen."

The pain in his voice stopped her cold.

"You and I...we're great together. I can see it, long term. I can see our future together; we can have it all, and be so happy together. Don't you see that, too? A family? A future?"

She swallowed hard. A safe, steady future with a man she cared for deeply. Yes, she could see it; she could be content with that life.

It was what she wanted, after all. Stability. A life partner. Someone who loved her.

But right now, she needed something else, something she couldn't quite name.

He added quietly, "I'm a sure thing. I will spend every day trying to make you happy. Can't you see it?"

She nodded slowly, her resolve wavering. "Of course I can."

"Then be done with that guy. Prove to me that I'm more important. Come with me to Atlanta."

Any softening feelings melted away. "I will not give up my oldest friend because of your insecurity, Anthony."

"It's not insecurity, *Gwendolyn*. It's an absolute fact. The man wants you for more than friendship. I'm in love with you, Gwen. And you know what that means? That means I can see others who are in love, too. And that guy—"

"His name is Reilly," she snapped, her patience at an end.

"I don't care if his name is Prince freaking Harry. The guy is in love with you. I think it's best if you just cut ties."

She gave him a tight smile. "That's enough, Anthony. I'll see you in Ireland. The time apart will do us both good."

He opened his mouth quickly, but snapped it shut as she held open the door and waited without making eye contact.

His jaw set, he gave her a jerky nod and, without another word, he stormed out.

She quietly closed the door behind him, seething. She *knew* if she ever wanted a chance at a life with Anthony, she would have to leave Reilly in the past. She didn't need Anthony to force it down her throat.

And I will leave him behind, she promised herself. *When I'm ready.* If she didn't, she wouldn't be able to fully give her heart to anyone else. But that would happen on her own schedule-with-a-k-sound, and not anyone else's.

CHAPTER 3

*G*wen smiled wanly as Ellie's aunt, Winifred, droned on about the latest on-dit in the upper echelons of British society. As Winnie was a prominent gossip columnist, the topic of conversation wasn't a surprise, but it was tedious, as Gwen didn't follow modern aristocracy.

That never stopped Aunt Winnie before, Gwen admitted to herself with a small smile, and it wasn't about to stop her today.

They were sitting in Winnie's Irish seaside cottage, counting the minutes until she ran out of things to talk about.

She glanced down at her weak tea and her stomach growled.

"I love what the Duchess is doing, but she better rein in that scamp cousin of hers," Winnie pontificated.

Gwen caught Ellie's eye and grimaced. Ellie scratched her eyebrow, their secret sign that one of them needed to redirect the conversation, so Gwen cleared her throat.

"Speaking of scamps," Gwen started, unsure of where to go with it.

Ellie immediately picked up, "We're hopeful not to run into any tonight." She glanced at her watch and stood quickly.

"We've got to go if we want to make our reservations, Gwen. We've got to dash, Aunt Winnie. Gwen's set up my hen party, and we've dinner plans before we get started."

"Off with you, I suppose," Winnie sighed. She adjusted her new spectacles and blinked owlishly. "I'm for London in the morning. Are you girls planning to stay the night here? I don't want you tripping in after eleven; there's no need for me to startle awake because you can't hold your liquor."

She directed a stare at Gwen, who squirmed uncomfortably. "I said I was sorry, Aunt Winnie. And it was seventeen years ago…"

"Still the worst night's sleep in my life, having to wake up to your uncontrollable giggles and then, when you fell down the stairs! Oh, to be your poor mother on the other end of the phone that night. Tsk tsk, Gwendolyn."

Ellie snorted. "Well, she did get five phone numbers that night. I'd call it a success."

"Eleanor!" Winnie exclaimed, as Gwen guffawed into her elbow. Winnie gave them both a censorious look before rising. "If your evening activities go past eleven, do get yourselves a hotel."

"Yes, Aunt Winnie," the women chorused. They watched her leave, then shared a silent look before bolting upright from their own chairs. They elbowed each other out of the way in a rush to get to the front door.

"Ha! I win!" Ellie exclaimed, slightly out of breath.

"Only because I *let* you," Gwen retorted, trying to even out her own breathing.

Ready with the front door open, Alan, Winnie's butler, kept a straight face when he droned, "Perhaps someday you two might act like grown women?"

"Perhaps," Gwen acquiesced with a grin, "but today is not that day."

He cracked a smile at that, and she gave him a quick kiss on the cheek before running down the steps to the parked car.

They piled in and slammed the doors, then burst into laughter.

"Oh, I do love her so," Ellie gasped.

Gwen wiped tears from her eyes. "Yes, but she just goes *on* and *on!*"

Ellie started the car and headed out of the driveway. "As if I truly care about a duchess right now. I'm getting married, Gwen! In less than three weeks!"

"I know!" They shared a moment of squealing glee before Gwen wrinkled her nose. "Okay, pull over. You have no idea where I'm taking you, and you know I love to drive on the left."

"You know I loathe crowds," Ellie reminded her as she expertly avoided two stray sheep in the road before pulling off to the side.

"I do."

And I can't handle them right now, either.

The thought came out of nowhere. Gwen shook her head, as if to dislodge it. She loved crowds. Right now, she was just in a funk. That was all. She'd shake out of it soon, she knew she would.

They switched seats and were on the road again in a moment. After a few twists and turns, Gwen's GPS told her to turn right…into a nice, open field, if she were to follow it.

"Uh oh."

Ellie laughed. "I think the surprise is up. Tell me what the plan is, and I'll give you directions."

In addition to being the life of the party, Gwen was also a master at event planning. She loved to throw huge get-togethers, plan major dinners, and mingle in a crowd of unfamiliar faces. Ellie, however, was the exact opposite, and in deference to her introverted nature, Gwen planned out the most low-key hen party ever to hit the shores of Ireland.

Ever.

"We're going to a private seven course wine tasting event."

"Oh, at that upscale wine bar by the sea?" Ellie breathed, excitement lacing her words.

Gwen smiled. "Yep. We have a private chef, dedicated waitstaff, and loads of different wines to try before the night is through."

"Will Colin be there?"

"El-*lie*," Gwen groaned, drawing out the name in complaint. "You have to have at least one night away from him!"

"I do?"

"Yes. It's written down in the *Gwen Allen Book of Pre-Wedding Etiquette*. Page thirty-six, section B, states, *You must spend at least one night away from your beloved before the ceremony, because absence makes the heart grow fonder.*"

Ellie snorted. "I call foul."

Gwen shrugged. "It was worth a try. No, he won't be there. It's just us."

Ellie reached over and grabbed her hand. "That sounds absolutely perfect. Thanks, Gwennie."

Gwen tossed her a wink.

"Oh, damn, you should've turned left back there," Ellie exclaimed, looking back over her shoulder.

Gwen let out another laugh. It was going to be a wonderful night. No pipe bombs, no gunfire, and no men.

Perfect.

IT HAD BEEN A LONG, DIFFICULT NIGHT.

Gwen almost rubbed the skin off her forehead as she leaned on her elbows on the perfectly polished stone counter. "I prepaid. I have the confirmation email right here." She slid the paperwork she'd printed earlier at Winnie's house across the counter to the apologetic hotel clerk.

"I'm sorry, miss, but there's been an overbooking due to the football match, and because of your late check-in, we had to give your room away. We did try to contact you."

Yes, she'd seen the calls come in on her phone, but she didn't recognize the number, so she didn't pick up. And they didn't leave a voicemail.

"How about a broom closet. Can I sleep in one of those?" Gwen grumbled. She was no stranger to being bumped; with the amount of travel she did every year, it was an inevitability. But she'd prepaid for just this reason.

And she'd prepaid for three weeks.

"I've already issued a full refund to your card," the woman added, again apologetically.

"Wait, a full refund? I have the room for three weeks!"

The clerk looked like she was about to cry. "When we released your reservation for the night, the system released you fully, and we immediately booked up, what with the championship game coming up in Dublin and all the festivities."

"You people and your soccer," Gwen sighed.

"Shall I ring about some other hotels in the area, to see if there's any availability for you? The night would be on us, of course, for the inconvenience."

Gwen gave her a tired nod, appreciative of the effort the woman was giving, and she checked her watch. Jet lag was catching up to her in a big way, and it was just after midnight. While Gwen knew she should've checked into the hotel earlier, she'd been too busy catching up with Ellie, since she'd picked up Gwen at the airport that morning. When Ellie dropped her off at the hotel a few moments ago, they said their goodbyes, and Ellie headed back to Winnie's, despite the old woman's dire warnings earlier in the day.

A few minutes later, the clerk hung up the phone, looking defeated. "Everywhere is booked, miss."

Gwen knew this already, as she checked her apps and the internet while the clerk made the calls. Not a single hotel room to be found for over fifty miles.

And Gwen had a dress fitting at eleven a.m. the next morning...and no rental car until tomorrow, either.

"Is there anyone you can call?"

Gwen nodded, and she thanked the harried woman before pulling her suitcase off to one of the lush sofas in the main entrance. She plopped down and took a deep breath, then dialed.

"Awfully late for a booty call. Welcome back, lass." The deep, rich voice immediately brought a smile to her face, and she sighed heavily.

"Not quite a welcome," she said, then quickly explained her situation.

"I'll be there in fifteen minutes."

"Put some pants on first," she teased.

A guffaw sounded and he replied, "Perhaps I'll put the léine on instead, just to be contrary."

He disconnected, and exactly fifteen minutes later, Reilly O'Malley pulled up, loaded her luggage into the car, buckled her tired body into the passenger seat, and drove them back to his house, where he had her tucked into bed inside of five minutes of arrival.

Sometimes, she thought as she snuggled into the covers, the man was too good to be true.

Right before she fell into a deep, dreamless sleep, her heart felt lighter than it had in far too long.

∾

James O'Rourke, the elder brother of Colin and Reilly's current training partner, leaned heavily on his sword, breathing hard. "Got some demons to fight today?"

Reilly bounced on the balls of his feet, feeling fresh and alive. "Questions will get you naught but more trials, cousin. Sword up."

They stood in the freshly tended lists at Reilly's sword fighting school. He opened it a few years ago after watching a particularly bad sword fight in a movie; though he catered to actors, he had a few die-hard reenactment folks as regulars.

No one walked away from his school and performed poorly in sword fighting again. He made sure of it.

James shook his head. "No way. I need water. I'm about to pass out. How long have we been doing this?"

Reilly checked his watch. "A pair of hours. Once more, lad."

James reluctantly raised his sword again, but not before throwing a longing look toward the drink machine. "I'm already regretting this. You know I'm here for vacation. For Colin's wedding. For relaxation. It's too early for sword training."

Reilly canted his head, bemused. "It's never too early for sword training. And this *is* relaxing."

"The sun has just come up over the horizon," James pointed out. "If the sun is sleeping, people should be, too. It's the way of the Universe."

"That's just the kind of attitude that'll get you killed while time traveling," Reilly explained patiently as he hacked at James. The metal-on-metal sound brought Reilly great pleasure, but here at his sword fighting school, the sound was not nearly as common as he'd like. The Hollywood stunt men he trained used a poor substitute of wooden swords to practice their skills, and eventually they were allowed dulled blades. He couldn't trust them with anything else.

But, when James, Colin, or Aidan came to visit, Reilly had

the joy of crossing sharp blades with them. And James would not deny him the sport because, above all, he was determined to learn how to fight for self-defense.

A few times in a dungeon would do that to a man, Reilly well knew, and during one particularly uncomfortable escapade —unfortunately, James's first—James was on the wrong side of a land border. It took Reilly a pair of days to free him, and once he did, James decided he needed more knowledge than simply how to identify the business end of a sword.

He needed to know how to use that end effectively.

And so here they parried, a few minutes after dawn, a few years into his training. Reilly took pity on the man—after all, they spent the majority of the last week in the lists, working on a new technique—and ended their session abruptly as James swayed. James gratefully made a beeline for the water and swigged it as Reilly checked his phone.

"You *never* check your phone. Got a hot date?" James asked, wiping his mouth with his arm.

"Gwen's at the house, sleeping. Lost her hotel reservation."

James paused, the bottle halfway to his lips again. "Wait, she had a reservation? At a hotel?"

Reilly shrugged off the feeling of irritation.

"What did you do to make her get a reservation?"

"Nothing."

James turned fully to him with a guffaw. "Gwen always stays at your house. She visits you so often that you even decorated one of the bedrooms just for her. Rumor has it that no one else is allowed to stay in her room."

"Colin speaks overmuch," Reilly grumbled.

James grinned. "Only when he's in his cups."

"Colin's never in his cups."

"*Never* is so absolute. A better term is *rarely*. Colin is *rarely* in his cups."

Reilly spared a glance for his sweating cousin. "What else did that fool disclose?"

"In fairness, I never confirmed it was Colin saying anything," James noted innocently. "You forget, I've been spending time with my almost-sister-in-law. You know... Gwen's *other* best friend? Once she trusts someone, it's a bit difficult to get her to stop talking."

Reilly grit his teeth. "Jests are unwelcome."

"Unless it's Gwen who's doing the jesting?"

Reilly started for him, but James laughed and put up his hands. "Down, boy. I'm just kidding. I'm no expert on relationships—hell, everyone but me knew my ex-wife was sleeping with everything under the hospital roof. But even I can see that something had to have happened to make Gwen decide on a hotel rather than her second home."

"Aye." Reilly unclenched his jaw and tried to ease the unfamiliar tension from his shoulders. "A bloke by the name of Anthony Ferraro."

"A boyfriend?"

"A fiancé."

James winced. "Ah."

Reilly jerked out a nod.

James stared at him thoughtfully for a moment. "And you're happy for her, right?"

"Of course." Reilly tripped over his words, though he hoped James didn't notice.

"Hmm. Well, back onto Colin and Ellie for a moment. So, if I remember it correctly, each O'Rourke Protector has a single soul mate, right?"

"Aye."

"And the souls of the two mates would never rest in peace until they're united?"

"Aye again, though the woman can live a happy life without the man. Unfortunately, it doesn't go both ways."

"Huh. The one time it sucks to be a guy, right?" James joked.

Reilly tossed his phone into the gym bag at his feet and raised a brow. "A smart man doesn't claim his mate unless he's certain the woman reciprocates. He's only bound to her once he's fully given himself over to the idea."

James finished off the water. "Colin had to admit it out loud, though."

"That's because Colin's a stubborn arse, and it made it an easier pill to swallow if he thought he hadn't a choice but to accept it."

"He would've come around."

Reilly snorted. "Perhaps. But it wouldn't have been in time. Ellie would've gone on to settle with someone else. I saved him a boatload of time and heartache."

"You also brought Bri and Nick together," James mused. "And let's not forget Aidan and Emma. You broke all sorts of rules with those two."

Reilly grimaced and wiped his brow. "Don't remind me. I'll be paying for that for the rest of my life."

"How?"

Reilly stretched his muscles. "Whenever I do something the Fates don't like, they saddle me with something that gives me a bit more of a headache than usual. They let me off too easy with MacWilliam."

James frowned. "What did they do?"

After he brought Aidan back from the past, the Fates sent him two young boys, not quite thirteen, who were desperate for an adventure. Corralling them had been a challenge and a headache, but eventually, Reilly got them to where they needed to be. And they had quite the tale to tell their grandchildren, though Reilly fervently hoped they left him out of it.

But he knew the Fates would never let him off so easily for bringing Aidan forward in time, against their plan.

Reilly shrugged. "They've brought me a few visitors who weren't as easy to control as others. But no worries, mate. Everyone is where they're supposed to be right now."

James raised an eyebrow. "Interesting, seeing as Gwen is at your house right now, slumbering peacefully."

"Her snores sound like a freight train."

James laughed. "Lies. And don't complain too much, O'Malley. At least you have someone to go home to today. I'd be content with that."

"You are well rid of your ex, and you know it." He clapped James on the shoulder. "Your mate is out there, O'Rourke. Let us both be grateful that the soul mate rule only applies to those who are both an O'Rourke and a Protector."

James raised an eyebrow. "*Us*? Do you mean *us*, as in all those clansmen who are both Protector and O'Rourke, or *us*, you and me?"

Reilly tested the weight of his sword, covering his apprehension. "You and me. We've each only one of the two criteria."

James dug the tip of his sword into the dirt, then rested his hand on the hilt. "Only applies to one of us, cousin. I'm an O'Rourke, but I'm not a Protector."

"And I'm a Protector, but not an O'Rourke."

James lifted his sword up and studied it in the brightening sunlight. "I must've forgotten to tell you. There's some pretty cool ancestry stuff available now, so I figured what the heck? I took a few weeks and traced our family line back to the thirteenth century."

A frisson of dread raced up Reilly's spine, but instead of acknowledging it, he merely stood up straighter. "That sounds…"

"Enlightening? You bet."

"I prefer the term boring."

"As you love your history so, being as you see it firsthand all the time," James continued on calmly, "I'm sure you've heard of Finn O'Malley, the chief clan advisor to Laird O'Malley, in, say, 1255?"

Reilly's mouth dropped open. *Nay.*

"This guy Finn, he was different for the time. He did the opposite of what normally happened when two people wed back then, because—and feel free to stop me at any time if you care to join in with the details, Ry—he left his own clan to join his wife's. Joining the O'Malley clan was a huge thing, and eventually earning the trust of the laird certainly seems like it was a testament to Finn's ethics."

"How did you...?" Reilly, at a complete loss for words, sat down on the dirt with a thud.

"His wife, Mary, must've refused to leave her clan for his. But at that time, Finn's clan wasn't so great, was it?" He paused and watched Reilly carefully, even though Reilly was certain the man already knew what he was saying to be factual.

"O'Rourke, bite your tongue," Reilly warned weakly, though he was surprised he could hear himself over the roar in his ears.

"I also found it interesting that Finn and Mary had two children. A younger daughter by the name of Sorcha...and an older son, born in 1245, by the name of Reilly. A fierce warrior, even at a tender age, who inexplicably disappeared when he was about thirteen."

Reilly's throat closed. "Enough," he rasped.

"Finn was an O'Rourke, Reilly. Your father was an O'Rourke! Did that have something to do with how you became the chosen one to lead all the O'Rourke Protectors?"

Reilly wiped a hand over his face, trying to regain some semblance of composure. "I can't tell you."

"Can't? Or won't?"

"It's a sordid tale, James, and it's been my cross to bear for more years than a man should have in his lifetime. Let it lie, for your own peace of mind if nothing else."

James released his sword, dropped to the ground in front of Reilly, who remained on the ground, and gripped his shoulders. "You know I'm a vault, Reilly. Words you say to me go no further than my own ears; I've never once betrayed anyone's trust. Think about it. I'm not a Protector, so I can't ever use your words to travel back to a time when I could change what's been done to you. But I am your family. A cousin—a *brother*—who will give his life for you without question or regret. Lean on me as your clansman. Let me carry some of your load."

Something shifted inside of Reilly, and he bent his head. Perhaps he had been carrying his secrets for much too long. He nodded, sweat dripping from the hair above his brow.

James grabbed their bags, stowed their weapons in the boot of Reilly's car, and gave him a hand up. "I'm listening."

Reilly led James inside the large half-gym, half-classroom space he'd built. They walked past the practice rooms, the sword displays, and the locker rooms, stopping once he reached the office.

"It goes no further," Reilly said heavily, though he knew he didn't have to worry. James's words were truth; once sensitive information was given to him, it was tucked away, never to be mentioned again.

"You have my word."

"Good enough for me." He ushered James inside, and even though it was barely past dawn, he pulled out a bottle of Irish whiskey and poured himself two fingers. He pushed the bottle toward James, not as an offering, but more as insurance that he wouldn't drink any more than what was in his glass.

James wisely said nothing, pulled the bottle from the desk, and placed it out of sight.

"In 1258, I was thirteen years old. I'd already been training for battle for four years by that point, and I was a fierce warrior in the lists. Men lined up to fight me, as my energy levels were what you'd expect of a teenage boy, though my talents were that of a tested warrior. I'd seen battles and come away the victor in more than a few. My parents were, as you might imagine, quite proud. But one day, my father proclaimed that I might grow to be the best warrior to ever grace Ireland. His boasting was not unnoticed. The O'Rourkes at the time were a mess. They were a disorganized clan, weak in their skills. They constantly battled each other to become laird, though laird of what? They had almost no land, their weapons were rudimentary, and they were very much the barbarians by which other countries judged Ireland. The Fates had been waiting for someone with O'Rourke blood, who had warrior skills and an almost inhuman desire to succeed at every task before him. That was where I came in.

"When the Fates approached me, they came to me first in my dreams. The Maiden enticed me, as only a maiden can. She offered herself to me, and you can imagine my reaction." He chuckled humorlessly. "She knew how to get inside a teenage boy's head. Then the Mother came to me, showering me with praise and adulation for all my successes. And finally, the Crone. She told me that I was destined for great things, if I were but open to them. One night, all three appeared in my dream together, and they told me of my future. The first option was to continue living as I was. I would be victorious in battle, but my family, they told me, would perish in a future, smaller outbreak of the plague. The second option was to become the most powerful warrior of all time; one who could not be defeated in battle, who could not be killed, who could not be contained. A warrior who would conquer all for a greater cause—and in becoming that, my family would be spared their lives, and blessed to live long into old age."

"So you chose option two."

Reilly laughed hollowly. "I did. I see now that it didn't matter, that they would've persuaded me one way or another.

But while they decreed the final outcome, I at least had say in how I got there."

James cocked his head. "Why was the O'Rourke clan so important? What did they want you to protect?"

Reilly closed his eyes for a moment. James asked the one question he'd been asking himself, without a clear answer, for far too long.

Finally, Reilly answered. "My first job was to somehow unite the O'Rourkes. They weren't the most warrior-minded of men, but they were ingenious in the ways in which they survived. I singled out the most level-headed man in the clan, convinced him to fight for the lairdship, then guided him as to the best way to keep his position. The Fates whispered in my ear the entire time, so it wasn't as though I simply walked in and the clan began to listen to me, of course. And once that was complete, it was time to begin my own training. Now, as you know, I train and mentor all the O'Rourke Protectors."

"Aside from teaching them swords and street fighting and ancient languages, what else do you do?"

Reilly folded his hands on the desk in front of him. "I'm responsible for seeing that the current Protector lives at least long enough for the next Protector to be born. Once that happens, I'm to ensure he stays well enough until I can train the new Protector in his duties. Once trained or once he finds his mate, the former Protector is relieved of his duties if he so chooses."

"Has anyone chosen to stay?"

Reilly met James's intense stare. "No. However, I can call them at any point in their lives prior to that time. Once relieved, they've always been most grateful, as you might imagine." He cleared his throat. "Once I turned thirty, the Fates decided I was in the prime of my life, and they stopped my aging process."

James blinked. "The Fates stopped you from aging?"

He nodded curtly. "Aye. I had developed all the muscle I

ever would, and they essentially paused my body's growth. It still changes, though at a rate that might seem incomprehensible. For every century, I age but a single year."

"Ah. That explains why you look the same now as you did in my youth."

Reilly nodded wearily. "But I've been alive much longer than that. It wears on a man. The things I've seen, the things I've done."

"Can you ever stop being a Protector?"

"I don't know. If so, I haven't figured out how. Whenever I've asked to be released from this hell, the Fates tell me that the time isn't yet right." He shot back the whiskey and let it burn all the way down his chest, into his belly, before he continued. "I've doubted for a long time that I'll ever be just a normal man again."

"What about the soul mate?"

Reilly rolled his eyes. "Again, I doubt that applies to me. I'm a special case. While I do train the new Protectors, my main job is to ensure that Brianagh's children, and her children's children, stay alive long enough so that we have enough time travelers to fight when the time comes. Bri and Nick have created an incredible blend of O'Rourke ingenuity with MacWilliam ferocity. Those in that line that are born with the gift are Protectors by choice; they can choose to refuse it, and if they do, I then wait for the next Protector to be born. A soul mate would distract me from the mission."

James chewed his lip, clearly hedging his next question. "What exactly is the mission, Ry?"

Reilly took a deep breath and let it out slowly. "I'm still not quite sure."

James blinked. "What?"

"Aye. I believe the O'Rourkes carry something of value to the Fates, but I've not been privy to the what of it."

"But...how can you know nothing of it? Your entire life

has been dedicated to the clan, without understanding what it is you're protecting? That seems highly unlikely."

Reilly pursed his lips. "And time travel is also highly unlikely. Yet here we are."

"Reilly. You must have some idea."

Reilly nodded wearily. "Aye. From what I've gathered throughout the years, sometime in the future, or perhaps in the past...all the people of Ireland must join together under a single ruler. I believe it will be one of Bri and Nick's direct descendants. They'll do so under the Fates. Until that time comes, the line must be protected. But truly, I don't know for sure. We simply protect the line, to ensure that the descendant can take his rightful place and save the people."

"And until that time, you're forced to watch everyone you love grow old."

"Aye," he agreed quietly. "Though I was given the body of an immortal, I am still just a man. And this time, it's more difficult than ever."

"Because of Gwen?"

Reilly avoided James's eyes. A moment ticked by, then another. He lowered his head again and let out a small breath. "Aye."

"Then you can't let her marry this guy."

Reilly barked out a humorless laugh. "When has Gwen ever allowed me that sway over her?"

James crossed his ankle over his knee. "She loved you once, Reilly."

"Aye. I've spent the last ten years ensuring she knew I thought of her as a brother in every possible way."

The troubled look on James's face echoed Reilly's fears. "And you were successful in that. To the point where she's agreed to marry another."

"Aye. Hollow victory, that."

"Nah. You've just made it harder on yourself."

"Because I waited too long."

"No, because it took you too long to realize you could've had her all along. If you'd known she would've accepted the idea of your time traveling, would you have let her love you, and love her in return?"

Reilly pushed his untouched whiskey around on the desk. "Like I said, it doesn't matter now. I'm too late. I was arrogant in thinking she would simply just be there for me. She's engaged to another man." The words physically hurt his chest.

James narrowed his eyes. "Oh, you're not too late yet, cousin. She hasn't said 'I do.'"

Reilly sucked in a breath, his eyes snapping to James's. "By the saints...you think I should steal her?"

"In a way. I mean, you are a warrior, are you not?"

Reilly's mind began to spin.

"And," James continued, breaking out in a grin, "you've never yet lost a battle. This one is no different, but the prize... damn, Reilly, you'd get Gwen. Forever."

"I've no idea where to start." He dropped his head in his hands.

James coughed, though it sounded suspiciously like a laugh. "I'm sure you can figure it out."

"I'd have to make her love me again."

"Do you think she simply stopped loving you? Or," James asked carefully, "do you think that with the right circumstances, you could show her how wrong you've been, and maybe she could see her way back to you?"

Reilly stood suddenly and grabbed his keys. "I don't know. But I need to find out."

$\mathcal{A}$n hour later, Reilly stared at the pot of coffee in his kitchen as it brewed. Water from his shower dripped into his eye, shaking him out of his reverie, and he slicked his wet hair back from his face, reminding himself that he was due for a haircut.

It was no coincidence that he was also due to visit his mother soon, and she always found it humorous that his hair was so short. He loved to make her laugh.

"Want to borrow my hair elastic?" Gwen asked, stifling a yawn as she grabbed a cup from his cabinet, poured some coffee, and handed it to him. "You're almost ready for a man bun."

His heart stuttered at the sight of her sleepy green eyes. Outwardly, he shuddered in horror. "Bite your tongue, lass. I've plans to shear it this very afternoon. Did you sleep well?"

She stuck her tongue out at him. "You know I did. Thanks for the rescue last night."

He sipped his coffee as he watched her prepare her own. Copious amounts of sugar were dumped in, then stirred. She then poured enough cream into the cup to ensure there wasn't any trace of coffee left and took a sip.

"Mmmm."

"Why bother with putting the coffee in at all?"

She batted her eyelashes at him over the rim of her cup. "Because drinking just cream and sugar would be uncivilized."

He chose his next words carefully. "Have you spoken to Anthony this morning?"

Her eyes shuttered. "No."

"He doesn't know you're staying here?"

Her shoulders tensed. "Not yet."

He noticed the tension lines around her eyes. "When does he arrive for the wedding?"

She looked anywhere but him. "I don't really know."

He blinked, assimilating this new information. "I thought he was coming with you."

"Plans changed last minute," she replied abruptly, her spine stiffening. "Let's not discuss it anymore."

That was fine with him. He had three weeks of Gwen, all to himself.

"Aye, so plans changed. They often do. What do you have to do today, lass?"

She tapped her chin, and with that simple movement, Reilly felt a rush of happiness at the familiar scene. How many times had this woman sat at his table, doing the exact same thing, over coffee? Or weak tea, her preferred beverage in the afternoon, or a deep red wine, her beverage of choice at night?

With a pang, he realized that if he let her go, this was likely to be her last stay at his home. But damn him if he wasn't pleased that her hotel reservations were canceled. Knowing she was in town, but not in the bedroom that he'd made hers years ago, felt all kinds of wrong. It felt like...fate.

She belonged with him.

When he saw her, worn out and exhausted, standing

outside that hotel…He knew that she was his, body and, dare he think it, soul.

He'd been so stupid all these years.

"I have to be at the dress fitting soon," Gwen said, reaching over and popping a biscuit in her mouth. Then, talking around the food, she added, "But nothing else for the next few days." She swallowed. "Ellie sent me a text that Colin has to return to Boston for some company emergency, and that she's going with him. They leave tomorrow night."

"I'm sorry, lass. I know how much you wanted to spend these three weeks with her."

Gwen shrugged. "Actually, it's okay."

He frowned. "Will you be heading back as well, then?"

She chewed her lip. "I'm not really sure."

Reilly paused, his cup halfway to his mouth. "Are you worried about getting another flight back? Are finances tight?"

She rolled her eyes. "No, but thanks for the concern."

"Then whyever would you stay, when your fiancé awaits?" He was digging, he knew, but he had to know so he could figure out ways to convince her to stay in Ireland.

She shrugged. "He's in Atlanta for a few weeks, working on another project. I just…would rather be here right now."

The elation he felt at that statement gave him all the push he needed.

Perhaps this is where he differed from modern men. Reilly sneaked a glance at Gwen's face, mostly hidden behind her cup as she drank, and he knew that he would never voluntarily choose anything over her. He would move heaven and earth to ensure that she knew he was always there for her.

In fact, he often did just that, and last night proved that she counted on him.

She continued, oblivious to his plotting, "Of course, I understand Ellie's position. She's in love with Colin and doesn't want to be away from him. I don't blame her one bit. In fact, I even suggested they elope while they were there, but all I got was a smiley face in return."

Reilly read the text she showed him and laughed, though inside, he wondered if she saw the difference between Ellie's desire to be close to her love, and her own decided lack of desire to see hers?

He merely replied, "Aye, Eleanor is blind to everything but Colin. He's a lucky man."

Gwen smiled, her eyes shining. "I've never been happier for her. I was—"

She was interrupted by the chirping of her phone, and as she saw what came across the screen, her face changed in an instant from happy to nervous.

"Everything all right?"

She started to respond, and he watched as she twirled a piece of her hair around her finger. The movement of the silky strands mesmerized him, and he realized with a start that he was staring as she was talking.

"Sorry, what was that?" he asked, embarrassed at his uncharacteristic lack of control.

"I know, right? It's silly of him to be so jealous of you. But like I just said, Anthony will freak out if he knows I'm staying here. But what other option do I have? There aren't any hotels for days, at least. And I like it here. I love spending time with you." Her voice became tight. "And I can do whatever I want. I'm not a cheater. He should know that by now."

Reilly wisely remained silent, offering little more than a nod, but inside, his mind was reeling.

Clearly, not all was perfect in Gwen and Anthony's relationship. And while he would never do anything to hurt her, Reilly saw his future without Gwen: Dark, bleak, and very lonely.

The only snag in his plan was, quite possibly, Gwen herself.

He couldn't live without her light...but, if she was in love with Anthony, he couldn't live with himself if he extinguished that light. He had no problem dimming it, if it meant it led her back to him, for he knew he could make her burn brighter than before. But only if she let him.

He feigned nonchalance. "I'm sure he doesn't think that of you, Gwendolyn. But if he's as in love with you as you are with him, perhaps he's feeling a bit insecure. I've seen it time and again. The poor sap thinks he has it all settled, but then the smallest thing knocks him for a loop, and he's not sure which way is up."

"I've given him no reason not to trust me," she protested.

Reilly couldn't help but remind her, "But *I've* given him no reason to trust *me*."

She rolled her eyes, but he didn't miss the color in her cheeks.

Burn, indeed.

Ready or not, he thought determinedly, *the battle has just begun.*

∾

GWEN PEEKED OUT FROM BEHIND THE CURTAIN AND GRIMACED. Reilly sat—well, he sprawled—in a dainty, off-white chair, meant to seat mothers and sisters and maids of honor. He looked broody.

She knew he would need food sooner rather than later, if she was to restore his good humor. Well, as good-humored as he got in public. The man loved to give off that *don't-mess-with-me* vibe when they were out, though she wouldn't complain about it. They never had a wait at any restaurant, they never were approached by unsavory characters, and people usually gave them a wide berth, which was quite helpful in crowds.

She needed that feeling of invincibility around her right now.

She took a moment to study him, and wondered what he was thinking about. He was not thrilled to be here; all around him, dresses shimmered and women tittered, exclaiming over laces, colors, and fabrics. The perma-frown etched onto his features was proof enough that, if she didn't hurry up a little, things were going to go downhill fast.

But underneath the grouchy outer layer, Gwen got the feeling that Reilly wasn't as unhappy about being here as he tried to make it seem.

Earlier, when her taxi driver showed up drunk, Reilly didn't need to say anything. One look at the driver and Reilly had him out of the driver's seat and passed out on his front lawn. Disgusted, Reilly called the taxi company, stowed the keys in the mailbox, and bustled her into his runabout car so she wouldn't be late.

Gwen protested, but if she didn't get the fitting done today, the dress wasn't guaranteed to be ready in time for the wedding. So, she thanked him with promises of a hearty lunch afterward. Reilly didn't complain, as he never did, but took it in stride and somehow got her to her appointment on time.

Gwen wrung her hands. How was it that the man was always so unruffled? Nothing ever bothered him. He somehow managed every situation as though it was a part of his plan all along, while she—

Well, any plans she made lately seemed to be tossed aside, trampled upon, and then spit at for good measure.

She nervously smoothed her hands down the soft satin of the dress and tried to calm her breathing. The dress clearly needed to be altered. Reilly was all elegant grace and refined strength; his clothing fit him perfectly, his hair was just mussed enough to scream *I-don't-care-because-I-don't-have-to*, and his large, well-formed physique had turned more than one eye since their arrival.

If it had gone right, as it was supposed to, the dress would be fine, and she would be out the door much faster. As it was…She glanced down again. It was so long it trailed a good six inches on the floor, accentuating her decided *lack* of height, and the waist was large enough that it made her figure look like she'd indulged in way too many pastries.

"Gwendolyn, I swear by all that is holy, if you don't stop fretting behind that curtain, I'll come in and drag you out here."

She jumped at his voice, then yanked back the curtain, fully frustrated. "It's awful," she moaned.

"Isn't the entire point of this escapade for you to have them make it *not* awful?" he drawled. His eyes raked her from head to toe, which took about, oh, three seconds.

"Stunning," he determined.

"Enormous!" she countered, gathering the copious amounts of satin.

"It needs some tailoring," he allowed, scratching his chin.

"Some?" she exclaimed, stalking to the mirror and almost tripping over the excess material. "It's not even close to the right size. I am drowning in this thing!"

He shrugged. "The color suits you."

The attendant bustled over, her eyes wide. "Oh, dear. This is the wrong size! It must be ten sizes too large!"

"No kidding," Gwen muttered, helplessly lifting the dress from the floor. "It's big everywhere."

The woman began pinning fabric with the speed of a NASCAR driver, rounding Gwen in dizzying circles. She made lots of "hmms" and loud sighs, but a few minutes later, she stepped back and eyed Gwen critically. "With some modifications, this dress will be lovely. You're such a petite thing, with such interesting coloring. This shade of green is simply perfect for you."

Gwen drew herself up to her full five-feet-two-inches and tried to imagine it. "Thank you."

The attendant moved aside, and Gwen turned to look at Reilly.

His face had a funny expression on it, like he'd been struck with something heavy and he was shaking off the resulting fog. She tilted her head at him, concerned. "Ry? Are you okay?"

He shook himself out of whatever was going on in his head. "Aye. The lady's correct, lass. Like I said: stunning."

Gwen wrinkled her nose. "Thanks. Hopefully it'll be done in time."

"Plenty of time," the woman assured her. "Do you need help taking it off?"

Gwen shook her head. "No, I've got it, thanks."

"I think we've found *the dress*!" another client called out excitedly.

The attendant flashed Gwen a quick smile and hurried over to a woman standing on a small stage. She seemed to glow with happiness as she turned this way and that, admiring in the mirror the wedding dress she wore.

"She looks radiant," Gwen murmured.

Reilly lounged back even further, threatening the stability of the tiny seat. "I bet you'll look even more so in your wedding gown. I can imagine you in it. Simple, elegant. Hair up, though you should leave it down. And none of that veil nonsense. Your groom should be able to see the love written all over your face."

She blinked at him, at a loss for words.

He cocked his head at her. "You should never hide your face behind anything. You're too beautiful."

Her eyes widened, and her heart thudded in her chest.

He gave her a quick smile, making her knees wobble a bit. "Am I so infrequent with the compliments that you've no idea how to take them? I'll have to rectify that. Off with you now. You promised me lunch, wench."

She laughed, her heart still pounding in her chest, and carefully picked her way back to the small dressing room. Reaching behind her neck, she slid the zipper down, but it snagged on something. She froze.

It's fine. You've got this, Gwendolyn. Just a little tug, and it'll glide right down.

A little tug made a rendering sound, and she pursed her lips. She stuck her head out the curtain, looking for the attendant. "Where's the saleslady?" she asked, biting her lip.

"She went to the other floor to get some sort of headdress," Reilly informed her. "What's wrong?"

"The zipper's stuck, and I'm afraid I'm going to rip it."

He stood in a fluid motion, and though there was nothing predatory in his walk, Gwen felt as though she was his prey. Which was ridiculous, as this was *Reilly*. He spent years ensuring she always felt like anything *but* prey.

Except once.

"I can unzip it. Turn around."

She complied and held her hair off her neck. A memory assaulted her; his hands, gliding down her back, just like this...

He let out a low whistle. "It's caught all the way down to here." He pressed gently on the curve of her spine above her bottom, and a cascade of butterflies took flight in her stomach. "You'll have to step into the dressing room for this, unless you'd like to bare yourself to the world out here."

Once they were behind the curtain, Gwen swore someone turned the heat up in the building. She concentrated on the ugly purple curtain that separated them from the main room as Reilly smoothed his fingers onto her back, slowly working the zipper free from the satin. His knuckles grazed her spine, and she shuddered.

"Cold?" he murmured, his fingers never stopping.

"Um, a bit," she lied.

He didn't reply, and she prayed he believed her, despite the fact that her entire body was turning red.

The curse of a redhead; every time she had any emotion at all, her skin showed it.

Reilly's hands were warm, his fingertips a bit rough, and his skin on hers brought her mind right back to where she swore she'd never let it go again.

Gwen, you know Anthony's touch will never give you this feeling.

Her knees were threatening to give out on her. She needed to get a grip. Gwen risked a look in the mirror she was facing, and her mouth went dry at the expression on Reilly's face.

She knew her mind was playing tricks on her, but she could swear that he looked like a man bent on seduction.

Holy hell.

If that's what a seductive Reilly looked like, she would combust before he even got her to the bedroom door.

Like an avenging angel, the attendant chose that moment to call out, "Did you get the dress off?"

"Um, no," she managed to call out. She swallowed past a very dry throat. "The zipper is stuck."

The attendant bustled in, *tsk*ed, and shooed Reilly out before tugging the last inch of fabric free from the zipper. The dress peeled off Gwen, and the woman readjusted a couple of the pins as Gwen tugged on her clothes.

"No damage done, thankfully. Men can never be trusted around satin. It makes them all sorts of crazy," the attendant confided with a knowing smile. "It's a tactile thing. Once they touch it, all rational thought goes, and they tend to simply shred it with their impatience."

Reilly hadn't seemed impatient to her; in fact, his hands had traveled maddeningly slowly. She nodded, thanked the woman, and exited the dressing room.

Reilly was waiting for her at the door, his face again an

implacable mask. Any trace of the desire, if there even was any, was long gone. "Food?"

She cursed herself ten times the fool as they left the shop together and promised herself she would call Anthony just as soon as she could.

THIRTY MINUTES LATER, REILLY WAS STILL TRYING TO RECOVER from the dressing room. He knew that if he was ever going to convince Gwen of his intentions, he had to lead her to her own conclusion…without letting her know he was doing any of the leading.

He could have her love. He reminded himself, for the sixteenth time that day, that he had to work for it, and show her his love first.

"So what would you care to do now?" he asked.

A thought entered his mind. He needed to introduce her to his family, but it had to be her idea, and she had to be certain of it. No backtracking allowed.

She sighed. "I don't know. I feel like I'm taking up your time. You didn't exactly plan on entertaining me."

"I've naught *but* time on my hands. All I had was a haircut and a tentative thought to visit my dam, but that can always be pushed to another week." He nonchalantly glanced down at her. "I don't mind at all."

"What dam? Like in a river somewhere?"

He gave her a half-smile. "Nay. *My* dam. My mother."

She gasped. "Your mom? You mean, you *were* going to take a trip? Oh no, is she expecting you? *Can* she expect you?"

He raised a brow. "Aye, but 'tis not a problem. I can see her another time. She won't mind at all, especially when I tell her I was with you."

"She knows about me?" Gwen asked, surprised.

He arched a brow. "Of course. You're the most important

95

person in my life; why wouldn't I tell her about you?" Her mouth formed a perfect O, and he took a moment to enjoy her speechlessness before continuing. "She's always on me about bringing you to her, but until recently, you didn't exactly know I could."

"She wants to *meet* me?" Gwen squeaked.

He easily maneuvered them onto the highway. "Well, aye. Colin's had naught but good things to say about you, and James, of course, told her all about your—"

"The O'Rourkes know her?"

"You're beginning to sound like a broken record, Gwen. Aye, they know her. She's been keen on meeting you since I first told her of you. But don't trouble yourself over it. Shall we visit Cork tomorrow?"

He held his breath.

"I'd much rather meet your mom," she admitted readily, and he let it out slowly. "I mean, your *mom*, Ry! I've always wondered what she's like. Is she sweet, or more of a tough love type? How old is she? Where does she live? Is she as beautiful as you?"

Her cheeks reddened.

"You think me beautiful, lass?" Reilly asked with a chuckle. He flexed his arm and gave her a sideways glance. "Go on. You know you want to."

Another one of their games. Gwen always found it fascinating that she couldn't wrap both her hands around his bicep. He would call her a wee thing, and she would try harder, to no avail.

His workouts weren't *solely* for the protection of the O'Rourke line.

She huffed out a laugh. "You're fishing for compliments, you know."

"Aye, I am. So be a good lass and humor this old man."

She wrapped her small hands around his bicep, and it shot

straight to his heart. She tested and stretched, but her fingertips were so far from each other, she quickly gave up.

"Yes, yes, your arms are huge."

"Eh, you're just a wee thing."

She rolled her eyes. "What about your sister?"

"What about her?"

"Does she still live with your mom?"

"Depends on when I visit her," he replied honestly. He cleared his throat. "It's the one thing the Fates gave me some control over. I can visit my family whenever I wish."

"So theoretically, if someone was to die of unnatural causes, you could prevent their deaths, if you were aware of it, right?"

"Nay. If I try to change their future, I'm immediately removed."

Which is why, after all this time, he still wondered how he was able to so thoroughly break the rules for Aidan and Emmaline MacWilliam. Aidan's fate was in the past, and Emma's in the future; he'd taken it upon himself to reunite them, despite what the Fates demanded.

Though it had been a couple of years, he was still half-waiting for the punishment the Fates would eventually mete out.

"Do you know when people die?"

"Only those that have died before this moment in time. I cannot go to the future."

She swallowed. "You seem rather cavalier about it."

"I've had more years than you know to come to terms with all of this. For the deaths of my family, I simply ensure my visits are between a certain set of years."

"How old are you, Ry?"

He shook his head. "Gwen, you don't want to know the answer to that question."

"I know what your license says. Are you much older than that?" she pressed.

"When did you sneak a look at my license?" he exclaimed, turning off the highway. He knew, of course. He always knew when his things were disturbed. It was a survival tactic of his, to remember just where he put important things, and to notice when they'd been moved.

"Let's not talk about that."

"I'll drop it when you drop my age."

"You're so sensitive."

"Aye, I cry into my cereal every morn over it," he deadpanned.

"You don't eat cereal. And fine, I'll let it drop for now. Let's talk instead about this visit with your mom. Mary, right?"

He nodded. "Aye, Mary. But you don't really want to go back then. It's even earlier than when you visited before, by more than a hundred years."

Her eyes widened, and he caught the sparkle in the mossy depths of her eyes when he risked a glance at her face. "Sure I would!"

He frowned, though inside he was preemptively raising a fist in victory. *Slow down, O'Malley.* "Lass, think about it. What would happen if you were to fall ill? Eleanor would never forgive me, and by association, nor would Colin."

"Oh, *pfft.* I won't get sick. I'll bring vitamins."

"What about a prolonged absence from your parents? Won't they wonder if you've not contacted them after a few days?"

She rolled her eyes at him. "They're on a two-week cruise in the Caribbean. They wanted to be tanned for Ellie's wedding. I hadn't planned on talking with them until then."

Reilly smothered his laugh. Gwen's parents were lovely, but they were walking stereotypes for wealthy, upper-crust Yanks. He turned serious. "What about your fiancé? Won't he wonder what's become of you?"

Her mouth turned downward into a small frown, and he wished he had the privilege to smooth it out. *Easy now.*

"Yes, probably."

"Probably? If it were me, I'd want to know."

"Control freak much?"

He snorted. "Hardly. My future wife can do what she pleases. I'd like to know of her plans so I could imagine myself rescuing her if her plans went awry."

"My plans always go awry," she muttered.

They do indeed, he thought. Which was why he liked always knowing what her plans were.

"I'll tell him that I'm going on a side trip and will call him when I can. He's pretty busy in Atlanta, so I don't think it'll prove too much of a problem."

"It would be if he knew you were going with me."

Gwen shrugged. "We're friends, Ry. He has to accept that."

"And if he doesn't?"

"He will."

He decided to let it lie for a bit, so he scratched his chin and affixed a perturbed expression on his face. "I don't know, Gwendolyn. There's always an inherent danger. When I travel with Colin or James, they have to abide by the rules."

"What are the rules?" she asked, excited. "I can follow rules!"

"Gwen, you're terrible at following rules."

"I am not!" she exclaimed indignantly, but immediately, she grinned sheepishly. "Okay, I am. But I won't be this time. I promise."

He put the car in park outside of a pub, then headed around to her side. He opened her door, unbuckled her, and leaned one arm on the dash in front of her, effectively filling her personal space. He searched her eyes, noticed her skin was flushing that delightful shade of pink he saw back in the dress shop, and he took a deep, even breath.

"Aye, Gwen. If you promise to do exactly as I say, I'll take you to meet my dam."

Her face lit up. "I can't wait."

He gave her a resigned smile, but inside, he was doing a victory dance. *Nor can I, lass.* He slowly backed up, allowing her to get out of his car, and he closed the door behind her.

A car parked a few spaces from them backfired, and Gwen let out the most ear-piercing, terrified scream he'd ever heard. Before he could blink, she was in his arms, trying to claw her way into his skin.

"Whoa," he exclaimed. "Gwen. *Gwendolyn.* 'Twas a car backfiring. You're safe."

Her body shaking, she nodded her head against his chest, but she didn't release her death grip on him. "Okay. Can we just stay here for a minute?" she asked, her voice raw.

His heart cracked at the tears saturating his shirt. *Oh, Gwendolyn, the things you must've seen.* He wrapped his arms more securely around her. "Aye. For a minute, for an hour, for a day. For as long as you need."

CHAPTER 5

"*R*eilly's upgraded his lawn furniture, I see."

Gwen and Reilly didn't leave for their time-traveling adventure right away. The car incident scared her witless for longer than she liked, but Reilly wasn't in a rush. They puttered around town, did some home improvement projects together, and basically just fell into their old pattern of being comfortable in the same space as each other.

Though Gwen was starting to get the feeling that Reilly perhaps was feeling slightly more than friendly towards her. And that had her all kinds of confused—if that was even what it really was.

Her Reilly radar was still broken from the last time she threw herself at him, so she wasn't sure she was the most reliable at interpreting signs.

Gwen grinned as she rubbed her hands over the smooth teak chair that matched the one in which Ellie sat. "Oh El, I'm so glad you're back. And no kidding. He's had those plastic things for much too long. I think the weather finally did them in."

"Colin told me it was one of Reilly's visitors who said something about it." Ellie sipped her iced tea thoughtfully.

"From what I gathered, it was a visitor who never encountered plastic before, and took a sword to it as a form of investigation."

Gwen's eyes widened, and a giggle escaped her. "Well, I can't say I blame him. They were pretty awful."

"These are as gorgeous as the rest of the furniture in the house."

Gwen nodded in agreement. "Reilly makes it all. He's very talented."

Ellie stirred her beverage with her straw without looking at Gwen, and said carefully, "So…you're sure you're over Reilly, Gwen?"

She choked on her own iced tea. *"Et tu, Brute?"*

Ellie grinned. "Excellent Shakespeare reference! Color me impressed!"

Gwen rolled her eyes. "I had to suffer through it in high school just like everyone else."

"Suffer?" Ellie gasped. *"Julius Caesar* was an amazing foray into—"

"Oh please, let's not discuss literature," Gwen implored, cutting her off. "I can't do it today!"

"Then let's discuss your love life. I admit that I'm a little surprised you agreed to marry Anthony. Not that you're unable to commit," Ellie hurried on, noticing her friend's color rising. "But you barely spoke about him. You worked with him a lot and have a respect for him, certainly. But when you talk about him, you don't have that joy."

Gwen laughed uncomfortably. "Not everyone wears their heart on their sleeve, El."

Ellie leveled a stare at her. "You do. And I know you, Gwen. I've known you all our lives. And while I wasn't privy to meeting your Reilly until last year, whenever you spoke of him, your eyes got almost starry. Your face lit up, and you became more animated."

Gwen swallowed hard, the stabbing pain in her chest almost unbearable. "That was before."

"Before Anthony?"

Gwen considered lying. She thought about how easy it would be to pretend, to let her best friend think that.

But Ellie would figure it out. She always did; she was so attuned to other people's thoughts and feelings that sometimes she almost knew Gwen better than Gwen knew herself.

She opted for the truth.

She took a deep breath, then opened her mouth. She promptly shut it, trying to form the right words, then opened it again.

Then shut it.

"I've got all day, but Colin and Reilly will be back from their run eventually. I suggest you simply spit it out."

Gwen chewed her lip for a moment longer. "I loved Reilly from almost the minute I met him. Obviously, he is gorgeous, and he was then, too. But there was something I recognized in him right away, like my soul settled into place when we first spoke. I thought we were destined to be together, you know? Even though I was so young, my heart just knew it'd found its other half. But he rejected me. And he did it in such a way that I was bruised, but I didn't give up hope. He offered me his friendship, and I took it."

Ellie nodded encouragingly, and Gwen focused her gaze on the tree line in the distance. "He always treated me as more than a sister, but less than a girlfriend. Best friend, I guess, which is what we are. I always wanted more, and I never made a secret of it. Good God, I made advances a lot, Ellie. A *lot*." She huffed out an embarrassed laugh. "More than any dignified woman should, for sure. But my pride never mattered. I just kept thinking, *He'll see it. He'll see that we are meant to be together, and it will all be worth it*. But then the years passed, and he didn't see it. He kept me at arm's length, and like a dog starved for attention, I was willing to take what he offered. Pathetic, I know. But I never cared about that, because just being near him, being part of his life, was enough for me."

"Ouch. Unrequited love. But you dated other guys…?"

"I did. And they were all right. But I kept holding them up to Reilly, and none compared. I mean, how could they? I was in love with someone totally out of my reach. They never stood a chance."

"But then Anthony came along, right?"

She adjusted her position and tightened her sweater around herself as a chilly wind blew through. "Not exactly. Before we had our time travel adventure, when Reilly was visiting me, I was sitting with him on the couch, fighting over the Doritos bag. We wrestled it back and forth a bit, and there was a moment when my mouth was close enough to his that if I was brave enough, I could kiss him. I could lay one on him and really feel if he was into me. But before I could, he handed me the bag, gave me a smile, then continued to watch the movie. He never felt the charge I did." Gwen paused a moment, pushing the lump in her throat down.

"So that was the moment you realized it was time to let go?"

Gwen swallowed hard. "I wish. But I couldn't. I physically couldn't handle the pain every time I thought about never seeing him again, because that's what I'd have to do in order to really move on. And I wasn't ready."

"What made you ready?" Ellie asked.

Gwen buried her head in her hands. "Last summer, when we fell into the Middle Ages, and after Colin saved you from the other laird, I saw Reilly covered in blood. It wasn't his, but it freaked me out. Before you fell asleep that night, you said something that struck a chord. You told me you had to try one more time." She paused, fighting the tears that threatened. "I left the chamber and went to Reilly's. He was awake. I'll never forget the picture of him, sitting by that fire, sharpening his sword. His hair was damp, and he smelled like soap. The blood was gone, but I had to say something right then."

Ellie's eyes were huge. "What did you say?"

Gwen pinched the bridge of her nose as she remembered. "Ry?"

He looked up from his task. "You should be abed, lass."

"I couldn't sleep. I needed to see you."

He didn't smile, but he did shift over on the bench and went back to his task.

She gingerly sat down. "Are you okay?"

"I'm always okay after these things," he replied. His tense shoulders told a different story.

She laid a hand on his arm. "Reilly…"

He froze. "Gwen, do you know what battle does to a man?" She remained silent, and his gaze dropped her hand on his arm. "It makes him…desirous."

"Too much testosterone flowing?" she tried to joke, but the words died on her lips when his eyes met hers.

"If you don't leave, I can't promise you'll be safe here."

Gwen searched his face. "You wouldn't hurt me."

He let out a humorless laugh. "Not intentionally. I beg of you, Gwendolyn. Leave me."

She gently cupped his face, knowing he needed her at that moment possibly more than she needed him. "I'll never leave you."

Slowly, he leaned toward her. "I've done terrible things in my life, Gwen, but I've never lost my honor."

Her voice barely above a whisper, she replied, "There's nothing you could do to stop me from loving you. There's honor in love, Reilly."

The admission shocked him; she could see it in his flared nostrils, his widened eyes. But then his mouth was on hers, devouring her, and her heart exploded with such love, she swore she'd somehow entered into heaven.

He said her name over and over again, through his kisses down her neck, across her cheeks, and into her mouth. His sword clattered to the floor, and he swept her into his arms, his lips never leaving hers. He tossed her onto the bed, and she watched him come close almost immediately. His hands traveled down her sides, to her hips; his fingers tightened around the fabric of her dress, and he began tugging it up. She lifted her hips to aid him, and he kissed her deeply, searing her soul. His hands were everywhere, and with them, he lit a trail of fire unlike anything she'd ever experienced.

She pulled at his tunic, and he whipped it off with one hand. Her breath whooshed out, as she took in the perfection of his chest. Enormous muscles, dusted with dark hair, flexed as he shifted himself over her.

"You're my light," he whispered feverishly.

"You're my life," she whispered back.

Their lips met again, slower this time, but with more intensity. He began to unlace her, and he revealed her inch by inch, until her breasts were free and her bodice at her waist.

"Perfection," he murmured, tracing her gently.

A knock at the door had him looking up, annoyed. He called out something in Gaelic, and a woman's voice replied. His face changed, and he looked down in horror at Gwen.

She sat up quickly, pulling her dress up. "What is it? What's wrong?"

"Dear God...I almost ruined you."

"What?" she half-laughed, a feeling of dread replacing the beautiful butterflies she had a moment ago.

"You must leave. Immediately." He launched himself off the bed and pulled his tunic on.

"I don't understand—"

"You're not a whore, and I won't use you as one," he said sharply. He shot her a glare. "I told you to leave. After a battle, I can't help myself. I've needs, Gwendolyn. And you're not the woman to see to them."

The sting of tears was instantaneous, and she didn't bother

trying to stem them. "How could you say something like that? I love you!"

"Nay, you do not. You think you do. But you mistake it. We've naught but friendship. I will not use you in such a way, to slake my lust after tonight's bloodshed." *He turned his back to her and picked up his sword from where it lay by the hearth.* "Go, Gwendolyn. Do not return to my chamber."

Ellie gripped Gwen's hand when she fell silent. "That was a horrible thing to do."

"The woman outside the door was coming to his room to *relieve his stress*," Gwen said, this time without inflection.

"I don't remember any tensions the next day," Ellie replied thoughtfully. "Though, to be honest, I had a lot going on."

"There was tension. I spoke about Claire MacWilliam being the next time traveler, just to irritate him. I know he *does* love her like a sister and the thought of her in danger would put him over the edge, so to speak. And I wouldn't let it go, either."

"When did you two talk about what happened?"

Gwen sighed. "The day we got back. He apologized, blamed it on the heat of the moment. He also swore up and down that he didn't allow the woman who interrupted us that night into his bedchamber."

"Do you believe him?"

"Not that it's relevant, but I do. And then we agreed to leave it in the past, and we made a promise to continue to be each other's best friend."

"How's that working out for you?"

Gwen used some colorful language that made Ellie grimace.

"I guess I never understood why he wouldn't choose me. I just don't get why I can't let him go."

"Can't, as in, *still* can't?"

"Couldn't," Gwen hastily replied. "Couldn't. Because I have. It's why I barely spoke to him over the last year. When I left for the States, I didn't call him or text him or anything. I video chatted with him when I was in Venezuela. When I realized things were a little off there, I think I needed someone to know where I was."

"Reilly's a good guy to have around for a rescue," Ellie agreed.

"Yeah." Gwen traced the rim of her glass before placing it on the small table between them. "That's probably the reason why I called him and not my parents or you." She let out a frustrated sigh. "God. I wish I could just understand why he rejected me. Every spurned woman's wish, I guess…"

"Has he ever told you about the soul mate thing?"

Gwen blinked. "The what?"

Ellie tucked her legs underneath herself. "The soul mate. No?" At Gwen's blank look, Ellie continued, "So, as I understand it, the Protectors are each destined for one woman. I can only assume it works for Reilly, too, as he's the leader of them. Once a Protector claims his mate, as she's called, he's bound to her forever. No matter how many lifetimes go by, he will only find happiness with his mate. But she has to return the claim."

"What happens if she doesn't?"

Ellie frowned. "The Protector is doomed to live half a life, never finding true happiness."

Gwen's heart felt heavy. "Well. There's my answer, I guess. All these years, I've offered myself to him over and over and over." Her voice caught on the lump in her throat as the realization hit her with full force. "That's the reason why he's never accepted my advances. I'm not his mate."

"I'm sorry," Ellie said softly, reaching over to squeeze Gwen's hand. "But Anthony…it just seems so sudden, Gwen."

Gwen explained with a shrug, "I think, deep down, I knew something like this was at play, that maybe Ry and I weren't meant to be. But I was excited that his secret was out.

I thought that must've been the thing holding him back. I mean, if there was any perfect time to tell me, that would've been it, right? But I realized, that day we got back from our adventure, that it wasn't ever going to happen. So I accepted his apology, and made the conscious choice to move on with my life."

"And so you came back, met Anthony, and fell in love?" Ellie asked skeptically.

Gwen grasped Ellie's hand, her eyes intense. "Ellie, I want what you have with Colin. I want the happiness, and the security of knowing that someone loves me. There's nothing wrong with that."

"Of course not."

"Anthony can give me that. I can be content with him. He's enough for me. I might not have that fairy-tale love, but I like him. I respect him. And I'm not getting any younger, to be truthful. I want children, and a dog, and a messy house."

"Gwen...you're settling," Ellie whispered, shocked. "Please don't settle. You deserve more than that."

"I don't *deserve* a damn thing," Gwen retorted. "Don't feel badly for me, Eleanor. Don't you dare. I've made my bed, and I'm perfectly willing to lie in it. Not everyone can get what they want all the time."

"What if Reilly were to walk through that door and tell you that you were making a mistake? That you belonged with him, and he wanted to marry you?"

Gwen felt a bubble of anger. "Why would you even say that?"

Ellie's mouth twisted into a sad smile. "Because I think you still love him. Answer the question."

Gwen shook her head. "You're wrong, El. I don't. I can't. I used to be blind with love, but I'm no longer that deep that I wouldn't see it for what it was. If, after all this time, Reilly were to declare his *undying* love for me, I'd know it was his pride speaking, not his heart. He's made it abundantly clear, over and over again. My pride can only handle so much."

"I wish it was different." Ellie's sadness darkened her whole face, and Gwen knew they wore matching expressions.

"He can't push me away, then expect me to be there when he's decided he's ready," Gwen said, her voice showing more resolve than she felt. "I've moved on. And I'll be happy with Anthony."

"Then I'll have to be happy with that," Ellie replied loyally. She offered her a small smile. "It'll all work out in the end. It always does."

"So says the glowing bride," Gwen smirked, relieved that Ellie was letting it lie.

Ellie began talking about the latest first copy of some book she received in her bookshop recently, but Gwen's mind was elsewhere. She wished she could feel the same way about Anthony that Ellie did about Colin.

REILLY STOOD JUST INSIDE THE KITCHEN, THE CONVERSATION outside leaving him dazed.

"I'd know it was his pride speaking, not his heart."

"You can't push someone away and expect them to be there when you're ready."

"I'll be happy with Anthony."

The words played on an endless reel, making him dizzy and slightly nauseous. He couldn't breathe.

Gwen truly *had* moved on.

He was too late, the "I do"s be damned.

"Come on," Colin murmured, physically pushing Reilly up the stairs. They were both covered in sweat, their run being more of a race. His win against Colin was a hollow victory.

Colin steered Reilly into the bedroom, then carefully shut

the door as Reilly leaned heavily on his bureau and dropped his head onto his arm with a curse.

"How are you going to fix this?"

Reilly's incredulous gaze snapped up to Colin's calm one. "Fix it?" he scoffed. "You heard her. She's moved on. By her own words, she's happy with Anthony, and she wouldn't believe me if I told her how I felt. Explain to me how I'm to fix that? Especially as she's made up her mind."

Colin grimaced and rubbed the back of his neck uncomfortably. "She's your soul mate, Ry. She's loved you for as long as she's known you."

"And I've pushed her away for just as long," he snapped. "By the saints, I am the worst kind of fool."

"You won't find me arguing the point. But you can't let her marry another man."

Reilly glared at Colin for a full minute before barking out his next words. "If your love wanted to be with someone else, would you force her lifelong unhappiness by separating them?"

Colin pressed his lips in a tight line.

Reilly carefully blew out a breath. "Exactly. You should go, cousin. I'm unfit company at the moment."

"We could go to the lists," Colin suggested.

Stonily, Reilly shook his head. "Not today. Take your love, and Gwen too, and leave me to my misery. I'll see you closer to the wedding."

Colin ran a hand through his dark blond hair, unsure. "I don't think you should be alone."

Reilly barked out a humorless laugh. "Oh, trust me, nothing untoward will happen to me. The Fates will make sure of it. Nay, I'm just destined to continue on as I've been."

He didn't say the word, but it hung in the air, as tangible as the floor beneath his feet.

Lonely.

"If that's what you want, I'll do it. But first—" Colin

waited until Reilly met his eyes "—think on this." At Reilly's continued silence, Colin continued, "For years, I've listened to, and taken, your advice. Even when I didn't want it. *Especially* when I didn't want it. But now we're in my territory, Ry. I'm the professional here, and so here's some free matchmaking advice. Show her you love her. Don't use the words, as you know she won't believe them. Actions only."

A long moment passed before Reilly finally admitted quietly, "I don't know how."

He frowned. "You've never had problems romancing a woman before, Ry."

"Aye," he agreed darkly. "But this time, I would need to romance a wife."

Colin's expression turned thoughtful. "Ah. That is a different beast altogether, isn't it?"

Reilly let out a frustrated growl in response.

"All right, mate. It won't be easy. But, as the saying goes, with great risk comes great reward. You have to make her feel special. Make her see that there is *no one* more important to you than she. It's in the little things. Put her first in *all* things, and she will start to see what you don't say."

"What if it isn't enough?" Reilly asked roughly. He slammed his hands on the bureau and pushed off it. "She's given up on me! By all that's holy, she's marrying someone she doesn't love!"

"And why is that?" Colin finally snapped. At Reilly's surly glare, Colin rolled his eyes. "To be free of you, you fool."

"Aye. And free of me she will be, but never I of her."

Quietly, Colin turned the door handle. "If she truly wants to be free of you, though, with everything she's gone through...and perhaps you might think a bit on the answer to this one...why, in her greatest moment of need, has *your mate* come running to *you*?"

Reilly had no answer, not that Colin seemed to expect one.

The door closed behind him softly, and Reilly sat down heavily on his bed. He'd never been so confused in his life. His mistakes were numerous and unforgivable. He didn't have to tell the world the name of his soul mate; as it was fully imprinted upon his heart, he'd already claimed her as his own. And now, he was destined to love only Gwen for all time, and she was pledging herself to another man, all because he fully convinced her he was nothing more than a friend.

A friend!

He dropped back, his arm over his eyes, and took measured breaths. She claimed happiness with Anthony, though her eyes told a different story. He knew she would be forced to choose between the two of them.

How could he walk away from her?

How could he *not*?

Colin's words were like a dagger in his chest. From her reaction in the car park, she was clearly suffering some degree of post-traumatic stress. Perhaps also survivor's guilt, if he knew her as well as he thought he did.

Colin was right. Gwen did come running to him. At the airport, she lost all sense of decorum and leapt into his arms, which he hadn't been expecting. And she hadn't been obvious about it, but since the moment she came into his home, she'd been keeping close to him, rarely more than a room away.

However, she'd promised herself to another man. He felt his anger at himself bubble to the surface.

A tentative tap on the door revealed a concerned Gwen, her beautiful face drawn with worry lines.

"Hey," she said softly. "Colin told me you weren't feeling well. I'll bring you some chicken soup, if you want?"

"I want nothing," he snapped. He sighed. "Sorry."

She blinked. "Okay, grumpy pants. I was just offering. I'll be back in a while; we're going to grab some dinner."

"Stay at Winifred's," Reilly replied darkly, placing his arm back over his eyes so he wouldn't have to look at her. He didn't want his eyes or his expression to give away any of his turbulent thoughts.

"If you want me to," she replied, her voice soft. "But I've been able to sleep through the night when I'm here."

He shrugged. "Fine. I'm going to shower. Have a nice dinner."

"I'll be home after I drop them at the airport. They're heading back to Ellie's over in London tonight," she added as he shut the door to the master bathroom behind him, cursing himself for his curtness, but wishing all the same she'd stay home.

Home, he scoffed silently. Her home was back in the States with her fiancé.

A few moments later, he heard Colin's car start, then head away from the house.

He swore when he realized he was out of towels, and headed toward the stairs to grab some from his dryer. On the way, he passed Gwen's room, and her scent wafted out of it.

Gritting his teeth, he blasted down the stairs, determined to ignore any more thoughts of her.

In the living room, her sweater lay across the couch. He turned his back on it, nearly grinding his teeth into powder, only to encounter a note on the kitchen table.

I forgive you, you big grumpy bear. And I'm bringing you chicken noodle soup, and you're going to eat all of it because that stuff fixes everything. Get some sleep, Grumplestiltskin. -G

A reluctant smile tugged.

Reilly knew he couldn't watch her marry someone else.

Feeling as though he was struggling for air, Reilly discarded the idea of a shower. He needed to be outside, to get some air and ground himself. He needed to get control over himself. And, he admitted, slipping her note into his pocket, he needed to make amends with Gwen. She didn't deserve his black mood.

~

"DO YOU EVER THINK, SOMETIMES, THAT THE FATES ARE JUST messing with you?"

Reilly choked on his beer mid-pull. When he could breathe again, he gave Gwen an incredulous look. "What?"

She shrugged, toying with her fork. They sat in the middle of a nearly empty pub, a fire giving off a pleasant warmth in the hearth nearby. The rain outside came down just hard enough to give the world outside the windows a fuzzy facade.

"I wonder if those Fates that you know are always pulling the strings just because they're bored, as though they see someone swimming along in life and think, *Hey! Let's make her life suck a little bit, just for giggles.*"

He shook his head. "They're too self-absorbed for that."

She sipped her soda, nonplussed. "How can they be self-absorbed if their entire purpose is to ensure the life span of others?"

Reilly pinched the bridge of his nose. "I dislike speaking of them."

"Why?"

He looked at her through his fingers. "Because it feels like giving them an open invitation to my life."

She wrinkled her nose. "I thought you said they dictate your every move?"

"If I said such a thing, it was said with contempt and distrust, and a bit tongue-in-cheek. They don't control everything."

"So what part of your life is destiny, and which part is fate?" she wondered.

He finished his meal and pushed the plate away. "They're the same thing."

Gwen studied him for a moment. He looked tired and a little stressed. How unlike him. She'd never seen him as anything but composed.

Well…except for the time he almost took her to bed. He was quite the opposite of composed then.

Rationally, she knew perfection didn't exist. Reilly had his faults as much as the next guy. But he was always self-assured, never seeming to doubt his actions or decisions, and always looked as though he was as fresh as the day was long.

The exhaustion lines on his face were concerning. "They're not, not at all. Did you have trouble sleeping last night?"

"Your illogical line of questioning has once again muddled my inept brain."

She rolled her eyes. "Stop fishing for compliments. Your brain is the furthest thing from inept. You look tired."

He rubbed his face. "Aye, I am. A temporary thing, that. I'm still able to best anyone in a sword fight."

"Always thinking of steel." She finished her soda and slowly swirled the straw in the ice. "So why do you think fate and destiny are the same?"

The gold flecks in Reilly's eyes sparked with interest. "Perhaps you ought to tell me why you think they're not."

"Nice evasion," she said, then promptly ignored his question and pressed, "but why do you think they're the same? And did you come to this conclusion on your own?"

"Are you a shrink now?" He pulled out his wallet and began counting bills. He shot her a dirty look when she reached for her purse.

"I can pay my own way," she protested, though she put her hands up in immediate surrender.

"We have this conversation at least every other meal," he replied patiently, placing the money on the table. "Consider it a blight to my honor."

"That's ridiculous."

Reilly raised a mock-supercilious brow. "Calling my honor into question, my lady?"

Gwen shook her head, wondering why she even bothered to attempt to pay. In all the years of trying to sneak the bill, she'd won only once. He'd been so distraught, she actually felt badly about paying. But she still felt the need to offer. "You know I hate feeling indebted to you."

"Gwendolyn." His suddenly serious tone had her looking up in surprise; the sincerity in his eyes was intense. "Believe me when I tell you that your presence is more than enough in return for a simple meal. To be honest, each time you deign to share your time with me, I am struck anew with how honored I am to be there, with you, in that moment. So no, you are not indebted to me, ever. The truth is, *I* am indebted to *you*."

Her heart melted into a puddle at her feet.

This. This is why you can never have a normal relationship. You've been spoiled by honest-to-God chivalry by an honest-to-God medieval warrior.

If she was anyone else, she'd be jealous of herself.

He didn't seem to expect her to say anything as he continued, "Aye, I came to the conclusion on my own. Fate and destiny are interchangeable terms, no matter the language."

She leaned forward. "It's hard for me to remember that English is your second language."

"Fourth."

She blinked. "Come again?"

"Old Gaelic, modern Gaelic, French, then English."

"You know *French*?" she exclaimed.

"Oui, mademoiselle. J'ai apprécié le son, alors j'ai appris cela."

She had no idea what he said, but she didn't really care. Reilly speaking French was doing inexplicable things to her insides.

He gave her a slow, seductive smile. *"Et cela en valait la peine, pour voir votre visage ce moment."*

Reilly was giving her a seductive smile? *No way. Imagination overdrive.* Apparently, the smooth sounds of a romance language addled her brain into seeing things.

She glanced at him from under her eyelashes, noted his smile again, and shivered.

For the first time in a very long time, hope flared to life in her heart. Before she could process that strange turn of events, he (unfortunately) switched back to English.

"I interrupted you. You were saying 'tis hard for you to remember that English is not my first language. Why does that matter?"

She shook her head to clear it. "Right. Well, in English, those terms—fate and destiny—aren't interchangeable."

He smiled, a bit indulgently. "Perhaps *interchangeable* is the wrong word. In Celtic lore, we've two distinct deities for them. The Fates, of course, and from ancient times, the Morrígan. Goddess of destiny. Her legend didn't last very long."

"Is she a real thing?"

He scoffed. "Nay, she is just a made-up story, told to frighten children at bedtime. Back to what you were saying, about what you think fate and destiny are. Enlighten me."

She stuck her tongue out at him, and he rumbled out a laugh. "Well," she said slowly, "fate is more the idea that someone else is, for lack of a better term, pulling the strings."

He rolled his eyes.

She chuckled. "Well, with fate, there's nothing you can do about it. Something—or someone—else is controlling your life. All the choices you make have already been decided for you. But destiny, that's controlled by you."

He sat forward a little, his shoulders bunching as he leaned his forearms on the table. "Lass, 'tis madness." He lowered his voice so that only she could hear him. "I know the Fates. I have *lived* with them. They, unfortunately, are not a made-up tale."

"I know, I know. Hear me out," she insisted. "Destiny is when we have control. Full control, as in, every decision we make results in an action, and that action directly results in another decision, and so on and so forth. Everything is decided by us; every choice is made with free will."

"Fate allows for free will," he argued. "But the end result is the same. You'll get to where you're going, regardless of the path."

She nodded her head. "Sure, to a point. But if the path always leads to the same place, what does it matter what the choice is?"

He opened his mouth to respond, but halted. Gwen watched, fascinated, as he internally debated some point with himself.

She'd seen him do so on only a few occasions prior. Normally, he was so convinced in his thoughts that trying to sway him to a different opinion was a waste of time. He called it experience; she called it stubbornness.

But when she did manage to give him food for thought, watching him war it out with himself always proved captivating.

Finally, he inclined his head. "You make a valid point. But I find it hard to come up with any example of your definition of destiny. I have plenty of them for fate."

"There isn't anything in your vast repertoire where you made a decision you knew would displease the Fates?" she asked skeptically.

"You remember Emmaline, from Celtic Connections, aye?"

"Of course. She's married to Aidan."

Reilly nodded wearily. "Aye, she is. A while back, Emma had her own adventure in the past. You know Aidan is Laird MacWilliam's brother. When Emma returned to the future,

Aidan remained in the past, as was his fate. And, as he's not a Protector, he had no way to return to her."

She knew her eyes probably looked like saucers, but she couldn't help it. "But he's in the future now! How did he get there?"

Reilly frowned. "I went back and got him, of course."

"Of course," she echoed. "That would be destiny, Reilly. You changed fate's plan for them. You helped them to create their own destiny."

In the second before the mask of indifference slipped back over his features, she saw a flash of vulnerability in his eyes. "I'm not so romantic as all that, Gwendolyn."

Yes, you are, she almost said, but held her tongue. Her point had been made; he either accepted it, or he didn't.

CHAPTER 6

"*I* will be back sometime next week," Ellie said. "I'm so sorry, Gwen."

Gwen adjusted the phone to her ear and pointed down a road, indicating Reilly should turn that way. "Honestly, El, it's no trouble. You know I could spend years in Ireland and never get bored. No, Ry, you were supposed to go that way!"

"I *do* know where to go," Reilly pointed out.

"I know, but you came all the way to Ireland just to be with me before the wedding," Ellie replied, "and I end up not even being there for most of it. Will you be quite bored over there?"

"Reilly has some plans to keep us busy," Gwen replied noncommittally.

"What kind of plans?"

Gwen wasn't sure how to tell Ellie without sending her into spasms of anxiety, but her silence went on too long, and Ellie gasped, understanding immediately. "Gwendolyn! I know your sense of adventure is well-honed, but really? There's no indoor plumbing! You were climbing the walls last time! What happens if you end up in a dungeon? Or kidnapped?"

The fright in her friend's voice had Gwen wishing she could reach through the phone and give her a hug. "Ellie, I'll be with Reilly. He'd never let anything happen to me." She turned to look at him, and noticed he sat up a little straighter. "Don't puff out your chest, caveman. You wouldn't let anything happen to anyone on your watch."

He nodded. "Especially not you. I vow my life upon it, lass."

"Okay, that sounded totally medieval," Ellie laughed, a hint of relief creeping into her tone. Someone said something in the background on Ellie's end, and she added, "Colin said to keep an eye on Reilly, and ensure he doesn't mar his features for the wedding photographs."

Gwen relayed the message, laughter in her voice, and Reilly rolled his eyes. "Aye, his concern for my well-being is truly overwhelming."

Gwen laughed. "Anyway, Ellie, we're not time traveling yet. So don't worry, okay?"

"Well, be safe when you do go. Tell me all about it when you see me next week. And don't worry about wedding details. Winnie has everything well in hand."

"She has loved this entire process," Gwen agreed. Ellie wanted a small wedding but didn't care very much about the details and gladly handed the reins over to Winnie. All she retained control of was the wedding dress, Gwen's maid of honor dress, and the cake.

Gwen was convinced that Ellie was the easiest, and happiest, woman in the history of brides.

"Have fun, Gwennie, and stay close to Reilly."

"You bet, El."

They hung up just as Reilly pulled into a parking lot. "I thought we were going to the supermarket." Gwen said. She glanced at the sign in front of her. "Finnigan's Feudal Fashions?"

He nodded and unbuckled. "Stay there." He opened her door and helped her out. "You'll see."

She gave a bemused smile. "You don't have to tell me to stay in my seat, Ry. I know not to move until you open the door for me."

"I never assume that what you did yesterday would hold true to today," he replied gravely, though a ghost of a smile touched his lips.

A moment later, they entered the shop, and Gwen's eyes nearly popped out of her head. Medieval gowns, ancient Grecian togas, Renaissance codpieces, Regency breeches… clothing from every time period filled the walls and shelves. A display of knives and swords sat in the center counter, and spinning stands of period jewelry lined the back wall. A Celtic pipe soundtrack played merrily in the background.

"Reilly O'Malley, it's about time you showed up!"

A round, middle-aged woman bustled over to them, her ruddy face beaming. "I've been awaitin' you nigh on a month! It's been ready since I called you!"

Her accent was so thick Gwen had to concentrate on the words the woman was saying, and even then she wasn't sure if she caught everything.

"Aye, but I've been waiting for the right time to pick it up," he replied easily. "Molly Finnigan, meet Gwendolyn Allen."

"Aye, she's a sight, isn't she? Just adorable, you are, lassie. Wait here, I'll get it, and you can try it on straightaway!" Molly grinned at Gwen, her face crinkling into smile lines, and disappeared into the back.

"Put what on?"

Reilly didn't so much as flick her a glance, and Gwen could see he was slightly uncomfortable. "I had a dress made for you."

Gwen laughed, delighted. "You had a dress made for *me*? Over a month ago, too, from the sounds of it! Why?"

If she wasn't watching for it, she might've missed the small tick in his jaw. A sure sign he was uneasy, she knew. She waited for him to school his features into a stony mask of indifference.

She nearly laughed when he did exactly that.

She tugged one of his arms free from the tight fold he'd assumed when Molly went into the back. "Tell me, Ry. You know I won't stop asking until you do."

"'Tisn't that the honest truth," he muttered. He looked at her, and some of the indifference warmed. "I thought perhaps, someday in the future, there may be a possibility that you might crave an adventure or two, after your first one with Eleanor. So I thought I'd best be prepared."

Her mouth dropped open. "You knew I'd want to go again?"

He snickered. "I would've been shocked if you didn't."

"I'm that predictable?" she asked, oddly saddened.

He touched her chin and drew her face up. "I didn't have you in my life for a year, Gwendolyn. You're never predictable. 'Twas merely a hope of mine."

The intensity in his stare made her pause, and a small tingle raced down her spine. A bit off-kilter, she licked her suddenly dry lips. "A hope?"

His smile turned smug. "Aye. And sometimes, I simply know you better than you know yourself."

"Oh, you're so arrogant," she exclaimed, pushing his hand out from under her chin. She rolled her eyes at his deep chuckle, but she wondered what that look had been about.

Stop it right now, she admonished herself. She was seeing things that weren't there.

"'Ere we are," Molly said, reappearing behind a mound of fabric. "You certainly were right about her stature. Tiny as a fairy, that one!"

"I'm petite," Gwen said staunchly.

"Like a fairy," Molly replied agreeably. "Come, come, hold

it up. The fabric was a hard one to get, you see, but your gentleman insisted it be authentic. No zippers or buttons, all hand-stitched with wool that was dyed in the old ways."

"This must've cost a fortune," she murmured, gingerly shaking out the dress. The lush garnet color was accentuated by the gold silk ribbons woven horizontally on the bodice. The tips of the sleeves and bottom of the skirt were all edged with delicate gold lace, and the wool, while warm, wasn't as scratchy or as heavy as she'd expected.

"Reilly, this is…" She searched for words, unable to convey her gratitude.

"Back in medieval times, this sort of dress would be worn only by the wealthy, or even royalty. Peasants surely had nothing like this, and the woman who wore it would be considered a jewel indeed." Molly stood back with a smile, admiring her own handiwork. "I've slippers to match, but I didn't make those. Mr. O'Malley wasn't sure of your shoe size, and isn't that funny, for he knew all your other measurements!"

"Sinead," Reilly said to Gwen, by way of explanation.

Sinead was the head seamstress at Brianagh and Nioclas MacWilliam's castle, and during her trip to the past, the woman had modified a couple of gowns for Gwen to wear. Sinead was magical with a needle and thread.

"I loved the color so much I ordered a few slippers in the same dye," Molly continued. "Be sure to choose some, aye?"

"Thank you," Gwen said, reverentially hugging the dress to her. "I adore it."

Molly grinned, then handed a worn piece of paper to Reilly. Gwen lifted herself on tiptoes to see what it was, but she didn't have to.

"Your design was flawless, Mr. O'Malley. It suits her perfectly," Molly gushed. To Gwen, she added, "May you find many occasions to wear such a lovingly designed dress, lassie."

Surprised, Gwen nodded.

"Go pick out your shoes, but for the love of all that's holy, please don't be all day about it," Reilly grumbled.

She tugged him down to her and kissed his cheek. "Thank you."

"You deserve it," he replied matter-of-factly.

"Deserve it?" she echoed, nonplussed. "I don't see how I—"

He leveled her with a look meant to silence her on the matter. "You deserve it," he repeated firmly.

"Aye, he's a gentleman, that one!" Moly exclaimed, patting his brawny arm. "He says you never do anything for yourself, and that every woman should have at least one thing made just for her. This one's mama raised him right, she did!"

She wondered briefly if he knew she didn't wear an engagement ring because Anthony felt exactly the opposite. *Of course he wouldn't know that*, she rationalized. Anthony felt that the money he would've spent on a ring would be better served if it went to a family in need, and she outwardly agreed, though secretly, she'd really wanted one. It didn't have to be fancy…she just wanted to feel special.

She felt her emotions begin to rise.

"Don't," Reilly warned, as Gwen looked up at him with tears in her eyes.

She tried to blink them back, but they both knew it was a lost cause. She sniffed and waved her hand in front of her eyes, as if that would somehow evaporate the emotions, too. She swallowed, then placed her hand on his arm and gave it a small squeeze. "Then thank you extra, Reilly. That means a lot."

He grunted in response and waved toward the shoes. "Choose your shoes, wench, and let us be gone from this place."

She sniffed again, then did just as she was asked.

GWEN'S FINGER HOVERED ABOVE ANTHONY'S NAME ON HER phone screen, uncertain.

She knew he was going to be angry. She also knew that if she loved him the way he loved her, she shouldn't want to spend so much time with another person, particularly the man she'd spent most of her adult life loving.

After the scare she had at the pub the other day, Gwen realized why she came to Ireland. It wasn't to spend loads of quality time with Ellie before the wedding, as she had been telling herself. It wasn't that she needed a break from Anthony, which had crossed her mind a few times since she'd been back from Venezuela.

She needed a safe place.

When Reilly's was the face to greet her at the airport, a weight had lifted from her shoulders. When he'd left her alone in her house that night, that weight fell back into place. When he left for Ireland the next day, the weight grew, pressing against her chest until she couldn't breathe. But when he showed up at the gala, she was floating, she was so light.

Oh, God, what have I gotten myself into?

She put the phone on the bedside table and chewed her thumbnail. She wanted to get married. That stability and security was appealing to her; she'd spent such a long time in dangerous places, devoting her time to people who needed it, but that kind of work drained a person. She needed a break from the insanity, some time to simply enjoy her own life. Have children, and a house filled with noise and joy.

Anthony thrived on his charity work. She understood the drive; the recipients were usually so wonderful and the feeling of accomplishment was unlike any other. The rush of feeling useful, of feeling like she did some good in a world full of bad, was addicting—but she wanted to begin her *own* life.

There was nothing inherently wrong with that, Gwen knew, but the guilty feelings were hard to overcome. Reilly once pointed out that there would always be another family in need, another orphanage to build, and she could only do what she could do; any more than that was unfair to herself.

At the time, she thought Reilly didn't understand. Now, she got it. If she only had this one life to live, giving *of* herself was important. But giving all of herself? That was a long, lonely road. A noble one, to be sure, but one she was increasingly seeing wasn't the path she wanted to stay on forever.

Anthony thought they were on that long path together. He always spoke of where they'd be in twenty years—maybe living in Ecuador, teaching the poorest communities how to become self-sufficient, or in Uganda, working alongside the local governments to get fresh water to everyone.

Gwen felt selfish for thinking that in twenty years, she'd like to attend her child's high school graduation.

But it's not selfish, she reminded herself. It was not selfish to want a family, and stability. She'd spent all of her twenties working to ensure others could have just that; why couldn't she want those things, too?

She glanced out her window and saw Reilly sitting on one of the low stone walls that surrounded his garden, talking on his phone. He looked at ease with the world around him. She smiled a little to herself. Even his clothing was made for comfort; his faded tee shirt strained at the arms but hiding what she knew was a washboard stomach and muscular back. Every pair of jeans the man owned was soft, fitted exactly to his body, with the back right pocket bearing the outline of his wallet.

Gwen sighed. She knew more about Reilly O'Malley than she did anyone else, save Ellie. But then he dropped the bombshell that he could actually move time, and it took her a while to get over the shock of that omission.

When she and Ellie found themselves in medieval Ireland last summer, and Reilly's secrets were blown wide open, Gwen was hurt that he'd never told her. His entire façade to her had been a lie; he claimed he was a simple woodworker from Ireland, with a close extended family who lived in America. His parents were dead, he lived alone in the woods on the outskirts of Dublin, and he was a simple man.

Of course, by simple, he meant a time-traveling, sword-swinging, medieval bodyguard.

But it was Reilly, and truly, she understood why he'd kept it from her. And she had continued to love him anyway.

Continued to love him now.

If only he wasn't so handsome. If only he wasn't so good to her. If only he wasn't such a good man. If only…

If only she could stop loving him, and give all that love to another, to someone who wanted it.

She watched Reilly continue his conversation, oblivious to her inner turmoil, and she wished things were different.

Why did I come back here? she wondered despondently. Did she enjoy torturing herself with Things That Could Never Be? She could be tucked into a nice hotel in Atlanta, enjoying the heat and all the wonderful things that city had to offer, with a man who was devoted to her.

But instead, she chose rainy Ireland, with a man who enjoyed her company but had no desire for anything more than that. And she chose it after avoiding him for an entire *year* so she could, in fact, move on.

I'm such a coward.

Gwen knew deep down that she shouldn't marry another man while her heart was so firmly attached to someone else. But that man wanted nothing to do with a forever with her. She had a chance at stability, at security. She could grow to love Anthony the way she loved Reilly.

She just had to admit she wanted that sure thing more than she wanted Reilly.

I do want that. I want to make a life with Anthony.

She picked up the phone and dialed. He answered on the first ring.

"I've missed you, Red. Tell me you're calling to come to Atlanta?"

"Still in Ireland, Anth. I had my dress fitting, and Ellie and I went out the other night. It was fun."

"Sounds like it. How's the hotel? Is it posh?"

She fiddled with her necklace. "I wouldn't know. They canceled my reservation." She told him all about it, and when she finished, there was a lengthy pause.

"So you're staying at Ellie's aunt's house?"

Well, Ellie and Colin had departed for the States, and Winnie had gone back to London...So, there was no reason for Gwen to be where she was. She knew that, but staying anywhere else was...

It was smart.

She was a smart woman. She knew she was. But her stupid heart kept getting in the way.

"No, I'm not at Winnie's. It was after midnight, so I stayed at Ry's. I didn't want to intrude on Colin and Ellie."

Anthony's silence was deafening. A moment passed, then another. Gwen's chest constricted, and she finally said, "Please don't be upset with me. I needed a place to stay, and he—"

"Is always there for you? Willing to drop everything in the middle of the night to rescue you?"

She stayed silent.

Another moment passed, and she could almost hear him gather himself. "Gwen, be honest here. Just, for once, be honest with me about this guy. If he asked you to leave everything behind, if he asked you to love him, to make a life with him, would you?"

She allowed herself to get caught up in the fantasy, and she hesitated a millisecond too long. "No, of course not."

"Gwendolyn." The heartbreak in his voice had her eyes filling with tears. "I love you. I want to spend the rest of our lives together. We work so well together, we get along so well. God, Gwen, we could save the world!"

"I want children," she blurted out. "And a home with a lawn, and maybe even a fence."

"I will give you all that and more."

"I don't want to travel around the world saving everyone else anymore. I want to save me."

He drew a sharp breath. "It's our lifeblood, Gwen. People like us were meant to help others, not ourselves."

"People like you," she amended, her voice wobbling. "I want something different. Something stable."

"And stability can be found in Ireland, in the home of a man who's kept you close enough to pine after him, but far enough to not love you the way you deserve to be loved? Solid logic, Gwen." The bitterness and anger lashed out of him, and Gwen felt the blows.

"This has nothing to do with Reilly," she said softly.

"Oh yes it does," he shot back. "But it also has to do with you, and your refusal to be honest with anyone, yourself included. I can't do this. I deserve more than to be the next best thing."

She gasped. "What do you mean?"

"You know exactly what I mean. You're in love with someone, and it isn't me." She drew in a sharp breath, but he barreled on. "I've known it, I think I knew it when I saw you two together, but I thought I could change your mind. Make you love me instead."

"I do!" she exclaimed.

He barreled on, "How long have you been in love with him? Months? Years? Since the moment you met him?"

"Stop it, Anthony."

Anthony snorted angrily. "You're refusing to answer the question. How long have you loved him?" he pressed.

"I *used* to love him," she said forcefully. "But he never loved me back. We are just friends, Anthony. This is more about your insecurities than mine."

The lie tasted bitter on her tongue.

He remained silent for one heartbeat, then two. "Do you want to marry me, Gwen?"

"Yes!" Gwen swallowed hard, knowing her answer had come out just a little too strong.

"Then you have a choice to make. Me or him. You can't have both."

"That's unfair! He's my friend, and you'll be my husband!"

"Life's unfair. I want to know that my future wife chooses me."

"I'll make a choice when you choose me over your charities," she shot back. She clamped her lips together, shocked that she'd said it, but unwilling to take it back.

"Done. After this, I'm all yours. If you want me to drop everything, take a nine-to-five job, I will. But I'm finishing here, because I'm a man of my word, and I promised a family that their house would be built."

She blinked. That was unexpected.

"But you come home," he continued. "I don't care if it's New Hampshire or Georgia, but dammit, Gwen, I want you away from him."

"After the wedding."

"No."

"You don't get to dictate the terms of my life." She felt her temper rising, but underneath it, a desperation. "I've got commitments here, too!"

His voice was laced with frustration. "Dammit, Gwen, all I want is your love!"

"You have it!"

The line was silent for so long, Gwen worried he might've hung up on her, but then he sighed heavily. "Which pains you more, Gwen? Never seeing me again, or never seeing him?"

She sighed, suddenly exhausted with their conversation. "Anthony, why are you doing this?"

"Gwen, if it doesn't break your heart, is it really love?" he asked, the fight leaving his voice as well.

Her throat clogged, and she made an inarticulate sound.

There was a gentle knock on her door, and it swung open silently. Reilly stood in front of her, his stance relaxed, a small scowl on his face. His black hair was effortlessly tousled, and his sharp hazel eyes found hers immediately, causing her breath to catch. His shoulders filled the doorway, and his head nearly touched the low ceiling.

She closed her eyes and imagined Anthony's easy smile, his teasing laugh. How he called her Red. How he wanted her to be his wife, forever. Life with him would be easy. He'd give her everything she ever wanted, and all she'd ever have to do was ask.

Life with Reilly would be so hard. He'd have to leave suddenly when called on a mission, strange visitors would show up without notice, and his time would be stretched thin between his Protector duties, his school, and her.

When they were out together, Anthony rarely frowned, and Reilly rarely smiled.

The choice should be obvious, but somehow, it just wasn't.

She drew a shaky breath. "I don't know what to say."

After another moment of silence, he swallowed loudly. "I know now that you were never mine, but losing you *still* breaks my heart."

He hung up, and she stared at the blank screen, her heart pounding, her stomach roiling.

"Gwendolyn?"

Reilly's voice, soft and low and too damn perfect, filtered

through her brain fog. She covered her face, her tears falling through her fingers.

She opened her mouth, but no words came out.

She tightened her lips against the oncoming sob, but it was useless. He opened his arms, and she fell into them as she fell apart.

"A fight with Anthony?"

She nodded into his chest.

"Oh, lass. He's upset you're staying here." His voice was gravelly, as though it caused him great pain that he might somehow cause *her* great pain.

She buried her head deeper into his chest. If he knew the truth of it, he would be wracked with guilt. She couldn't tell him. He'd insist she leave, go to Anthony, and try to fix it. He'd put her on the plane himself, and away from him was the last place she wanted to be.

But it was probably the only place she should be.

"Do you care to talk about it?" he murmured.

She took a gulp of air, then let out an unsteady breath. "No," she whispered.

He tightened his arms in response, and for once, she was more than grateful for his silence.

Allowing him to comfort her was something she'd always done, but suddenly she realized that she couldn't have it all. He couldn't be the one to comfort her if she married another. He wouldn't be the one to comfort her when *he* married another. Her heart hurt with the knowledge, and she cried even harder.

She was destined to love a man who would never love her back, and she knew she could never give her heart to someone else. Her soul demanded one thing, but her mind demanded another.

And her heart was caught in the crossfire.

∼

GWEN'S FACE WAS CONTORTED BY THE ANGUISH. HER TEAR-stained cheeks, her red-rimmed eyes…and pain etched into the lines around those eyes. This despair was different than anything she'd ever shown him; perhaps it was the strongest she'd ever experienced.

And he was the cause of it.

Reilly felt ill.

He pulled her off the bed and tucked her into himself, and she tried, unsuccessfully, to take a deep breath.

"Cry as long as you need."

The words were enough for the dam to burst even further open. She twisted so that they were chest-to-chest, then buried her face into the crook of his neck, clasped her hands around him, and sobbed.

It was, he realized, the sound of her heart breaking.

He'd never felt so helpless, or so worried. He wasn't a worrier, by any stretch of the imagination. He was one of the very few who had supreme confidence that he was always where he was supposed to be, doing what he was supposed to do. It helped that the Fates vowed to tell him when his time as a Protector was finished, and that until then, his life was secure.

She continued to cry, albeit softer now. In a way, it was worse, for it sounded as though she had lost the best piece of her soul, without any hope of getting it back.

It seemed, from the noises she was making, that she did indeed feel something deep for Anthony. She told Anthony she was staying with him, and the man—rightfully—was upset by that. But by the saints, the man needed to get off his arse and start putting Gwen first. Other people could wait; Gwen deserved to be treated better. She deserved the best of Anthony, not what was left over after he'd given it to others.

Why wasn't Anthony on a plane out there? Why wasn't he rushing to show her that she was his?

For a man to be the recipient of such love, and to not cherish it?

Reilly sighed heavily, seeing the irony in his thoughts. For years he hadn't given Gwen the best of him. In fact, she sometimes got the worst of him, especially if he'd had a particularly rough go of things during his travels. He knew he could be ornery, and in his foulest of moods, he'd call her just to hear her laugh.

And she worked so hard to cheer him. She'd coax a chuckle out of him, and after the really bad trips, she'd take the time to come to him. Once, she'd flown over, knocked on his door, handed him a beer, then made herself comfortable on the couch until he'd finished it. No words were spoken; she was simply there for him.

He needed her then, and she knew it. She gave him the best of herself, because she was an angel, and he was a beast.

He'd been so blind, and he was terrified the price for his stupidity was too high to bear. If she would but give him a chance, he would spend every day of the rest of their lives, and the rest of forever, showing her how much she meant to him. He would treat her better than anyone ever could. He may not be perfect, but he was perfect for her.

But did her heart belong to another? It would appear so, as she cried herself dry on his shoulder.

What a mess.

Later, after she'd cried herself out, he held her close as she slept the sleep of the emotionally drained.

Eventually, he placed her on the bed, and tucked the covers around her. He watched her sleep, the pain a physical one, her beauty suddenly too much for him to bear. He looked at the pale green walls—her favorite color—and tried to swallow past the enormous lump in his throat.

Was all truly fair in love and war? he wondered, James's words coming back to him in a rush. He knew he could make her happy. She was his soul mate. But was he hers? He looked at her sleeping figure, his heart as tangled as his thoughts.

He wouldn't be able to live with himself if he didn't try. He would take Colin's advice, and show her how much she meant to him. He would shower her with chivalry, show her his best side. Keep her smiling and safe. He would make her happy, or die trying.

The dress was a good start, but it was only a start. She needed to see his heart. Words wouldn't help him now; actions only. If she didn't see it, if she didn't return his feelings…

He'd let her go.

Reilly loved her too much to do anything else.

Her phone buzzed, and he picked it up to silence it. The text showed across the locked screen, and Anthony's name jumped out at him.

I won't stop loving you. And maybe that'll be enough someday. I'll wait, Gwen. I will. Maybe it'll be enough, and you won't allow the person who doesn't love you keep you from the one that does.

Reilly stared at it until the screen went dark again, then flipped the volume switch to silent. He stood another moment, wondering, and finally left her to her sleep.

CHAPTER 7

The next morning, Gwen shuffled into the kitchen, her eyes still a bit puffy and her nose a little red.

"Good morning," he greeted her. He pushed a coffee mug toward her.

She gratefully accepted it, then took a step in the direction of the refrigerator. She pulled up short when she realized that it already had cream in it, and took a long sip. It was sugared up to the point where she could barely taste the coffee.

Perfect.

"That's really good, Ry, thanks. Where did you go last night?" She looked anywhere but him. "I heard you come in."

She didn't have to worry about making any eye contact with him, as he didn't even look up from his paper. "Just an errand," he replied nonchalantly, though he did wince a little as he shifted in his chair.

"Are you okay?"

"Aye, just slept wrong. Don't worry yourself over it." He turned the page.

"I'm—I'm sorry for last night."

He looked up in surprise. "Whatever for?"

She shrugged uncomfortably. "For crying all over you?"

"You've done it before, and I hope you know you can do it again. Think nothing of it, lass." He went back to the paper, engrossed in the day's news.

Her head began to throb. She sat down, silently contemplative. Last night, when she awoke in the middle of the night, it was easy to rationalize her choice. Anthony was stable, and didn't she just decide recently that she would be happy? She needed to fix things with Anthony.

In the light of day, though, the question actually became the one Anthony himself posed: could she be happy without Reilly in her life?

"So what do you care to do today?" he asked, interrupting her turmoil.

Gwen paused, the cup halfway to her lips again. "Do? But don't you have to work?"

"The school is on break until next month," he informed her, turning the page. She craned her neck to see what he was so engrossed in, then rolled her eyes. Rugby scores.

"The comics are way better than rugby scores," she felt compelled to point out. "Also, no one actually reads a newspaper anymore. The internet has all that."

"Rubbish," he retorted, his eyes tracking the small print. His face lit up with a smile. "Tickets go on sale in a couple weeks. Looks like we play Poland to start the season."

"Thrilling."

"'Tis if you've ever seen our boys play…Eh. So, back to the topic at hand. What do you wish to do? Do you want to get off island, head to the Continent?"

Gwen wouldn't mind taking a day trip to Paris for the day. She loved that city, with all its sparkling lights. And, though she could be as rough and tumble as the next tomboy, there was something about the Tiffany's store on the Champs-Élysées that brought her to an unnaturally happy mental place.

She wasn't shy about the fact that she'd grown up

wealthy, and Gwen wasn't one to turn her back on the finer things in life. She just made sure to balance it with giving back as much as she could.

"Paris?"

"Mmm...nay," he murmured.

Daydreams of drowning herself in window shopping fled quickly. "Okay. How about we head to Temple Street?" she asked, referring to one of her favorite streets in Dublin. It was always bustling and great for people-watching. They also had some of the best coffee shops and bars in the city.

He shrugged. "If that's what you'd like."

She folded her arms and sat back. "Do you have something better in mind?"

He raised an eyebrow but didn't look up from the paper. "Not particularly, nay."

Frustrated, she blew out a breath. "I want you to understand that we could be sitting on the couch together, staring at paint dry, and I'd still have a good time. But I have to wonder, Ry. When's the last time you let your hair down? Had some fun?"

He did glance up then. "I've my school."

"That's work. I mean *fun*. You know, something that you do only for amusement?" she teased. "In all our years, I swear I've never seen you dance, or sing, or really let loose."

"I prefer to redirect my energy in other ways."

"Such as...?" she prompted him.

"Woodwork. Sword play. Flying metal beasts in the sky. Knife practice. Training legions of O'Rourke Protectors."

She snorted. "Oh, yeah. That last one sounds like loads of fun."

He frowned and canted his head at her. "So you think I'm starchy?"

"Starchy?" she giggled. "Maybe a little. Or maybe you're just a homebody. Either way, I'd love for you to try my brand of fun."

He headed to the counter and began to make some toast. "Your brand?" he echoed. "Are you talking about how you like to stay out until the wee hours of the morning at dance clubs? Or that you like to eat at various restaurants, but the fancy ones are your favorite?"

She laughed because there was no heat or accusation to his words. "I call it embracing my youth. We won't have it forever, you know. Though I don't stay out all night anymore. It got old." He didn't answer her, just grabbed the bread when it popped up and began to butter it. She soldiered on, "But when you stay in all the time, it makes it a bit hard for others to get to know how wonderful you are."

"I don't need others."

She rolled her eyes at his stubborn tone. "Oh, let's not go there. Everyone needs others. Sometimes, don't you wish you could just let go of all your responsibilities, and be a little bit carefree?"

He stayed silent for so long, Gwen began to worry that he was irritated with her. But then he turned and met her eyes. "Aye. But I've never done it."

His bleak expression stopped her in her tracks. Selfishly, she wanted to be the one to make that look go away. She racked her brain for a moment until the lightbulb clicked on.

"Up for a little game?"

He brought the plate back to the table and sat down. "I'm listening."

"Pretend that we only have until Ellie's wedding together before we can never see each other again."

"This is a terrible game."

"Well, you said the school is off for a month," she rushed on, her cheeks heating. "So just go with it."

He set his jaw. "I don't care to tempt the Fates with such talk."

"That's the first rule of our game. Rule one: Forget about the damn Fates. Don't let them have this time. This is all yours, Reilly. You hear that, Fates? Leave him alone for three weeks!" she called out.

Alarmed, he put out his hand. "Gwen, truly, please don't."

She pursed her lips. "If they are as all-knowing as they'd like you to believe, they knew this was coming. You and I both need a vacation, and I'm just the person to plan such a thing."

"That sounds ominous," he deadpanned, but his mouth quirked. "I'm certain this is a bad idea."

"You are certain of no such thing," she retorted, reaching across the small table and snagging his plate. The toast was still warm, and she popped it into her mouth.

"No, please, go right ahead. I'm no longer hungry," Reilly grumbled, though she saw the smile tugging at the corner of his mouth.

She grinned and spoke around the food. "How fortuitous, as I'm starving."

She swallowed and realized with a start that the toast had strawberry jam on it. She loved strawberry jam.

Reilly didn't eat jam.

She looked at her empty coffee cup, which was made exactly as she liked it, and looked back at the toast.

Reilly drank his coffee black, if he even had coffee, and he only had butter on his toast.

She was probably making too big a deal of it, but...he had made her breakfast. He'd never really made her breakfast before. She'd stolen his food, and he hers, but it was more that they co-existed in the kitchen in the mornings. She studied him as he re-opened the paper to the business section.

It's just me overanalyzing everything. He is trying to make me feel better after last night's sobfest. That was it. She watched him find nothing of interest, then fold the paper and stack the sections in front of him. He sat back in his chair, his torso eclipsing any view of the perfectly crafted woodwork that made up the chair back. The nip in the air outside had him wearing a flannel over his dark tee shirt, and his facial scruff only added to the lumberjack look he was wearing.

Gwen never before had a thing for the lumberjack look, but she couldn't help being attracted to it when it sat directly opposite her over a breakfast made especially for her.

Totally inappropriate train of thought, she chastised herself.

But still, she was a straight female, and there was a fine specimen of a male sitting directly in front of her, on a chair that he built, in a cottage that he restored with his own two hands.

He could also pull off the leather jacket and jeans look, she admitted. And a suit. Oh, Reilly in a tuxedo or a suit was a sight to behold. Typically, she shied away from men in suits; her parents' circle was full of well-dressed, stuffy men who wouldn't know a Phillips head from a flat head. But dressing up Reilly in a suit and tie, or a tux and bowtie, did something to her insides every time.

And don't even start her when he wore his medieval garb.

What was wrong with her? She needed to get herself back under control. For years, she had been so good about corralling her thoughts. She had them on lockdown, and the only time they came to the forefront was at night; she accepted long ago that she couldn't (and didn't want to) control her dreams.

Reilly chortled, noticing her sudden blush. "Oh, the coin I'd pay to know those thoughts."

She rolled her eyes, trying to play it off. "In your dreams, O'Malley."

His eyes darkened, and Gwen felt a corresponding pull. She sucked in a breath, but before she could overanalyze *that* reaction, he said quickly, "Describe what sort of things you'd like to do with me."

The thoughts *that* command inspired made her go thermonuclear red.

"Uh...." she stuttered, trying to lighten her tone.

He gave her a satisfied smile. "Pull your head out of the gutter, lass, and tell me what you'd like to do with me on this vacation of yours."

She blushed hard and cleared her throat. "Well, it'll be a staycation, unless you want to travel."

"Staycation is fine with me. What do you plan to start with?"

She thought for a moment. Clubbing would be fun, maybe, if he wouldn't glower at everyone who wanted to dance. And dinner out was always a good time. But she needed something unexpected, something that he would never do on his own.

Her eyes drifted over the kitchen before landing on the ancient stove, and the idea took root in her mind. "Baking!"

He stared at her for a full minute. "Have you gone mad? You've never baked a damn thing in your life!"

She shrugged, deciding it was actually a very good idea. "No time like the present to try something new, right?"

He gaped at her, but after a moment, he shrugged good-naturedly. "If it's baking you want, it's baking we'll do. But I'll be the first to tell you, your idea of fun doesn't quite match up with mine."

"What would you do, then?" she challenged.

His eyes darkened again, and immediately, Gwen's body temperature rose a few degrees. Mind in the gutter, indeed.

When it came right down to it, she was helpless *not* to play this game with Reilly. If she lost, she knew she'd never recover. But if she won…

Her heartbeat tripled.

First things first: She needed to determine if this game had only one player, or two.

～

THREE HOURS LATER, REILLY LOOKED AT THE ASSORTMENT OF "baking needs" on his counter, a dubious expression on his face. Aside from the expected flour, eggs, and butter, there was now a hand mixer, a baking sheet, and flimsy plastic mats that the saleswoman promised would "evenly distribute the heat," whatever that meant.

Gwen bought everything the saleswoman recommended, determined to make these cookies. Reilly told her once that Colin's mom made the best chocolate chip cookies in the world. Evelyn O'Rourke didn't follow a recipe; she just knew how much of what went in where. Gwen desperately wanted to be like that, but alas, she didn't understand the difference between baking soda and baking powder, so she resolved herself to baby steps.

Cookies seemed simple enough. The online recipe she found called it "easy" and the one on the back of the chocolate chip package looked to be exactly the same one, so rationally, it seemed easy as well.

"So how do we turn all of this into cookies?" he asked.

She held up the crinkly package. "It says we need to mix the dry ingredients in one bowl, and the wet ingredients in another."

"Sounds like a waste of a bowl to me," Reilly grunted.

Gwen shrugged. "Me too. It's all going to end up mixed together, so why don't we just add it all in now?"

"That sounds reasonable." As Reilly dutifully measured "dry ingredients" as instructed, Gwen dumped in the sticks of butter, eggs, and vanilla flavoring on top of his large pile of flour and some other ingredients that she already forgotten about. She plugged in the hand mixer, turned it on, and stuck it into the bowl.

It took a few seconds for the cloud of white to settle around them.

"Was there too much flour, you think?" she asked in a small voice.

Amused, he glanced down at his previously clean shirt. "Perhaps."

"Oh, you have egg all over you!" she gasped. She choked back a laugh. "Oh, Ry, your hair! It's white!"

He reached out and snagged her ponytail, which was liberally streaked with flour. "You didn't escape it either, I'm afraid."

She wrinkled her nose. "Hmm. Maybe I should put the mixer into the bowl first, then turn it on."

Wisely, he took a step back. "Perhaps. Or we could head to Letty's Bakery—"

"No way! We've already come this far. Let's finish it out." Determined, she put the mixer back into what was left in the bowl and turned the power on low. Nothing flew out of the bowl this time, so Reilly cautiously looked in.

"It doesn't look like cookie dough," he noted, watching the stick of butter clunk around the bowl.

Gwen set her jaw. "Well that's because it hasn't mixed up yet. Give it a minute. Wait a second, why is the butter stick not mixing in? It's all hard."

Reilly leaned forward to see, sending a jolt of pure lust zinging through her veins. She accidentally hit the speed on the hand mixer.

Flour-covered butter pieces splattered onto his cheek, and the rest joined the egg on his shirt. She clapped a hand over her mouth, trying to contain both her mirth and her horror.

Reilly heaved an enormous, weary sigh, then reached down and, in one fluid motion, whipped the flannel over his head. He was left in just a tight-fitting black tee shirt that did absolutely nothing to hide his biceps.

Her mouth suddenly dry, Gwen snapped her gaze on the bowl in front of her. Reilly in tight-fitting clothes always had the same effect on her as it did every other woman in a twenty-five-mile vicinity. She felt hot, off-balance, and more than a little light-headed.

"Sorry again. Um, so…" She fumbled for the bag, desperate to focus on anything other than Reilly's arms, which were the largest she'd ever seen. Or his trim waist. Or his flat stomach, or…"Once this is all mixed together, we have to preheat the oven to 190 degrees. Oh, wait, that's Celsius. Is your oven set for Celsius or Fahrenheit?"

"Celsius?"

"Oh my God, we are so bad at this," she laughed. She shoved him out of the way and glanced at the dials. "This oven is really old. It works, right?"

The appliance looked like something out of a bygone era. It was a cream-colored wall oven with a panel of colored circles that seemed to have no purpose other than decoration. The knob on the left had numbers on it, though they were faded almost to the point of unreadability.

"Aye, it works." He reached around her and turned the knob to, hopefully, 190. "It'll take a few minutes to heat up. In the meantime, we can start cleaning, aye?"

She looked around them and wrinkled her nose. Flour dusted everything, there was a square of butter on the ceiling, and the egg also hit the refrigerator.

"I didn't think of cleanup," she admitted.

He laughed. "Nor did I." He handed her a sponge. "Letty's would've been an easier bet."

"But not as much fun?"

He rolled his eyes. "You and your ideas of fun." But he was smiling when he said it.

As Gwen profoundly thanked the firemen once more, Reilly was struck anew with how absurd her idea of "fun" might be.

The firemen hopped in their truck and drove off, giving a friendly honk of their horn on their way down the driveway.

"Well, that was an adventure!" she sighed.

He glanced back at his cottage, which luckily had very little damage from their grease fire. Which, as one of the firemen pointed out, seemed strange, as they were baking, and cookies rarely used any form of grease.

"Oh, aye. A blast," he muttered.

"Blast. I get it. Funny. Ha ha. Stop, I'm dying from the laughter," she replied dryly as they reentered the house, the smell of smoke still prevalent. They headed to the kitchen to scope out the damage. Reilly's stove was completely out of commission. The charred wall directly behind the stove would need a cleanup and a fresh coat of paint, and his cabinets could use a bit of love, too.

"I'm glad it didn't reach the second floor," Gwen added, staring at the ceiling.

His eyes traveled up, and he sighed at its blackened condition. "Looks like I'll have to do that kitchen remodel sooner than I'd planned."

She brightened. "When were you planning to do that?"

"Never."

She looked suddenly crestfallen. "Oh, Ry, I'm so sorry. I truly am. I'll help pay for it. I'll pay for all of it, if you want. I didn't mean to light your house on fire."

She looked so earnest, with flour dusting her forehead and shirt. Her hair was loosely held back, curls escaping and caressing her cheeks. He bumped her shoulder with his arm.

"Don't worry yourself over it, lass. I'm teasing. Colin's been after me for years to do something with this room. His kitchen is something out of a movie, with all its gadgets. I'll remodel it to look exactly the same as it was. It'll make him insane."

She smiled a little, but it was a half-hearted effort. He needed to make her happy again. Seeing her without a smile was crushing him. She looked close to tears, and as he'd already had enough of those the night prior, he readily admitted to doing anything to avoid them again.

"Let's stay somewhere else tonight. Let the house air out a bit," he suggested. "Go pack an overnight bag and we'll drive."

"Where?"

He herded her toward the staircase, pushing her up a couple of steps. "Does it matter?"

She turned around, still not eye level with him, but closer to it. Her eyes were filled with regret. "This was a stupid idea. I'm sorry, Reilly."

He gently cradled her face in his hand, and for a moment, she buried her cheek into it. He momentarily lost his breath, mesmerized by the sight and feel of her. "'Twas not a stupid idea, Gwendolyn. I had fun, mostly. And I very much look forward to the next adventure."

She smiled tremulously. "Really?"

"Aye, really. But this one is my turn. I'll show you my kind of fun."

"Does it involve weapons?" she asked cautiously.

He laughed. "Nay, not this time. But don't disparage it until you've tried it."

"I love your laugh," she whispered. Her eyes widened, and she yanked her head back.

His heart leapt, though he strove to keep his reaction relaxed. "'Tis easy to laugh when I'm with you. Now, go pack a bag, and I'll see what I can do to secure us some smoke-free lodgings this evening."

She nodded once, then bolted up the stairs, leaving him to watch her hasty retreat.

So, she loved his laugh. It was a small thing, Reilly knew. Perhaps a slip of the tongue, or just a compliment to a friend.

But it definitely didn't feel like she meant it as a friend. Something was shifting between them, and though he initiated it at the dress shop a few days ago, she couldn't seem to help her response.

That was very, very good for him.

If he fully turned on his charm, would she be able to resist him? Would she *want* to resist him? He had much to atone for, with his past actions. And she would need much convincing, as well, to believe him to be sincere. And, for the first time in as long as he could remember, he wasn't sure of his charm anymore. While he'd never had a problem with women before, this time it was different.

This time, it was Gwendolyn.

This feeling of uncertainty would be the death of him. He headed to his room to throw together his own overnight bag and texted James.

Weird message on Gwen's phone last night after a fight with the boyfriend.

James texted back almost immediately.

Creepy that you're looking at her messages. Don't do that.

He snorted. He wasn't a complete idiot.

It wasn't intentional!

Sure. So what was the weird message?

Reilly shoved some things into his backpack and thought about how much he should tell James. He passed his phone from hand to hand, stalling. Finally, he typed:

Said he wouldn't stop loving her and that maybe someday it'd be enough.

That was the general message, though when he looked at it now, it seemed a bit overdramatic. He couldn't abide dramatics. Was he now being dramatic by texting James? Thankfully, James's response popped in, stopping Reilly from further traveling down that road of thought.

Ouch. And this was after a fight? Did they break up and call off the wedding?

Unsure.

Well? Are you going to ask her if she did?

Reilly snorted. As though he would ask such a question the morning after she said she didn't want to talk about it!

Last night she said she didn't want to talk about it, so nay.

James responded almost immediately.

That was last night. This is today. You need to know where she stands. Ask her if she's in love with the guy.

A sense of panic built in Reilly's chest.

What if she says aye?

He shoved more things into his bag as James replied.

She won't say aye, she's American. She'd say yes instead.

Reilly smiled at that.

> Wise arse

The smile died from his face, though, as he read the next text.

> So, what *if* she says yes?

Reilly stared at the screen. That was the question, wasn't it? He didn't know. He was in fully uncharted territory. Women had never been particularly difficult to get into his bed, and he never had a pressing need to keep them in his heart. Gwen had always been different, though. She was special.

But he couldn't write that to James, else the teasing would be torturous. He texted back.

> That's why I'm texting you, though I can see it was a mistake.

> Get your panties out of a bunch. Seriously, I think the bigger question you're asking is, what if she says nay?

He let out a frustrated sigh. Aye, that was the question, wasn't it? It was easier to know what he'd do if Gwen didn't want a life with him, knowing what he was, what his life was like. If she didn't, he could ensure she got whatever it was she wanted, and try to be happy that she was happy.

He clenched his jaw at his lack of confidence. The feeling was unsettled and, if he were to be fully honest, he was beginning to annoy himself.

> Aye. I've never done this before.

Reilly grit his teeth when he read the next text.

Woo a woman??? *smiling devil emoji*

The next time they were in the lists, James would pay dearly for his teasing. But at the moment, he really needed James's advice, so he texted:

Woo *the* woman.

After a few moments of radio silence, the incoming text notification sounded, and Reilly swallowed hard.

Then it's time to prepare for battle. Winner takes all.

He shoved his toothbrush into the bag and zipped it before replying.

I've yet to lose a battle.

James took his time with his final reply.

Probably true. But you've never battled for something this important, so tread carefully, and keep your wits about you. The rules change daily, if not hourly, so don't even try to figure them out. Good luck, cousin. Let me know if I can help further.

Reilly groaned. If that was James's definition of help, the man needed a new dictionary.

CHAPTER 8

*R*eilly was nervous.

It was a new feeling he was unaccustomed to, and he found that he didn't much care for it. The changes in his mind were, he knew, driven by something he couldn't control. He suspected 'twas love that was behind this particular wheel, and he understood a bit, perhaps, as to other men's actions when they too found themselves similarly afflicted. But this was Gwen, not some medieval maiden who desired flowers and ribbons and courtly gestures. Gwen made it plain early on that all she required was him.

Why was that enough to make his palms sweat?

Most likely because, even though she may not require them, she deserved flowers and ribbons and courtly gestures and everything else his feeble brain could come up with. She deserved every good thing in the universe.

And he had *eleven years* to deliver them, but he hadn't. All because he was too busy making up excuses. First she was too young, then she needed to experience life on her own terms, then she was too important.

Too important? he scoffed at himself. Ha. When a lass is too important, you grab her and never let her go.

Easier said than done, though, as he was learning firsthand.

As he strapped the last dirk about his calf, Reilly glanced around his bedroom. It was tidy, though smaller than the ones his family members called their own. Colin's was an entire floor of his home in Boston; Aidan's was most of a floor in his cottage by the Irish Sea. Even James's room in his new house in the States was at least twice the size of the one in which Reilly now sat.

Reilly loved his house. He lived with much more and much less, yet the humble, daub-and-wattle cottage he restored over years was perfect for him. He ensured every detail wasn't too modern, for the comfort (and sanity) of his time-traveling visitors. So many lost souls wandered into his garden over the years, sent to him from the Fates for various reasons; Reilly knew what could be accepted and what could not, and he took that knowledge into consideration from the placement of his light switches to the width of his stairs.

If he managed to win Gwen's love, he'd give it all up for whatever she wanted. Gwen too lived with much less and much more. She grew up in a life of luxury, but she remained the most down-to-earth person he knew. Oh, she loved her fine things—she owned not a single piece of costume jewelry, and her clothes were high quality, though she never cared for labels much. But there were days when her nails were dirty from digging in the soil, or her hair was wild and her face red from sweating in the sun while working outside. She could swear like she'd been born a king's warrior, and weep with the gentleness of a finely-bred lady.

And she could read him unlike any other. Even Colin couldn't tell Reilly's thoughts when he didn't want him to, but Gwen could. She knew him almost better than he knew himself.

Well...she used to. Now, he wasn't so sure.

"Ready to go?" Gwen asked, appearing in his doorframe.

He glanced up, taking in her appearance. "As ready as I'll ever be, I suppose."

"It's just an overnight trip," she pointed out.

Aye, it could be. But the hair on the back of his neck was lifted ever so slightly, and he knew to take care when that happened. Hence the myriad of weaponry currently attached to his limbs. He glanced longingly at his sword, but knew he couldn't safely carry that around modern-day Ireland. He just hoped the Fates would give him what he needed, should he need it.

He flashed her a smile and tucked the phone into his back pocket. "Aye, you're right, of course. Let's see where the road leads us."

REILLY OWNED FOUR VEHICLES.

Gwen didn't begrudge him his toys, but to her, four did seem a bit excessive for a single guy living in the woods north of Dublin.

His forest green Rover was outfitted with all sorts of medical gear. He explained that it was easier to have a mobile hospital for some of his more damaged visitors; explaining them to a hospital staff might prove to be more trouble than it was worth.

His little red Renault was what he called "the runabout car." He used it to putt around town, and he never really cared if someone opened their car door into his, or if the mirror got scratched up. Gwen half-suspected he wouldn't care if it was stolen, either, as he didn't bother to lock it whenever they were out. The trouble with the Renault was it was tiny, and Reilly was not. The driver's seat was pushed so far back that the backseat was slightly squished.

Reilly also owned a Ford SUV. It was comfortable, with all the bells and whistles, and he liked to take it out when the weather was bad. Gwen never complained about the seat warmers, and he never complained about the four-wheel drive on icy Irish roads in the winter. It was a beautiful winter white. He always hit the alarm on that one, and parked it a bit further away from the shops.

But she knew that his love lay with his custom, shiny, black Victory motorcycle. Built for comfort and long distances, the bike was outfitted with deep seats, seat warmers, plenty of storage for bags, a high windshield, and even matching helmets. His helmets weren't just run-of-the-mill full-face ones, though. They were wirelessly connected with the radio and each other, and made speaking between the driver and passenger a breeze. They were also soundproof; with the visor flipped down, there was very little road noise. Gwen loved the Victory almost as much as Reilly did.

She wasn't surprised when he handed her a riding jacket, in just her size. She grinned like a fool as she shrugged into it. She zipped it, loving how well it fit her, and tucked her overnight bag into the storage case. He followed suit, then handed her the helmet.

She reached out to take it, but he didn't let go. It hung, suspended between them, and she frowned at his serious expression.

"Gwen...about last night." He took a step toward her, the helmet now pressing into her chest and his stomach. "I need to know. Did you end things with him last night?"

The zipper on his black leather jacket was zipped about three quarters of the way up, leaving his shirt exposed. She let go of her side of the helmet, which wasn't going anywhere, and tugged the zipper fully closed.

She raised her eyes to his and caught her breath. There was no mistaking the look on his face. His eyes, darkened with desire and hope, roamed her face, looking for something, though she couldn't decipher what. "No."

His shoulders tensed and his nostrils flared as he inhaled sharply.

Before he could say anything, she added softly, "He did."

His eyes widened, and her hope flared anew.

What the hell? No. No hope flaring. Nope.

"Is that acceptable to you?"

He waited patiently, but Gwen understood his deeper question. Did she love Anthony enough to fight for him?

She had the same question. Which, she knew, was all the answer she really needed. If she loved him, it would be a no-brainer. But deciding she could consign herself to a lifetime of almost-love was a lot harder than actually doing it, and that dose of reality was a cold one.

"I think so," she whispered.

He moved the helmet out of the way and took a step closer. "Are you *certain*, Gwendolyn?"

Their eye contact hadn't broken. He was stalking her with his eyes, and she couldn't help the frisson of anticipation that tingled up her spine.

If you do this, your friendship could be ruined, her brain cautioned.

If you do this, you'll know if he's the one, her heart whispered.

If you do this, you may never get me back, her soul warned.

Confused, and a bit afraid, she stepped back, panicked. For years, Reilly put her off. For years, he told her that friends was all he was willing to be. And she got it—she didn't want to lose him if things went bad.

And that was her answer. She didn't want to lose her best friend. She trusted him with her life, but he'd never exactly proven himself trustworthy with her heart. And she couldn't handle it if he pulled away from her again.

She grabbed the helmet from him and placed it on her head, then flipped up the visor. "Yeah, Ry. I'm certain."

He reached for her, and she tensed. But he only flicked the nearly invisible switch by her chin, then put his own helmet on and did the same. He didn't raise his visor, and his voice filtered through the small speakers in her helmet.

"Are you happy about that?"

His voice returned to normal. Grateful, she flipped her visor down and forced a chuckle as she got onto the back of the bike. "Turns out I'm a bit of a commitment-phobe. Who knew, right?"

He clucked as he locked the storage case, then swung a leg over his seat. "You're not a commitment-phobe. He's a fool for not fighting for you." He started the engine, and the machine purred to life under her. He slowly walked it, backwards, out of the garage. "You know that, aye?"

Mutely, she shrugged, though he couldn't see her.

His voice lowered, grew almost hoarse. "Gwen. You are worth fighting for. If I were in Anthony's shoes, you know what I would do to get you back?"

She didn't answer, because she didn't think she wanted to hear it.

They headed down the driveway at a sedate pace. "I'd drop everything to be with you. I'd show you that my sun rises and sets with your breaths, that your triumphs were my exaltations. I'd tell you every day how much more beautiful you are than you were yesterday. Hold onto me, we've got some turns coming up."

She wrapped her arms around his waist, and they turned onto the main street.

"Ry…"

"I'd write you terrible poetry about my love for you, and sing it to you through a window each night."

She choked on a bubble of half-cry and half-laughter. "Terrible, huh? That wouldn't be much of an incentive, I don't think."

She could hear the smile in his voice. "I'm a terrible poet, but the truth of the words would be there, all the same. You're worth that and more, Gwen."

Sighing, she laid her head on his back as they picked up speed. "Thanks, Ry."

"What would it take to win you back?"

Gwen's heart leaped into her throat. Was he asking hypothetically?

She was silent for so long, he prodded, "Gwen, you must have some idea as to what would be the way to get back in your good graces. A grand gesture, perhaps?"

Ah. It was about Anthony, then, as Reilly had never been out of her good graces. Her heart fell all the way to her toes, and she cursed herself.

Someday she wouldn't wish so hard or hurt so badly for what she couldn't have.

"No grand gesture," she finally said sadly. "Just love. Real love. Reciprocated love. The kind that lasts forever, even when you're at your lowest."

"Are you at your lowest right now?"

She closed her eyes, focusing her attention on the wind whipping at her jacket and pants; on the solid man in front of her, real and wonderful and damn near perfect for her.

And she wondered if she would ever be able to really move on from him. She wanted to, but she wasn't at all sure she could. Right now, at this moment, she wasn't scared of anything. She wasn't anxious or thinking about her friends who died a terrifying death, or how close she herself came to dying. She was enjoying the day, knowing that no matter what happened, she was protected.

Because of Reilly.

"Not anymore," she finally replied.

"How can I help to lift your spirits?"

She tightened her grip on him as they rounded a particularly sharp curve in the road. "Just be you, Reilly."

In response, he placed his gloved hand over both of hers and gave them a squeeze. They merged onto the highway, and they rode westward.

THREE HOURS LATER, REILLY CUT THE ENGINE AND STRETCHED. The drive had been an easy one, without much traffic and somehow without rain. The clouds hung low in the sky, promising a good soaking at some point in the near future, but he hoped to have them fully ensconced in a quaint bed and breakfast well before then, and his Victory in a secure garage.

"Where are we?"

Her voice, which had been mostly silent for the drive, came through his helmet. He stepped off the bike and pulled it off, motioning for her to do the same.

She did, then tugged the elastic from her riotous hair and tried to fluff the curls with a head shake. The fiery copper and red strands tumbled over her black-clad shoulders.

She always looked even more beautiful after they'd been out riding.

"We're on the west side of the island," he answered, unzipping his jacket a little.

"This looks weirdly familiar, but I don't think I've ever been out here."

"Oh, you have. But not in this time."

A little V appeared between her eyes as she processed that. He watched the wheels turn for a moment, then pointed up the hill. "There's Bri and Nick's castle. Or what's left of it, anyway."

Her eyes widened, and she followed his finger toward the spectacular ruins overlooking the ocean.

Her face conveyed her feelings more than words ever could.

"Aye, 'tis strange to walk over these stones in different times," he mused, staring at it. "I know she lived a good life. A happy one."

"But it still hurts that she's gone," Gwen said softly. She

stood and placed her hand on his arm. "I understand, Ry. And it sucks."

A pang hit him squarely in the chest, because he knew that she did understand. She met Bri. She stayed in the woman's castle, became friends with her, her husband, and children. Gwen lived through an experience that brought her an idea of what he lived with every time he came out to these ruins.

Before, no one save Colin or James could ever have truly understood what the feeling was like. The walls between time were fragile here, in this place. He'd have to warn her to be careful, to watch her step. Time gates were all over Ireland, and he set up his cottage near the busiest one, but the ones in the west were fickle. All manner of folks popped up in the strangest of places.

The breeze shifted just slightly, the hair on the back of his neck stood at full attention, and Reilly felt the familiar pull on his soul. His senses went on full alert, and he stiffened his back.

Back when Aidan was in the past and Emma was in the future, Reilly broke the cardinal rule of time traveling: No traveling for personal gain.

With certain exceptions, Reilly was allowed to see Brianagh whenever he liked, as long as he didn't interfere with history. He was also allowed to visit his family, again without changing anything. And he was not, under any circumstances, allowed to change the fate of other people.

But he blatantly ignored that rule when Aidan and Emma were separated. Seeing two people—even if one of them was the man who had made his life difficult when Reilly first brought Bri back in time—who were so clearly meant to be together, hurting so desperately, made him angry. Sweet Emmaline, whose tough outer shell protected a fragile heart for so long, did not deserve to be at the mercy of the time gates. So, when he decided to act without regard to the rules set forth by the Fates, he knew the proverbial other shoe would drop in a major way. There would be punishment, possibly retribution, definitely revenge.

The feeling that swept over him was instant, and he knew his comeuppance with the Fates was finally upon him. He admired their timing; of course they'd want his Gwen to see his downfall.

As a stiff wind kicked up, lifting Gwen's hair and swirling it about her, his stomach lurched.

Damn them, she wasn't going to watch him; it was going to *involve* her.

"Whoa!" Gwen exclaimed, wrestling her hair back. She secured it with her elastic again and glanced worriedly at the sky, where the clouds were now rolling. "I hope we can get to a dry place before the storm hits."

An old woman shuffled toward them, a withered staff in one hand. Her back was hunched, her kerchief was anchored over her white hair, and her skirts blew in the breeze. Her skin, papery thin and more wrinkles than not, was nearly translucent.

Reilly evened his breathing, reminded himself that he was tired of their games, and assumed his intimidation position. Legs spread shoulder-width apart, arms folded over his chest, feet planted firmly on the hard-packed earth.

"State your purpose, old woman, and be quick about it," he snapped.

"Reilly!" Gwen gasped, her eyes turning to saucers. "That was so rude!" She hopped off the bike and hurried to the old woman, who stood now only about ten feet from Reilly. "I'm so sorry, ma'am. Please excuse my friend."

The woman gave her a wizened smile, then patted her hand. "What a kind soul ye have, Gwendolyn."

"Thanks," she started to reply, then froze. "How did you know my name?"

Reilly stalked over to Gwen and yanked her behind him.

"Don't touch her. Leave her out of this, Crone. What is it you want from me now?"

"You've disappointed us, Protector," she replied, her voice steely. "We've spent much time deciding what your future will hold."

"And what did you come up with?" he demanded. Gwen tried to peek around his back, but he roughly shoved her back in place. He didn't want any of the Fates near her, especially not the Crone. She could be the cruelest of all, if she hadn't the other two nearby to temper her. And as the Maiden and Mother weren't anywhere to be seen, he couldn't—wouldn't —take any chances. She'd have to go through him to get to Gwen.

"Many ideas, to be sure."

Gwen stepped out from behind Reilly, and he shot a prayer heavenward that she would keep her mouth closed. Pissing off a Fate would bring her nothing but trouble.

"Do not say a word," he warned her in a low voice. At the flash of anger in her eyes, he gave her the first, and hopefully last, pleading look he'd ever given anyone. "Please, Gwendolyn."

She mutinously clamped her lips together, and he breathed a short-lived sigh of relief.

The old woman cupped her hand and gently blew in Gwen's direction. "She's deaf and mute for the moment," the Crone informed him. Her eyes narrowed. "She's a mortal woman, with no right to know who I am. Naming me in front of her? You have been taught better. Another rule broken. Your list of transgressions is multiplying, child."

"I'm not a child," he stated flatly. "Speak your piece."

"I could take her life," the Crone warned him. "There is one too many lives here in this time. One who shouldn't be here."

"Make it work," he growled.

"Oh, we've forged a new path for young MacWilliam. The

fabric of time has an abnormality in its weave, now that he will be allowed to remain."

"As he should be," Reilly replied evenly. "To place two soul mates together, only to rip them apart, seems a cruel game, meant to amuse you."

"In your case, Protector, we've placed your soul mate with you time and again. Yet still you resist, and any humor we may have had has vanished. So the question becomes," the Crone said slowly, her eyes taking on an unholy light, "do we take your love from you as a payment for young MacWilliam to keep his? Vows were broken. There must be amends."

Reilly felt a panic unlike any other rise up, choking him. "Do not use her as a pawn in your game. I've given you almost two hundred years, Crone."

"And she wants to give you three weeks. Oh, aye, we heard her demand. Cheeky of her, to think she could issue a demand to us."

"State your purpose, Crone," Reilly ground out.

"Colin O'Rourke shocked us, you know. He decided to remain a Protector, even though he found his mate. He's the first one in all the Protectors to do so. Of course, he's your most loyal clansman, so looking back, it shouldn't have surprised us quite so much. But he did, and we do love a good surprise."

"By *good surprise*, you mean one that benefits you," he growled.

She shrugged. "What benefits us, benefits all. 'Tis the nature of life."

"Tell me your plans or be gone from here. I've no more patience for your stall tactics, woman."

The old woman straightened, and the clouds dropped from the sky, encircling them. Reilly pulled Gwen flush against him and wrapped his arm around her. Gwen's eyes, wide with fear, met his. Her mouth moved, but no sound emerged.

"You are safe," he mouthed clearly to her. She clung to him, confused, and he pressed her head into his chest. To the Crone, he snarled, "Get on with it, then."

The dense fog swirled harder around the ground, creating a pressure around them. He could see the Crone from the knees up, gripping her staff tightly, anger creasing her brow.

Another figure appeared out of the thick mist, and Reilly narrowed his eyes. The Maiden, resplendent in her beauty and grace. She was the polar opposite of the Fate in front of him.

"Crone, release your anger," she commanded, her voice gentle. "We've already determined his immediate path."

"He speaks out of turn," the Crone spat.

The Maiden looked at Reilly and gave him a sweet smile. "Aye, but he's been loyal to us for centuries. A mishap is to be expected. He is, after all, merely human. He went without incident even longer than we believed him capable of, aye?"

The Crone's eyes narrowed, but she dipped her head in acknowledgement. "Aye, 'tis truth enough in that."

Reilly remained tense. When he traveled back in time to bring Aidan forward, he knew he was overstepping the boundaries set forth by the Fates. Aidan was supposed to live out his life in the Middle Ages, and Emma in the present.

But instead, Reilly couldn't stand to see such suffering, and, in a moment of either weakness or clarity, depending on how he chose to look at it, he knew he could bring the two souls together. So he did.

The Fates were not pleased he had stepped in where he wasn't allowed.

Gwen's shaking brought him back to the present moment. He glanced at her and had a flash of terror unlike any he'd experienced before. To his knowledge, no one other than the O'Rourke Protectors had ever seen the Fates, in any form. Their individual power could easily overwhelm a human, and their collective power could easily frighten a person into a heart attack or worse.

His voice cold, he said clearly, "If your plan is to take Gwen's life for MacWilliam's, be warned that I will be forever done with you and your schemes. Finished. I will refuse any more assignments. If I cannot return to the moment before you take her, I will actively seek out danger, so that I may join her in the afterlife. You will not take her from me and continue to use me to your liking. This woman is mine to protect, and you will not take her from me."

The Maiden blinked slowly. "Reilly O'Malley...are you declaring her to be your soul mate?" Softly, she added, "The time to choose your path is upon you."

The Crone smirked, but he held his reaction in check. Whatever the Fates claimed to do, they could not read minds, nor control free will. Despite the conversation he had with Gwen, Reilly understood better than any that destiny was merely a set of paths, set out by the Fates, allowing a person to choose which direction his life will lead. One of the paths was the easy one. That path ensured a smooth road, with as few bumps as possible. *A charmed life*, people called it. If the person took one of the other paths, then life became longer and more difficult. Reilly watched as people who made the right choices along the wrong path reap the rewards at the end of the tough stretches, and those rewards were all the sweeter for the trials they overcame.

He was never allowed to choose his own path...until now. Suddenly, with great clarity, he understood what his punishment would be.

He was going to choose his path, and come hell or high water, they were going to make him do it without their aid.

"Well?" the Crone demanded, crossing her arms. Her staff pointed away from them, clutched tightly in her gnarled knuckles, almost vibrating. "You took the fate of another in your hands before. You have the power to do so again. Claim your mate, and she will be spared. For now."

He looked down again at Gwen, who had buried her face into his jacket.

He looked back at the Fates and gave a decisive nod. "Aye. I'm claiming my mate, and her name is Gwendolyn Allen."

The Maiden nodded and the Crone lifted her staff above her head. "Be warned. She demanded we give you three weeks, so three weeks you shall have."

The Maiden added, "Use it well. If she does not claim you as her soul mate by the twenty-first night, it'll be her place in time for MacWilliam's."

"And if she does claim me?" Reilly challenged, though his heart was beating hard.

The Maiden smiled easily. "We'll not reveal *all* our secrets so easily, warrior. But be warned, Reilly O'Malley. You shall do this without our aid. And you must not take her free will from her, either, or else our agreement is void. Do you agree to these terms?"

Reilly nodded once, tersely, and the Crone slammed her staff to the ground. The fog surged, encasing the two Fates.

The mist dissipated almost immediately, and Reilly caught Gwen as she crumpled.

CHAPTER 9

The eerie-green of the lichens in twilight captured his attention first, then the impressive trunk of the tree to which it was attached. His eyes traveled up, adjusting to the fading light of day, and he saw the notches he'd placed there as a child, as he learned how to climb it. The branches, thick and sturdy, jutted out proudly, as though welcoming him home again. As was his custom, he slowly refocused his senses: first, he allowed the chill in the air to reach his skin; they'd need a fire tonight. He then attuned his ears to the sounds of the forest, listening for either the stealthy slip of an enemy's knife from its sheath, or the welcoming song of the birds as they sang their lullabies.

A feeling of peace settled over his soul as he looked down at the small body coming to in his arms.

He drew in a deep, cleansing breath, trying to assimilate the sensation of having his past and present collide.

"What the hell…?" She glanced at him. "What are you wearing?" She glanced down at herself. "What am *I* wearing?"

He helped her to her feet. The deep garnet brought out the fire-red streaks of her long curls, which rained freely down her back. The strands at her temples were braided and tied together behind her head, highlighting her pixie face and vibrant green eyes.

"You are…" Struggling to find the right words, he stood to his full height, and allowed himself the pleasure of truly seeing her. "Captivating."

She blushed prettily. "Thanks, Ry." After a couple of seconds, she paled. "What the hell just happened to us?"

He busily checked himself for his weaponry. Thankfully, all of it seemed attached to the places he'd attached them to, so he was relatively happy about that.

He was not relatively happy about anything else.

"The Fates," he answered succinctly. "You just met the Crone and the Maiden. Who knows where the Mother was."

"Maiden, Mother, Crone," Gwen whispered. "I remember that from my Greek studies class! In those stories, they never moved from a hearth, where they spent their time snipping pieces of yarn to end people's lives."

He let out a sigh. "It's close enough to the reality that you don't really want to know more."

She finally noticed their surroundings and her eyes widened. "Um…where are we, again?"

He swore suddenly, then gave her a look of pure agony. "My bike!"

Confused, she shrugged her shoulders, as if to say, *Is that really the issue at hand here?*

He dragged his hands through his hair. "They better protect that bike. I love her."

Gwen merely watched him fret about his Victory, but she didn't know how much time and energy and money he'd sunk into that motorcycle. *Love* wasn't a strong enough word.

"Reilly, I know you're missing your baby right now, but could you please focus for a minute? I'm still a little fuzzy on the details. You know, like *where the hell are we* and *why are we dressed like this*?"

"When. The better question is *when* are we? And I'm not entirely certain." He patted himself down, relieved to find that though the Fates took his keys, they'd left his more practical metal. He shoved his hands through his hair; he hadn't wanted to introduce Gwen to the less savory side of medieval Ireland, if that was indeed their time period at the moment, but he knew better than any that danger could be just behind the next tree. "Promise me you'll never fear me, Gwen."

She frowned. "Why would I ever fear you? Because of your unhealthy love of a machine?"

He tugged the sleeve of his tunic up, revealing a sheathed dirk tied to his forearm. "Nay. Because of this."

He slowly tugged up his other sleeve, revealing an identical dirk. Then he showed her each thigh, each calf, and the ones tucked inside his medieval boots.

"Well," she managed.

He would've like to flatter himself that her sudden short breaths were a reaction to his baring all sorts of places on his body to her, but alas, her gaze remained fixated on the various bits of steel on his person.

The Fates certainly dressed him well for his unexpected fall through time. He was grateful they didn't strip him of his knives, though he would do almost anything at the moment to feel the comforting weight of his sword against his back.

By the time he finished revealing the various weaponry on his person, her eyes were glossy, and he worried that she would start running. But she needed to know. He needed her to understand.

"Every one of these blades has ended at least one life. A life who tried to take mine, or the life of someone who is under my protection. There may be more lives taken with this steel, but it is never for naught. Do you understand, lass? I kill not for the sport of it, but for the survival from it. We may be in a dangerous time, and the best policy is to act first and ask questions later."

She was about to see a side of him that she had never seen, one he never wanted her to see. She knew of it from her last foray into the forest, but when he fought with Colin for Ellie, Gwen was safely tucked away at Brianagh's castle. She saw him in the aftermath of that battle, covered in blood.

Bri often told him his chivalry was only a veneer to his uncivilized side.

Bri was not wrong.

Gwen's face softened. "Reilly, fear is the exact opposite of what I feel when I'm with you. You would never hurt me, and I am so honored you would even think to protect me with your weapons."

"With my life," he corrected her.

She smiled, though serious. "I couldn't have asked for a better guardian, then. Thank you. I'm not scared, Ry, not with you."

He let out a breath he didn't realize he was holding, and though he kept his face impassive, inside, he smiled with relief, though he hoped not to test her statements. He unsheathed his most wicked-looking dagger and held it loosely in his hand.

Couldn't be too careful, especially as he wasn't quite sure *when* they were. How was he to protect them without his sword? Daggers were useful, but they weren't a sword.

"Are we near Brianagh again?"

He shook his head. "Nay. We're about a three-days' walk from the O'Rourke castle." He smiled at her, allowing a bit of his dimple to show. "Welcome to my other home, Gwendolyn. Looks like we're visiting a bit sooner than even I expected."

She started to reply, but her eyes grew large and she made incoherent noises and pointed behind him.

She didn't need to, though. The glancing blow off his back

told him all he needed to know about what stood behind him. He took a chance and trotted out his medieval Gaelic. "Truly, lad?" he asked. The blade the man threw at him fell off his shoulder and landed at his feet. Gwen cried out in distress.

"Not a lad," the man replied, also in medieval Gaelic. "I'll be wanting my dirk back, ye know."

Well, there was proof enough of the general time in which the currently found himself. He knew, of course, based on his and Gwen's clothes, but he didn't entirely trust the Fates. He could admit to being grateful they didn't send him somewhere like 17th-century England, where, garbed as they were, he would've had to use most of his wits and all of Gwen's charm to extricate them from a stay somewhere unsavory.

He refocused. The very medieval bloke in front of him was dressed in MacDermott colors.

By the saints above, how Reilly loathed the MacDermott clan. They caused no end of unnecessary grief and annoyance to all they crossed paths with.

The man was eyeing him speculatively. "You'll pay for walking upon my clan's land; I'll be taking all you've got."

"'Tisn't your land, lad. And all I have is what you see," Reilly replied easily, ignoring the slight burn on his shoulder blade. "A dirk worth nothing."

The man looked past him. "Oh, you've got something else, I'll wager. You'd be an O'Malley, and I've never been one to trust one of your ilk. I'll be having your weapon, and your woman there too." He drew his sword casually. "I won't make her scream loudly if you'll hand her over without complaint."

Reilly's dagger found its mark before the man finished his sentence.

The man's eyes opened wide, and he staggered back. He looked down at the dagger protruding from his chest, and his mouth formed a silent O before he fell over.

Quickly, Reilly yanked the knife from its resting place, cleaned the blood on the man's tunic, and grit his teeth.

He wondered how he was to protect Gwen without a sword. Well, the Fates certainly gave him the opportunity to answer that question.

He pulled the sword from the dead man's fingers, then braced himself to view the horror on Gwen's face. Slowly, he turned.

If he thought her pale a few minutes ago, her face was now a ghostly white.

"I think I need a drink," she whispered, then promptly fainted.

He swore, then vaulted over a log and felt her head and body for any signs of broken bones. It seemed like she missed hitting anything important, but she was fully unconscious.

Reilly rubbed his hand, hard, over his face, and swore again. He needed to hide the man's body, and fast, before anyone happened upon them. He could handle one, but an entire clan? The rules were kill first, and don't bother with questions, ever. If an O'Malley was found with what he suspected was a MacDermott, especially a dead MacDermott, his head would be removed from his shoulders without much fanfare.

He took another breath, looked heavenward for a moment, then dragged the man off into the woods. He returned swiftly, then decided the past wasn't the place he wanted to woo Gwen.

He grabbed hold of Gwen's limp arm, held out his right hand, fingers splayed, and murmured the ancient Celtic words the Fates had given him the night he swore his loyalty to them. More guttural words, long forgotten by all living beings, burst from his lips, and he quickly twisted his outstretched fingers into a tight ball, curling in from his smallest finger to his thumb, and...

Nothing.

He cursed. Did those witches strip him of his time travel ability? He and Gwen couldn't be stuck in the past; they had too much to live for in the future.

But he knew he was without aid, and that his decisions needed to be more measured now. They were serious when they said he was on his own.

His instincts kicked in then, and he knew he had to get them away from the MacDermott border and closer to the O'Malley stronghold. He raced into the woods again, keeping Gwen's unconscious form in sight, and gathered a few plants that smelled altogether revolting. He ran back to her, crushing them in his hands as he did so, then tucked them under her nose. He praised himself on not flinching too much when she vomited all over his boots.

It was going to be a long night, for certain.

GWEN BLINKED SLOWLY, THE SOUND OF REILLY'S VOICE realigning her senses. She wiped her mouth, immediately embarrassed about losing the contents of her stomach all over Reilly's leather boots.

She focused on them. They were not the riding boots he'd had on earlier. There were no laces to the shoes he now wore; instead, they looked like they'd been stitched out of large pieces of leather and crisscross tied, all over, with smaller straps of leather.

Ry's words filtered to her brain, but they arrived in a different order than how he spoke them. She raised her eyes to him, still unable to process what was happening, but wanting very much to do whatever he said. He sounded anxious.

That couldn't be right, though. Reilly was never anxious.

He was saying the words again, and she concentrated hard to understand him.

"Gwendolyn, we need to move. We're too close to the border, and we risk discovery on unsafe land."

She nodded, swallowing past a very dry throat, and wished for water. He understood what she needed, and he helped her up.

"We will stop by a stream a bit further on. Hurry, Gwen."

They began walking at a pace mall walkers the world over would envy.

"Too fast," she managed.

He shook his head. "Nay, lass, not this time. If you can't keep up, I'll carry you."

Well. She didn't care to be carried. She picked up her pace.

"Was it real, Reilly?"

He didn't pretend to misunderstand, for which she was grateful, and replied grimly, "Unfortunately, aye. He was a MacDermott. There's a large clan war happening in this time, if we're in the time I think we're in, between the MacDermotts and the O'Malleys. He was going to kill me and take you." He slid a look to her. "Your fate would've been worse than what was promised to Eleanor."

Gwen felt the bile rise again; with effort, she pushed it back down. Ellie had been kidnapped in medieval Ireland, where she was almost forced to wed a very unpleasant, very forceful, and very nasty man. Ellie had been shell-shocked for quite some time after that affair, and still had flashbacks every once in a while.

Gwen had enough flashbacks of her own, but she was rational enough to know that Reilly did what had to be done. Death was never easy…yet it was sometimes necessary.

It was that man's life or Reilly's. There was no gray area there, and, understanding the difficulty of that stark contrast, Gwen understood the necessity of it. The brutality of the times.

It wasn't so different from her time. She had many dreams where she redirected that grenade back to the ones who threw it at their caravan, and she knew that, if she had been given that chance, she probably would have done just that.

Their lives, or her friends' lives. Black and white.

"Thanks," she finally whispered.

He nodded curtly. "Keep up, lass."

Mentally girding her loins, as it were, she put everything out of her mind and hurried onwards.

An hour or so later, after being bodily placed on a sturdy log, Gwen felt a little more like herself. She looked around and wondered if Reilly knew where they were. Imposing evergreen trees stretched toward the darkening sky above them while birds called out their goodnights to each other.

"Are we in the right place?"

Reilly began gathering twigs and fallen branches. "Depends on what you mean by *the right place*."

"All right then. Are we in a safe place?"

"For the moment, aye, I believe so. In the morning, we'll head to my mother's cottage, see if she's in attendance. We'll make our plan from there."

She propped her chin in her hands. "Okay. So, tonight, what's next? Shelter?"

"Aye."

"Fire?"

"Aye."

"Anything else?"

He grunted, and she rolled her eyes. "Easy, Ry. Don't overwhelm me with details."

He slid her a sideways glance. "I'm merely looking out for your delicate constitution."

She snorted. "I had a bit of a shock back there. All that walking helped clear my mind." *If I don't allow myself to remember that man dying in front of me.*

He nodded briskly. "Good. We'll also need dinner."

"When you time travel, do you always get to choose where you're going? And do you get there every time?"

He huffed out a laugh as he dumped some sticks in front of her. "Now I truly believe that you're back to normal. Can we postpone the questions?"

"Nah," she replied with a smile. "Talking helps pass the time, right?"

"Oh, aye, of course it does," he returned dryly. "Aye, I usually end up where I want to be. I'm never off by more than a day or two, and I haven't gotten my location wrong in more years than you'd believe. But this time, I had naught to do with when, where, or how we got here."

"Yeah…about that. How exactly did we end up here? Why were two Fates visiting you? And why couldn't I hear or say anything? I didn't like that very much."

A wry smile touched his lips. "Aye, I imagine you didn't. They had a debt to settle with me, and I fear you're part of my payment plan."

"Me?" she squeaked. She cleared her throat. "Explain, please."

He motioned for her to start picking up sticks, and they continued to gather wood for a fire. Gwen didn't see much dry kindling, so she set about gathering leaves and tree needles.

"Remember when I told you that I brought Aidan to the future?"

"Yes…" she trailed off uncertainly.

"His fate was to remain in the past, and Emmaline's fate was to remain in the future. I displeased the Fates greatly by bringing him to Emmaline."

"But you always say Aidan's a 'pain in the arse!'" she exclaimed, using finger quotes. "Why would you help someone you so obviously dislike?"

Reilly shrugged. "I don't dislike him, per se. He *is* a pain in the arse. He made my life hell when I brought Bri to the MacWilliams. The crafty bastard had me locked in the dungeon for the wedding ceremony. He slipped something in my drink, then had the guards chain me up."

Gwen gasped. "Well. I'd be pretty mad at him, too! Obviously, you escaped."

"Chains can't hold someone who isn't there," Reilly agreed with a mischievous smile. "I traveled back to the present day and waited until the Fates called me again. It wasn't long before they sent me back to Brianagh and her beau. Aidan again tried to chain me, but I was smarter that time. He didn't trust me at all—he knew nothing about the magic then. I've never said he wasn't intelligent."

"And after all that, you still went back for him."

"I went back for Emmaline," he corrected her, and her heart melted a little at the obvious half-truth. "Besides, Aidan and I have moved past his previous actions. Mostly."

A sharp cry from a bird made her glance up at the darkening sky. "Um, are we very far from your mother's house?"

He dumped an even more impressive pile of sticks onto the ground and began to form them into a circle. "Far enough. We're safe for the moment, though. Travel at night is dangerous in this time, and I can much better protect you here, where I know the dips and swells of the terrain, and where to hide you in a pinch."

"I like the sound of that. Well, the hiding, not the need to do so. Can we get back? Will those two Fates allow us to?"

He snorted. "Eventually, I expect so."

She took a moment to gather her thoughts, which were swirling even faster than the words she was speaking. "That was the Maiden and the Crone, right? What was the other one again?"

"The Mother is the third one. I've no idea where she was, but I'm glad you didn't have to see them all together. Their collective power can overtake most people, which is why it's a rare thing if they allow a person to see them."

She cocked her head. "I still half-believed they were a myth."

"Not a myth," he confirmed.

Silently, she chewed on that for a few minutes. "You know, I don't think I want to know any more about all that magic for the moment."

He sighed audibly. "Praise the saints."

Gwen added her bounty to the pile, the silence of the night pressing in on her. About five minutes passed before she couldn't take the quiet any more. "So you grew up here?"

He smirked, as though he knew she couldn't hold out.

She didn't care.

"For a bit," he replied, focused on arranging the wood. "I left when I was thirteen."

Reilly never spoke about his past. She knew now that he couldn't while she was ignorant of his time traveling abilities. But perhaps now was her chance to plumb the depths of Reilly O'Malley. She had, after all, spent more nights than she could count wondering about him. When they first began their friendship, he refused to answer anything. He dodged questions, or redirected the conversation. By the time she figured out what he was doing, he moved on to ignoring her questions altogether. At the time, she suspected he had a rough go of it, and decided to respect his boundaries. But now that she knew it had been off-limits because she didn't know his secrets, well...

As he finished setting up the fire pit, she hoped he would tell her now. She risked a glance at his face; his eyes remained fixed on his task, and his arms flexed as he placed large rocks around the wood.

He stood and brushed his hands together. "Come, we must catch our dinner before the light fully disappears."

She frowned, but dutifully followed him until they reached a quick-moving stream. She helped herself to a long drink, and he removed a dirk strapped to his arm. He quickly fashioned a long, thin branch into a spear. Within just a few minutes, he'd caught three good-sized trout. They headed back to their camp, Reilly instructing her to pick up as much dry wood as she could find on the way.

She brought her meager offerings to the pile and sat down on a fallen tree he'd helpfully pulled over, then used one of his dirks to begin preparing the fish. "So, you left when you were thirteen? Was that normal?"

"Nay. What was normal was to leave your parents at nine. I stayed longer because my sire requested it of our laird, and he agreed because I was already an accomplished warrior."

"You were a warrior at thirteen?" Gwen echoed, a little horrified.

He raised his eyes to hers. In the rapidly fading light, she couldn't see their hazel color, but she could see the corners of them crinkle with humor at her surprise.

"I was a warrior at seven."

Gwen tried to digest that. A child, sent into war, to kill for his clan. She shuddered.

"If your dad had to ask permission from the laird…where did that leave you on the society scale?"

"Just another member of the clan." Reilly created a nest of dried leaves and grass, then, from the small bag at his waist, pulled out a stone and a small, C-shaped ring of hammered steel. "We weren't wealthy, but we always had food in our bellies. My mother is a master weaver and tapestry seamstress; it brought in a good amount of coin for us and the clan." He swiftly struck the flint onto the steel, and a small wisp of smoke curled from the nest. He blew it gently, and within seconds a small flame burned brightly.

"Wow," Gwen noted, impressed. "I've never seen that done so fast."

"I'm an expert level Boy Scout," he quipped. After another moment spent coaxing the nest, he carefully placed it into the kindling.

"Do they have Boy Scouts in Ireland?"

"Don't know. Colin and James were in it in America growing up, though. I went on many camping trips with them."

Gwen nodded, then furrowed her brow. "Reilly?"

He sat back on his heels, satisfied, as the fire caught. "Aye, Gwendolyn?"

"Can I ask you...*questions*...now?"

His body stiffened, and she gulped.

She quickly added, "About your past. Questions about your past. I'll understand if you don't want me to...but you can trust me with your secrets, Ry."

She patted the ground next to her, then continued to clean the fish. He rose, brushing his hands on his red and gold léine, then squatted in front of her, his thigh muscles bunching as the léine fell between them.

He took her hands in his, warming them with his thumbs. "Thank you for your loyalty. I regret that I was never able to tell you of my past."

She clasped his hands to her chest. "Ry, you don't need to apologize. I get it. You have a lot on your shoulders. I might not be able to carry some of your load, but I can certainly share it from time to time."

He speared her with a look, and she shivered from its intensity.

She was either fully misreading his intentions—which, based on her past history, was more than just a little possible —or Reilly was showing interest in her. Which was ridiculous. He loved her like a best friend. Yes. A platonic best friend.

"Your hands are like ice. Move closer to the fire," he said, his voice low and gravelly.

She hated herself for wanting him the way she did. Rationally, she knew it was because just a few days ago she was ready to commit herself to someone else for the rest of her life, and letting go of all those feelings was, naturally, quite difficult.

At least, that's what she told herself.

They both stood, and he dragged the log toward the flames. When they settled back down, she took her courage in hand and asked, "How did you become what you are now? A Protector? The boss of all Protectors?"

The firelight danced over his features, and he stared straight ahead for almost a full minute. Gwen held her breath, hoping he'd satiate her curiosity, but willing to let it drop if he refused to talk.

She was, she thought wryly, quite good at accepting his reluctance.

He reached for some of the large leaves he'd gathered earlier and began to weave them together. Finally, his voice still low, he replied, "Are you sure you want to hear the tale?"

She snorted, relieved he was even considering it, and bumped his arm with her shoulder. "Are you kidding? I've been trying to get you to open up to me for more than ten years. You bet I want to hear the damn tale. So if you're talking, let's go back a second and start with how old you are."

"Two hundred and twenty-nine."

She looked at him for almost a full minute before replying, "Come again?"

He repeated it, and she blinked owlishly at him. "Something doesn't add up."

"If it helps, I was born in 1245."

"Reilly!" she exclaimed. "You know that just makes it more confusing!"

He fully turned himself to her. "Aye, I know."

"Walk me through it. And feel free to talk to me like I'm two, so I'll understand fully."

Reilly placed the fish over the fire in the makeshift basket he'd made. "All right, lass. The important thing is that I was 183 when Brianagh was born."

Her mouth worked, but no sound came out for a moment. She swallowed hard. "I think your driver's license is a little off."

He rubbed the back of his neck. "Not exactly."

She frowned at him. "If I'm supposed to be figuring this out myself, I'm failing pretty hard."

"I stopped aging normally at thirty."

Gwen furrowed her brow. "Stopped aging? What have you done during all this time?"

He sighed. "'Tis confusing even for me, and I've lived it. At thirteen, the Fates took me in. I'm not even sure where it was, save that there was forestry. For the first decade, I stayed with them, going only where they told me to go. I needed a full education in all things relating to what my life was going to be like."

"Sword skills and stuff?"

"Swordplay was part of it. I had to learn languages, mythology, history before it happened. My days were filled with tales, books like I'd never seen, experiences that no man had ever experienced. The first couple of years, I walked around in a fog of shock. But sometime in the third year, I began to realize that this was all real." He stared into the fire. "Time passed then the same way for me as it does for you now. When I was twenty-three, I was sent on my first mission. 'Twas a small thing—rescue a child from a tree where he'd been stuck for a few hours. I had to travel backward in time, locate the boy, convince him to trust me, return him to his parents, and return by sundown."

"Did you find him?"

"Aye. But it took me much longer to convince him I was trustworthy, and I almost didn't make it back in time."

"What would've happened if you were late?"

"It would be over. All that training for naught."

"Trial by fire," Gwen murmured, awed.

He nodded in agreement. "'Twas more difficult than I anticipated. Later, there was more mercy. If I didn't complete the mission within the Fates' time table, I'd be stuck in that time period for maybe a day, sometimes a week. But I learned more about people during those early missions than I ever did in the tales and books."

"Like what?"

"Well, each argument has more than one side. And each situation can have different outcomes, depending upon the words chosen. And I learned patience."

"You do have legendary patience," she broke in with a smirk.

He arched a brow at her. "It well prepared me for you and your smart mouth."

She grinned at him, then motioned for him to continue.

Sobering, he folded his hands, then leaned forward and rested his forearms on his knees. "Eventually, time began to slow, though the years passed still. It was strange, watching those around me grow old, while I remained the same."

"So you kind of...froze in time?"

"Aye. I was to be at my peak, my most battle-ready, for my most important task. A child was to be born, one who would be the bearer of all other time travelers, all of whom would be destined to protect the family line for a greater purpose."

"Brianagh," Gwen guessed.

"Aye. An O'Rourke, the Fates told me. One of my own distant relatives. She was to be protected at all costs, but she had to learn independence, confidence, and grace. And she was not to be told of her legacy, for it was her trial to be had."

"Last summer, when Ellie and I, um, got lost in your woods after being chased by the paparazzi, we could've landed anywhere in time?"

"Aye."

"How did you know we were at Brianagh's?"

He paused long enough for her to suspect she was going to get only a piece of the truth. "Colin was—*is*—tied to Eleanor. They're soul mates. Each Protector only gets one, and once he claims her, he's bound to her for eternity. I knew their connection would lead us straight to her."

"So he claimed her before he got to us?"

He didn't reply, instead, adjusting the fish. The fire popped, and the smell of their dinner filled the air.

Gwen watched the flames for a moment before asking a different question. "Why did it take so long to get to us?"

Reilly tossed another log onto the fire. "Colin needed some time to admit it to himself. Once a Protector admits such a thing aloud, he's bound to her, even if she doesn't return his feelings. If she doesn't love him back, if she doesn't claim him, which she must do without his interference, he's tied to that woman forever…it's a situation no Protector wants to find himself in."

Gwen frowned. If Colin needed time to admit that Ellie was his mate, and he needed to have claimed her to get to her in the past…how did they get to Ellie and Gwen?

Something wasn't adding up.

"Have you claimed your mate?"

Reilly froze. It was a small thing, unnoticeable if one didn't know his every expression and body language, but Gwen wasn't just anyone.

"Aye."

Her stomach plunged to her knees. Of course he had a soul mate. She had sensed it, but it was another thing entirely to hear it fall from his lips.

She reminded herself that it was a good thing she was moving on from him. She wasn't the one for him, and he could only find happiness with that person.

She didn't want to be the source of his unhappiness.

He continued with his story. "Anyway, Brianagh was to be raised by someone else, but my life centered on her protection. I knew every move she made. Every holiday she went on, I was there, though she wasn't always aware of it."

"Was it always Brianagh?"

"Aye. Before her, the Fates sent me various O'Rourkes who needed training in the ways of a Protector. I became the teacher. When Brianagh grew into a young adult, it was her cousin, Colin, who was the next trainee. I was to not only watch over Brianagh, but train Colin as well. It was a challenge I needed, for being Brianagh's babysitter was not exactly the most thrilling thing I'd ever done, though 'twas the most important. She was almost a full-grown woman; I needed something more to do than simply sit around and watch over her."

The fire popped again and Gwen jumped. She scooted an inch closer to him, a little spooked by the stillness of the forest around them. "You had your hands full. But what happened after Bri married? Was your task over?"

"Aye."

"Did you go back to teaching other Protectors? Do you have new missions?"

"I haven't had any as of yet, as there's been no new Protectors since Colin. I've had various visitors drop by my humble home, lost souls who traveled by accident or those who need my services. But lately, I've had little to do. It's why I opened the school."

The firelight was in full play on his face now; the angles of his cheekbones cast long shadows, painting his skin with dancing shades of orange and black. His eyes shone in the light, though his expression remained somber.

"Will you ever die?"

"I hope so." His throat worked, and he rubbed his hand down his face. "I enjoy life, but..."

His jaw twitched, and she instinctively grabbed his hand between hers. "But?"

He swept his eyes over her meaningfully, leaving her

breathless and breathy at once. "But I'm only a man. A man destined to watch the ones I love grow old without me."

"You can always travel back in time to see them, though. Right?"

"Aye. But never for long periods of time. And I'm always brought back to the furthest point I've seen in the future. Right now, that's your time."

Gwen frowned. "So, theoretically, when I die, you'll be able to come back and visit me in the life I'm living now?"

"It'll give you pains in your head if you think on it overmuch. But aye, I would have to live the rest of my life with only glimpses of you. If I stick around you until the day you die, I'll never be able to interact with you the way I am now. I can't double back on myself, if that makes sense. And only the Fates know how long I'll live."

"Oh, Ry." Sadness swamped her. Of all the people in the world, Reilly shouldn't suffer like that. He always gave so much of himself to others; for him to live forever by himself was more than her heart could bear.

He reached over and squeezed her hand. "Do not grieve for me, Gwendolyn. I've made peace with it."

"I can't imagine the loneliness you must feel," she whispered.

He wrapped his arm around her shoulders and pulled her against him, and she snuggled into his warmth. "I'm never lonely when you're near, Gwen."

She took a moment to bask in the glow of *that* statement before asking, "Are we stuck here?"

He shook his head slowly. "Nay, I don't think so."

She breathed a sigh of relief.

"But I don't know when we can return. During the few times I've been sent places, I've some purpose in being there at that time. I can't go back until that purpose has been realized."

"Do you know why you're here this time?"

He seemed to work out his response for a moment before replying. "I have a suspicion, but only time will tell, Gwendolyn."

The sadness in his voice hurt her heart. She didn't fully understand the weight he carried, only that it was a hefty one. She could be a sharer of that weight, if he would but let her in.

No more of those thoughts, she told herself firmly. Tonight, and for their time in the past (however long that was going to be), she was going to enjoy the company of the man she now understood why she could never have.

REILLY LEFT GWEN IN CHARGE OF TURNING THE FISH OVER THE fire and quickly scouted the area for long sticks to create a bed for them. He still could only guess at what year they'd landed in; his plan was to head toward his childhood home and hope someone still lived there.

He had a feeling his mother would be waiting for him.

He wondered what his mother would make of Gwen. She knew so much about her already; he suspected that she knew Gwen was the one for him, though she'd never come out and said it before. She always asked what Gwen was doing, or where she'd been recently. His mother, he knew, was a little bit in awe of Gwen. Her independence, her strength of character, her desire to help others.

He felt the same.

He returned to the delicious smell of dinner, with Gwen gently shaking the basket over the fire, and began to set up the bed frame. Longer sticks on the bottom, filled in with smaller sticks. Test the resistance, fill in with more sticks. He made it a point to sleep off the ground anytime between August and May; though an unexpected warm front was always possible in the fall, more often than not it'd be a sudden frost, and he'd rather wake up without frostbite in case of the latter.

Once the frame was built, he pulled soft moss, lichen, and leaves to lay over it. By the time he was finished constructing, the fish was thoroughly cooked and Gwen was pulling it off the fire and laying it on a plate she made of leaves.

"It's not gourmet," she laughed as she slid him a perfectly filleted piece, "but I bet it's tasty."

"Where did you learn to clean a fish?" he asked.

"Mozambique. Our group ran out of rations and one of the locals taught me how to clean and fillet fish in exchange for some English lessons."

He chuckled; he shouldn't have been surprised. "Your life experiences are indeed varied, Gwen."

She snorted. "Um, I think this is a case of the pot calling the kettle black, yeah?"

They enjoyed their dinner in companionable silence, and when they finished, Reilly buried the bones. Then, with a glance to the nearly-full moon overhead, said, "If we turn in now, we should be able to start early in the morning and arrive by the noon meal." A look crossed her face, but he wasn't sure how to interpret it. "What ails you?"

She fidgeted. "Well, let me say that I don't doubt your abilities at all. But what happens if someone tries to sneak up on us while we're sleeping? Should we take shifts?"

Reilly reached behind his back and slowly pulled his sword from its scabbard, the sound making a satisfying *cccchk* sound.

"I've never been caught unawares. You may rest easy, knowing I am here to defend you, should the need arrive."

Her pupils dilated and she sucked in a breath; Reilly's chest puffed a little at her awe.

"Okay," she whispered.

She lay down on her side on the bed, the sticks barely moving under the thick blanket of flora he'd laid, and he settled against her back. Carefully, he reached over her and laid his sword in front of her. "Now you're protected on all sides. Sleep well, Gwendolyn."

She murmured something, and within moments, was fast asleep.

Reilly placed his lips on her hair and kissed her. He breathed her in, held her tightly, and took simple pleasure in the feel of her in his arms.

He did not sleep.

CHAPTER 10

"*H*ow should I greet her? Do I curtsy? Do I shake her hand? Is that even done here? Do I hug her? Oh my God, what if I step on her toes when she hugs me? *Will* she hug me?"

The next morning, while Reilly silently erased all evidence of their fire and dismantled the bed, Gwen continued to work herself into a cold sweat over meeting his mother. He smiled to himself as she gasped and jerked to a stop.

"What if your mom doesn't like me? Oh no. I couldn't handle that. I mean, I'm pretty likable, right?"

"Very likable," he agreed, though she didn't seem to be listening. He withheld his smirk as she paced nervously and wrung her hands.

"Maybe you could tell me a little about her, Ry. You're not exactly forthcoming with the details. Is she sweet? Or tough? Does she speak English? What should I be expecting?"

She bumped into him, unaware of herself as she fretted, and he gently took her by the arms.

"Gwendolyn."

She looked up at him, her eyes clouded with worry.

"Assuming she's there, things will be fine. She speaks

peasant's English, so she will be able to understand most of your words, and you hers. A simple, 'Pleasure to meet you, Mary,' is all that is required of you. Nothing else."

She bit her lip. "Should I call her Lady O'Malley?"

Reilly gave her an incredulous look. "She's not married to the laird. You remember how it's done from the last time you were in the past—laird and lady titles only go to the leaders of the clan. Everyone else goes by first names, as we all share the last. Call her Mary. And no, there's no need for a curtsy, she's not a queen. She's just a woman."

Gwen's eyes softened. "No, Reilly. She's more than that. She's your mother, and that makes her even more important than a queen. To me, at least."

His heart clenched, and in that moment, he loved Gwen even more. He wanted to swoop down and claim her lips with his own to show her how much she meant to him. How much her words meant to him.

Because she was right; his mother was that important to him, too, and he wanted Gwen to like her, and her to like Gwen. They were more alike than not, though he couldn't ever see his mother building a schoolhouse for poverty-stricken children, not in her time, anyway. She was stern, fair, stubborn, kind, and loved him unconditionally.

All the things Gwen was…and hopefully would be in the future.

"What do you call her?" Gwen asked, her nerves returning.

Reilly released Gwen's arms and continued to break camp. "Mam. It's a form that's still used in Ireland today."

"And your sister?"

"Ah, Sorcha. She's a good lass, though her tongue's a bit sharp. She should be here, unless she's visiting friends of another clan. And the Fates know not to send me to my da's time period," he added in his ask-me-no-more-questions voice. It was the same voice that made enemies think twice before opening their mouths, and all other men clamp their lips closed for worry of what might come if they don't.

Unsurprisingly, it was ineffective on Gwen. "Why not?"

Reilly let out a long-suffering sigh. "Because, Gwendolyn, he asked me not to."

His da wanted Reilly to always look forward, not back. *"Though ye can travel freely throughout time,"* his da said as he lay in his sickbed, his face pale and his eyes bright, *"I want ye to rely on your memories. Someday ye might not have this ability, and ye must keep the mind strong."*

While he'd understood the reasoning at the time, Reilly hated it. But he respected the old man's wishes, and now all his memories of him were fuzzy. He couldn't quite remember his da's voice, but he remembered the feeling of security. Of pride.

It took Reilly decades to realize that he remembered exactly what his father wanted him to remember, so that he may one day recognize it again. Security. Pride.

Love.

"Okay," Gwen replied slowly, in the tone of voice that he knew meant, *I'll let it go for now, but when you're ready, I'd love to hear more.* "So. How do we get there?"

Reilly surveyed their campsite, which now bore almost no trace of them, and brushed his hands on his léine. "We can walk or ride. Your choice."

Gwen pursed her lips. "Horses seem to be a bit scarce at the moment, so that leaves us with only one viable option."

"Ye of little faith," Reilly chuckled. "We walk for now. In a couple hours, I'll whistle and see what comes our way."

"Because wild horses roam the medieval Irish countryside?"

"Because well-trained horses within hearing distance come when they are called," he countered. "Ready?"

"Not really."

"Don't get cold feet on me now," he said, mock-seriously.

"You've already come all this way…doesn't a few hundred years in the past seem like a long way to go, just to back out with a few hours left?"

"Oh, shut up," Gwen laughed. "Let's go, tough guy."

He held up a hand. "A quick review of the rules, if you please."

"Do we really need those still?" she asked. At his unyielding look, she scowled. "Fine, fine."

"Tell me what you remember of them."

She rolled her eyes. "I will do exactly as you say, when you say it, without questioning you." She paused, then added quickly, "In public."

"And the other rule?" he prompted.

She nodded. "We leave when you say we leave, and not a minute later."

"Aye. They're important for your safety, Gwen. I wouldn't want your pretty neck severed."

"Aw, you do care," she teased.

"Only insofar as I don't want to be the one to tell your parents that you weren't on a safari somewhere."

She tried to pretend outrage, but the flash of her teeth ruined the effect. She sobered. "Seriously, Ry, I get it. You have my word. This is your world, and after what Ellie went through, I am more than willing to be the helpless maiden here."

"Helpless is hardly the word I'd use to describe you."

"I'm going to take that as a compliment, as I'm sure you meant it to be. Can we go already?"

He drew his sword. "Aye."

GWEN STOOD NERVOUSLY, HER ARMS WRAPPED TIGHTLY AROUND her middle, and stared in wide-eyed amazement.

The smell of a peat fire thickened the air, and Reilly's

childhood cottage stood proudly, a wattle-and-daub, thatched-roof affair. It looked as though the cottage sprung from the earth, which had in turn gripped the abode with lush emerald vegetation that extended up the walls. A beautiful, arched, solid entry door stood on the right side of the home. The long wall to the left held three tiny windows, each with a rustic flower box attached to the bottom. A dirt path extended from the front door outward, then wrapped around the dwelling and disappeared from view.

Gwen studied it a moment more, fascinated, and eventually let out a low whistle. "Well, well, Mr. O'Malley. Just when I think I've uncovered all of your secrets…"

The cottage resembled Reilly's present-day home so closely, she half-wondered if they hadn't simply walked back into the future.

He cleared his throat. "Aye, well…you know. It's a good structure, so I thought by, uh, recreating it, it'd provide a safe place. For travelers," he added hastily.

"And memories?" she guessed.

He gazed at it fondly. "Aye," he admitted. "And memories, too. Let's just be grateful it's here, and that it's occupied. Come on, I'd like to introduce you to my mam."

Gwen's stomach tumbled over itself as she slowly followed Reilly. Her throat dry, she remained silent as he called out a greeting in medieval Gaelic.

Someone answered from inside, and his face lit up. "That's her. This is…"

His excitement was palpable, and Gwen couldn't help smiling back. "Weird?"

"Wonderful," he corrected her. "But also unexpected, my worlds colliding like this. It's wonderfully, fantastically unexpected."

He took her hand and led her through the wooden arched door that was all the way to the right of the cottage. Stepping inside, Gwen was surprised to find that the long room was walled off halfway into the house, splitting the first floor into two rooms. In front of her was a matching door to the one through which they entered, presumably leading to the back gardens. To Gwen's right, within arm's length, sat a large, solid table with high-backed chairs tucked in around it. Above, in varying heights, bunches of drying plants hung from the low ceiling. More herbs lined the short wall, giving off a heady fragrance, countering the peat scent. To her left, the room held an empty, suspiciously modern-looking rocking chair. A basket overflowing with all sorts of materials sat next to it on the stone flagged floor, on which a beautiful spun wool rug lay. A long wooden bench pressed against the back wall, decorated with fluffy, pretty pillows and blankets.

Gwen was enchanted.

An older woman serenely walked through the archway to the other room. Unmistakably Reilly's mother, her features were softer, her stature not nearly as tall, and her pride nearly swallowing the entire room. Gwen bit back her smile.

"Ah, you've finally brought her to meet me! I thought the day would never come!"

Gwen gave her a friendly smile. "Hi. I'm Gwen—"

She was cut off by the strongest hug she'd ever received. When her vision began to swim, the woman released her and stepped back, eyeing her critically.

"You've the look of a Scot about you, Gwendolyn."

Gwen pressed her lips together. The way she said "about" sounded like *aboot*, and she spoke quickly. Decisively.

Just like her son.

"I'm Mary," she continued, oblivious to Gwen's thoughts. "Welcome to me home. I've been waiting for years to meet you! Reilly, be a good lad and fetch us some ale? I've a batch all ready, sitting in the kettle by the hearth. Go on with you." When Reilly good-naturedly kissed his mother's cheek on his way to do her bidding, Mary gave his wrist a loving squeeze before turning back to Gwen. "My, you really *are* a wee thing, aren't you?"

"It's a blessing and a curse," Gwen agreed.

"Och, I think I like you!" Mary looked her over, then ushered her to the bench. "Forgive an old woman, but Reilly's told me so much about you, I feel like I've known you forever. You're even prettier than he said, and he did say you were quite the most beautiful creature on God's green Earth."

Gwen blinked. "Um...he did?"

Mary took her own seat in the rocking chair. "Of course!" She made the word sound like *cairse*, echoing strongly of Reilly's accent, and Gwen gave her a small smile.

"Well, that was very kind of him. He's told me precious little of you, I'm afraid. Not that he didn't want to," she hurried to add, "but I've only recently found out about his, um...special talent."

She flushed dark red. That came out wrong! Oh god, did she just make an innuendo in front of Reilly's mother?

Reilly reentered the room at that moment, smirking at her. She must've looked as mortified as she felt, because he took pity on her.

"Gwen took a little trip back in time and needed a rescue." He handed Mary and Gwen each a cup made from smoothed wood and continued, "Lucky for her, I was there to save the day."

"He didn't show up for three days," she informed Mary.

Mary laughed. "Made you worry, did he?"

"Pfft. There was nothing to worry about," Reilly boasted. Gwen chuckled, and he arched a brow at her. "There wasn't."

"Actually, there was, but that's not what I was smiling at. Your mom and you say the word *about* exactly the same way. I always thought you said it strangely, even a little bit different than the Irish of our—my," she quickly corrected, "time. But now I see it's your own accent. Your medieval one."

Mary beamed. "Aye, he was raised right proper by his da and me! Said his first word when he was less than a year, he did. 'Twas amazing. He spoke clearly just a few months after that. Smartest lad in the clan, to be sure, and the most handsome, too."

"Mam," Reilly protested mildly.

As Mary went on to tell all about Reilly's childhood (the good, the bad, and the embarrassing), Gwen soaked in every last detail. Reilly brought food at some point, but Gwen was too enthralled with Mary's stories to ask what it was, so she ate it as the daylight waned.

She traded stories of her own childhood, trying to omit anything that would be too difficult to explain to someone who had no knowledge of modern-day conveniences. She told of her parents, her lack of siblings ("a true tragedy," Mary clucked), the people she knew, and the work she did.

It was one of the most pleasurable days she'd ever had, and all she'd done was listen, talk, and listen some more.

When the sun began to set, Reilly lit some oil lamps in the house and stoked the fire in the other room. Gwen couldn't cover her yawn fast enough.

"Time travel does wear on a person," Reilly noted. "Last night couldn't have been comfortable for you. Let me show you where you'll be sleeping."

"Go, go." Mary waved at her. "Tomorrow I'll show you me garden and we'll talk more. I've great interest in your bravery and helping with the unfortunate folk. I'd like to hear more about those places."

"Absolutely." She turned to Reilly. "Thanks. I'll follow you."

He led her into the other room, which consisted mainly of a massive hearth set into the far wall, which was fully opposite the table in the sitting room. Clay and steel pots and pans hung from these walls, and a large island stood in the center, clearly where food was prepared.

"I thought that these houses usually had farm animals in them," Gwen whispered.

"Those are called longhouses, and they do. But my mam never kept any animals until after my da died, as he spent his days at the castle and didn't have time to tend them."

Gwen followed him up some rickety steps to the second floor, and he continued, "When she got around to having some, she hated having them in the cottage. I built her a little barn in the back where she keeps the cow and the chickens. I insulated it sort of like a greenhouse, so in the winter, the animals stay warm from the heat of the sun. And when the sun is too weak to warm it, Mam burns a peat fire in there during the day, and when it dies out, the barn holds the heat of the fire through most of the night."

"That's pretty smart."

"Having lived as long as I have, I had time to figure out ways to modernize for her that wouldn't raise any eyebrows."

The second floor had three rooms, all without doors. The far room had clothing and chests, the middle and first rooms each had a four-poster bed with bed hangings.

"This is adorable," Gwen declared.

Reilly shrugged. "I suppose. You'll be sleeping there, in Sorcha's bed." He pointed to the middle room. "She's probably visiting a friend. Usually she's home."

Pointing to the bed in front of them, she asked, "Is this one your mom's bed?"

"Aye. She goes to bed late and is up before dawn, to tend the animals. Though I do it when I'm here, she insists on standing out there, watching over me like I'm an errant lad of six summers." He rolled his eyes, then muttered, "I vow, family will bring out the child in anyone."

"Too true," she laughed. "Wait a second. Where will you sleep?"

"Belowstairs, by the hearth."

She shook her head vehemently. "No, Ry, you take the

bed. If you're our last line of defense out here, I want you fully rested—"

He snorted. "I'm your first, last, and *only* line of defense."

"Isn't that a line in that *Men in Black* movie from the nineties?"

He blithely ignored her. "In the far room, you'll find nightclothes. Dress warmly for it does chill up here. In the morning, choose a dress from the chests on the left. Those are Sorcha's, and though they'll be too big, Mam will fix it for you before I've even finished collecting the eggs."

"That sounds…"

"Provincial?"

She frowned at him. "No, Reilly. It sounds lovely. Stop fretting. This is amazing. Thank you for bringing me. It's more than I ever dreamed."

"Are you saying you dream of me, lass?" Though he was teasing, his eyes darkened and his nostrils flared as he inhaled.

It was the same look she'd seen at the dress fitting. Gwen felt the flush start at the base of her spine and rapidly travel up her body. She was off-balance, the desperate wish of a thousand nights filling her senses. She worked to form words, but none would come out.

"Breathe," he commanded softly, and she forced the air from her lungs. He searched her eyes for a moment before slowly touching her face. "Things are changing, aye?"

"Are they?" she whispered.

He pulled his hand back and dropped it to his side. "It feels like it."

His expression didn't change, sending a frisson of alarm —or thrill, she couldn't tell which—racing through her veins.

"Well, then," he replied, his voice almost hoarse, "Sleep well, Gwendolyn." He kissed her knuckles slowly. "I do hope your dreams are as vivid as mine."

"Goodnight," she whispered, confused and more than a little short of breath, and he quickly descended the stairs.

She touched her cheek, his light touch burned into her skin, and held her knuckles to her mouth. She wondered, not for the first time, what someone like Reilly O'Malley dreamed about.

∼

WHEN HE WAS CERTAIN GWEN WAS DEEPLY ASLEEP, REILLY SAT down with his mother and told her everything, from the time Gwen announced her engagement, to the Fates, to their arrival.

"Those Fates gave you but three weeks?" she exclaimed. She smoothed her features into one of supreme confidence. "Of course, if anyone can make a lass fall in love with him, 'tis you."

"I'm not to interfere with her free will."

Mary sat a bit straighter. "What does that mean, exactly?"

He bounced his knee. "I can't do or say anything that will affect her own decisions."

"I don't understand…?"

Reilly stood, unable to sit any longer. "I think that, if I were to tell her that she is my soul mate, she'd claim me back simply to ensure my happiness. She has some understanding how it works."

"Ah."

"And, though she's no longer betrothed, she stated that she would be doubtful of my true intentions. How am I to convince her that I'm the one she is destined for, without claiming her openly?"

"Well, seeing as she's yet unmoved by your sweet self, I'd say you need all the aid you can get with wooing her."

"Aid?" Reilly exclaimed, breaking his tension with a laugh. Oh, he had no doubts that his mother loved him, and that she was indeed full of pride when it came to talking about him, but she'd made certain over the years to keep his head from getting too big. She would take him down a peg— or three—whenever she felt he needed it.

Which was almost every time he visited her.

"Aye, aid. Don't you laugh at me, lad. This, at least, is one area where I know more than you."

"You know much more than me about many things, Mam."

She patted his cheek. "Of course I do. I was just trying to make you feel a bit better."

He threw his head back and laughed again. By the saints, 'twas good to be home.

"So, her former betrothed told her he'd wait for her?" Mary repeated, bringing him back to their conversation. "And he spoke those precise words?"

Reilly nodded his head curtly. "His exact words were, *I'll wait, Gwen* and *Maybe it'll be enough, and you won't allow the person who doesn't love you keep you from the one that does.*"

Mary rolled her eyes and settled herself in her rocking chair, which Reilly had pulled closer to the light of the fire. "'Tis a man we speak of, aye? Not a green lad?"

Reilly sat heavily in the stool by the hearth. "It doesn't matter what I think about him, only what Gwen does."

"Your future wooing is overly complicated. Your da decided he wanted me as his wife, then he set out to prove he was the best one to care for me."

"How did he prove it?" Reilly asked curiously.

Mary pulled a dress from her enormous sewing basket and settled it over her lap. "He told the laird, and the laird saw it done."

"Aw, Mam, things are different in the future. Women don't need surnames for protection in Gwen's time. Also, the people of Ireland and Gwen's country frown upon arranged marriages."

"Pity. 'Tis much more effective."

"Agreed, but if it were as easy as that, someone would've claimed her long before I came along."

"Nothing to be gained by griping about it. What do you plan to do now?"

Reilly grumbled, "By the saints, woman, you claim you know more than me in these matters. I was hoping you would have some ideas."

She gently rocked back and forth, carefully stitching. Reilly, for his part, stoked the fire, hoping something brilliant would come to one of them.

Wooing Gwen wouldn't be as easy as a bauble and a kiss, no matter how much he wished it to be.

His mother lowered the dress. "What does the betrothal contract contain? What did she lose when it was broken?"

He explained that engagements were based on the word of two people instead of the transfer of goods and belongings. When Mary had fully wrapped her head around that notion, her eyes were watery.

"How far our fair isle has come in its view of women," she murmured.

"According to Gwen, it has huge amounts to go before she would agree with you." Reilly sighed. "I'm at a full loss here."

"Surely you've some idea, aye? You know her quite well. Do you think she's reconsidering her betrothal? I don't think any man would want his betrothed to sleep under another man's roof. Would you? Of course not," she answered for him. She held up the forest green dress and inspected the seam, then tied off the final stitch.

Reilly groaned. "I've never said—or thought—so many words about *feelings* and such nonsense in my life as I have these last pair of days. My head spins from the lack of sense pummeling it. Truly, Mam, I can't make head nor tail of it."

"What a strange saying," Mary scoffed. She pinned him with her deep brown eyes. "Are you still smitten with her?"

"Still?" he grumbled.

Mary rolled her eyes, then rocked, contemplative. Reilly remembered the day he finished that chair for her; she'd never seen a moving chair, and her excitement when she realized how soothing it was for her mind made him smile each time he thought of it.

"Do something with your hands," she instructed him suddenly, noting his bouncing knee. "Carve something. And don't mince words with me, lad. You *are* smitten with her. But do you think you can love her? *Forever?*" she added pointedly.

"I don't think there was a time I didn't love her, Mam." He took out his smallest dirk and selected a nub of wood from the kindling pile. He began to gently shave the bark from it.

Mary's eyes softened. "Oh, Reilly. She's the one, isn't she? Your mate?"

"Were I to admit such a thing aloud, I'd be tied to her forever, even if she didn't love me back," Reilly reminded her.

"Do you want to be tied to her forever?"

He chipped a little too hard at his almost-formed wooden figure. "Aye, I do indeed want to be tied to her forever. 'Tis one of the reasons why I claimed her, out loud, in front of two of the Fates." He smiled a little at his mother's gasp. "I never thought I would claim anyone."

"Well, you've never had reason to before," Mary pointed out sagely. She leaned over and patted his arm reassuringly. "Now, you've got to build a relationship with her, which won't be too difficult for you. The secret to any relationship is compromise, and we both know you've no troubles with that. Your Gwendolyn is a lovely lass, though a bit headstrong. Do you think you can rein her in a bit?"

Reilly blinked and paused his hands. "Why would I ever want to rein her in?"

Mary chuckled, delighted, and reached for her sewing basket. "That's a good answer, lad, and she'll appreciate you not wanting to change her to your liking instead of liking her for what she is."

"Aye. But it might not matter. I had her love for so long, but I couldn't tell her about my life. My…gift, as you like to call it. And so, rightfully, she decided to be happy with her own life. She moved on, and that included—" he swallowed past the distasteful words "—someone else."

Mary tapped her cheek, lost in thought for a moment. "If a lass gives her love freely to her mate, does she ever really stop loving him?"

"I've no answer to that."

Mary eyed him speculatively. "Ah, but that's why you've come here. To find out."

"Perhaps." He carefully continued his carving, the small shavings pile at his feet growing. "The Fates sent me here. I had no hand in it this time."

"What is the one thing Gwendolyn has with you?"

He thought for a moment. "Trust."

She nodded slowly. "Aye, Reilly. Trust. She *trusts* you. Do you ken why?"

He looked up wearily. "Mam, please don't make me guess. I've used enough words with Gwendolyn over the past few days that I'm fair certain my tongue will fall out of my head soon."

"Exactly! She trusts you because she can talk to you! Have you told her how you feel? Give the words to her on a trencher and see how palatable they are to her?"

He sighed heavily. "'Tis the trouble, right there. Gwen is clever. Very clever. If I were to suddenly claim that she should be with me now, she'll believe I'm saying the words because of her betrothal, not because of her. She'd compare herself as a prize to be won in a jousting match."

"Well, isn't she just that?"

"Nay!" he exclaimed vehemently. At his mother's smug look, he took a deep breath and tried to regain control of the conversation. "Nay, she is not. She is…" He struggled to find the words.

"Something else is holding you back, lad."

Reilly sighed. "I made a mistake, Mam. A big one. She and I…well, our passions were…"

Mary chuckled. "I see. Did you take her maidenhead?"

He bit back a smile. If Gwen had any idea what they were speaking of, she would be mortified and horrified and generally ready to castrate him.

"Nay. I stopped us before it became too late, but I did not handle it in a graceful way."

"Ah. So you shamed her."

"Nay, never! I told her that I had needs, and she wasn't the woman to see to them." He felt the rise of his own shame in his neck. "I didn't want to use her like that, and I was angry. I was driven by battle-lust."

"I can only think that she heard shaming, as though she wasn't good enough for you," Mary said gently. "As a woman, 'tis a vulnerable position to place oneself in. And to be roundly rejected, with words such as those…it's shame. Shame for not reading the situation clearly, or shame for doing something you'd never meant to do, or shame for simply not being enough. But 'tis shame, Reilly, and that lays on your shoulders."

"I never meant to hurt her," he said hoarsely. "I wanted to protect her."

Mary stood and padded to him, then sat down near him on the bench. "These emotions, they're big. Bigger than you, and you've no idea how to control them." She softened her voice, watching him dig at the wood in his hand. "Perhaps you've yet to learn that you can't control everything."

"Lately, I can't control anything. But I *can* control this," he muttered. He drew his hand over his face, wiping the beads of sweat that had inexplicably formed on his forehead. "I *will* control this. 'Tis naught but my next lesson."

"Aye, everything's a lesson with you," Mary replied, holding her hand out for his latest piece of art. "But perhaps this time, this is a lesson best learned from someone other than yourself." She held it up to the lamplight, delighted with the small fairy he'd started. She handed it back to him and headed back to her rocking chair, where she picked up the tapestry she'd been working on. "Perhaps, this is one time you mustn't rely on the Fates for aid."

"I haven't had their aid for more years than I care to count," Reilly said after a moment of companionable silence.

"Haven't you, though?" Mary mused. She carefully pulled a bright red thread through the thick fabric. "Answer me this, Reilly. How many swords should've cleaved you in two? How many times should a horse's hooves pounded you into the ground? How many times were you sent somewhere, with naught but a vague message, and a helpful sort of person was placed in your path?"

Reilly considered her words, but ultimately, he shook his head. "Mam, I haven't died, but only because I'm still useful to the Fates. And I haven't been trampled to within an inch of my life for probably the same reason. I'm worth more alive than dead. There are more Protectors to train, more lost travelers to direct."

Mary snorted delicately. "Oh, you poor man. Are you truly believing you understand the Fates' plan for you?"

"Stay strong, take care of lost wanderers, protect the O'Rourkes. There's not much else for me."

Mary held her tapestry up to the firelight, then brought it back to her lap. "When Sir Colin decided he didn't want to be a Protector anymore, those long years ago when he was but a young warrior, what did those Fates do?"

"You know the story."

"Humor your dam," she demanded.

His stomach rumbling, Reilly walked to the side table and loaded a trencher with some food. Over his shoulder, he said succinctly, "He was given three tasks by each of the three Fates, and upon completion of each task, realized the deep and lasting impact in his sacred vow."

"Three again. They do love that number—three tasks, three Fates, three weeks." She fixed a snag in her fabric, then continued. "And with the other Protectors you've trained. How do you know they're ready for their own quests?"

"They must complete three trials after they've been properly instructed in swordplay, knife fighting, history, and the how-to of time travel."

"And what were *your* three tasks?"

"I had many more than three."

"Aye, I suppose you did. And at some point, when those Protectors found their mates, they were released from their Protector duties. Isn't that what you told me?"

Reilly glanced up and replied quietly, "You know what goes for them doesn't necessarily go for me."

"Because you're their laird?" she asked mildly, her eyes following the path of the needle. "I don't want to know how many years you've been doing this. But as your mother, I see the weariness in your eyes. Your shoulders are strong. Your mind is brilliant. But your heart? It's losing itself. You're only human, lad. The Fates know this. You can't be this forever. 'Tisn't natural, and at some point, they'll know your time with them must end."

While Reilly would have loved to believe her, the cold, hard facts said otherwise. He'd been wandering through hundreds of years, doing exactly as the Fates decreed. When did his determination to follow their exact orders begin to fade?

He didn't really have to ask himself the question. It was when he broke the first rule he ever learned about time travel —that he could only do so to protect the O'Rourke line (or visit his family, as was the contract his da made with the Fates). He saw, back when they were unfathomable distances apart, how miserable Emma and Aidan were, and he went directly against his orders to not return to medieval Ireland… the Fates were sure to punish him for that. He knew it was coming.

It didn't make it easier, though.

Mary smoothed out her tapestry, pleased. "Aye. Look here at this. I've been working on it for months now."

He stood over Mary's shoulder, ensuring he did not block the weak light. He admired the small, tight stitches and rich colors of thread. The main focus of the tapestry was a woman in a chair by a blazing hearth. She cradled a small child in her arms. Behind her, in an open doorway, stood a man with long hair, home from battle. His attention was focused on his wife and child, and his bloodied sword hung above the door. Woven into the blood on the sword were the Latin words, *Pro domo focoque pugnamus.*

We fight for hearth and home.

"This hangs in the MacWilliams' castle," Reilly remembered, running a finger over the intricacies. "In the laird's solar."

"Well, that's a high honor, indeed!"

"How did it get in a MacWilliam castle, though?"

Mary smiled with satisfaction. "Sorcha."

"How would my sister have anything to do with a tapestry that hangs in another clan's castle next century?"

"Sorcha married a MacWilliam. I believe she's very in love with him. He's a good lad."

Reilly frowned, certain he heard his mother wrong. "I thought she was to marry an O'Rourke?"

Mary frowned. "Sir Lochlan O'Rourke perished last year in battle. She didn't grieve overmuch, as she'd never actually met her betrothed. But our laird never sought to renew the agreement with any other of that clan."

"The MacWilliams, though?" Reilly shook his head, disappointed. "They are a weak clan right now. They will be for years to come. And the strife they must endure… O'Rourkes would be a better choice."

"Aye, 'tis the truth. But love had other ideas. She's safe enough, Reilly. I've no concerns."

He frowned, unconvinced. "If there's a way out of the betrothal, Laird O'Malley should rethink it." Not that it would matter, he thought to himself. He knew his sister wouldn't marry. He visited her once, as an old maid, a respected elder of the O'Malley clan. She had no children, but was happy. "When are they to marry?"

Mary's voice went soft. "'Twas all so unexpected. They met at a tournament a few months back. Cormac approached the laird within days, and they wed shortly thereafter."

"What? They've already married?" Reilly laughed. "Mam, no, she couldn't have."

Mary raised a brow. "I can assure you they have."

"I know you're wrong, Mam."

Her eyes flicked up to him, a touch of sadness in them. "Oh, the things you must know, my dear. But for this, she did marry him. And she seems quite content."

"No, Mam, you don't understand. Sorcha doesn't marry. I *know* this. I've visited her, later in her life. She never married."

"Well, methinks the Fates have changed things up on you."

Reilly shook his head, an unfamiliar sense of dread rising. "Mam…no. They've never done that before; they've never changed the past."

She canted her head. "And how would you be knowin' that for certain? You've always claimed you'd never try to understand women, especially those particular ones. Why wouldn't they change things to suit their purposes?"

"But Sorcha…"

Mary stood resolutely. "Perhaps you ought to take it up

with those Fates, Reilly. For me, I was at that wedding, saw it with me own two eyes. Vows were spoken, bedding happened, and a tasty brunch was had by all. Sorcha is happy, her new husband is proud, and both clans have exchanged dowries and goods. This tapestry is the final part of my wedding present to her; it's late because it took so long to get the red thread, you see. She's a MacWilliam now, and may she have a long and healthy life as one."

Reilly's eyes flicked to the folded cloth, confusion fogging his brain. That tapestry hung in Nioclas MacWilliam's solar.

If it hadn't been handed down, as Nioclas himself told Reilly it was, then how else would the MacWilliams have gotten it?

His mother, bless her, quietly left him to his troubled thoughts.

CHAPTER 11

*G*wen carefully stretched and took stock of her surroundings. Beautifully stitched canopy, soft bedding, and the smell of something roasting mixed with peat moss; she knew immediately where she was. She rarely had any issue remembering where she was when she awoke in a new place; perhaps it was due to all her travels, or maybe it was just part of her DNA. But, after many sleepovers with Ellie—who forgot where she was when she woke up in her own flat, much less if she woke up in a strange location—Gwen was grateful for the small blessing.

She briefly wondered if her friend still had that problem when she was with Colin. Ever since meeting him, Ellie had seemed calmer and more even-keeled than ever, though she couldn't quite overcome her clumsy tendencies. Ellie was always a quiet, steadfast, sweet person, but with Colin by her side, she was a brighter, more vibrant version of herself.

Gwen thought that might be what love looked like.

Her stomach clenched. If Reilly did have real feelings for her, and not just a passing fancy, what would that mean? Aside from the fact that she didn't understand why he would want to make a life with her, after all he told her the other night. He admitted he already claimed his soul mate, for crying out loud. Gwen knew soul mates were a one-and-done deal. And because he found his soul mate, could he even love another person? She didn't really know. Maybe that's why he held everyone at arm's length.

But not her. Never her, except for in those early days when she foolishly threw herself at him over and over. When she did so, he'd shut down swiftly, but not absolutely. He easily could've written her off as a silly young woman with too many romantic notions in her head, but instead, he fostered their closeness. He made it a point to talk with her often. He spoke with her about everything, and by his own admission, he didn't often speak so openly with any of his cousins, with whom he was as close as brothers. The ins and outs of his days, his frustration with a family member, the thousand small victories when he was woodworking—he came to her with all of it.

Why her?

Perhaps Reilly had lost his chance with his soul mate. Perhaps she hadn't claimed him back. If that was the case, Gwen wondered, would she be willing to live a life with Reilly anyway, knowing that he loved another woman more fully than Gwen loved him?

Her questions weren't going to answer themselves, and though she wasn't quite ready to confront Reilly with them, she could feel her courage building. She'd get there, eventually.

Just not today.

She was also keenly aware that while Reilly readily showed her one side of himself, there was another, more uncivilized side. The last time they'd been in the Middle Ages, she remained at the castle while Colin, Reilly, and a slew of others headed off on a rescue mission. He came back covered in large, damp, dark, reddish-brown spots. His sword was caked with dirt and grime, and his forehead was smeared with dried blood. He assured her that none of the spots on his clothing were his blood, and he redirected her attention to her friend, who had needed her very badly at the time.

Gwen never let herself think of what Reilly actually did whilst he was about the business of saving Ellie. But now, she'd seen for herself what he was capable of; he killed a man. One minute, the guy was having a chat, and the next, he was lifeless on the ground.

She felt the bile rise up again, but she forced it to stay down and swiftly tucked the memory into a box in the deepest recesses of her mind. She locked it in the same area labeled *Venezuela*, then decided she needed some fortification.

Swinging her legs over the side of the surprisingly comfortable mattress, Gwen's feet found the lamb's wool floor covering. She dug her toes in, relishing the softness, and glanced around her. Mary's bed next to her was empty and fully made. All of the walls were chalk-white, and the ceiling above her canopied bed was the thatch of the roof. She read once that the bed hangings were originally to catch any vermin that would fall from the thatch, preventing a nasty wakeup in the middle of the night.

She strongly hoped that her bed hangings were for decorative purposes only.

The room itself wasn't quite cold, but a draft from the thatch drifted down to her. She hurried toward the clothing at the other end of the house and saw with relief that a gown of forest green had already been laid out. She quickly changed, grateful the laces were in the front, and realized with a start that the dress fit her perfectly.

Baffled, she slipped her shoes on and cautiously made her way down the staircase and into the kitchen, where a delicious warmth and smell emitted from the large hearth. Mary stood, stirring something in a large kettle, and greeted her with a sunny smile.

"Gwendolyn, good morning! Reilly will be back in a moment. He's gathering my eggs, the good lad. He always insists on doing the chores when he's home."

"He's a good man," Gwen replied, accepting a steaming cup from her. She looked into it. Oatmeal? Maybe. She didn't care; she was hungry. But first…"Um, where's the gardrobe?"

"Oh, we don't have one. We've chamber pots in the rooms and Finn—that's Reilly's da, God rest his soul—built a little house a ways away. Reilly calls it an *outhouse*. That lad and his future words." She chuckled, and her dark eyes twinkled. "Anyway, it's out the back, to the right. You'll see it. I'll keep your porridge warm."

Gwen thanked her and gratefully handed her back the cup. She went in search of the outhouse, and, after taking care of her needs, she headed back toward the house, only to almost run fully into Reilly's chest.

"Good morning, Gwendolyn. Sleep alright?"

She immediately noticed the lines around his eyes were tight; a sure sign that his guard was up. While Gwen could usually read him like an open book, when he shuttered himself, even she couldn't penetrate his self-made fortress, though she liked to believe *he* thought she could.

"I did, thanks. Any ideas where the dress came from?"

He smiled. "Aye. My mother altered it last night for you."

Gwen sighed with jealousy. "I wish I could sew like that. She got my size almost exactly right!"

"She's a master seamstress. She's one of the tapestry weavers for the laird, and she sells some of her work. It's what supports her out here. The nearest house is almost two kilometers away." He handed her a basket with some eggs, then picked up two buckets filled with milk.

"So just her and your sister live out here?"

"Well, it turns out my sister married a few weeks ago."

"You sound a little put out by that," Gwen noted. "Did you want to attend her wedding?"

He shook his head. "Nay, I'm not upset by that. But the Fates have changed things. I've visited my sister in her future, and in that visit, she…" He looked heavenward. "She never married."

"Whoa," Gwen breathed. "They can change the past?"

"I didn't think so. But it seems they can."

"Can they change the future, too?"

Reilly frowned. "I've no idea." He shook himself a little and looked ahead to the house. "But now it's just my mam. I'm going to have speech with her about moving closer to the castle for protection. It was dangerous for the two of them to be out here, but it's even more dangerous for a woman living alone."

They reentered the kitchen together, and Reilly put the milk on the floor by the hearth while Gwen placed the basket on the center island. They brought the bowls of porridge to the table and sat down to eat together.

"What do you want to do today, lass?"

The question from Reilly had Gwen raising her eyebrow. "This is your show, Ry. I've no idea what's available."

"The final harvest finished just this past moon," Mary offered. "The village games start today."

Gwen's eyes lit up. "Village games? What does that mean?"

Reilly answered. "They're a celebration. In your time, 'tis called Mabon. It's the autumnal equinox, and here, 'tis an important point in the year when we have one more night by the light of a full moon to finish the harvest. Once that happens, a week of celebration and games are held by the clan in the village center."

"Aye, the games are a sight. 'Tis a time when the men show their strength, and the laird chooses new guardsmen to bring to his castle," Mary added.

"What kind of games do they play?"

Reilly pushed his empty trencher away from him and sat back slowly. "Games of strength and warrior skill, mostly."

"Like the Highland Games?" she asked excitedly. "I saw those one year in New York. It was crazy, these guys were lobbing telephone poles!"

Mary look intrigued. "Pray tell, what are telephone poles?"

"Never you mind," Reilly muttered. To Gwen, he replied, "'Tis much different than those games. There are sword fighting competitions, wrestling, archery, and strength tests. Arm wrestling, if you can believe it. Endurance challenges, too. But the highlights are the songs and poetry."

"Really?" Gwen asked skeptically.

"Aye," Mary confirmed. "The celebration reconnects us to our ancestors, and we do that through our storytellers."

"While the prize for the strength contestants is to become part of the garrison, the prize for storytellers is the equivalent of one year's salary and an invitation to the castle to entertain important visitors," Reilly informed her. "'Tis a great honor, bestowed to only one."

"Oh, let's definitely go to this." She rubbed her hands together. "Can women enter any of the contests?"

"Aye, though we're not allowed to join the castle garrison if we win," Mary replied, gathering their trenchers. "Do you care to try your hand at something, lass?"

Gwen shrugged. "I wouldn't say no if there was something that interested me."

Mary beamed at her, then carried the dishes to the hearth. At Reilly's pointed look, Gwen shrugged, bemused. "What? I wouldn't."

"You would say nay if I said not to, aye?" he prompted.

She grimaced. "Right. Or if you said not to."

"Good answer," he murmured, so only she could hear. "The rules, Gwen. 'Tis for your safety."

"Then we shall go," Mary declared, bustling back over to

them. "Your dress is too fine for the games. You'll need something else."

Gwen waited as Mary pondered, then reflexively smiled when Mary's face brightened. "Ah, yes! The cobalt dress."

"Blue?" Gwen replied dubiously. She fingered a lock of her hair. "I think it'll clash with my hair."

Mary frowned. "Clash? Do you mean mismatch?" At Gwen's nod, Mary *tsk*ed. "Think of a fire. The hottest part of the flames is blue, and the cooler parts tend to be a blend of colors, including the exact shade of your hair. They all work together in nature; why wouldn't they work on you?"

"Listen to her," Reilly advised. "She's not a master seamstress without merit."

"I'll wear whatever you want me to wear," Gwen replied, unsure. "It'll just be new for me, that's all."

A few moments later, Mary had the dress downstairs and was holding it against Gwen, as Gwen studied herself in the smooth mirror on the wall.

"I had no idea I could wear this color," she breathed. "I always thought it'd make my hair look more orange."

"Nay, not at all." Mary smoothed her hand over Gwen's long tresses and placed them over her shoulder against the material. "'Tisn't it a wondrous thing when we give a second chance to something we thought was a lost cause?"

It took everything Gwen had not to scan the room for Reilly; instead, she merely inclined her head. "Yes," she agreed quietly. "It certainly is."

GWEN WATCHED IN WIDE-EYED WONDER AS TEN MEN GRUNTED, sweated, and fought to tug a massive rope. A small ribbon marked the center, and it flapped in the wind as each team tried to move it over their line, which was drawn in the grass using the tip of someone's sword. The rope was thicker than both Reilly's wrists, and all Gwen could think was how those warriors must be getting the worst kind of rope burn.

"What do they get if they win, again?"

Reilly winced as one of the men slipped and fell. The contestant recovered quickly, though, and his team was able to hold steady. "Bragging rights, for certain. And a silver coin each."

"Who pays the winners? The laird?" Gwen wondered.

"Aye. He is generous," Mary replied, with obvious delight at the game playing out. Another man on the same team slipped, and this time, the other team was able to yank the ribbon over their line. Cheers, swears, and a fistfight broke out almost immediately.

"Let's see what we've got over here," Reilly said, herding the women away from the spectacle. "Today's events happen all day long; each team or competitor continues until there is but a single winner. From what others are saying, today we have the rope tug, the anvil throw, swordplay, and trick sword fighting."

"Ooh, trick sword fighting! What's that?" she asked, intrigued.

Reilly looked above the crowd, his eyes searching. "It's where a magician comes in and waves his magic wand over the swords. Then they up and fight themselves."

"Oh, listen not to him," Mary chided. "He jests. Trick sword fighting is for the children; it's done with wooden swords instead of steel. Because the balance is different, it makes sword play a bit less…"

"Exciting?" Reilly chimed in.

"Dangerous," Mary finished. "I'll remind you it's for the younger lads to try their hand at swordplay."

"Oh, that sounds cute!" Gwen exclaimed. "I think it'll be fun. Let's check it out!"

Reilly capitulated easily, probably because his mother and Gwen were insistent. Gwen noticed the way the other members of the clan greeted Reilly and were slightly deferential to Mary. She seemed to have a deep respect from the clan; Gwen wondered how much of that was due to her tapestry work, and how much was due to her son.

Reilly stayed close to them both, shielding them from the press of the crowd when it became too intense. His hand frequently stayed on her lower back, guiding her through the throngs of people, and she shivered every time.

She suspected that he lingered much longer than was necessary, but she couldn't pull away.

Everywhere she looked, Gwen saw villagers, dressed in their daily garb, cheering on their loved ones. They watched the boys, who seemed to be around seven or eight years old, parry with the wooden swords. The winner of the day, it was promised, would have his very own sword made of steel; with such reward, the boys fought hard. Reilly, Gwen, and Mary didn't stay to see who the final winner was, but there were a few definitive front runners.

"Did you ever participate in these?" Gwen asked Reilly as he bought her a pasty from one of the food stalls.

"Aye."

Mary puffed up with pride. "He not only took part, he won every game he entered! 'Twas a wondrous sight to behold. When he was but six, he won his own steel sword. When he was eight, he threw a lead ball further than any of the grown men! And the anvil toss—"

"What's that?" Gwen interrupted, fascinated.

"Mam," Reilly tried to put an end to her maternal bragging, but she hushed him with a wave of her hand.

"The anvil toss is just over there. See those beams set up, with the beam across them?"

Gwen stood on her tiptoes and looked in the direction Mary was pointing. Two tall poles stood with a bar across them, about a third of the way up, looking almost like a giant H in the middle of the events field.

"I see it!"

"My Reilly," Mary boasted, "stood at just ten years old and put the other competitors to shame! You see, lass, you must stand with your back to the beams. Then, you reach down, lift an anvil weighing your own weight, and toss it up and over your head. If it clears the beam, it's a successful throw." She beamed. "Reilly was the only one to clear it!"

"Is there anything you can't do?" Gwen smirked at his discomfort.

He noticed the smirk and smirked right back at her. "At these games? Probably not."

"He's not the best with a bow and arrow."

"Mam!" Reilly exclaimed with a good-natured laugh. He turned to Gwen, his eyes twinkling. "Don't listen to her. Though I'll admit, I'm much better with swords and jousting."

"So there *is* something I could beat you at," she teased.

He raised a brow. "Think you?"

She folded her arms and raised her own eyebrows (both of them, as she couldn't do just the one, no matter how hard she tried). "I do."

"Lass, I said he wasn't the *best* with a bow and arrow," Mary said worriedly. "He won that game as well."

"You said earlier that women participate in these games?" Gwen looked at Mary for confirmation, and at her nod, Gwen grinned. "Perfect."

Suddenly, someone shouted, "Mary!"

The three of them swiveled their heads toward the man calling out her name, and Mary flushed. "'Tis the laird."

"Go on, we shall wait for you here," Reilly encouraged her. Mary quickly headed over to the man, who looked more than a little fierce.

"He's scary," she remarked.

Reilly guffawed. "Darragh? Nay, he's a lamb. At least when it comes to my mother."

Gwen's eyes grew round and she looked up at Reilly. "Do you mean that he likes her?"

"He's proposed to her no less than twice a year for at least five years."

Gwen's mouth dropped open. "Why has she refused him?"

"She claimed she and Sorcha had everything they needed." His brow furrowed. "But now, with Sorcha married...mayhap she's a bit lonely?"

"Perhaps she'll agree, if for nothing more than companionship," Gwen agreed. She frowned. "Wait a second. If she agrees, does that change the past you know?"

He frowned. "Aye, damn those Fates."

Gwen's heart constricted at his bleak expression. She needed to distract him. Thinking fast, she turned fully to him with a cheeky grin. "So, since you're basically the reigning Mr. Medieval—"

He flexed his bicep. "Medieval is so restrictive. Throw the word *Modern* in there, too. It'll be more fully representative."

"Oh, you're so arrogant," she scoffed, laughing. "Back home you're so far from earning that title, it's laughable."

"Is it now?" he asked, his eyes glittering dangerously. He took a step toward her, and she restrained the smile pulling at her lips. "Who could possibly take that title, if not me?"

"Well, your competition includes Chris Hemsworth—"

"That Australian actor who played the god in your superhero movie?" he exclaimed. "His accent was terrible."

"No way, it was sexy. And he's a *god*," she added, just to get under his skin.

"I'll have him as my competition then. So far, I win."

"You also are up against Hugh Jackman. I mean, hello, male perfection. He's also been married for what, twenty years? That's dedication and loyalty. He's adopted children, does loads of charity work, looks amazing without a shirt..."

"You seem to enjoy the Aussies," Ry replied darkly.

"Aye," she mocked in his accent, "though I be likin' yer Irish lads Colin Farrell and Liam Neeson as well."

He growled at her, and she squealed as he grabbed for her. She avoided him once, but he caught her with his second attempt and hauled her against him. "Makin' craic av me accent, aye?"

His breath fanned over her, and her heartbeat picked up. His body heat seared through her gown, sensitizing her flesh. His hard body, honed by so much more than a gym, combined with the indefinable scent that was intrinsically Reilly threw Gwen's hormones into overdrive.

With her intense and unexpected reaction to his nearness, Gwen's traitorous knees did what they'd never before done. They gave out on her.

Reilly caught her before she fell fully, and he lifted her, clasping her against his chest, so that they were almost eye-to-eye.

Oh, why did he have to smell so good? It should've been impossible, because they were in medieval Ireland, and the other people didn't smell nearly so nice, and he had bathed that morning outside in the freezing creek…where could he possibly have gotten a bar of soap that didn't smell like the one she used? And was it her imagination, or had the yellow flecks in his eyes turned a deep golden color? His gaze was hooded, but when her eyes met his, the connection between them surged to life. A spark, almost tangible, crackled the small amount of air between their faces. Her insides pooled, and her entire body softened, as though it didn't care what her mind told it, as it wanted Reilly.

She wanted Reilly.

He released her slowly, sliding her down his body. His nostrils flared slightly, and his eyes focused on her lips. She didn't step back when her feet reached the ground; if anything, she pressed herself further into him. The world shrank to just the two of them; nothing existed but the moment. She forgot to breathe, forgot to blink…she forgot everything, except Reilly O'Malley, and the golden flecks of his irises, and his strong arms encircling her waist, holding her where she most wanted to be.

Her breasts felt heavy, and her arms ached to slide up his and twine themselves around his neck. Her fingers flexed on his forearms, and she just barely stopped herself.

"Gwendolyn." His voice, merely a whisper, was laced with something that echoed her own thoughts.

She watched him, mesmerized, unsure what was going to come out of his mouth. Silent, crushing hope flared in her heart, while her mind called it ten times the fool.

"Reilly!"

Gwen blinked then, shaking herself out of spell, embarrassment flooding her. *Oh God oh God oh God. No. I can't go through this again.* The rejection. It was a sure thing. And hadn't she promised herself she wasn't going to feel this way anymore? *Nope, nope, triple nope.* She was moving on with her life.

Yet no matter how many times she had that thought, her unruly heart wouldn't pay the words any heed.

Reilly smoothly extricated himself from her and turned to face Mary, who was hurrying toward them from behind the laird as they pushed through the crowd to get to them. The laird spoke in rapid-fire Gaelic, slapping Reilly on the back multiple times as he spoke. Reilly nodded a few times, then responded and gestured to Gwen.

"Oh, forgive me, lass. I'm no' one to accept the English, but as you're with Reilly, that's to be overlooked, of course. I'll speak in your tongue so as to not upset your beau." The laird patted her hand, and she tried to smile at him, though she was sure her face looked more like a contorted mess of uncertainty than delight.

Apparently done with her, the laird turned his attention back to Reilly. "I've been asking yer mam to marry me for years. Claims she's useless as she doesna want any more bairns. But I've got me three sons, so what do I need more bairns for? Nothing, I tell her. So now that Sorcha is settled, she's agreed to be me wife, with yer blessing."

Reilly looked at his mother seriously. "I'll need speech with you first, Mam."

Mary nodded meekly, and Gwen's BS radar went on full alert. Mary didn't strike her as someone who would be meek about anything, much less about her decision to marry.

"Do excuse us, my laird." Reilly nearly dragged Mary away, and Gwen followed, unwilling to be left with the English-hating laird, no matter how nice Mary claimed him to be.

"This is what you want?" Reilly demanded.

Mary lifted her chin a notch. "Well, he's been asking long enough. Makes me think he's serious."

Gwen couldn't help the giggle that escaped.

"Oh, you find this humorous?" Reilly snapped, though there wasn't any heat to his words.

Gwen ignored him. "Mary, do you love him?"

Mary looked over at Darragh, who was unabashedly watching them. "Perhaps."

"He'll provide great security," Reilly conceded. "You'll move into the castle, so there's that. And your position would be greatly elevated. Lady of the clan; you're well-suited to it." He lapsed into a slew of Gaelic, and Mary simply continued to nod thoughtfully.

"Will you be safe if you don't marry him?" Gwen asked, concerned.

"Well, aye, of course," Mary replied, a bit taken aback at the vehemence in Gwen's tone.

She pressed, "Ok, so perhaps you love him. That's the only thing to consider, right? Because if you don't...well, just be sure."

Mary blinked. "At this point in my life, lass, love isn't the most important thing—"

"Don't marry him if you don't love him," Gwen interrupted desperately, grasping the woman's hands. "Don't settle if you don't have to. You're worthy of love. Great love. We all are, right? I mean, too many women have to marry someone just to find that peace you've already found. Don't throw that away for greener grass!"

Mary stared at her, and Gwen watched as understanding dawned on her face. "Aye, lass, I ken your words. I ken."

Gwen nodded, her eyes filling with tears, though she didn't understand why. Or maybe she did.

She didn't know anymore.

Mary looked at Reilly, though she still held Gwen's hands. "Aye, Reilly. This is what I want." She looked back at Gwen. "I had my happiness with my first husband. When he died, a piece of me died, too. But Reilly's da, he knew what he was about. He told me to wait until my heart healed, for heal it would. And so I sat, in my little cottage, waiting." She patted Gwen's cheek. "I've waited long enough. I vowed I wouldn't settle for something less than everything." She leaned in and whispered, "Don't wait as long as I did, Gwendolyn. But don't make anyone make *you* settle, either."

Gwen nodded, a slight movement that barely registered for anyone watching.

"Then of course you have my blessing. My lady," he added with a grin. Mary headed back over to the laird, leaving them alone again.

"Greener grass?"

Gwen stared at Mary's retreating form, her mind a million miles away. "She's a wise woman, your mother."

"Aye."

~

REILLY STILL WASN'T SURE HOW HE ENDED UP WITH A BOW IN HIS hand. Gwen stood a few feet away from him, also holding a bow, and she seemed not ill-at-ease with it.

Curious.

"Why did I agree to this?" he asked again, drawing an arrow from the quiver on his back. He inspected it, decided it was straight, and nocked it.

"You didn't," she informed him, smoothing her fingers over the string of her bow. She nodded, satisfied, then glanced at him. "I merely wanted to see you try your hand at archery, after your mother exposed it as the one thing you might not be amazing at."

"There are but few things I'm 'not amazing at.' But there's no need for me to put on a show about them," he grumbled.

"Oh, relax. No one is even paying attention to us."

That, at least, was true. Archery wasn't set to begin until after the noontime meal, and the archery site stood empty. At Gwen's insistence, Reilly reluctantly procured arrows and bows for them both.

He got the impression that Gwen thought herself to be a good archer. He didn't care to trump her, but he truly was an expert-level archer himself. Part of his training with the Fates, they ensured he could get out of a tight spot with any weapon. While it wasn't his favorite weaponry, he wasn't opposed to its uses, especially when one's foe was too far away for swords.

"My arrows look straight, and my bow is tight," Gwen announced. "I think they'll be fine. You ready to give this a go?"

She looked like a warrior princess, her hair escaping its plaits, the wind blowing her cobalt blue dress around her as though it was encouraging her.

He sighed. "If you'd like, you can simply shoot them all."

"Afraid I'll make you look bad?" she asked sympathetically.

He straightened. "Hardly. I don't care to disabuse you of the notion that you're any good at this." When she openly laughed at him, he narrowed his eyes. "Lass, I've never even heard you speak of arrows before. What makes you think you're better at them than me?"

She smiled mysteriously. "Wouldn't you like to know."

He leaned forward. "What's your confidence level?"

"Exceptionally high," she replied without inflection.

"A bet, then. Winner takes all."

"All what?"

"We shall allow the winner to decide," he demurred. "We each shoot three arrows into the target. The one with the closest bullseyes wins."

"Done. But I'll have to think on what you'll be giving me when I win."

His eyes glittered dangerously. "Oh, lass, you've no idea what you're baiting when you boast about things you can't possibly do."

She smiled sweetly at him. "Do your worst, O'Malley. Do you need a practice shot before we start?"

He snorted. "Nay, but perhaps that's your way of letting me know that *you* do. So, ladies first. Take your practice shot."

She shrugged, then took up her stance. She nocked her arrow, set up her bow and string, and aimed. She drew the bow back—*rather well*, he thought with some surprise—and let the arrow fly. It hit a few inches off the bullseye.

"Step aside, and watch how 'tis done," he said with exaggerated patience.

She barely contained her grin, but he ignored her. He did the same as she did, and landed his arrow significantly closer to the center.

"Last chance to back out," he warned as they retrieved the arrows.

She pursed her lips. "Reilly, shut your trap. I agreed to this, as did you. Any ideas what you'll demand if you win?"

"Ah, that's the way of it," he replied approvingly. "You'll find out when I win."

She rolled her eyes and took up her stance again. But this time, Reilly noticed she was a bit more focused. Her head was up, and her shoulders were relaxed. With supreme confidence, she set herself up, then, with precision archers the world over would weep for, she let the arrow fly...into the center of the bullseye.

He stared in shock.

"Would you be a dear and grab that for me?" she asked, trying—nay, purposefully failing—to keep the smugness out of her tone. "I'd hate to split that perfectly good arrow with my next shot."

"You've never split an arrow," Reilly protested.

"Well, no," she admitted. Then she gave a sly smile. "Rather, the arrow slides in next to it, ruining the wood and sometimes splicing the feather. I hate doing that, too."

"I don't believe you," he declared.

She shrugged. "Okay. But if those guys over there demand someone replace these two arrows, that's on you."

"Deal."

She selected another arrow, and, with frightening accuracy, slid it home next to the other one.

"What the devil...?"

She brushed an imaginary piece of lint off her shoulder, then ruined the effect by grinning at him. "United States Archery Association's Outdoor Archer of the Year, five years in a row. Youngest ever to hold the title, back in high school and college."

He gaped at her. "You never mentioned a word of it to me!"

"Guess it never came up." Smoothly, she shot her third arrow, aiming it slightly to the left of the first two, then gave him an exaggerated bow. "Your turn, Mr. Medieval."

He clenched his jaw. Once she removed her arrows, he

carefully took his stance, relaxed his shoulders, and picked his chin up slightly. He released his arrow...bullseye. He just barely resisted the urge to pump his fist.

"Excellent shot," she said approvingly. "Shall I remove the arrow?"

"If you wouldn't mind," he replied through gritted teeth. He was going to win if it killed him.

Not because he wanted to beat her, though of course he did. But if he won, his "all" would be to finish what they started earlier. His lips, on hers, where they were meant to be.

He needed to kiss her, and he needed her to want to kiss him back as much as he needed air.

Carefully, he shot his next arrow, and it, too, landed in the bullseye, though it was almost on the line. He wondered...

"If you're thinking of a tiebreaker in which you distract me, think again," she called out.

He glowered at her. "Reading minds, are we?"

"Didn't need to. It was written all over your face."

He grunted in response, wishing he'd never agreed to this nonsense. But agree he did, so he yanked another arrow out of his quiver.

Gwen, for her part, didn't try to distract him. She merely watched silently, waiting for him to make the next shot.

He held his stance, the arrow nocked, and an idea came to him. He caught her eye. "What's your prize, if you win?"

She tapped her chin thoughtfully. "I'll show you when I win."

He waggled his eyebrows. "If I hit the center, I win."

"If you hit the center, it means we're tied."

He huffed out a laugh. "Oh, nay, lass. You roundly beat me when you ruined two arrows. I'll still show you what I would've won."

She shrugged. "As long as I don't have to hold a sign reading *I'm a loser*, okay."

"I'd never make you wear a sign," he retorted. He lined up his arrow, pulled back the string, and released.

The arrow hit home, and for possibly the first time in his life, he felt that this was something that wasn't driven by anything but his own skill. No Fates behind it, no unseen force determining the outcome.

A feeling of elation went through him at the thought.

"Nice shot!" she exclaimed. She retrieved the arrow and brought it over to him. "I figured you'd be good, but—"

He cut her off by sinking his hands into her hair and slanting his lips over hers.

~

REILLY WAS KISSING HER.

Reilly.

Was.

Kissing.

Her.

And it wasn't a mere brushing of lips or tasting of tongues, Gwen dimly noted. It was a branding kiss, searing her soul, fusing her to him like nothing else could. Full of desire and heat and need and something deeper.

As soon as the shock of his mouth on hers faded, Gwen surrendered to the kiss. She dropped the arrows in her hand and slid her fingers into his hair, her fingertips exquisitely sensitive to the softness.

She wanted this more than her next breath.

She dragged her nails against his scalp, pulling him closer, pressing her body flush against his. He slid his arms around her waist and easily lifted her, never breaking their kiss. He fitted his mouth more securely against her lips, lazily swirling his tongue with hers. A fire ignited low in her belly, and she growled, half-desperately. He bit her lip, then sucked it gently, and she lost all semblance of control.

She opened more fully, pouring every ounce of pent-up passion into her response. Years of longing, lifetimes of understanding. *This* was why she came to Ireland. This was why she existed. For this man, and this moment.

He eased back from her, his eyes dark with desire, and Gwen couldn't contain the tremble that wracked her at his gaze.

"Wow," she whispered.

His breathing ragged, he placed his forehead against hers. "Feel free to slap me at any time."

"Why would I do that?"

He closed his eyes. "Many reasons, but the biggest one is perhaps because I probably deserve it."

"You probably do," she agreed. Then, gathering her courage and her breath, she quietly added, "It's probably time we spoke about what happened at Bri's castle."

He searched her eyes with his for a moment. She felt his chest expand against hers with each breath he took; he held her securely, her arms still looped around his neck. A moment passed, and he inclined his head. "Perhaps it is."

She swallowed hard, then pressed her lips against his once more.

His eyes showed his surprise, but without hesitation, he obliged willingly, smiling against her mouth.

She closed her eyes and allowed the happiness of the moment to overshadow her fear.

CHAPTER 12

$\mathcal{W}$hat Gwen wouldn't give to have just ten minutes to talk with Ellie.

That was at the forefront of her mind the rest of the day, walking from event to event, holding Reilly's hand.

She. Was holding. Reilly. O'Malley's. Hand.

Her thoughts were reduced to one-word sentence, and she wasn't even worried about it.

She felt as giddy, and as nervous, as a teenager. She worried that their discussion later would kill whatever this was, but they were adults, and they discussed things. They worked them out. And the thought *did* cross her mind that perhaps this wasn't real, that perhaps Reilly was swept up in the moment. But her rational side reminded her that Reilly didn't get "swept up" in anything. He only let show what he wanted to let show, and when he gave his word, it was forever.

He hadn't declared undying love, but she didn't believe for a second that he would've kissed her to simply start a fling. In fact, he worked so hard and so long to do exactly the opposite, she wondered if maybe he resisted for so long because he was a little bit afraid of what they could have.

She knew she was.

But the thought of forever with him made her insides jump in anticipation of it.

She wondered if that's what everyone always talked about when they said, "Oh, you'll just know when you've found the one." Was this feeling the "just knowing" part? The feeling where she wanted to hop out of her skin and into his, then repeat it for the rest of her days and beyond?

If so, she was there. She'd *been* there for years.

She steadfastly refused to contemplate that her version of forever might be different than Reilly's version of it.

She didn't want to think about that too much.

"I wonder," Reilly murmured to her as the crowd pushed them close for a moment, "how long you care to stay?"

"Until your mom gets tired," Gwen said without hesitation. "I could look at this stuff all day."

He gave her a meaningful look. "Nay, I mean how long do you want to *stay*."

Oh. In the Middle Ages. "Um, well, I haven't got a timetable, so…whenever you want to leave?"

He gestured toward the far side of the fields, and, nodding, she followed him to the edge of the festivities, out of earshot from anyone.

He looked at her gravely. "My, er, *gift* failed me once already. After the incident in the forest when we first arrived."

Gwen blanched a little at the memory.

"I wonder, if I were to try again, if it would work the way it always has. I'm hopeful that my purpose here has been served."

"We've been here for less than two days. You think you've done whatever it was you were supposed to have done in that time?"

"I certainly hope so," he muttered.

"Did you go somewhere last night?"

He shook his head, surprised by her question. "Nay, of course not."

"So what, exactly, do you think you've accomplished?"

He gave her a small smile. "Well, us."

She laughed, right in his face. "*Us*? That's your purpose here?"

"I can't think of anything else they'd send us back for, can you?"

"Why does it have anything to do with me?"

His smile faltered. "I've a suspicion, is all. We are together now, aren't we?"

"Define together."

He sighed. "Together. Us, in a relationship. You'll move in with me, we'll get married. I'll get my time traveling power back. You know. That kind of together."

She blinked at him for a few seconds, unable to form words. She crossed her arms and put on her fiercest frown. No mention of love, or any other emotion, actually. And he didn't even address their past.

"Once we're settled, I'm certain everything will go back to the way it was, and I'll have no trouble moving through time again."

"If the only reason for this"—she motioned between them —"was so that way you could get your *gift* back, then you can rest assured that we are certainly *not* together."

"Well," he said with a slow smile, "'tisn't the only reason, lass. You can't deny, 'twas quite the kiss you gave me back there."

Any residual happiness faded. He was using her to get his time travel back?

A wave of anger, mostly at herself, shot to the surface. When would she learn? "*Not* that it matters, but it was you that kissed me. And as you're the one who stopped kissing me the last time…"

"Aye?" he prompted.

At his utterly blank, confused look, she stared at him in shock. "You are not serious, Reilly."

He seemed completely serious, so she stopped herself from taking him up on his earlier offer to slap him. Though, perhaps it would knock some sense into him.

She narrowed her eyes at him. "I think now is a good time to have that chat about what happened before. When you and I almost became more than friends, at Bri's castle."

He remained silent, though his expression became wary. "All right, lass. Ask your questions."

She stepped back to put a bit of distance between them, and she was jostled from behind by another villager. She refused Reilly's ready hand and steadied herself.

"Why did you stop us?"

He frowned. "I told you then why. I didn't care to use you that way."

"Was that really why, though?" she prodded.

Affronted, he crossed his arms. "Aye. What other reason would there be?"

Gwen regarded him for a few seconds before stating, "Ellie told me something."

He scratched the back of his neck. "Sometimes, keeping up with your conversations are powerfully difficult, lass. What has Ellie to do with us?"

"She said," Gwen barreled on, "that Colin told her that once a Protector claims his mate, and she claims him back, he can leave his time travels behind and be released from his obligations to the Fates."

Reilly nodded, once.

"You've never lied to me, right?"

"By omission I have," he muttered.

She rolled her eyes. "Other than not telling me who you really are. But everything else, Ry. Have you ever lied to me?"

He shook his head. "Never, lass."

"Will you ever?"

He frowned. "Gwendolyn. Make your point."

"If you claim your mate, and she claims you back, are you free from your life with the Fates?"

He shrugged. "I don't know."

She crossed her arms and stopped walking to face him fully. "Could it be that simple, though? You claim someone, and she claims you back, then Fates give you your life back?"

"'Tis never that simple with the Fates. But if it were to follow the pattern of all other Protectors, then aye, you have it aright."

Gwen narrowed her eyes. "When we first arrived, you told me that you claimed your mate already."

He swallowed hard, but she barreled on.

"Reilly. Did she not claim you back?"

He took almost a full minute to reply. "She has not yet claimed me, no."

Gwen blinked. That answer made it seem like the woman could still claim him.

What?

He shook his head. "You wouldn't understand."

Gwen's eyes nearly fell out of her head, and she had to count to ten before she spoke again, lest she wrap her hands around his neck and squeeze. "I'm not simple-minded, Reilly. I can understand lots of complex things. Try me."

He folded his arms and the all-too-familiar look of stubbornness descended upon his face. "Nay."

She almost stomped her foot in frustration. She took a deep breath. "Fine. You don't want to talk, don't. But if you're serious about us, if you're serious about wanting us to work, you need to answer this." She took a deep breath. "Who is your soul mate?"

He swallowed hard before looking away. "I cannot tell you that."

Her mouth dropped open. "You can't? Or won't?"

He remained mute.

Tears gathered in her eyes.

"Oh, you look as though you could skin a chicken with your teeth," Mary interrupted, materializing beside them.

Gwen gave her a tight smile. "Oh, I'm okay. Truly. I'm fine."

"Ah," Mary replied, understanding in her voice. She looped her arm through Gwen's. "'Tis like that. I also am *fine*. Darragh announced to the clan elders that I've agreed to marry him, and they decided—without me, mind you—that the wedding is three days hence!"

"What?" Reilly exclaimed.

Mary nodded indignantly. "Aye! He took away my right to refuse."

"Would you have refused?" Reilly demanded.

Mary shrugged. "Does it matter? I deserved the chance to, if I so wished it. But now that he's told the world, I'm beholden to the marriage."

"I'm sorry," Gwen murmured. "Having your future taken away is a terrible thing."

Reilly's expression was tortured, and Gwen refused to meet his eyes as his mother continued, "Don't worry yourself over it, lass. I probably wouldn't have refused. But three days! We can't have a wedding in three days! It takes weeks to plan, to ensure there's enough food for everyone, that all family is notified. And I thought we'd have a proper hand fasting ceremony! A year and a day, to get me used to the idea of becoming Lady O'Malley!" She sniffed, thoroughly put out, and patted Gwen's hand. "So, let's walk for a while longer, then go back home, where I've a warm fire, many knitting supplies, and a tasty meal for our supper."

"Go on, and I'll meet you in a moment." She resisted Mary's tug for a moment more, then watched as the woman waved down another clanswoman. Gwen turned to the man staring at her.

"Reilly." She gathered every last bit of her courage around

her, sent a prayer flying, and asked quietly, "Am I your soul mate?"

Say aye. Tell me I'm the one, that I haven't waited in vain.

He swallowed hard. "No more questions, Gwendolyn."

And her poor heart shattered.

REILLY HAD ENOUGH.

After a bowl of cold soup, a silent dinner, and being glared from the room, he was done with being the bad guy.

He told Gwen that a Protector could have no influence on his mate's claiming. She either didn't remember, or didn't want to know. But he wasn't sure if he could speak openly with her about it; the Fates were, again, horrendously vague with their details. What would happen if he told Gwen that she was his? Would that be an influence on her decision in claiming him back?

He was tired of the gray areas; his life had been very black-and-white until recently, and he longed for it to return to that.

After Gwen was asleep, Reilly stood in front of his mother, placed his foot on the rocking chair to halt its movement, and assumed his most intimidating position. He took a deep breath, expanded his chest outward, and crossed his arms. He stared down at her, his face a stony mask.

"Your da used to give me that same look," she informed him without looking up from her sewing. "I remain as unimpressed with you as I did him. And believe me when I tell you, I was *quite* unimpressed with him. It takes more than brawn to intimidate me, lad. If anything, I should be giving you a talking-to!"

"About what?" he exclaimed.

"Honestly, what were you thinking, kissing the lass in full

view of everyone like that?! Now the entire village thinks you're to be married!"

"That is the point of all this," he snapped back. He rubbed the back of his neck. "Though I'm not quite sure that Gwen wants to marry."

His mother's face didn't change. "And why not? She'd be lucky to be married to a strong warrior such as yourself!"

"Aye!" he agreed.

She rolled her eyes at him. "You've too much pride, Reilly O'Malley. She has her choice of many men. What have you done to earn her attention? Simply be you?"

He wrinkled his forehead. "Ouch, Mam."

"Think on it. Have you wooed her?"

"Nay, I suppose I haven't. But she's my mate. My more pressing need is to obtain her claim on me."

Mary shook her head in disgust. "Reilly O'Malley, *you are an Irishman*."

"I'm aware, Mam."

"Then how can you be so thick-headed? If you want her to claim you, she must be in love with you first. And more than the kissing-in-the-field kind of love," she chided. "Were I in her position, after all she did to show you her affections during all of your acquaintance...Oh! Your first language should be romance! Gaelic second, of course."

He massaged his temples. "Aye, that is sensible. But Gwen doesn't like all that romantic drivel. She's said so, many times. So, do I simply tell her I've claimed her?"

Mary snorted. "Oh, aye, because 'tis every lass's dream to be told she now belongs to you."

Reilly conceded the point. He knew he'd taken her for granted over the years. He could remedy that, though; it was a blunder, but she would forgive him for it if he worked hard to reassure her that it would never happen again.

Maybe.

His throat closed, and a feeling of extreme uncertainty

almost overcame him. If he were a lesser man, he would've said he panicked.

"I'm a bit lost here, Mam," he whispered. "I love her. And I can't live without her."

Mary placed a gentle, weathered hand on his head. "You've got much work ahead of you to convince her that you're serious in your pursuit of her. Kissing her senseless is a good start, but as you know, that won't be enough. Not for someone like her. She demands truth, Reilly."

"Then I'll tell her," he decided, though his heart was beating entirely too fast and his palms were as damp as a lad's. "And I'll hope for a miracle."

Mary laughed and stood, stretching her back. "A miracle 'tis hardly necessary. The lass loved you once; she can love you again. Use what the good Lord gave you, and what the Fates taught you."

He banked the fire. "I'm beginning to realize that I don't quite know how to do that. And, of late, I find myself wishing that I'd never agreed to any of it. I want to forget so much of what I've seen." He hung his head. "Whom I've killed. What I've done."

Mary placed her hand on his shoulder. "You wouldn't have shed any less blood as an O'Malley warrior. You may even had shed it for a less noble purpose."

"I'm not worthy of her love, Mam. I've never been. She is all good, and—"

She held up her hand. "Stop right there, lad. None of this nonsense. You know you're deserving of the same love all those other Protectors found. You've waited more years than any human should. If there is anyone who deserves the love of a good woman, 'tis you, and not because you're my son. Because you have a bigger purpose, and love is the only way to fully achieve it."

"Do you know what my purpose is?" he asked. He stood, rising to his full height. "Did they ever tell you?" Angrily, he dug his nails into the palms of his hands. There were moments he hated his life; always in the service of someone else was indeed noble, but when would he get some happiness of his own?

Mary immediately stepped onto the stool he'd been sitting on, so that they were eye level, and put her hands on her hips. "If you're wanting an argument, you'd best choose another to spar with, because if you think I would willingly hand over my only son to a trio of women with dubious intent, you know me not at all." She huffed out a breath. "Of course I know your purpose. You're Ireland's savior!"

He blinked, momentarily thrown. "What? Nay, I'm an O'Rourke Protector."

"Oh?" She crossed her arms. "Perhaps you ought to explain what you think you've been doing since they took you all those years ago?"

"I've been learning, and teaching others what I know of ancient, medieval, and modern warfare. That knowledge will aid me, and the other Protectors, when the descendant of Brianagh and Nick, who has yet to be born, rises up to save Ireland. All the legend and lore, stories, families and clans— they'll all be destroyed in an act of war if we don't band together and fight with our collective knowledge."

"And you are their leader."

"Well...aye," he agreed. "But—"

"*You* are the laird of the O'Rourke Protectors. *You* are the savior, Reilly. You are the one who has been taught to lead, to understand, and to rally those who are able, to travel to the time and place where you'll all be needed the most, to save your land and your people. You've been building a clan of the best warriors from all times, Reilly."

Shocked, he stared at her. He couldn't draw a full breath; she couldn't be right. He was the chosen bodyguard, not the chosen one. The Fates told him...

Nothing. They never actually told him what his purpose

was; they allowed him to tell them, but they never really told him if he was correct in his assumptions.

He dragged his eyes to his mother's, his world tilting on its axis. "Nay."

She held him steady with her gaze. "Aye, Reilly."

He sat down heavily, all the anger fleeing his body. How could that be? He groomed one O'Rourke from each generation to protect their line. They were to give up their own life to ensure the next Protector would reach adulthood, so that the next could begin his training. And throughout it all, each man swore his loyalty to...

Him.

"This is what they told you?"

She nodded cautiously. "Aye, 'twas. And they warned me not to tell you until you asked me directly. Think about your men, Reilly. *Your* clan. All direct descendants of *yours*."

His men. All those he'd trained, befriended, saved. They swore their loyalty to Reilly, and to the O'Rourke clan. Of which, of course, Reilly was one, thanks to his father's blood. But it didn't matter to the Protectors that Reilly's last name wasn't O'Rourke, and he'd never told any of them about his connection. Only James figured it out.

They swore loyalty to him all the same.

"That's why I was to protect Brianagh," he realized out loud. "So she could begin the line of time travelers, whom I would train, and those Protectors would come when Ireland needed them most?"

"Aye."

"This changes...everything."

"How?" Mary asked, climbing down from the stool.

He dragged in a breath. "I knew I was protecting the O'Rourkes for some greater purpose. My entire life has been to serve them—"

"Us. Use *us*, Reilly, for as much as I love that you bear the

O'Malley name, your father's clan was—*is*—the O'Rourke clan."

"My entire life has been to serve *us*," he amended. "I'd hoped, now that I claimed my mate, that I too would be able to finish my time with them. That I could live as a normal man. Die as a normal man. How can I be with Gwen, knowing that I've no end date? I can do many things, but I can't watch her die, too, Mam."

"'Twas vowed to me, as your mother," Mary replied, "that your soul mate would make you stronger. That your obligation to the Fates ended with her."

"I've claimed her, yet I've not had to battle for Ireland, as is my purpose. So how is my obligation to the Fates complete?"

"Do you think she will claim you?"

Reilly heaved a sigh. "I don't know. But I'm running out of time."

Mary paused. "Perhaps you tell Gwen directly, after all. You won't be holding a sword at her throat, demanding she return the sentiment. She can refuse or receive you at will, but she needs to know what's in your heart. Don't be a fool. Claim her properly, Reilly. The Fates assured me, those many years ago, that your mate would give you everything she had, and more. She would love you with every breath in her body. But, after you said such cruel words to her in her moment of vulnerability, how can you expect her to claim you? Especially if you haven't told her that you love her? No matter how strong the woman," she added softly, "there are only so many times one can expose one's heart. She may have used up all her bravery, Reilly. Perhaps it's your turn to be brave enough for the both of you."

He dropped his head. "Aye. But with all she knows of me...all she's *seen* me do..." He flashed back to the moment she realized he killed the man in the woods, and his stomach roiled. "Mam, *she* needs to decide her future. If I tell her she's my soul mate, she knows that means I would never find happiness if she didn't claim me back. She'd give up her own happiness to ensure mine."

Mary's face softened. "Och, lad, you have much to learn about love."

"I'd be taking her future from her, much as what was done to you."

Mary lifted his face up, forcing him to meet her eyes. "These are but excuses, Reilly. Love requires so much blind faith. You are worthy of her love, and she yours."

He closed his eyes. "I need her to be happy above all else, no matter how that comes about. I don't think she loves me the same way she once did, and even if she does, she may not be able to forgive me for all I've put her through."

"Her love. Your transgressions." Mary kissed his cheek. "You will make her remember one, and she will make you forget the other."

∾

GWEN FUMED.

The morning before Mary's wedding, she sat in a medieval chair, in a medieval cottage, during a medieval rainstorm, and she seethed at herself.

She did what every other woman of his acquaintance did when presented with his affection: she swooned. *Swooned!*

And, to make matters even worse, then she went ahead and did exactly what she swore to herself she wouldn't do: tumble head over heels for him. All it took was one kiss, and she was braiding rainbow ribbons into the manes of unicorns.

And nothing had changed. She *still* was not the woman for him.

She dashed a tear from her cheek and took a deep breath. She was made of sterner stuff than this. She was *better* than this. Yet, as he stood outside and chopped wood (*in the rain, for crying out loud!*), she couldn't help but watch. His tunic was plastered against his chest, his dark chest hair easily visible through the wet fabric. The damn thing had the gall to stick to his abs, too, giving her a perfectly good outline of what she knew was a ridiculously sculpted torso.

She didn't want to think about his ridiculously sculpted *anything*, but alas, Mother Nature didn't care about what she wanted.

Hell, no one cared about what she wanted.

And her chest hurt.

The physical pain was almost too much to bear. She alternated between close to tears and spitting fire.

The tiny part of her that wasn't angry was disappointed. She always harbored a spark of hope that Reilly would one day wake up and realize they were meant to be together. He would show up at her door with chocolates in hand (because really, what good are flowers if they're just going to die? At least chocolates taste good as they disappear.). He'd tell her he'd been so blind, and to please allow him to spend all of eternity showing her how much he loved and appreciated her.

That they were soul mates, destined to each other before time began, and would last after time ended.

She snorted at that image. That wasn't Reilly. It never would be.

The crack of the axe drew her attention back to the man in question, and she looked out the open door at him again. He claimed he needed something to do, so Mary suggested he make himself useful with the axe. It did seem to be depleting the excess energy he held around himself all morning.

The village games were postponed until "later," though Mary admitted that could mean days or weeks from now. With nothing else to do, Mary began to teach Gwen how to knit.

Surprisingly, she enjoyed the rhythmic clacking of Mary's

needles. Unsurprisingly, her needles didn't clack rhythmically or otherwise. She kept dropping them.

After a while, Mary showed her instead how to finger-knit, and Gwen found that to be much easier. Boring, but easier.

"What do you do when you don't have any games to attend?" she asked, trying to loosen one of the yarn loops that had tightened around her forefinger.

"Sew, mostly. Sometimes I'll visit a friend in the village."

Gwen smiled, but inside, a piece of her began to wither and die. She couldn't stay in this tiny cottage and finger-knit until the rain stopped. She'd lose her mind.

"Can I cook something for you?" she offered, placing the yarn tangles aside.

Clack, clack, clack. "Nay, lass, you just enjoy your yarn."

Gwen forced a smile again, then looked with despair at the tangled mess. "Okay, well, I guess I can—"

Thankfully, Reilly chose that moment to enter the house. "'Tis a deluge out there. Mam, you're set with wood, though you'll have to dry it out longer than normal."

She thanked him, though they all knew she wouldn't be using the wood he split, as she'd be moving into the castle well before it dried out.

Clack clack clack.

Did Gwen ever think she enjoyed that sound? Because suddenly, it felt like the sound of death chimes.

Gwen stared morosely at the fire.

"Gwendolyn?"

She snapped to attention, then realized it was Reilly talking. Her expression turned cool. "Yes?"

"Would you care to join me?"

Huh? Clearly, she missed something, though admittedly she hadn't paid any attention to their conversation. She glanced out the small window and raised an eyebrow. "Are you planning to swim somewhere?"

"Nay," he replied off-handedly. "I'd planned to row us there."

Mary snorted out a laugh, and Gwen clenched her teeth. "No, thank you."

"I've much sewing to be done," Mary said helpfully. "Is your needlework better than your knitting?"

"You know it's not," Gwen sighed. She glared at Reilly. "Fine, I'll go with you."

Mary handed her a shawl, which Gwen wrapped around herself, and she and Reilly stepped outside.

Reilly grimaced as he pulled his shirt away from the back of his body. "Let's go to the barn." They walked around the house, and, as promised, there was a small outbuilding. "I need a favor."

Intrigued despite herself, she followed him in.

He pulled his shirt over his head, revealing...

Well, Gwen lost all train of thought at the perfection staring back at her.

He smirked, then flexed a little. She blinked, then gave him a dirty look. "What's the favor?" she barked.

He turned around, his muscled back on full display. "I'm afraid I've—"

"Jesus, Reilly, what happened?" she cried out, rushing to him. An angry red line slashed across his shoulder. "It looks painful!"

He admitted it was slightly painful before handing her a small jar. "When we first arrived, the man's dirk scratched me. I admit I forgot about it until yesterday, when it began to burn."

She carefully opened the jar and wrinkled her nose. "That's pretty strong stuff."

"Aye. Organic, too."

She couldn't contain a small laugh, then gently spread the ointment over the wound. It looked a little bit angry, as it was red and warm to the touch. His muscles jumped as she smoothed her fingers over it.

She finished her ministrations, then handed the jar back to him.

"Thank you."

She shrugged. "Anything else?"

"Aye. There's a wedding to attend, and I find myself in need of a date."

"Have you tried asking anyone?" she replied evenly.

He stepped close to her, and rational thought fled. All she could comprehend was, in order: a) Reilly O'Malley; b) Reilly O'Malley without a shirt; and c) Reilly O'Malley, looking as though she was his most favorite meal, and he'd been fasting for weeks.

"Gwendolyn Allen." He stepped closer, their bodies almost touching, his voice gravelly and his breathing as uneven as hers. "Will you do me the very great honor of standing by my side at my mother's wedding tomorrow morning?"

She gritted her teeth against her initial reaction and stepped away from him. "No."

He nodded. "I deserved that. And what I don't deserve is an answer to my next question, but I pray you might find it in your sweet soul to provide me one."

She remained silent, waiting.

"I've made mistakes with you, Gwen. Big mistakes—"

She held up her hands, her traitorous eyes filling with tears. "Stop. I don't want to hear any more."

"Please, Gwendolyn. Can you forgive me?"

She shook her head. "There's nothing to forgive, Reilly." He stepped towards her, but she matched it with a step backward. She shook her head. "No. I can't do this. Not again."

She heard his words trail after her as she fled from the outbuilding, back to the house.

"I will have my words with you, lass. And they will be soon."

~

Watching his mother depart with the laird's messenger, Reilly wondered at the changes that were happening. History as he knew it was being rewritten, and he wasn't quite sure he liked where 'twas going.

While he was glad that his sister had found love, and he was relieved that his mother would be secure in her marriage to the laird, the unsettling feeling in his gut gave him pause.

The feeling was similar to the first time he rode in an airplane. His stomach felt as though it was floating uncomfortably in his body, alternating between shooting up to his throat, then hovering somewhere under his ribs, then dropping to his knees.

Reilly turned and caught sight of Gwen in front of the mirror.

He had the same kind of feeling now, though he suspected his stomach wasn't the only organ that danced about.

He watched her wind her plaited hair around her head and was reminded of the first time he watched her do the same. He still wasn't sure why she agreed to fly to a country she never been to, to see a man she barely knew. Perhaps it was her sense of adventure, or the folly of her youth. But he was grateful she took the chance all the same.

When she'd been staying at his cottage for a pair of days, during that first trip out to see him, he recognized that her attraction to him made her a little nervous. It didn't put her at ease that he ensured he gave off no reciprocal response; after all, she was but twenty-one, a mere child in the modern world. To pursue her would end in disaster; he had just handed over Brianagh to Nioclas and didn't know if he was to have another assignment, or if he'd be sent back to the past to live out the rest of his days. Gwen hadn't seen anything of the world, and she was eager to get out there and conquer it.

That first night she was in town, they planned to go into Dublin city center. Twenty minutes after she said she'd "be just a minute," Reilly went looking for her to see if she perhaps forgotten the way out of her room. When he came to her open door, he halted, struck witless at the sight in front of him.

Gwen had been seated at the small vanity he placed in the room before she arrived. Masses of red curls tumbled over her hands as she struggled to grasp it all, her eyes closed as she wrestled with it. Her elegant neck was fully exposed from the back, and Reilly stared at it, unable to comprehend why the sight of it was more alluring than any of the pretty faces he'd seen in all his years.

She had let out a frustrated sigh and her eyes popped open, immediately catching sight of him in the mirror. "I know I'm taking a long time. I'm sorry. I just can't get all my hair up. I banged my wrist this morning, and it's really sore," she rushed to explain. "If I leave my hair down, I'll get really hot while dancing."

"May I assist?" he asked.

She nodded and explained to him how to gather it all and pull it through the hair tie. He gently gathered the silky strands, the feel of each one branding his skin. The fruity smell wafted to him, enveloping his senses fully, and he was rendered immobile for a long moment.

"Reilly?" she had asked uncertainly.

He'd shaken himself out of his reverie. "Just trying to figure out how not to snap this," he covered, testing the elasticity of the hair tie. He managed to do as she asked, and though it was far from perfect, she gave him a beatific smile and didn't touch it for the rest of the night.

Pulling himself back to the present, Reilly reminded

himself to breathe. He was a seasoned warrior. Battle-hardened. He stared death in the face and laughed outright.

Looking at Gwen's profile now, he didn't feel much like laughing. In fact, he felt as though he might cast up his accounts all over her beautiful red dress.

Dealing with a feisty redhead who was still angry with him was a battle he was ill-prepared to fight.

He needed to apologize to her, ask for her forgiveness, tell her he was hers for as long as she'd have him (which, he hoped, was for eternity). And then, perhaps, he could dust off his chivalry and woo the lass the way she deserved to be wooed.

She caught sight of him watching her and rolled her eyes as she slid the last pin in place. "I won't make us late for your mother's wedding. Come on."

He held out his arm.

"I don't need you to pull some Neanderthal move to let everyone know I'm yours," she sniffed. "I am quite capable of walking myself to the castle."

He merely continued to hold it out.

He watched her struggle with herself before she sighed lightly.

She frowned at his arm, but finally took it. "Fine."

She tried to charge toward the open door, but he slowed her. "We need speech, Gwen."

She set her jaw. "So this is why you sent your mother ahead? You want to do this now?"

"Aye. I need your forgiveness."

She kept her eyes on the sodden ground as they trudged forward, almost ambling, toward the village. "Can we just pretend like this never happened?"

"That what never happened? My feelings for you? Our kiss? The attraction we've fought for years?"

"All of it?"

"If there's one thing we've always had, Gwen, 'tis our

trust in each other. Trust that we'd always be honest with each other. 'Tis what makes us work." He let her think on that for a moment. "Ready for the hard questions, Gwen?"

"No," she grumbled.

He paused. She could be stubborn, but once she forgave, she didn't hold a grudge.

She seemed to be holding a grudge at the moment.

He focused on the real point of their conversation. "What happened in Venezuela?"

She gasped, her hand fluttering in an entirely un-Gwen-like movement, to her throat. "What makes you think anything happened there?"

"It was on the news, you know. I know about the deaths. And you haven't been quite yourself."

She looked away. "I've been fine."

He drew them to a halt. He gently grasped her chin and drew her face toward his again. "Have you, Gwen?"

She took a step back, out of his reach. "Well, I've had some tough moments, I guess. But overall, I'd say I'm the same as I ever was." She held her hands out and gave him a false, bright smile. "See? Still me."

"Don't jest about this, Gwen. I know you. You *know* I know you. So perhaps you can do as you always have, and be honest with me. What was your real reason for coming to, and staying in, Ireland?"

Her entire body went still.

"You could easily had your dress for Colin's wedding sent to America," he pointed out. "You could have stayed in your lovely house by the sea, during your most favorite time of year, and fiddled with your investments, as you love to do. You could've gone to Georgia, and spent time enjoying the pleasures to be found in its cities. But you didn't. And even when Ellie went back to the States with Colin for who knows what—"

"Investors," she supplied.

He arched a brow. "Not that it matters, but all right, when they went back for the *investors*, you stayed. So, I'll ask again. Why did you come, then *stay*, in Ireland?"

Her shoulders dropped, as though a hundred-pound sack had fallen onto them, and she covered her face with her hands.

"Stop," came the muffled reply.

"Have I ever told you that you frighten the daylights out of me?" he asked. She kept her hands on her face, but she shook her head, so he continued. "Aye. I've felt no fear when a sword's come at my neck. Actually, I rather look forward to those moments, as they make me feel alive. The moments that follow make me feel grateful to be alive. But it's the moments well after, once the swords have been put away and 'tis just me and my cup in front of a fire, that make me feel the most. You know what I feel, Gwen?"

She peeked at him from between her fingers.

"I feel so damn lucky. I've my head atop my shoulders, my feet warm by a fire, and you in my life. And though you may not be sitting next to me at that moment, you are always foremost in my mind."

She shuddered, and he took that as a good sign.

"You and me, Gwendolyn. You're a part of me, a part of my soul."

"Not all of it, though."

"All of what?"

She didn't bother to clarify. "Anthony asked me not to go to Ireland. He demanded it, even. But I had to. I needed to feel like the world couldn't get me. A safe place, you know? And I went to the safest place I knew."

"Where?" he demanded. He needed her to say the words, to realize what she was saying. A primitive, visceral need that wouldn't be fulfilled unless she understood what she was saying to him. How she was claiming him.

She dropped her hands and looked up. Her eyes, the exact

color of the lichens he'd always associated with home, held an emotion he wasn't sure how to interpret.

"Where's the safest place you know, Gwendolyn?"

She gulped. "In your arms."

An enormous burst of elation engulfed Reilly, and it took every ounce of his self-control not to crush her into him.

She continued, "I just…needed that. Everything was so bad, Ry…I was helpless to stop the panic, because those were my friends, and I watched them die. And I was almost in that van."

His heart ached for her. He knew the pain she felt, the survivor's guilt she experienced. He told her he understood it because he'd lived it, time and again.

She nodded, but the shadows in her eyes didn't vanish, so he pulled her close.

"I don't need you to save me," she murmured softly. "I like it, sometimes. But I don't need it."

He stepped back and gently grasped her hands. He searched her troubled, wet eyes, noting that he'd seen her tears more in the last few days than all their time together. "Aye, Gwendolyn. I know."

He watched her throat work to swallow and her eyes attempt to look anywhere but in his. She started to speak, stopped, started again, then stopped again, stuck in an endless loop of silence.

"Whatever you need to say, say. But give me the truth, Gwendolyn."

She looked at him with clouded eyes, and a small frown formed around her mouth. "I'm scared."

"Of what?"

"Of us."

He rubbed circles on her palms and remained silent.

"If I let myself love you the way I stupidly seem to need to, then…don't you get it? I won't survive it, Reilly."

"Would loving me be so bad?"

"Maybe." She pulled away from him, and he let her go. "Since the day I met you, I've been living half a life. I gave you my heart over and over, but you kept on rejecting it. Do you even know what that does to a woman?"

He absently rubbed his heart. "I was a fool."

"Yeah, you were! But I could handle that, because you didn't make me any promises. When you give your word, O'Malley, you keep it. So if you make me a promise, I believe it with my whole heart. But if you break that promise, I won't be able to survive it." A sheen of tears blurred her eyes. "Moving on from you was the smartest thing I've ever done. And now here you are, twisting everything up. I'm not sure I can give you my heart again. And I don't think I'm willing to take that risk."

His chest constricted with such force, Reilly almost lost his breath.

"I want to be someone's everything," she whispered, her eyes luminous and open. "I want to find happiness where I can, because I know now that life can end at any second. I came to Ireland because I told myself I needed to restore my soul. But I stayed because, as it turns out, I didn't really need to restore it. I just needed the other half of it."

His constricted chest loosened, and he felt a swift, staggering sense of relief. "Gwen—"

She waved him off. "So I have to ask, and you have to be honest with me, Reilly." She searched his eyes. "Do you know who your soul mate is?"

"Aye."

"Did you know immediately that she was the one?"

He swallowed hard. "Aye, I did."

"And did you claim her?"

He closed the distance between them. "I did. But—"

She shook her head quickly, halting his next words, her expression tortured. "Stop. I don't want to hear any more."

He frowned. "But—"

"No," she said, her voice clear. "Please. Not right now. Let's go see your mother married, then see if we can get home. I need some space to think."

"But Gwen—"

"Please, Ry." Her face held such emotion, it rooted him to the spot, and he was filled with the need to ensure she had whatever she asked for, no matter what it was. The chapel bells chimed in the distance, signaling the start of the wedding procession, and she started jogging towards the sound. Over her shoulder, she said clearly, "I know we're not soul mates. I just have to figure out if I'm willing to be anything less." Her eyes, luminous behind the tears, beseeched him. "Please drop this Reilly. For now, at least."

He'd never known true pain until this moment, and he had to admit, it wasn't anything he'd ever desired to experience in the first place.

"Gwen, you're—"

"*Please*, Reilly."

And, like the coward he didn't know he was until that moment, he did as she asked, and dropped it.

Reilly watched, his arms folded and his face expressionless, as his mother promised to honor and obey Laird O'Malley for the rest of her days.

If he were to give into any sort of expression, he wasn't sure what would win out: one of relief that his mother and sister were settled, protected, and very possibly loved, or one of laughter that the laird seemed to believe Mary would obey him within the castle walls. Or one of profound despair that his love was heartbroken.

The priest droned on, and Gwen began to fidget. Reilly smiled inwardly; she was terrible at sitting still. He doubted that would ever change, and he wanted, with a desire bordering on desperate, to be by her side forever, so that he may enjoy that energy for all his days.

Not soul mates. What utter rubbish. He should've claimed her the first night they met while they sat at the bar drinking their whiskey.

He leaned closer to her. "Careful, lass. You don't want to bring attention to yourself. Did Emma ever tell you how she ended up married to that toothless beggar of hers?"

"Aidan's not toothless," she whispered back, her lips barely moving. "And he's definitely *not* a beggar."

"I've yet to determine why all the womenfolk find him so pleasing."

"Perhaps it's due to his smiles and charm," she replied. "You ought to try it, see where it gets you."

He snorted. "Emma was an unwed lass at the MacWilliam castle. From what I was told, her beauty caught the eye of a MacWilliam ally, and he wanted to have her. Needless to say, she found herself engaged and married in the same day."

"Was it what she wanted at the time?"

He kept his eyes forward and murmured, "Who would want to marry such a one as Aidan MacWilliam?"

Gwen rolled her eyes. "I'm going to tell him you said that."

"Nothing he hasn't heard before, I assure you."

"I'm trying to pay attention to the wedding. So cut bait already. Why are you telling me all this?" she whispered, exasperated.

Meaningfully, he dragged his gaze to the other side of her. Against the chapel wall, an older clansman was openly ogling Gwen. When she caught sight of him, he gave her a nearly toothless smile and a waggle of his bushy brows. Then he blew her a kiss, pointed to her, then himself, then the priest.

"Toothless beggar," Reilly whispered, laughter lacing his words.

Gwen's head snapped forward. "Did you put him up to that?" she whispered furiously.

Reilly chuckled softly. "Nay, lass. 'Tis Niall, and he's a clan elder. If he goes to the laird to demand you become his wife, I'll be forced to either hand you over or wed you myself."

"I think I'm going to be sick," she said faintly.

"There, now. Niall's a nice enough lad."

"You wouldn't do that to me. He's old enough to be my grandfather!"

Reilly fought a smile. "Age is but a number…"

"Shut *up*, O'Malley," she hissed.

The priest placed Mary's hand in Darragh's, then began winding a rope around their wrists.

Reilly kept his face neutral and his voice low. "I'd like to point out that I still have all my teeth. That should put me at least a bit ahead to win your affections?"

"You're so funny," she managed.

He took pity on her. "The other option, of course, is a bit of travel. New destination, new time."

She stiffened. "Because your *purpose* has been realized?"

"Aye. And I was quite mistaken in what it was."

Mary repeated her vows in a crisp voice. They turned to sign the dower papers which, Reilly saw his mother realize, had been taken care of by him.

There was no way she would be giving up everything of hers to Darragh, no matter that he was laird. The woman had been through enough, having lost her husband to an early death and her son to otherworldly activities. She could keep her cottage, her land, and her gold.

Mary looked at him, and she gave him the tiniest of smiles. He winked.

"What's happening?" Gwen asked, noticing their exchange.

He leaned down to her ear. "When a widow marries a second time, she gives over everything she has to her new husband. That includes all her land and gold. But I had speech with Laird Darragh to ensure my mother is well taken care of."

Gwen smiled softly. "That was kind of you."

He cleared his throat. "Well. She's my mam."

Gwen fell blessedly silent, and they watched the rest of the ceremony in silence.

Later, when the festivities were well underway, Reilly felt the hairs on the back of his neck prickle, and he knew it was time.

He looked down at Gwen and found her looking up at him. "Do you feel it, too?"

"I do," she replied quietly. "It's an odd feeling. What's it mean?"

"It means that I had the right of it, and I realized my true purpose in coming here. And now 'tis time to take our leave," he concluded. "'Tis my experience that we have just enough time to say our goodbyes, then find a secluded spot."

He made his way to his mother, who, despite complaining loudly about having little time to plan a wedding, looked quite happy.

Her smile turned a bit wobbly upon his approach. She murmured something to her new husband, who waved her off toward Gwen and him.

Mary calmly took Reilly's other arm, and he maneuvered both women outside the castle. As soon as they rounded the corner, Mary teared up.

"Oh, Mam, no," he exclaimed, aghast. He'd seen his mother cry exactly three times in his life, and each time was worse than the last.

Gwen pulled Mary into her arms. "Why are you crying?" she asked tenderly. "You know he'll come back to see you."

Mary shook her head, her voice catching. "N-no he won't." She wiped her tears, though they continued to fall.

"Reilly, my love, I saw them. The Mother, she came to me, and she told me you'd be saying your final goodbye."

"Seems a bit overdramatic," he soothed. "Mam, you've no reason to be so upset. I'm taking Gwen home. I'll be back when I can."

Mary sniffled; then, in Gaelic, she said, "Nay, Reilly, you won't. This is it. We've new paths now. I'm not sure how I was when you saw me in my other future, but the Fate visited me before I walked into the chapel today. She told me that changes have begun. I know not what your future holds, but I know that for mine, this will be the last *I* see of you."

Speechless, he looked at her tear-stained face. What was this madness? Why were things changing? How were they changing?

She tugged him down to her and cradled his face in her hands. "Love her well, son. She's a good woman. I fear that she, as your mate, has many trials in front of her. Have patience. But mostly, just love her. Marry her, give her bairns. They'll keep her company on the cold nights when you might not be able to warm her bed."

He looked at her in alarm. "Are you trying to tell me that my life is in danger?"

"It's always been in danger," she confessed. "But you've had the guiding hands of the Fates to help you along. I fear that time has also come to an end." She swallowed hard. "Be safe, Reilly." She turned to Gwen, and in English, she managed, "I'm so happy to have met you, Gwendolyn. Love him."

Gwen nodded wordlessly, sadness etched into her features. While he knew she didn't understand the exchange he and his mother had, she seemed to understand the gravity of it.

Mary hugged Gwen, then she hugged Reilly. And if he held her a bit tighter, a bit longer, than he ever had previously, and if perhaps the dust from the ground at their feet made his eyes water fiercely, he rather thought no one could blame him.

"Go," Mary rasped, slipping from his arms. "Be off. Be safe." She kissed him on the cheek, her tears spilling onto her cheeks. "I am grateful, you know. Many mothers do not see their sons to manhood. Most mothers do not see their sons happy in life. I'm blessed to have had both visions."

With that, she turned and fled back to the castle, leaving Reilly staring helplessly after her.

Gwen tugged gently on his arm. "Come on, Ry. It's time to go."

He nodded once, not trusting himself to speak past the lump in his throat, and allowed her to lead him away from the small but safe pile of stones where his mother would live out the rest of her days.

After ensuring no one had followed, Reilly tucked them against a copse of trees. Gwen placed her arms around his waist, but he wasn't taking any chances. He easily lifted her, and she wrapped her arms around his neck.

"I don't want to lose you," he explained hoarsely.

She smiled gently. "Nor I, you."

The iron fist that had locked itself around his heart eased slightly. He drew a breath, then tightened his hold on Gwen with his left arm. He extended his right arm, held out his right hand, fingers splayed, and murmured the ancient words and sounds that would take them home. He quickly turned his fingers inward to his palm, and the air began to shimmer around them. He clasped Gwen to him with both arms a half-second before shards of light began pelting their bodies. The trees spun away, the currents lifting Gwen's hair to encircle them both in its radiance, and a dizzying moment later, the air settled.

CHAPTER 13

"*I*'ll be glad to see a coffee shop." Gwen strove for a light tone as she beat the dust from her gown.

"Not a fan of medieval ale and wine?" he teased, though his eyes were alert to their surroundings.

Gwen glanced up at him curiously, her heart constricting a little at the sight of him. His hair blew around his face in the wind, and his tunic, while not pristine white, was clean enough that the scent of soap wafted in her general direction. The léine danced around his knees, and he loosened his sword from the straps on his back.

"Why are you looking around like you're expecting an ambush? We're home...right?" Almost as soon as the words left her mouth, voices called out in Gaelic, and Gwen groaned, "Oh, come *on!*"

Reilly called back, and Gwen let out a sigh. He gave her a small smile. "Looks like I was sent somewhere other than my planned destination."

"Which was home, right?"

He nodded, then tucked her protectively behind him as riders approached. They spoke in rapid-fire Gaelic, and it ended with the men on horseback welcoming him with much happiness.

One of the warriors slipped off his horse and handed the reins to Reilly, then joined one of his clansmen on his horse.

"I explained you were fatigued," Reilly told her as he lifted her onto the animal.

"I'm not!" Gwen replied indignantly. "I can walk!"

"So can I. But as we have no idea where to go, and haven't quite figured out how far we are from where we might want to be, I thought this would be easier."

"Oh. Good plan." She fell silent as he swung himself up easily behind her. The group of men and beasts swung around and began trotting through the thick forest.

Minutes passed before Gwen ventured, "Do you know where we are?"

He had just begun speaking to one of the others when she'd asked, and he said, in English, "Of course." It came out as *ov cairse*, his accent thickening due to the switch in languages, and he gently rubbed a circle on her arm. "It's the *when* I'm not quite sure about. Worry not, lass. I'll keep you safe."

She looked around her with a touch of wonder and resignation. "Is this really what your life is like all the time?"

His chuckle vibrated against her back. "What, you mean walking through a forest, in a time unknown, with a dozen heavily-armed lads speaking in foreign tongues, leading us to a castle?" He paused, then deadpanned, "Aye. You can't say I don't know how to show a lady a good time."

She laughed despite herself. "We're safe, really?"

"Never safer, except were we sitting in my living room, sipping that coffee you were looking forward to but a few moments ago."

"Thanks for the reminder," Gwen muttered. But she wondered if she'd ever again sit in his living room, sipping coffee as though she hadn't a care in the world.

Things had changed, and she was still reeling from it.

They passed more trees, meadows, and tended fields, and Gwen wondered how Reilly was able to tell *any* time apart, language aside. Rural Ireland, to her, looked exactly the same, no matter what century she was in. Thousands of shades of green, pretty vistas in every direction, low stone walls, and sheep.

So. Many. Sheep.

Eventually, Gwen caught sight of a castle, rising majestically against the glittering sea behind it, and she sat up straighter.

"Is that...?"

Reilly's arms tightened around her, sending a thrill through her.

"As I said. Never safer. At least in medieval Ireland."

A small village came into view, and Gwen saw the tidy village green where she'd danced to a medieval song in the firelight. She remembered the faire, with all its food, music, and activities, and the swell of joy almost overwhelmed her.

That night, so long ago, before everything went to hell in a hand basket.

How times have changed, she mused morosely. Now, she'd never been so unsure of anything in her life.

"Well," she managed after a moment, "I think someone might be disappointed at our arrival."

"Lady Brianagh is never disappointed in my visits." Reilly twisted her slightly, so that she was looking back at him. "The laird never dares question my appearances, either."

"Not them. Claire. You arrived without a gift, and you always bring her a gift."

He searched her face for a moment before a slow smile spread. "Ah, lass. You underestimate me. Of course I've brought the spoiled chit a gift."

Gwen furrowed her brow. "What'd you bring her?"

He turned her forward again. "A visit with you."

"Sir Reilly! Lady Gwen!"

Reilly swung down from his horse and gently lowered Gwen to the ground. Around them, the courtyard buzzed with activity, and amid it all stood a serene, radiant Brianagh MacWilliam.

"Lady MacWilliam," Reilly intoned, affecting a deep bow, keeping Gwen's hand in his.

"Oh, shut up already and give me a hug," she snorted with an impatient smile as she approached them.

Reilly lifted Gwen's hand and gave her knuckles a soft kiss, then turned and swept Bri into his arms. "Lass. 'Tis good to see you so well."

"A bit more gray hair than the last time I saw you, but all in all, I couldn't be happier," Bri replied, hugging him tightly. She lowered her voice to a whisper. "It's 1485. And I see Gwen hasn't aged a day, so I'm guessing it hasn't been that long since you last visited me?"

"Mere months," he confirmed.

"Time is a strange thing," she murmured, releasing him.

A long-suffering sigh sounded from behind him, and Reilly smiled into Brianagh's amused face as a voice intoned, "O'Malley. Why is it that every time I see you, I must remind you to remove your hands from my wife?"

With a serious expression, Reilly faced Nioclas MacWilliam. "And why is it that every time I see you, you look a wee bit softer than the last time I saw you?"

"You'll pay for that slight in the lists," Nick warned, before a small smile graced his handsome features. "Welcome back, cousin."

"Good to be back, my laird." Reilly embraced him and they slapped each other on the back. "I've brought Lady Gwendolyn, as she was most anxious to visit with Lady Claire. Is she home?"

Nick's features darkened for a moment. "She is. Is aught all right?"

"We'll have speech later."

Nick nodded and they joined Bri and Gwen, who were animatedly discussing Colin and Ellie's upcoming wedding.

"Come, you must be exhausted from your travels," Bri declared. "I sent for a bath upon word of your arrival."

"Your scouts are impressive," Reilly noted, following them into the grand doorway of the castle. "We made excellent time."

"New steeds," Nick explained. "I've been breeding faster horses from a pair of Arabians I bought from a trader on the mainland."

"There will be time for that later," Bri said gently, laying her hand on her husband's arm. Her sapphire eyes twinkled. "All I've been hearing about for the last three years are these horses, and while I'm sure Ry and Gwen would love to also hear about them, let's allow them to take a few moments of rest before supper." To Reilly, she said, "Your room remains unchanged. I've put Gwen in the east wing—"

"Nay. She takes the room adjoining mine," Reilly cut in swiftly.

Bri blinked. "Reilly, you know we can't do that."

He firmed his jaw. "Then she stays in my room."

"O'Malley," Nick said sharply, "she's an unwed lass. Have a care for her reputation."

Reilly remained silent. He knew that reputations were important to the laird's direct family, and less so for the rest of the clan. He also knew that Nick would never allow Gwen to stay in his room, but Nick didn't know what Gwen had been through. He didn't know that she still had nightmares at night, or that the only thing that soothed her in her sleep was his arms.

Even Gwen didn't realize that.

But he refused to be so far from her. He would explain

nothing, and, glancing at Bri, knew she understood that truth. She canted her head in agreement and said softly, "We'll move you to Gwen's adjoining chamber, then, if that's amenable to you?" She looked at Gwen questioningly.

"If it's no trouble," she replied uncertainly, clearly wondering what had come over him.

Reilly gently took her hand in his. "'Tisn't any trouble."

Shafts of light fell across the great hall, catching in Gwen's eyes. Momentarily lost in the green depths, Reilly snapped back to attention when Bri tapped his arm.

"I think it best if I deliver Gwen to her bath, and you go with Nick." She lowered her voice. "He's been worried about Claire lately. She's been preoccupied. And she's refused every suitor he's brought forth. I fear she's trying to make herself unmarriageable."

"Is that even a word?" Reilly asked dryly.

"How old is she?" Gwen wondered.

"A score and two."

A small knot appeared on Gwen's forehead. "Weren't you thirty when you married?"

"Twenty-nine," Brianagh replied matter-of-factly, "but my circumstances were a bit different than Claire's."

"Oh, aye. Was the greatest difference how you were so very willing to meet MacWilliam at the altar?" His dry tone remained unchanged.

"It's a simple thing to ignore him when he prattles on," Brianagh murmured to Gwen.

"He does make it so easy," Gwen agreed, a smile playing about her lips.

At Reilly's narrowed eyes, unable to contain their mirth, the women started laughing.

"You dare tease a warrior?" Nioclas asked Gwen curiously. "Have things changed so much since your last visit?"

"I think I was a little…surprised for the duration of my

last visit," Gwen mused. She slid a glance to Reilly, who still held her hand in his.

"But aye," Reilly added, his eyes never leaving Gwen's. "Things have indeed changed."

"I see," Bri murmured, delight in her voice. "I cannot believe I have, in my castle, the woman who's brought Reilly O'Malley to heel."

"I'm not a dog," Ry snapped.

"My love, be sure to set guards at the coastline," she continued, as though he hadn't spoken.

Nioclas closed his eyes for a moment before asking, "Though I know I'm going to regret asking…why would I do that?"

"For the scores of women sure to throw themselves into the ocean once it's known he's no longer available, of course."

"Brianagh…" Reilly warned, an uncomfortable feeling settling between his shoulder blades.

Gwen stifled a laugh behind her hand.

"Oh, think that's funny?" he demanded.

Bri fluttered her hand to her chest in an over exaggerated gesture. "Oh, Gwen, the stories I have for you. You know, he used to brag all the time how the lasses adored his—"

"Come, O'Malley," Nioclas interrupted loudly, "and let's leave the women to their…"

"Inanities?" Reilly supplied.

"Payback for a dateless teenage experience?" Bri suggested sweetly.

Reilly grit his teeth. "I was keeping you safe from those worthless lads."

"I appreciate that effort," Nick put in.

Gwen's head went from person to person in a desperate attempt to keep up with the fast banter. "Dateless? You began a matchmaking empire, though…"

"She did, because she's uncommonly clever and can read people very well," Nioclas boasted.

"Not all people," Reilly replied smugly.

Bri snorted. "Please. Even had I tried to match you, your stubbornness would've ensured that any woman I put forth would've had a wonderful time, but no followup. And I knew you well enough that when, at my first truly big wedding— remember? The Bouchement wedding?—you said your life had changed in an inst—"

"Lass, here's your chamber," Reilly said hurriedly, pushing open the heavy wooden door.

"What happened at that wedding?" Gwen asked Bri, her eyes going wide as she craned her neck around Reilly's hulking form.

Reilly gently pushed Gwen into the room. "Bath, then food, then sleep. I daresay we all need it."

Bri looked uneasily at Reilly, then she nodded slowly. "Aye. Rest from your journey, Lady Gwendolyn."

Reilly continued, desperate to move the conversation to safer waters, "Look, lass, your bath stands at the ready. Wouldn't want it to get cold."

Gwen's face took on a calculated expression, and he just barely managed not to gulp.

He was a warrior. A man without fear. "Take your bath, lass. We'll have speech later."

She threw him one last, searching look, then acquiesced and closed the door.

Brianagh chewed her lip. "I'm missing something."

"You usually are."

She canted her head at him. "I'll figure it out, if you won't tell me. But I'm on your side, Reilly. I'm always on your side."

He dragged his hand down his face, then silently marched himself out toward the laird's solar, Nick following at a more sedate pace.

A reckoning was coming, and he hadn't a clue how to prepare for it.

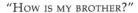

"How is my brother?"

Reilly folded his arms and leaned against the wall of Nioclas's solar, schooling his features into a mask of inscrutability. "He's alive and well, living a good life with his lady wife."

"Any bairns?"

Reilly did smile a little at that. "Aye, she's carrying their first right now, though they've not announced it."

Nioclas laughed. "That lass, she is amazing."

Reilly tipped his head in agreement. "Aye. She deserves so much more than what that lout can give her, but she seems happy, so I merely observe, standing ready to rescue her once she comes to her senses."

Nioclas settled himself on the edge of the desk, a small smile gracing his features. "Ah, but 'tis love. It makes no sense, there's no direction to it. It simply is."

"Well, that's terrifying."

Nick barked out a laugh. "Though it's been almost three decades, I well remember the fear I felt when I realized I loved my own sweet wife." He took stock of Reilly and let out a hearty sigh. "Ah, what I wouldn't give to be as young as you, lad."

"Careful what you wish for," Reilly warned. He pushed off the wall and paced. "Believe it or not, Nick, I want what you have."

"I'm a lucky man," Nick agreed immediately. "I've a wife whom I love with every breath in my soul, four sons I've seen into adulthood, and a daughter who, while trying at times, is more intelligent than anyone I've ever known."

"And you haven't had to watch them die."

"Aye, you've the right of it. My blessings are great indeed. But yours are as well. 'Twould seem you're finally beginning your life."

"My life was to protect Brianagh."

Nick nodded. "Aye, and grateful does not convey the depths of gratitude I have for your careful attention to her over those years."

Reilly waved that away. "Since her, I've been given no specific task from the Fates. No one to protect, no one to teach."

Pensively, Nick stroked his chin.

Reilly paced faster. "I've no purpose right now. I'm at a bit of a loss as to what I'm supposed to be doing."

"Must you be doing something?"

Reilly shrugged. "I've known nothing else since the day I was chosen by the Fates. I've always had something to do, someone to watch over. But for the last pair of years…just watching out for Claire."

"Strange, how but a pair of years has passed for you, yet so many more have passed here," Nioclas murmured softly. "Stranger still, how it continues to give me pains in my head when I overthink it too much."

"I admit to never having the problem of overthinking anything before," Reilly grumbled, accepting the cup of ale Nick held out. He took a sip of it and stared into the brew, as if it held the answers to the questions he didn't know.

"Before?"

Before Gwen. Before he realized that, for the first time, he hadn't the answers in front of him. He wasn't certain that the Fates would allow him to live a full life. He wasn't certain he could convince them to do so. He didn't know how he and Gwen would make their lives together work, when he was constantly pulled to different times. He wasn't certain that Gwen would still love him, when she could only have part of him. He wasn't sure if Gwen could handle growing older, while he remained frozen in time.

He simply wasn't certain, and that was a first for him. And he had no idea how to deal with it.

He realized he'd spoken aloud when Nick slapped him on the back. "Uncertainty is a difficult thing, cousin. It can eat you alive, turning you from a warrior into a weakling if you let it."

"I've no idea what to do next."

Nick downed his own ale. "You make a decision, then see it through. And if, when you're in the midst of seeing it through, you realize that the decision needs to be changed, you change it. *You* change it. Not Fate. Not circumstances." He held Reilly's eyes. "*You.*"

With a start, Reilly saw how Nioclas had been so powerful for so long. Since the tender age of twelve, Nick shouldered more responsibility than anyone Reilly knew, save himself. He'd matured quickly, then sharpened into a clever, compassionate clan laird.

Nick led a mostly peaceful existence since his marriage began, yet his clansmen were still battle-ready, willing to die to defend their laird. Reilly heard them even now, the sounds of steel on steel from the lists a faint sound through the alcove window. Nioclas ensured that those around him knew things could change in an instant, and he was ready for that instant, whenever it may happen.

Living a life of peace did not make Laird MacWilliam complacent; nay, it only made him profoundly grateful for what he'd worked to achieve, and it made his clansmen eager to preserve it. They had something to fight for.

Reilly understood, with a sudden clarity, that he also had something to fight for, were he brave enough to march into the fray without knowing the final outcome.

"Aye," he said slowly, gazing up at the tapestry his mother created so many years ago. The Fates certainly marred the fabric of time in whatever ways pleased them. Perhaps, Reilly mused, it was time for him to mar his own tapestry. He handed Nick his cup. "'Tis about time I took my life in my own hands."

"You might fail."

"Thanks for the confidence."

Nick didn't look perturbed. "It's a fact we all must face at some point in our lives, Reilly. 'Tis only then that we begin to truly live."

"The Americans have a saying. Failure is not an option. And it isn't, not now, not with Gwen."

"Ah. So we *are* talking about her."

Reilly chuckled. Nick's nonchalance fooled no one. "I claimed her to the Fates. So it's out there, swirling about the universe."

"The Fates aren't the ones who make this decision, O'Malley. 'Tis but you and your lady love. You have to give her the choice. Look at what happened to Colin. The fool almost lost his soul mate because he tried to make the decision for her."

"I don't want to make the decision for her," he admitted, shoving his hands through his hair. "But her happiness is more important than mine. For a long time, I went back and forth. Do I let her go, and allow her to live a lifetime of peace with another man? Do I push her into his arms, and revel in the fact that she doesn't have to grow old while I don't, or wake up to a cold bed because I've been called away for some mission?" He stopped and drew a deep breath, then looked at Nick. "I never was so undecided about anything before. With everything else in my life, every path was clearly marked out. I knew the consequences of my actions before I took them. But in this? I've no idea which way is up, nor down."

"Blind faith," Nick said knowingly, although his tone was one of understanding. "You must trust in something, O'Malley. May as well make it love."

"Love seems a risky trade."

"Oh, 'tis. But the riches of it can be worth more than you can imagine."

～

GWEN SEPARATED THE STRANDS OF HER HAIR, HOPING IT WOULD dry faster in front of the fire. A lady's maid laid out a beautiful gown of deep navy with silver trim.

The MacWilliam colors.

The chambermaid helped Gwen into a long white nightgown, then bobbed a curtsy before leaving Gwen with her thoughts.

Easing back onto the small-backed stool, Gwen tried to relax her shoulders. The window in her chamber showed night had fallen in full.

As she looked around the luxurious chamber, she admitted to being grateful for accommodations such as this. The large, four-poster bed had its curtains drawn back, showcasing the sumptuous furs and coverings that looked soft enough to bury into on a cold night.

And, being that they were in Ireland, in September, the nights weren't exactly tropical.

She knew from experience that the feather and straw mattresses in the MacWilliam castle were free of vermin and fleas; a luxury, to be sure. And she dragged her bare toe over the uneven but smooth stone on the floor, marveling that it didn't feel gritty. When she was in the castle last, Reilly told her many stories of staying in various places where the floors were covered in rushes filled with rotting foodstuffs and the mattresses were so infested with fleas that the stables were a preferable chamber in which to pass the night.

Brianagh had very high and exacting standards, and though the chambermaids might grumble about the extra work, they all slept in fine beds, ate good food, practiced twenty-first century hygiene habits, and were healthier than anyone had a right to be in the Middle Ages.

A gentle knock on her door revealed Brianagh, carrying a

tray of food. "I thought you might be hungry. Time traveling tends to do that to a person."

"Sorry I missed supper." Gwen smiled at the trencher, which was laden with meat, vegetables, and bread. "I didn't really care to socialize."

Bri filled her cup with wine and nodded her head. "Reilly won't tell me what's going on. And you don't have to, either. But you're among friends here. So you do whatever it is you need to do."

"Thanks." Gwen chewed thoughtfully. "What makes a good match, Bri?"

"Well," she replied slowly, "it depends on the goals of each person. Sometimes, it's for a life partner. That's what I specialized in. But there are other matches, too, like when two people marry for legalities such as insurance purposes."

Gwen toyed with the cup. "What if one person loves the other person more?"

Bri's eyebrows knit together. "That's part of any relationship, really. Can you give me an example?"

Gwen rubbed her temples. "I have two scenarios for you. In the first, the woman loves a man. She's loved him for as long as she's known him, but he loves another woman—*but* that second woman is, for all intents and purposes, out of reach of that man, so he settles for the woman who is there, and who does love him."

"Ah. So this woman, she loves him despite his love for another woman?" Bri asked.

"Unfortunately."

"Hmm. What's the second scenario?"

"That same woman is in the reverse situation. A man loves her very much, but she loves another. But the man who loves her can offer her everything the one she loves cannot. Stability, a home, children. Normalcy."

"Ah. Normalcy is a variable term," Bri replied matter-of-factly. "It means something different to everyone. But for this woman, that's what she wants, yes? In a perfect world, she would have the man she loves, in the life she envisions for herself."

"The world is far from perfect."

"Then perhaps it's time for her to redefine what normalcy is, or what perfect is." Brianagh smiled softly at Gwen. "But the reality is, she has to determine what will be the best choice for herself long-term. Will she grow to resent the man she loves, when she believes his heart is with another? Or would she be content in the knowledge that he chose to be with her, despite loving someone else, no matter how far out of reach she is? Only the person deciding could know the answer to that."

"Or," Gwen said glumly, "she knows when to cut her losses and try to love the man who loves her."

"And that is certainly possible," Bri agreed. "Love is as much a choice as anything. That fiery passion that consumes people is often mistaken for love. But you and I both know that's naught more than lust. And lust is intense, but it burns out over time. Love is what's behind that emotion. It's in the choices you make. It's your love's best interests, no matter the personal cost to yourself. It's in the words you speak to him, the way he cares for you when you're sick, the sweetness in everyday gestures. That's love. And if it's true love, the kind that lasts forever, the lust doesn't actually burn out. It simmers, always there, but no longer as consuming as it once was. It can easily be stoked into flames again, but then it's the knowledge of what awaits when those flames calm again. And they will calm."

"What did you mean, that one person loves another more, being a part of a relationship?"

"Well," Bri mused, her cobalt eyes speculative in the firelight, "the thing many people don't understand is that love is a give-and-take. There will be times when you want to wring your partner's neck, or he yours. In those moments, during those arguments that last for longer than either of you care to admit, one of you has to make the choice to love the other enough for both of you, until the other person regains his or her balance. And it changes throughout the years. The secret is to never fall out of love at the same time."

Gwen pushed the trencher away and stared at the dancing flames. "So you think it's possible to grow to love someone?"

"Absolutely."

"Even if your heart belongs to another?"

Brianagh reached over and touched Gwen's arm. "Listen closely Gwen, for this advice comes not from the matchmaker, but from the old married woman in front of you. For the man who loves the woman more—does he love her enough for the both of them right now? And does she think that she could truly grow to love him out of mutual respect and tender feelings?"

"I want to believe that," Gwen whispered.

"That's good. But the other scenario, the woman loving the man enough for the both of them, that doesn't necessarily work in this case, does it? Because," she guessed, "the man in this case has a soul mate who possibly isn't the woman who loves him so desperately. The man might be tied to another person, never to be fully happy with anyone but her, whomever she would be. Is that correct?"

Gwen nodded miserably.

Brianagh got up and wrapped her arms around Gwen; it was only then that Gwen felt her own tears.

"I wish I could help you with this," Brianagh murmured, "but only you can make the decision, Gwendolyn."

"Do you know who his soul mate is?" Gwen asked, half-hoping Bri would say no.

"It wouldn't matter if I did. The words have to come from Reilly, not me. And I think you know that."

"I asked him if it was me."

Bri pulled back. "That was very brave of you."

Gwen swallowed past the lump in her throat. "Was it? It didn't feel brave."

"Of course it was brave. Reilly doesn't lie, so you know you would be getting the truth from him."

"He refused to answer me."

Bri's face fell, sadness eclipsing her. "Oh, Gwen. I'm…"

"I know," Gwen whispered. "Me too."

"What will you do?"

Gwen laughed miserably. "I have no idea."

CHAPTER 14

"Supper last night was indeed a solemn affair without your presence."

Claire MacWilliam spun around, her hand on her chest, and nearly fell into Reilly's lap. He stood and easily righted her. Once he ensured she was well, he carefully pushed his sword further onto the table at his hip. He'd been sharpening the blade when he saw her breeze into the great hall from the stairway; he was grateful she fell onto him instead of the sharp steel.

She threw her arms around his neck in a most un-lady-of-the-castle way and squealed. "Oh, Ry, I'm delighted you're here! I've missed you so." She released him and stepped back, peering at his tunic for, he well knew, signs of a specific present. "Did you perhaps bring me anything?"

"Spoiled wench," Reilly replied with a smirk, but it faded quickly. "Alas, I apologize for the disappointment, but nay, I haven't any of what you seek."

Being, of course, Nutella. Claire developed a fondness for the thick paste years earlier, and Reilly made it a point to bring her a jar each time he visited.

This time, though, he obviously didn't have time to stop at the local Tesco and grab her any.

He didn't explain why to Claire, though. The less the headstrong lass knew about time travel, and how it was or was not working for him, was best. The saints only knew what sort of plan she'd devise to attempt to fix his current misdirection.

He laughed lightly at her crestfallen face. "Cheer up, Lady Claire. I've brought you something even better."

Claire pursed her lips. "I don't believe there is anything better."

"What about a visit with your friend Lady Gwendolyn?"

Claire's eyes widened. "Nay, you jest!"

He shook his head. "I do not. She has yet to rise, but she is staying in the east wing, in the chamber adjacent to mine."

Claire gave him a strange look, but he merely raised an eyebrow at her. For all Claire's boisterous ways, she did draw the line at questioning Reilly's decisions. She understood that if he had a reason for keeping Gwen close to him, 'twas a good reason, and that was enough for her.

Smart lass.

"So before you rush off in haste to wake her, perhaps you can tell me why you secreted yourself away in your chamber all evening, with instructions to all that you weren't to be bothered?" he asked mildly.

Claire wasn't fooled. She took up her normal stance—one of immediate defiance—but then paused. Slowly, she unfolded her arms, dropped her shoulders, raised her head, and clasped her hands demurely in front of her stomach.

Reilly was instantly suspicious.

"I take many nights to myself, reflecting upon my life choices."

He frowned. "Do your clansmen actually believe that pathetic bit of drivel?"

She smiled easily at him. "'Tis easy to believe when 'tis the truth. I've many difficult choices ahead of me. And very soon, I'll have to decide which path to take. So I'm using my time wisely to reflect on how my life has been, and how I'd like my life to be."

"Your da presenting you with ever more suitors?"

"Always."

Reilly shook his head. "You'll make someone very happy someday. Unbalanced in the head, perhaps, but happy nonetheless."

"Reilly!" she exclaimed, giving him a light punch on the shoulder.

Actually, Reilly thought, *that punch was a bit more than light.* "Have you been training?"

Her face lit up. "Aye!" Her expression changed to one of concern. "Oh! Did I injure you?"

He snorted. "Nay. But I certainly did feel a difference. You're stronger. Does your sire know about this?"

"You know he wouldn't approve." Claire twisted her hands into her dress. "But I've no idea what the future holds for me, and Mami has always told me to hope for the best, but prepare for the worst. So I'm preparing."

Claire was one of the mightiest women he knew; Reilly often thought it such a waste for her to be born the only daughter of a powerful laird. She was destined to marry for clan alliance more than love, though Brianagh was trying for both.

Hence why Claire was allowed to turn so many suitors away, though Reilly knew Nioclas faced pressure to marry her to one of the Maguire lads. Erin and Donovan had six sons, but Claire had been brought up like a sister to them.

"I've the utmost faith in your abilities to make the correct choice," he finally replied.

She smiled widely at him. "That means much, Reilly. My thanks." She threw her thumb over her shoulder. "I'm going to find Lady Gwen."

Reilly gave her an indulgent smile, and she hurried off, waving to people as she went.

Aye, Lady Claire was a special young woman. Reilly only hoped that her future husband did not attempt to clip her wings.

~

GWEN PULLED THE WOOLEN CLOAK TIGHTER AROUND HERSELF, warding off the chill coming from the ocean. Up here, on the battlements, she had space to think, and to breathe.

It was the first time she'd been out of Reilly's presence for days, and she was both elated and sad. Her emotions, she admitted, were all over the place.

The sea glittered in the weak sunlight, and in the distance, there was nothing but the horizon line and a few puffy clouds.

"There you are!"

Gwen turned, surprised, as a figure emerged from the battlement steps, huffing. "Claire!"

They embraced, and Claire blew out a breath, frosting the air. "'Tis uncommonly cold today for October, isn't it?"

"I thought it was September?"

"Nay, 'tis the first of October."

Gwen frowned. She was having a hard time keeping track of the days; she hoped they would return to the future soon. She could not miss Ellie's wedding.

"Reilly said you were in your chamber. I've been looking for you for over an hour, and my feet are fair to freezing off!"

"I've been up here the whole time," Gwen replied, tucking her numb fingers back inside her cloak. She shivered. It *was* colder than the day before. "Do the trees change color here?"

"Oh, aye. 'Tis a wonder. But they're mostly barren now."

The women looked across the ocean again, as a few birds dipped and flew over the waves.

"It is beautiful here," Gwen said wistfully. "It looks much the same on my side of the sea. If you were to travel west and a little south, on the other side of the horizon lies my country."

Claire shook her head in wonder. "My mother has told me of such things, but I confess to not quite believing it." A moment of companionable silence passed. "If I were ever given the chance, I would but love to see such a thing."

Gwen half-smiled. "There's so much about this time that's good, too, though. The simplicity. The anonymity or the notoriety, if you want it. The sound of the rain, the smell of the earth. In too many places in my time, these have all been lost."

"How can one lose the sound of the rain?" Claire asked curiously.

Gwen glanced at her friend, who was almost the spitting image of her mother. "Imagine thousands of cows within your village, and they are all constantly mooing. Now put them in the rain, but don't stop the moos. The sound of the cows becomes all you hear."

"You have that many cows in the future?" Claire asked, wonder in her tone.

"Not quite," Gwen hedged, wondering if she could explain horns and cars and buses. She opted not, and instead added, "But it's similar to that."

"The adventures you must have," she murmured.

The Venezuelan jungle rose in her memory, and she swallowed hard. Determinedly, she focused her eyes on the swooping gulls, the waves crashing in the far distances, and the uncommonly blue sky.

All good things. All soothing sights and sounds. Just blue, blue, and more blue. Gwen breathed through her nose and exhaled slowly out of her mouth. In again. Out again.

Claire continued, her voice melodic, and her bearing relaxed, as though she was remaining calm so she could lend some of it to Gwen. "'Tis wondrous, the place I find myself in now. For the entirety of my life, I've watched my mother unite people. Good people, ones who might never have thought to be with the other. They marry and lead happy lives together. I was brought up to believe that one day, I would share that same fate. I would meet a man and fall in love. The tales my mother used to spin were so romantic!"

"Did your brothers roll their eyes a lot?"

Claire smiled in memory. "Nay, not at all. Mami told great tales of knights and warriors, full of chivalry and bravery. Men who would march proudly into battle, thoughts of protecting their clan at the front of their minds. They were defenders of women and children, with fierce outsides and soft underbellies. Romantic words fell from their lips as easily as a battle cry."

"We have fairy tales like that, too. Unfortunately, knights in shining armor are scarce where I'm from."

Claire gave her a sad smile. "Do their mothers never tell them all that they can be?"

Gwen paused. "I don't know. If they don't, they should."

"Mothers are important. But so are sires. My own told me tales of brave ladies who, while the men fought the battles to ensure the enemy never reached the castle, the women did the job of both. They raised the children to be fine clansmen and protected the castle if an enemy attacked. They used their wits and what resources they had to save their children and themselves. They were sisters first, coming together whenever the need called, to ensure the greater benefit for the clan." She sighed. "But marriage and children were always their main purpose. And I grew up with these tales in my head, believing that I, too, would love nothing more than to do just that."

"Has something changed?" Gwen waited, curiously, for the answer.

Claire drew her eyebrows together. "I've been asking

myself the same question. A few years back, when I was in the village, I delivered some food to one of our sick clanswomen. She was coughing, then asked me to make a tonic for her with the herbs she had on her table. I did as she said, but when she told me to put meadowsweet in it, I hesitated. I picked up nettle instead, and I somehow just knew that would stop her coughing. Meadowsweet relaxes the muscles in the stomach," Claire explained, "but nettle actually heals it. So I put it in, instead. She knew when she drank it that I'd used something else, and she was quite angry. But she already drank it. And, when I finished my rounds a few hours later, I went back to her home. She wasn't coughing, and she told me she was feeling remarkably better. In fact, she was walking around, which she hadn't been able to do for days. When she took my hands and told me I had a gift, I felt lightheaded. And when I left that cottage, something in me changed."

"Wow." Gwen gave a slight shake of her head. "Claire, that's a really special gift."

She grinned. "Aye, 'tis! James and I have had many a discussion on herbs and remedies. And I want to use what I've learned, what I know. But each man my sire has brought forth refused to allow me to continue my healer ways, so I've rejected them. And Da's lost patience, and he will force me to marry someone soon. I very much doubt whomever that is will allow me to continue, either. It's strange, isn't it, that when you're forced to look at yourself because of new experiences, that you're not the person you once thought you were?"

Gwen froze, Claire's words striking a distant chord in the back of her mind.

She always thought of herself as a worldly sort, having seen some terrible situations and human living conditions, but there was nothing in her repertoire like what she experienced in Venezuela. In fact, the thought of going to another country to volunteer again had her simultaneously terrified and, oddly, disappointed in herself.

Gwen didn't want to feel that kind of fear ever again, but she made it a point to dedicate her life to helping others. She thought of all the people she knew who also saw truly terrible things, just as she had, and went on to volunteer more, give more, *do* more.

She always thought she'd be one of those people, if she ever had a worst-case scenario. But when she held the reality of a worst-case up to the idea of a worst-case, everything was so much more complicated than she thought it would be.

"Does that make sense?"

For a moment, she'd been so lost in her thoughts that she'd forgotten Claire was sitting next to her. Gwen nodded slowly. "More than you might know."

Claire looked at her curiously, her eyes holding compassion and insight far greater than her years. "Some adventures seem better in our imaginations than in real life, aye? But then, as my sire tends to remind me, imagination stems from reality. We can use our minds to make things better, or worse. But rarely are those two ever the same."

"Your father is a wise man." Gwen shuffled further against the wall as two guards marched past, their helmets glinting. They gave a deferential bow to Claire before continuing on their way.

"He is. But being wise does not always mean knowing what is best. He wants me to marry and have children. And maybe I do want that, some day. But right now, I want so much more. I have skills with herbs; healers come to me for advice. And I'm not quite sure how I know so much, but when I see or smell a plant, in my mind, I can almost picture what it can do to help. I've eased the pain of a difficult birth, and healed deep hunting wounds. I can be so much more than the lady who approves menus from Cook. And I want more than those maidens in the tales he would tell me at my bedside."

Gwen wrapped her arms around herself. "We all have a purpose. It's the finding of it that is challenging."

"Aye, 'tis the truth. I wish..."

Gwen turned fully to Claire. "What do you wish?"

Claire smiled, a faraway look on her face. "I wish to do more for this world. I'm not sure what that means, exactly, but I wish for adventure. To see the best and worst of what people are, and somehow make things better. However...I am but a woman, and my world does not see me as much more than chattel. 'Tis why I would love to go to your time, when women are freer to do things that men can."

"Claire..." Gwen wasn't really sure what to say. She had reservations about the reality of Claire's ability to assimilate to all the advances made from now until the future.

But didn't Claire just say that reality and ideas never really matched up? Gwen glanced at her friend. If anyone could succeed in the future, it'd be the young, determined woman next to her. Who was Gwen to judge?

And who was anyone to judge Gwen? If she wanted to be done with volunteering, she could be done with volunteering. It didn't make her less of a person. It just made her a different one.

She wanted something different now. A vision of a home, with children and a husband, flitted through her mind.

The promise of forever. Someone who wouldn't always leave her and their family to go out rescuing the world.

She swallowed hard. *Oh, God.* She knew what she wanted. She didn't want to be someone's second-best. She wanted to be important to someone, and have that person be just as important to her.

"I know," Claire continued, oblivious to Gwen's inner turmoil. "I've heard it all before from Mami. She is certain I'd be overwhelmed, but she tends to forget that I am her blood.

There's a part of her that makes up a part of me, and I need to explore that. I need to find out what I can do."

Gwen reached out from her cloak and impulsively hugged Claire, and said fiercely, tears burning her eyes, "Then you do that. If we're only given this one life to live, then you live it the best way you can. If you do get a chance to take that adventure, then do it. But do it knowing that things change. Ideas change with experience, and sometimes, those grand plans become living nightmares. Don't be too proud to decide it was all a learning experience, and return to a simpler life. Make the choice that best fits what you want, Claire. Because you're important, too."

"Thank you," Claire whispered, tightening the hug. "Thank you for understanding."

∼

REILLY STOOD QUICKLY AS GWEN AND CLAIRE ENTERED Brianagh's private solar. They removed their cloaks and handed them to a waiting servant, who murmured something to Claire.

Claire smiled at Reilly. "Apparently, my parents need speech with me in my sire's solar. Another potential husband, no doubt. I'll return when I can."

A few seconds passed after Claire left the room until Gwen glanced his way.

The sadness in her face ripped him apart.

She slowly made her way over to him. "I'd like to go home, Reilly."

He frowned. "Is something wrong?"

She refused to meet his eyes. "Can you take me back?"

"I can try," he replied slowly, "but I'm not yet sure why I was sent here."

She took a shaky breath. "I don't think we came here for

you." She raised her eyes to his, the unshed tears making them shimmer. "I think we came here for me."

He shook his head. "I doubt that, lass. We've—"

"I'm not a lass," she interrupted. She stood taller. "I'm a full-grown woman, Reilly. Stop calling me a child."

He stepped back, surprised. "'Tis a term of endearment."

She firmed her lips. "I don't want your terms of endearment anymore. What I want is to return home."

His gut tightened. "What does that mean, you don't want my terms of endearment anymore?"

She straightened her shoulders, and Reilly felt a moment of pride for her. Whatever she was about to say was going to take a lot of courage, though he wasn't sure why she needed courage to speak to him.

"Because," she said, her voice catching slightly, "I'm not yours to endear. I want to go back and live my life the way I want to live it, Reilly. I know it's not a popular thing to want anymore: the husband, the two-point-five children, the dog and white fence. But I *do* want it. I'm tired of living this life, trying to prove some point. I don't even know what that point is!" The tears fell down her face, unchecked.

He offered a smile. "'Twould be my privilege to give all that to you, Gwendolyn."

"No," she said quickly. "No, it won't."

His lungs seemed incapable of drawing in air. She continued on, as though she wasn't breaking his heart and stomping on it with daggers attached to her slippers.

"I want a husband who loves me, Reilly. I want to love someone who can love me back."

"And you think I can't love you?" he managed, his breath coming in short gasps.

She looked at him incredulously. "You said yourself that you were destined for one woman only, and that you already claimed her. So no, I don't believe you love me. Not in the same way I love you."

"Would *you* claim me, Gwen, if you knew you would bind yourself to me for all time, regardless of how I felt for you?"

She furiously wiped at her face. "Don't you see, you foolish man? That's what I did for years!"

"I can't live without you," he said hoarsely.

"You don't have a choice," she whispered.

He grasped her arms and gave her a small shake. "*I can't live without you,*" he said, more desperately this time. "Please, Gwen, answer me. Knowing me as you do, knowing *me*, the man, not the Protector…would you claim me?"

She sobbed in earnest now and wrenched herself away. "No, Reilly. I would not."

He roared, and she jumped backward as he picked up a stool and chucked it at the wall behind him.

"You don't get to do this!" she cried out angrily. "You already have your soul mate, Reilly! Let me go, so I can find mine!"

Brianagh and Nioclas burst into the room, Nick with his sword drawn.

"Are you all right?" Brianagh asked, her eyes wide as she took in Gwen's tears, Reilly's fury, and the now-broken stool laying uselessly on the ground behind him.

"He needs to let me go," Gwen said unsteadily.

"Did he hurt you?" Nioclas asked, his sword pointed at Reilly.

In any other circumstance, Reilly would've laughed at the idea that Nick would run him through. But at this moment, when Gwen had so fully rejected him, he would gladly stand with his arms open as his brother-at-arms ran him through.

"He did not," she said, her voice still shaky. "And he won't. But I want to go home."

"Not until we fix this," he growled. "You are my soul mate, Gwendolyn!"

She clenched her jaw. "No, I'm not."

"I'm confused." Brianagh looked between the two of them as Nioclas bolted the door shut.

"She refuses to claim me," Reilly explained curtly. If it came out as more like a wheeze, Brianagh was certainly kind enough not to point it out.

Bri covered her mouth with her hand, but Gwen clearly wasn't having that be the only explanation. "I've lived my life for everyone else for too long." To Reilly, she said, "I've loved you for too long, and I got swept up in the madness of thinking you might someday love me back. But the truth is that you didn't want your backup to abandon you, too. Right?"

He shook his head. "Backup?"

Her mouth dropped open. "Are you serious? For eleven years, I follow you around like a damn puppy dog. I can't have a normal adult relationship because I'm so blindly in love with you that I can't see straight. So I decide it's time to move on, and you know what? I find someone who loves me. Someone who wants to be with me. And that is conveniently when you decide to make your move."

Nioclas folded his arms and frowned fiercely. "Poor form, O'Malley. Poor form."

Reilly ignored him. "Nothing is convenient about this!" he snapped.

Brianagh blinked. "Reilly, watch yourself. You've never even yelled at me like this."

He turned to her, his eyes blazing. "Perhaps that's because you weren't damning me to an even longer eternity of hell!"

He could actually feel Gwen freeze, and he knew he'd slipped up. He swore silently, then glanced at her.

Oh, aye. He was in for it now.

"*What* did you just say?" she asked softly. So softly, that he had to strain to hear her.

"It's time for us to go," Bri said quickly. Nick, bless the

man, threw the bolt on the chamber door, pulled her out, and slammed it shut behind them.

If fire could fly, Gwen would be shooting him with sparks from her eyes. Her voice lowered more than he'd ever heard it before. "Reilly O'Malley. Explain yourself immediately."

He closed his eyes, his nostrils flaring. When he opened them again, she'd taken steps closer, until she was nearly upon him.

"You told me," she continued in a measured tone, "that you knew your soul mate the moment you met her. Were you lying?"

He shook his head, unable—unwilling—to say the words. The devastation on her face was killing him.

He did that to her.

He deeply hurt the one person he loved above all others. The pain in his chest was physical.

"I asked you. I asked you point blank. Why? " she asked softly, her teary eyes searching his.

He tried to answer her, but he was rendered mute. He didn't have any words to make this better; his mind was swirling with too many thoughts, too many reassurances, too many questions. His normally glib tongue deserted him.

"You've kept me on a string, knowing how I felt about you?" Her voice rose in pitch. "Knowing I was desperate for any of your attention? I was so stupid! Were you waiting until I had to make a choice? Did you *enjoy* seeing me suffer?"

"Nay—" he started.

"I can rationalize a lot of it away," she barreled on, her hand fumbling for the chamber door as she gazed at him with a blazing emotion in her eyes.

Disgust? Pity? Hard to tell through the tears.

He felt ill.

"Sure, you didn't trust me with your secret. That hurt a lot. But I accepted it without holding onto any anger about it, Reilly. Because that's what I do. I forgive those I love." She bit her lip. "And I went out to make a life for myself, thinking that you didn't want me. And I did that, Reilly! I did it, and I was ready to get married to someone! Have a family and live my own life! And it's then that you step in? Then? *Years* after you knew we were meant to be together?" She stifled a sob. "Who the hell do you think you are, screwing with me like this?"

"Gwendolyn..."

With an obvious effort, she drew in a deep breath, then pulled the door open. Brianagh stood against the far wall, looking unsure. "Can you travel through time?" Gwen demanded.

Brianagh hesitated.

"Is Reilly the only one who can get me home?"

"I am," he answered for Brianagh.

"He's not," Brianagh said in a quiet voice. "There is one other."

"Who?" Reilly demanded.

Gwen looked steadily at Brianagh. "Can you arrange for him to take me home, please?"

"Absolutely not." Reilly's entire body tensed at the thought of anyone taking Gwen from him.

Gwen dragged her eyes back to his, and Reilly felt it like a slice in his gut. The mixed emotions all over her face made him want to weep for being the cause of it, but he couldn't say anything.

What was there to say?

"It's all just a game to you, isn't it?" Before he could voice protest to that, she held up her hand and shook her head. "It's over, Reilly. I'm done playing. I want to go home."

"I'll take you," he said hoarsely.

A tear escaped her eye. "No, thank you. I'm choosing option B, whatever—no, *whomever*—that may be." To Bri, she added, "Please send him to my chamber." To Reilly, she said firmly, "If you ever cared for me at all, let me go. And believe me when I say I *never* want to see you again."

She swept out of the room.

Reilly was left staring at a shocked Brianagh. She twisted her hands and glanced at him, anguish in her eyes.

"Did you claim her, Reilly?"

He nodded mutely.

"Then why didn't you say anything?" she whispered, horrified. "You could've told her you were a fool, you were stupid, you made a mistake. You could've apologized. But you didn't say *anything*! You're losing her!"

"I suspect," he said with a deathly quiet as a desolation swept across his soul, "that I already have." He flexed his hand, then loosened his sword. "Don't send anyone to her chamber. If you do, I'll never return here again."

He heard Brianagh's gasp as he strode down the hallway.

Gwendolyn was right.

He *had* played a game, and he just lost everything.

CHAPTER 15

*T*he fight in her was gone. She was left exhausted, and all she wanted to do was crawl into the big bed she woke up on this morning and sleep until her heart healed.

Unfortunately, if that was to happen, she might never wake.

So instead, Gwen had slid to the floor of her chamber, placed her arms on her knees, placed her head in her arms, and waited.

Maybe Colin would come. Perhaps Bri had a system where she wrote a note, stuck it in a bottle, then sent it off into the time warp, where Colin would receive it.

Gwen thought it said a lot that she would rather live out her days in this chamber than face Reilly again. She hadn't been joking when she told him her heart couldn't take any more from him.

A knock at her door forced her to croak out a feeble, "Who's there?" before dropping her head back down.

"Gwendolyn."

She laughed, a hollow, wrung-out sound dredged up from the darker part of her soul, no doubt. "Go away, Reilly."

"I will never go away," he replied, his voice low.

"Then I will never come out." She said it without inflection, without emotion. She was tired of him, of his deceit and his lies. She trusted him, and he blew that trust away.

She might've been a fool once, but she wasn't going to be a fool again.

She stuffed her fist in her mouth, stifling the sob that threatened. How could she possibly have more tears in her?

When she was certain her voice wouldn't fail her, Gwen responded, "I want to go home."

"I will take you."

"I want to go home with anyone but you," she revised.

There was a thunk, which she thought might be his head against the other side of the solid door. "Gwendolyn, you know that's not truly possible. Bri won't send anyone here to take you."

"How do you know?" she shot back.

"Because I told her I would never return if she did."

Anger like Gwen had never felt rose in her chest. She jumped to her feet and threw open the door, fury emanating from every pore of her body. "How dare you," she hissed.

He quickly stepped inside and slammed the door shut behind him. "I dare much," he countered, "because I only now understand what I've done. I've made a mistake in not telling you sooner."

She laughed incredulously. "That's your mistake?"

He frowned. "Aye. And I'm sorry for that."

She fisted her hands at her sides and corralled all her anger into one pulsating ball, held in the place of where her heart used to be. "No, Reilly, that's not your mistake. Your mistake started the day you met me, then decided that you were going to lead me on a merry chase, taking *years* away from my life. And before you even think to speak to me, you're damn right that I allowed it to happen. I was stupid, I was young, and I was in love. Hell, you could do no wrong in my eyes! For so long—*eleven years*, which I realize to you is a

blink of a freaking eye, but to me actually means something—
I thought something was wrong with me, that you couldn't
love me back for reasons I couldn't figure out. And believe
me when I say that I spent more nights than not agonizing
over the whys of it. And you know what?" she demanded,
jabbing her finger into his chest and relishing in the surprise
in his eyes. "Every moment that I wasted on you is one that I
am going to claim back. I am going to live my life, without
you in it, and I am going to be *happy*. Because I deserve that.
Every person deserves that except, maybe, *you*." She drew in
a deep breath. "You cheated us, Reilly. There isn't a single
reason in the world that would be good enough to forgive
that."

Rationally, she knew her words were harsh. But Gwen
was so far past rational, and she'd never blown her top
before, and it felt *good*. There was a release in the words, a
feeling of power that she'd never had when dealing with
Reilly O'Malley, and she wasn't going to take any of them
back.

"You said you always forgive the ones you love," he
replied hoarsely.

She remained stonily silent.

"So that's it?" he finally said. "That's it, after all we've
shared? We're done?"

"We haven't *shared* anything. *Sharing* infers there was
some sort of equality between two people, but that's not what
we had. No, *I* gave and *you* took. And I'm done." The despair
in her voice had him rearing back as if she'd struck him. "You
waited too long. I tried to give you all of me, but you
wouldn't take what I offered. The offer has been rescinded."

He stepped closer again. "I will wait for you to offer again.
I will wait for you today, and tomorrow, and the next day. I
will wait for you forever, Gwendolyn Allen, and not because I
have claimed you as my mate. I will wait for you forever
because I will love you, no matter where you go or what you

do. I will always love you, because you are the one for me. The only one."

Gwen could feel herself draining of energy again, and she did the most sensible thing she could. She put her hands over her ears.

Because, the truth was, she didn't want to forgive him.

He reached for her hands, but she stepped back. A shaft of light beamed between them, lighting the room. A small breeze ruffled their clothes, and the air shimmered between them. A matronly woman materialized between them.

The woman looked blandly at Gwen. "I am the Mother, and, should you wish it, I've come to return you to your time, if you've made your decision, Gwendolyn. Would you like to return?"

Gwen glanced at Reilly, who's face had gone completely white. She felt a pinprick of unease, but he said the one word that reminded her that only she was in charge of her destiny.

"Nay." Reilly stated it forcefully, as though his word was the final one. The only one.

She lifted her chin. "Yes."

"So be it," the Maiden said, and, the next moment, Gwen found herself surrounded by trees…with a plane flying overhead.

And she was completely alone.

Nioclas found Reilly on his knees, his chin against his chest, in the middle of the chamber.

There was no sound and no movement from him for a long moment.

"They took her."

The words, spoken in a voice so hollow, had Nioclas loosening his sword. "Then we will get her back."

"We cannot get to where she is," he said, raising his

head. The agony on his face was painful to look at; his countenance was one of utter despair. "The Fates. They've returned her to her time and left me here. Someone had to take Aidan's place. And that someone is me."

Brianagh poked her head around the open door, and, seeing Reilly, rushed to his side. She dropped to her knees and wrapped her arms around him. "Oh, Ry."

"Aidan wasn't meant to be in the future, but I had to bring him and Emma back together. They deserved their happiness. But the Fates didn't like that I'd overstepped and marred the fabric of time. They always have a way of evening things out." He rubbed a shaking hand over his face. "I should've known. I should've figured it out."

"So they brought Gwen back to the future, but left you here?"

He nodded, then dropped his head back down.

"Then you must go to her," Brianagh said gently. "Quickly. Nick, close the door."

"Don't bother. I've already tried, and my powers are gone. I can bend time no more."

Nioclas and Brianagh shared a look that lasted for more than a few long seconds, before Nioclas closed the door anyway.

"O'Malley...there might still be a way." Nioclas's words seemed torn from his throat, given unwillingly.

Finally, Reilly rose, Brianagh still holding his arm. "You are mistaken, my laird. I've already tried to call to my men, but none have heeded the call. I suspect I've been stripped of everything. All power."

Someone banged on the door. Nioclas opened it to find his captain, Kane. "Aye?"

"Battle. The guards at the gate have been slain, and they are almost at our courtyard now."

"Get to your solar," Nioclas barked at Brianagh. To Kane,

"Find Claire, send her there with no less than ten guards. Raise the alarm."

"I have already," Kane called out as he sprinted down the hallway, Nioclas on his heels.

Reilly pulled his sword out and hauled Brianagh out of the room.

"There's an easier way," she gasped, surprised by the force he used.

"Show me."

She went back into Gwen's chamber and stepped inside the small hearth. On the left wall, she pushed as hard as she could, covering her gown with soot, and the wall gave a groan.

Reilly pulled her out and took her place. Putting his whole weight against it, the wall gave, revealing an ascending staircase.

"It'll bring us to one of the chambers close to my solar," she explained. "We can close it once we're inside."

"Once you're safely in there, I'll find Claire."

"And then, Reilly?" she asked.

His eyes became hard. "Maybe, if I'm lucky, there won't be an *and then*." He dragged Bri into the staircase and shifted the wall back into place behind them.

"We can get you back to her," Brianagh whispered.

Grimly, he retorted, "If I'm alive after this skirmish, then we shall have speech. But until then, hold your tongue, bolt the door, and say your prayers. Just…leave me out of them."

GWEN STUMBLED FROM THE WOODS, SIMULTANEOUSLY RELIEVED and dejected that she landed at Reilly's cottage.

Would he be there? Did he make it back before her? She didn't want to deal with him right now.

She was still dressed in the blue and silver gown, and for a moment, she lamented the loss of the beautiful red one.

She refused to think about how Reilly had it made just for her. She trudged onward to the little cottage, determined to gather her things and book the next ticket out of Ireland.

Ellie came flying out of the back door, her long hair trailing behind her, and Gwen remembered with a start that she couldn't leave; she had a wedding to attend.

The things one forgot while traveling around the time continuum, she supposed.

"Gwennie!" Ellie cried out. "Oh, Gwen, we've been so worried! Is Reilly with you?"

Gwen stifled a sob and stumbled toward her, losing her footing in the hem and going down into the grass. Ellie was upon her a moment later, holding her against her chest. "Oh, Gwen, it's all right. Come on. I'll make some tea."

Tea was Ellie's answer to most of life's problems, so Gwen heartily wished that it might somehow solve some of hers.

Shakily, they stood, and Ellie supported her as they made their way back to the cottage. She jerked in surprise when she saw the kitchen nearly back to the way it was—with not a speck of soot anywhere on the walls.

Or ceiling.

"When you stopped answering your cell phones, Colin finished his business quickly in the States," Ellie explained quietly. "We got here, and the kitchen clearly had some sort of fire. But there was no sign of you or Reilly. Col checked the garage, and all the vehicles were there. We hadn't any idea what happened to you."

"He'll be happy to know his motorcycle made it back in one piece," Gwen said absently. "He's going to hate the new stove."

The shiny Aga nearly sparkled. And while it was certainly an upgrade, she knew Reilly would have no use for that.

Not that she would be around to hear him complain about it, though.

"Where have you been?" Ellie asked, seating her at the table and putting the water on. "Colin wasn't able to time travel at all. He wasn't called to anywhere, and he couldn't figure out where you two were."

Gwen explained how the Fates dumped them with Reilly's mother, then at Brianagh's. "We were gone for only a few days."

Ellie's eyes widened. "Gwen...you've been missing for almost two and a half weeks."

"What?"

She nodded emphatically. "We thought you were lost in time. You weren't gone for just a pair of days."

Gwen frowned. "That's...bizarre. I don't understand how that happened. No matter, I guess. If it's all the same to you, I'll take that cup of tea to go. I want to stay at Winnie's, not here."

Ellie drew her eyebrows together. "Is there a reason?"

Gwen's shoulders dropped. "There is, but I'd like to get out of here before Reilly returns, so I'll explain it to you later."

Ellie watched her for a moment, then impetuously threw her arms around her in a quick hug. "Go pack. I'll wait."

Gwen nodded, then ran up the stairs. She quickly shucked the gown onto the bed, then changed into a comfortable pair of jeans with a cozy sweater. She shoved her clothes and belongings into her suitcase, then retrieved the dress. It landed over the headboard of the bed, and when she pulled it off, she noticed the headboard was a different one than the last time she'd stayed at his place.

While the color was the same as the old one, this one had intricate Celtic knots expertly carved all over it. They twisted and turned, each slightly different than the others. She glanced over at the armoire; it was done in a similar style, the craftsmanship and attention to detail unlike anything she'd ever seen. Each of the two pieces were polished to a high shine. She slowly opened the armoire drawers again, noticing that even the drawer pulls were hand-carved. The drawers slid silently open, the tracks well-oiled and perfectly placed.

She closed the large doors, then ran her hand over the knot work.

She started to turn away when something caught her eye. She peered closer, then, her jaw sliding south, began to frantically search the rest of the door.

Hidden in the knot work were letters. Words, maybe. They didn't seem to be in any order; one word read *Trí*, and another was simply the letters *na*.

Did Reilly make this furniture? she wondered, lightly dragging her fingertips over the letters. They certainly weren't placed there accidentally.

She went back to the bed and studied the headboard. Letters there, too, she could easily discern the word there.

Gwendolyn.

"You almost ready, Gwen?" Ellie called.

"Uh, yeah," she called back, her voice tight. "Down in a minute." She grabbed her phone and opened the note app. She typed in *Trí*, *na*, and her name, then studied the armoire. It held no clues.

On a hunch, she headed into Reilly's room. It was tidy, with the covers only slightly mussed from when he last slept in it. She quietly closed the door behind her, then studied the furniture in there. The armchair had an even stranger word on it: *haoiseanna*. She added it to her list. She turned her attention to the biggest piece in the room; the four-poster bed wasn't overly large, but it was impressive. She searched for only a minute or so when she saw the letters *mo* on one post. Another post had *thar*, and another, *am*. The final post had the letters *mo* again. She moved to the chest and saw *ghrá*.

She hadn't any idea what those words meant, but she knew it meant something. Suitcase forgotten, she ran down the stairs. "Ellie, do you know what this means?" She showed her the list of words, but her friend shrugged apologetically.

"I don't, but it looks like Gaelic."

Gwen smacked her own forehead. "Of course! That would make sense. Do you think Colin would know?"

"Maybe. He's in Galway at the moment, doing something for Celtic Connections. He should be back tomorrow morning. I can try texting him, but he won't respond until tonight at least."

"No, it's okay. I can wait until tomorrow." Gwen stared at the words again, trying to make sense of them. She plugged them into a translator app, but that was no help.

A taxi honked out front, and Gwen retrieved her suitcase. A sense of dread filled her as she left the house, but, as there was nothing more for her there, she placed her bag in the trunk and didn't look back as Ellie locked up.

THE NEXT MORNING, AFTER A FITFUL NIGHT SLEEP, AND OVER A sumptuous breakfast in Winnie's sunroom, Gwen relayed everything to Ellie, start to finish. And when she was done with the tale, Ellie sat in stunned silence for a long moment.

"Wow," she finally said.

Gwen sipped her orange juice. "That's a good way to sum it all up, I suppose."

Ellie crossed her arms and sat back in her chair but ruined the effect by nearly falling out of it. When she'd righted herself, she tapped her chin. "Are you still angry with him, now that you've had some space?"

Gwen nodded. "I am. I'm not spitting-nails-mad, though. More like…disappointed-mad."

Ellie raised an eyebrow.

Gwen rubbed her temples. "I placed my trust in him for so long, believing that he could do no wrong. I gave him the key to my happiness, and I felt like he held onto it just because he could. I don't understand why he didn't tell me."

"Shall I play Devil's advocate?" Ellie asked pertly.

"I wish you wouldn't."

"Ah well, wishes don't always come true, so let's give it a go anyway. How old were you when you met Reilly?"

"Twenty one."

Ellie nodded sagely. "And he was..."

"Thirty-something, I guess." *Just like he is now. Would he ever age?* She supposed she would never have the chance to find out.

"Uh huh. And when you were twenty one, were you looking for anything long-term?"

Gwen thought for a moment. "No. My parents wanted me to get married, and they put boys in front of me starting around nineteen. I purposefully went in the complete opposite direction; I didn't want anything serious."

"Why not?"

"Because I was twenty one?" Gwen asked in an *of course* tone.

Ellie gave her a look. "Exactly. You were twenty one, and you were just starting to find yourself. Do you think maybe Reilly saw and understood that right away?"

Gwen folded her arms across her chest. "No."

"Don't be stubborn," Ellie said mildly.

"Fine," Gwen grumbled. "I'll allow for the *possibility* that he *may* have thought about something like that."

"Excellent. A fifteen-year=plus age gap does seem a bit large, doesn't it? Think of all the life experience you packed into your twenties. Would you have had those same experiences, had you been tied to Reilly? Would you be the same person you are today? Would you still want the same things?"

Gwen held up her hands in defense. "Whoa, El, whoa.

Slow down. You know I'd be a different person today. As far as the other questions, I don't know."

She paused. But she did know, didn't she? She'd spent so long trying to save the world, that she'd forgotten to save a little of herself. And it took a terrible act of war, and the loss of her volunteer friends, for her to finally admit what she truly wanted at this point in her life.

Huh. The realization must've shown on her face because Ellie smiled at her.

"So did you really give him the key to your happiness, Gwen? Or did you merely leave it in his hands for safekeeping until you yourself were ready to turn it?"

Gwen shoved another piece of pancake into her mouth to avoid answering, but maybe Ellie was right.

She recognized that she had a lot of growing up to do in her twenties. And, looking back, she regretted none of it. She learned so much, not the least of which was how to trust her instincts.

And her instincts were screaming at her that perhaps she needed to hear Reilly's side of the story before coming to any concrete conclusions about her future. She'd fought for Reilly for so long; was she really going to walk away from a lifetime of happiness without trying to understand his side of things, misguided though they may have been?

She wasn't that rebellious young woman anymore.

Colin interrupted her thoughts when he strolled into the room, snagging a biscuit off a tray and dropping an entirely-too-involved kiss on Ellie.

"Glad you're back, Gwen." He took a bite, then swallowed. "So. Where'd you go?"

Gwen gave Ellie a defeated smile. "Do I have to repeat it?"

"Probably," she replied ruefully.

"Before I do," Gwen said, rummaging in her pocket and pulling out her phone, "do you think you could tell me what this means?"

"*Trí na Gwendolyn haoiseanna mo thar mo ghrá.*" He reread them silently, then asked, "Are these in a specific order?"

"I don't know."

"Well," he said slowly, "if you shift them around a bit to read *Trí na haoiseanna thar am mo ghrá, mo Gwendolyn*, it translates to *Throughout the age, beyond time, my love, my Gwendolyn*."

Ellie's face softened. "That's beautiful."

"It's a well-loved saying of the Irish. You can hear it in Gaelic songs and poetry." Colin looked at Gwen closely. "Where did you see this?"

"Carved into the bedroom furniture," she whispered. *What have I done?*

"Why don't you just ask Ry?"

And she repeated the entire story, but unlike Ellie, Colin interrupted with many questions. Another hour passed, and she was exhausted by the end of it.

"I think I made a mistake," Gwen said in a small voice.

Ellie patted her hand. "We all do at some point, Gwen. It's what we do when we figure out that the mistake's been made that matters."

"But how do I fix this one, if he's there, and I'm here? Colin, can you take me back?"

He shook his head. "I can't. I can only travel when the line's in danger, or when Ry calls for me."

"What's that?" Ellie asked, noticing the large parcel he'd placed on the table when he first came in. "Sorry. I'm not trying to change the subject."

Gwen laughed. "I know. But it looks like a book, and if it looks like a book, you need to know what it is. I get it."

Colin picked it up. "I had the family genealogy book rebound. The cover was showing a lot of wear, so I brought it to that place you recommended in the town center." Ellie nodded, and he handed it to her. "Check it out. It looks really good."

"I love this book," Ellie said with a small smile as she flipped through the pages. "Of course, I have a partiality to the late 1400s. It's nice to see some names that I—"

"Something wrong?" Colin asked, pouring himself a cup of coffee from the pot on the table. He glanced up, then immediately put the cup down and rushed to Ellie, who had gone white.

Gwen also came around the table, then searched the pages open in front of Ellie. Colin gasped, and still she didn't see anything that would make them so visibly upset.

"What am I missing?"

Ellie twisted in her chair and grasped Gwen's hand. "I'm so sorry, Gwen."

"Sorry for what?" she asked, a feeling of panic descending. She tried to read faster, but Colin placed his hand over their two.

"Here."

Reilly O'Malley, unknown relation to MacWilliam clan, d. 1485
Cause of death: wound infection
Burial: Traditional Irish burial, with clan honors

"But…no," she exclaimed, alarmed. "No. Because he can't die, right, because…because why, Colin?" She turned begging eyes on him. "Why? How?"

Colin was already dialing on his phone. "I don't know, Gwen. But I'll be damned if we don't find out. James? You need to get to Winifred's immediately…No, it's got nothing to do with the wedding. Just get here."

AROUND MIDDAY, AIDAN AND EMMA SHOWED UP WITH LUNCH. They joined the effort of trying to find out what happened to Reilly, but every lead fizzled out.

Gwen threw up her hands. "This will take forever, and we don't have that kind of time! We don't even have a date!"

"We know it happened sometime between early October and the end of December," James said patiently. "It has to be in these certificates somewhere."

"But he wasn't a member of the O'Malley clan in 1485, and if he was to have a certificate within the MacWilliam clan, he had to share in the last name," Aidan said heavily. "'Tis how we did things."

"This is going to take too long," Gwen repeated. She stood up. "There has to be something we can try that we haven't already!"

Wearily, James wondered aloud, "How does it work, Col, when you travel?"

"The Fates appear to Reilly, and then he sends out the call. Usually he heads first to wherever the clansmen he needs are at that time, then we make our way to where, or *when*, we're needed together."

"Can any of you go back in time and stop this?" Gwen asked as Aidan and Emma joined them.

"I already tried. But we can only go to where we're needed," Colin said softly. "The only one who can bend time to his will—"

"...is Reilly," Gwen finished for him, her voice hitching.

"I wish I could change it," Colin said brokenly. "I would do anything to change this."

An idea took shape in Gwen's mind and was out of her mouth before she knew what she was saying.

"*Anything*, Colin?"

He dragged his hands through his hair, his face tortured. "Anything."

"Excellent. I know what we need to do." Three heads swiveled to Gwen. "We need to get to Reilly's house. I'll explain on the way."

311

CHAPTER 16

"*N*o," Colin said flatly. "He'll rip me limb from limb."

Gwen clenched her jaw. "Well, as of this moment, he's *not alive* to do any such thing. So are you going to help me, or am I going to help myself?"

They barreled toward Dowth, a monolithic structure to the west of Reilly's cottage, in Reilly's Ford, which was the only vehicle big enough to hold everyone. She quickly changed into her medieval blue dress again, and, with the help of Colin and Aidan, strapped five blades from Reilly's chest to various parts of her person.

Colin took a hard left, then continued on at breakneck speed. "I'll not call those harpies, Gwen. They'll kill you just for sport. We try it my way."

"They're the only ones who can get us back there," she replied—and rather rationally, in her opinion.

Another hard turn had her gripping the dashboard.

Behind them, another conversation was happening over theirs.

"I find it grating that I'm wearing an O'Malley léine,"

Aidan grumbled from the backseat. "A travesty. If anyone should be in this monstrosity, it should be Gwendolyn."

"You're just upset that it's too big for you," James said with a snort. "You wouldn't go wrong with a few days in the gym, you know."

"So says the soft-bellied healer," Aidan shot back.

"Who saved your life. Twice," James reminded him blandly.

Colin hit the horn in warning as a sheep herder began moving his flock toward the road. "You're being unreasonable, Gwen."

"You've said yourself you don't have the power to open the damn rock," Gwen argued, tightening her hold as he swung around another turn. The sun dipped low into the sky. "We'll never make it by sunset."

"What does your cake look like?" Emma asked Ellie.

"Oh, it's gorgeous. It'll be three levels. The frosting will look like lace, to match my dress, and there will be red poppies all over it."

"Red poppies?" Emma asked, surprised.

Gwen could hear the grin in Ellie's voice as she responded shyly, "It's our flower."

"We're here," Colin said curtly, slamming the brakes.

The sun was almost touching the horizon as everyone piled out of the SUV. Ellie took Gwen's hand, and the group raced toward the nearly-abandoned site. The overgrowth obscured part of the entrance, and, as the shadows lengthened, they ran to the far side of the structure.

Aidan, James, and Colin were dressed in Reilly's spare léines, and Gwen smoothed the front of her dress nervously. This had to work.

It *had* to.

Colin shot her a disgruntled look, and she threw up her hands. "Fine!" she exclaimed. "You got us here in time. Now, please, *just get us there*."

They all fell silent as Colin cleared away the small vines and leaves to reveal a slim crack. "Stand close, because if this opens, it closes fast." He turned to Ellie and kissed her hard. "I love you."

"I love you too," she whispered. "Be safe. Oh! And take this." She handed him a paper bag. "For Claire."

Aidan kissed Emma, then leaned down and kissed her stomach. "I will return. We've unfinished business."

Her smile was wobbly. "We always seem to, in these situations."

Gwen waited impatiently. It was decided that Ellie and Emma would stay behind, mostly because they had no desire to travel back to the Middle Ages. James, laden with modern-day antibiotics, would be rendering aid to Reilly once they found him; Aidan would be of help in navigating and fighting their way through Ireland, if they ended up somewhere they didn't expect. Colin would bring them all there, and Gwen...

Well, she was going, no matter what, because this was Reilly. *Her* Reilly.

Colin placed both hands on either side of the small opening and closed his eyes. A charged moment passed. *"De réir an cumhacht ag an gods, ordaímse duit a oscailt le haghaidh dom, an Protector."*

Gwen held her breath.

Colin pushed against the rock again. More forcefully, he repeated, *"De réir an cumhacht ag an gods, ordaímse duit a oscailt le haghaidh dom, an Protector!"*

And when nothing happened, save a bird calling in the distance, James swore, and Colin's shoulders dropped.

"What happened when Reilly would do this?" Ellie ventured.

"It would open, then, when the last rays of the sun hit the chamber inside, it would bring him directly to the

MacWilliam lands," Colin muttered. "Looks like that was a gate for Reilly's use only."

"Well," Gwen said decisively, "now we do it *my* way."

She walked a few steps away from them and threw her head back. "You best show your cowardly faces, Fates! I have a big bone to pick with you!"

"Not the best way to get their attention, Gwen."

"I'm past caring, Colin. These Fates have done enough playing with people's lives." She narrowed her eyes. "They're not in charge of us."

"They rather are, I think," Aidan murmured.

She pointed at him. "Stop it. *They are not.* We are in charge of our destinies. And Reilly's destiny is not to die in some medieval castle from an infection that could probably be fixed with today's medicine."

"Probably," James agreed. "Let's just hope we can get to him."

"Oh, we're going to do more than hope," Gwen snarled. "Come out, you useless old hags, and live up to your fearsome reputation!"

If she felt any fear at all, Gwen ruthlessly buried it deep in her chest. She couldn't afford to be afraid. Reilly's life depended on it, and he'd lived too long—and they'd been through too much—for it to be over before it had even begun.

The air began to shimmer, and Colin instinctively put Ellie behind him. He then replaced himself with James, and ran out to Gwen.

"They don't scare me," she told him with a huff. "You hear that?" she called. "You don't scare me!"

"It makes one wonder what would scare you, Gwendolyn Allen."

Colin tried to tuck her behind him, but she sidestepped him and faced the Mother, who stood between them and the rest of the group. She glowed, the light surrounding her making it nearly impossible to see anything beyond.

"Send us back to him."

"Do you think you're brave, child, standing here and making demands?" the Mother asked curiously.

"Not brave. Just right. Send us back to get him."

"Such indignation," the Fate replied calmly. "I've already granted one request of yours. What motivation have I to grant another?"

"Motivation?" Gwen echoed, her anger rising. "How about one hundred and eighty-two years of being your minion? Isn't that enough? Or maybe, now that he isn't of any use to you, you think you can just throw him away and deny him the right you've given to all the other Protectors?"

"Ah. But you denied him. You took away that right when you rejected him as your soul mate. He is of no more concern to you."

"I did not reject him as my soul mate," Gwen retorted, standing her ground. The Mother glowed brighter, but Gwen refused to look away. "I was angry, and I was wrong. But I never said I rejected him."

"You did deny him, though. You chose to leave him. He chose to fight in a battle not his own. And therein lie your fates."

Gwen refused to believe that. "No. You asked if I was ready to go home, and I said yes. You did not ask if I was refusing to claim him back."

A second figure joined the Mother, and Gwen felt her alarm grow. The Crone's staff loomed, and the Fate herself seemed larger than the last time Gwen saw her.

"You are quite desperate, summoning us," the Crone snapped.

"Bold," the Mother corrected. "I believe her to be bold."

Gwen folded her arms. "Desperate, bold, call it what you will. But you owe him more than what you've given him."

The Crone glowered. "You are but a speck in time. Your

life will happen and end in a fraction of the Universe's existence."

Gwen jumped on that like a lifeline. "Yes! Exactly! And that's why it shouldn't matter to you that someone is pulled out of their time, such as Aidan was. Or that another man, who dedicated what tiny slice of time is allotted to him within this Universe to *you*, is spared from an unnecessary death."

The Crone opened her mouth, then paused.

The Mother smiled. "What a wise point you've made, Gwendolyn. Our young warrior did indeed give his time in this world to us."

The Crone leaned heavily on her staff. "You understand that we could end your life right here."

"I do."

"And yet you still are determined to make demands to spare his life, regardless of your own?"

"I am."

A third figure materialized, and the land around them lit up so brightly, Gwen had to cover her eyes; even then, the light penetrated her hands and eyelids.

"She's proven herself dedicated to her mate," the Maiden's voice carried.

"Only a true soul mate can go to him," the Mother added.

Gwen stood as tall as she could. "I am Reilly's soul mate. And he is mine."

"We will send you back to him," the Crone said decisively. "We will send you with your three warriors here. But you have only three hours in which to find him. At the end of those hours, you all must be with him if he is to return to this time."

"Done," came a faraway voice from behind the Fates. Gwen couldn't be sure, but she suspected it was Colin.

And Gwen felt the Crone's staff shake the ground.

~

His time had finally come.

Though he wished to be allowed a natural death, Reilly thought it would be nice to die of old age rather than a dirty sword through the side. But, he reasoned, beggars couldn't be choosers. When one's time was up...well, 'twas up.

And he hadn't anything to live for, anyway. He lived an unnaturally long life. He knew joy and pain. His was a life well-lived, for the most part. As long as Gwen was safe... Colin would ensure it, he knew it deep in his bones.

His breath shallow, he tried to lift his head. He recognized Bri's voice as she urged him to lay back. He blinked his eyes open. He may be dying, but his mind was still alert. Foggy from pain, to be sure, but he was not dead yet.

It took a moment to focus his gaze. "Bri."

"I'm here, Ry. I'm right here. I won't leave." Her voice, strained with tears, sounded faraway.

Well, he thought. *That's probably not the best sign.*

He tried to take a deeper breath, but his lungs seized and he began coughing violently. She made sounds of despair, placing her hands over his oblique muscles. "Stop, stop, you're making the blood loss worse! Oh, Reilly, please..."

He covered her hands with his, and dimly realized hers were covered with blood.

His blood.

"Be happy," he whispered.

She sobbed over him. "Reilly, can you try to move time? I'll go with you. We can get you to James, to a hospital. They can help you."

He shook his head, the motion making him feel ill. "Nay, lass, my time is here. Leave a message for her to find, please."

Bri sobbed, but nodded her head.

"Tell her I will always love her. And that I'm sorry."

Bri smoothed his hair back from his forehead. "It's not supposed to end like this, Reilly O'Malley. You, more than any of us, deserve a happy ever after."

He smiled a little at that and closed his eyes. "Maybe next time, Bri." The pain was becoming more intense, and he licked his lips. Words wouldn't fall from his tongue as well as he'd like them to. "Want to…say goodbye to…everyone."

Bri bolted up from his side, her sobs in the distant part of his mind, and for a moment, he hovered somewhere between life and death.

"Jesus, Reilly, what a mess you're in."

Reilly tried to open his eyes, but his side was on fire, and his head was going to explode. He couldn't get enough air. But he would've sworn that was James's voice.

A cool touch to his forehead gave him such comfort that he wanted to weep.

"He's so cold." Gwen's frightened voice filtered through the darkness that threatened to swallow him whole. "Please, Ry. Please hang on."

Was this heaven? he wondered in amazement.

"He looks like hell," Aidan's voice said bluntly.

Definitely not heaven.

But Gwen wouldn't be in hell, would she?

"I've got the IV going. Colin and Aidan, hold him down. I've got to stitch him up as fast as possible so we can move him."

James again. He wanted to open his eyes, tell them that they were too late. But instead, he took a final breath, and relaxed into the hands that cradled his face.

• • •

Brianagh stepped outside of Reilly's bedchamber. Nioclas met her in the hallway, looking grim.

"He's going to die," she said bluntly, though her voice wobbled.

Nioclas nodded, his mouth tightening.

"His fever has worsened and both wounds are infected." She dabbed the corners of her eyes with her sleeve. "His breathing is labored. It won't be long now."

Nioclas held open his arms, and Bri fell into them, pressing her face into his chest, muffling her words. "He deserves so much more than this. He's given so much of himself to everyone else...and he's had nothing in return."

"I'll bury him with full MacWilliam honors," Nioclas said, his voice hoarse. "We will honor him with all we have."

"It's all we can do now," she whispered. "He's asked for everyone, to say goodbye."

Claire came down the hall, a tray in her hands. Her own face was tear-stained, her eyes puffy from crying. "Is he better?" she asked, though they all knew the answer.

Brianagh drew her daughter into their embrace. "It's time to say our final goodbyes."

Claire shook her head, her eyes shiny. "I never thought this day would come."

Brianagh closed her eyes against the onslaught of fresh tears. *Neither did I.*

Nick kissed the top of Bri's head. "Aye." He held her for a moment longer, then took her hand. "Come, loves. We shall grieve together." To the guards outside the room, he said, "Leave us."

Once they'd left, he opened the door, and together, they stepped inside.

Claire's tray fell with a clatter. The room was empty, save a single jar of Nutella atop a brown paper bag.

Brianagh collapsed. "They found him," she sobbed.

Claire sank to her knees and clutched her mother. Nioclas held them both, and sent a prayer of gratitude heavenward.

∾

My eyes feel like sandpaper.

Swiftly following that thought came another: *I'm on fire.*

Blinking slowly, he tried to open his eyes, but they were too heavy. A cup materialized at his lips, offering cool water.

It was the most delicious thing he ever tasted.

He drank slowly as he came into consciousness. He kept his eyes closed, for opening them was too much effort, and he instead concentrated on his surroundings. He heard naught but the even breathing of the person administering the water.

He'd know her smell anywhere, in any time.

He finally opened his eyes, and met hers, though his vision was somewhat blurred. The soft green he'd fallen in love with all those years ago stared back at him.

"I thought," he croaked slowly, "I heard the sounds of a lady in distress," he croaked. He cleared his throat.

"Well," she said, her voice catching, "it wasn't me. *I* don't need to be saved."

He cleared his throat. "I'm sorry."

She burst into tears.

He attempted to sit up, but a searing pain across his side and stomach made him gasp and freeze in place. Still teary, Gwen helped him to lie back down, and he realized a few things simultaneously: 1) He was in his own bedchamber in his little cottage; 2) Gwen was wearing modern-day clothes; and 3) They were not alone.

"You were sliced," she said without preamble, wiping the tears from her cheeks.

"I remember," he groaned, the battle flooding back to him. He hadn't pulled his sword from the body of his last opponent fast enough; two of the dead man's clansmen had attacked him.

He was groggy and had many questions, but the one that pushed to the forefront was, "How am I here?"

She smoothed his hair. "Don't worry about the details. There will be plenty of time for that later. James is going to give you more medicine right now."

"For what?" Reilly asked, wishing desperately to sit up, to be in command.

James's voice came from somewhere behind him. "Both

wounds were severely infected. No major arteries were hit, but you lost a lot of blood. Your fever is going down. You're lucid again."

He tried to shift, but the pain nearly rendered him unconscious. The fire on his stomach and back was going to burn him alive.

"Just a scrape," he wheezed. Why was everything so blurry? "No medicine necessary."

She shook her head, dislodging more tears. "No, Reilly, not this time. Without it, you'll die."

"Can't. They're not done with me yet."

Colin's face swam into view. "Mate...we're not just saying this. We *know* you'll die. You already did once."

Reilly felt the absolute certainty of the words sink into his mind. Colin wouldn't say it if it wasn't true.

Memories assaulted him in rapid order: The feeling of the sword slicing through him; the transport from the MacWilliam courtyard to a bedchamber. Nick grimly telling him the injury was severe. Brianagh sobbing at his bedside.

The sounds of James and Gwen.

Gwen rested her cool forehead against his hot, sweaty one. "Please don't fight us," she whispered.

"James?" Reilly asked uncertainly.

"Right here, cousin. Antibiotics. If you'll let me, I'll set up an IV. Easier that way, and we can do it now that you're not thrashing about."

He nodded wearily. "I'm so tired."

"Sleep," Gwen murmured, gently climbing into the bed next to him.

"Stay," he mumbled.

As he slipped back into a dreamless sleep, he could've sworn he heard her whisper, "Forever."

∾

A WEEK LATER, GWEN SAT IN THE ARMCHAIR IN HIS BEDCHAMBER, serenely reading the comics.

"No one actually reads a newspaper anymore. I've it on good authority that the internet has all that," he grumbled.

She merely smiled. "Rubbish."

"Instead of reading that drivel, why don't you explain to me how you traveled back to me?"

The first day he was home, he woke up only once. Over the last few days, he'd been improving, but he was still groggy, and his mind was not nearly as sharp as it usually was.

He'd been asking her the same question every day. At first, she told him she'd tell him later. Then she moved on to avoidance. And lately, she would flat-out ignore him.

But today? Today, he would have answers.

"Damn it, Gwendolyn, why can't you travel to St. Croix, like every other trust fund baby?"

She placed the paper down and joined him on the bed. Slowly, she brushed her lips against his and smiled. "Because I'm not *like* every other trust fund baby." She lovingly caressed her fingers over his cheeks. "Besides, I think you know me by now. I prefer to hang out in more rustic locations."

He smiled, but it didn't reach his eyes.

"What is it?" she asked, immediately concerned. Her eyes roamed his face. "Are you in pain?"

He shook his head, loving how her hands never left his face. He leaned into her a little more. "I've much to atone for, lass." She tried shushing him, but he covered her hands with his own to still her, and continued gravely, "The night you came to me, at Brianagh's castle…"

Gwen's lips turned downward slightly, but she stayed silent.

Reilly cleared his throat, shame creeping into his voice. "I told you that you couldn't see to my needs. That I wanted someone—anyone—else."

"It's in the past," she replied softly. "I've forgiven you for it."

"And I'm grateful for it, Gwendolyn. But I must apologize. I said the words in anger, trying to convince myself that you and I should never be together. I said them to wound your heart enough so that you'd leave me to my personal hell." He rubbed his thumb in a circle over the sensitive part of her hand between her thumb and forefinger, a wash of emotion overcoming him. "Yet, you saved me."

"We *all* saved you."

He slanted her a look and pursed his lips. "You rescued me in more ways than one."

"How many more rescues do you think you'll need?" she asked, a smile hovering at her lips.

"How many do I get?"

She leaned closer and placed her mouth at his ear. "As many as you need."

He laughed, delight spreading as she parried his own words back to him. "Never change, love." Swiftly, he changed the subject, hoping her good mood would encourage her to speak freely at last. "Tell me, please. I need to know, Gwendolyn. How did you get there? The line wasn't in danger, so Colin couldn't have brought you on his own."

She pulled back and patted his hand. "We can talk about the details later."

"Now."

"Later," she insisted. He glared at her until she capitulated. "Okay, fine. I did something."

He raised an eyebrow.

"Don't be mad."

"Never a good start to a confession, for certain."

She closed her eyes and took a deep breath, then rushed

the words out. "Colin-told-me-how-to-get-the-Fates-to-come-to-me-and-I-made-them-send-us-to-you-and-don't-yell-at-me-because-I-would-do-it-again!"

His jaw set, albeit slowly. His eyes hardened, and his body stiffened. He carefully pulled his hand away from hers, then, without moving his eyes from hers, he bellowed, "Oooooo'Rourrrrrrrrrrke!"

"Oh, he's not here," she rushed on. "He figured you would get the story from me today, so he took Ellie and left."

"Coward. Since I can't kill him, that leaves you."

"You won't," she whispered, taking his hand again.

He kept it stiff, thoroughly angry with her. "I might. What the hell were you thinking, Gwendolyn? The Fates could've killed you! Easily ended your life, simply by showing themselves in all their power!"

"Reilly. Calm down. If I didn't go back, you would die. In fact, you *did* die!"

That stopped him cold. "What?" He knew he had been close to death, but...

"It's true. We saw it in Colin's family genealogy book. And I refused to lose you, so I had to change it. The only ones who could get me to you were the Fates. And if my life was the price to pay for yours, I'd gladly pay it over and over again."

He closed his eyes, images of all the things that could've happened to her flashing in his mind. "The risk wasn't worth it, Gwendolyn."

She stood and pressed her hands into her hips, and he was struck by her fierceness. She was an avenging angel, a fairy sprite, a fiery goddess in her own right.

And he was so in love with her, he could barely see straight.

"It *was* worth it, Reilly. And like I said, I'd do it again, and again, and again. Because *you're* worth it. I love you. I will *always* love you. Forever. *Trí na haoiseanna thar am mo ghrá, mo Reilly.*"

He grinned. "Snooping about in my bedchamber, lass?"

She snuggled in. "I saw the words on the furniture in my room the day I got back here. And I had a hunch, so I went into your room and found the rest. Colin put the phrase together for me."

"I should've told you. I should've told you from the moment I met you."

"We both should've done things differently, but we cannot change the past. No more regrets, Ry. Just you, and me, and a good life. We can start over."

"I don't want to start over," he murmured, stroking her hair. "I've too many memories of your sweet self in my life."

"I love you," she whispered.

He held out his hand, and cautiously, she placed her own in it. He pulled her slowly, inexorably, up his body, until she was merely an inch from him. "You."

Her face softened.

"You, Gwendolyn Allen, are a fierce and brave warrior. I love you, I love your determination and your stubbornness. I love your smiles and your light."

He drew her face down until he was breathing her air. "I love you with everything I am, was, and will be. And I love you for loving all of me."

"You're stuck with me for eternity, you know," she whispered. "I claimed you. To the Fates."

"I am indeed a lucky man," he whispered, wiping the tears from her cheeks with his thumbs. "It's over, you know."

At her confused look, he added, "My days of time traveling."

"Will you miss the adventure of it?" she asked, resting her forehead on his and releasing a shuddering breath.

"I think that my greatest adventure starts now," he replied honestly.

She pulled back and her eyes searched his. And, instead of saying anything, she did, in his opinion, the most sensible thing she'd ever done in their long acquaintance.

She kissed him.

CHAPTER 17

One Month Later

Gwen gently floated Ellie's veil over her shoulders, and her eyes shimmered with tears. "Oh, Eleanor."

Ellie blinked rapidly, her own eyes misty, and she grabbed Gwen's hands in her own. "I don't know what to do with all this happiness inside of me!"

Gwen sniffed. "I'm so happy for you. And Colin's out there, wearing a hole in the floor, waiting for you to come out, so we'd better get a move on."

Colin and Ellie insisted on pushing out their ceremony and reception until Reilly was recovered. Reilly protested, but the collective power of Colin, Ellie, Aidan, Emma, James, and Gwen won out.

It also helped that Colin admitted to Reilly that he and Ellie already married in a short and sweet ceremony in the States. It was a small courthouse affair, just what Ellie always wanted. Only Colin's parents, brother, and Winifred attended.

Ellie's dream day, she later confided to Gwen.

But today was the wedding day Winifred planned, and Ellie…

Ellie was radiant.

Both women turned, and Winnie's face softened into a genuine smile. "Oh, girls. You have something special, do you know that? All these years of friendship between you. You've seen ups and downs and all arounds, and here you stand, together. My girls."

Ellie waved her hand in front of her eyes, trying to dry the tears before they fell.

"Waterproof mascara," Gwen reminded her, sniffing a little.

"Puffy eyes and nose," Ellie shot back with a sniffle of her own.

Winifred enveloped Ellie in a hug. "This is all I've ever wanted for you, my love."

Gwen discreetly stepped out of the room and quietly closed the door. She turned and caught sight of a man watching her from a few steps away.

He was enormous, and dressed all in black. A different black from the first time she saw him; back then, it was a black leather jacket, and today that was replaced with a tuxedo jacket. Instead of jeans, the bottom of a léine, in O'Malley colors, wrapped about his waist; his legs were bare, and in place of scuffed work boots were formal, shined shoes.

"That dress is loads better than that orange disaster."

His voice, gravelly and low, had the same effect on her now as it did then. Her insides pooled, and she could only be grateful that they belonged to each other.

"It wasn't orange. It was shrimp."

"It was ugly."

She laughed as he drew her into his arms. "It most certainly was that."

"But this…I admit to not liking you in the O'Rourke léine." He fingered the small ribbon in the O'Rourke colors under her chest, that matched his léine. "You should only be in the O'Malley one."

She went up on her tiptoes and tugged him down so her mouth was at her ear. "I'm in O'Malley colors...under the O'Rourke dress."

He groaned and crushed his mouth to hers. She laughed into him, and he pulled back with a mock-frown. "Feisty wench."

"Always."

The door opened, and the two looked at Winifred, who smiled indulgently when seeing them in each other's arms. "We're ready."

~

"Drinking away your troubles, mates?"

Reilly grimaced as Aidan joined them at the table, but 'twas more of a habit than a reaction. Despite the lack of blood between them, they still annoyed each other as only brothers could. It was a relationship for which Reilly was profoundly grateful, though he'd never admit to such out loud.

He suspected Aidan felt the same. But he'd cut off his sword arm before asking him to admit to such drivel.

"He's under strict orders not to drink," James intoned. "It would interact with the pain meds."

"Haven't taken any," Reilly shot back.

James blinked. "For how long?"

Instead of answering, Reilly lifted his glass in James's direction and took a sip. It had been a long month of recovery, but the time passed so much faster with Gwen as his nurse. Just the thought brought a smile to his face.

He still had a long road ahead of him, but 'twas perhaps one he could take his time following. After all, he hadn't anywhere to be, except in the arms of his love.

Aidan flipped the nearest chair around and straddled it,

then signaled to a server for a new round of drinks before continuing, "So, since the patient can drink, are we commiserating on Colin's shackles, or are we toasting his intelligence for marrying such a wonder?"

All three men swung their gazes to Colin, who was gazing with adoration at his new bride as they swayed slowly to the music.

"Toasting, of course," James replied with a smile. "Look how happy he is."

"Bloke could float off the floor in his Doc Martens at this point," Reilly agreed. He signaled, a server placed three tumblers in front of the men. They raised their glasses toward Colin. He happened to look up at them, and the grin on his face couldn't help but be returned threefold.

"Poor bastard," James murmured, smile firmly in place.

"He's done for," Reilly readily agreed.

"Pathetic," Aidan snickered, his eyes glinting in amusement.

The song changed, and the couple in question headed straight for their table.

"You gentlemen all look so handsome in your tuxes," Ellie exclaimed, her cheeks a pretty pink. "Aidan, the restaurant is stunning. Thank you for letting us use it with such short notice. I've no idea how you managed to make it so magical!"

"I stepped aside and allowed your aunt to hire a decorator," he deadpanned.

"Surely a smart decision," Emma said, sliding into the chair next to him. She gave him a small smile. "Have I told you how amazing you look tonight?"

Smiling at them, Ellie turned to Reilly. "Where's Gwen?"

Reilly glanced pointedly at the empty seat next to him. "Not here?"

She laughed. "I meant has she returned from dealing with her parents?"

Reilly frowned. "I didn't realize she was."

Colin placed a hand on his shoulder. "They were trying to set her up with one of my coworkers, last I saw of them."

Reilly frowned. "She wanted to wait until after the ceremony to tell them about us. That, and I need to speak with her sire."

Ellie bit her lip and pointed. "She's over there, and she doesn't look very happy."

All four pair of protective male eyes swung to Gwen, who stood alone, her arms wrapped around her middle. Her light green eyes watched as her parents exited the restaurant.

"You think O'Malley is the one to make her happy?" Aidan asked, stroking his chin.

"Surely not," Colin agreed. "He's always so moody."

"Foul-tempered," Aidan agreed.

"Don't forget high-handed," James put in.

Ellie rolled her eyes. "Honestly, gentlemen, he's not all of those things!"

"Ignore these idiots, Eleanor, for I vow they're struck dumb by your beauty, and are therefore running their mouths without thought, as per usual. Love looks wonderful on you," Reilly added, leaning over to kiss her cheek.

Ellie's radiant smile grew as she carefully pulled him in close for a hug. "You are the sweetest man, Reilly."

"Don't tell anyone," he whispered. He straightened and smoothed his hand over his tux jacket. "Watch how 'tis done, lads."

"Finally decided to woo her?" James asked with a snicker.

"We'll have to speak with her about her life choices," Aidan said with a sigh. "Clearly, if she's contemplating a lifetime with you, she needs an intervention."

Reilly observed his love for a moment. Her fiery copper curls were placed artfully around the top of her head, leaving her long, slender neck exposed. Reilly could see her pulse beating rapidly against her translucent skin. The long, emerald-green bridesmaid gown highlighted her slim waist, and except for that blasted piece of O'Rourke color on her, it complemented her well. She was magnificent, and if her parents made her cry, they would feel the full wrath of Reilly O'Malley.

Pushing his wayward thoughts aside, the crowd parted easily for him.

She saw him coming, and she blinked rapidly. "Ry! Are they doing the cake cutting yet? I wasn't sure when..." She trailed off as he wordlessly pulled her onto the dance floor. "Okay, so we're dancing."

Silently, he pulled her close, and she willingly went into his arms, laying her head against his chest. She let out an enormous sigh, and simply let him hold her.

"Go slow," she whispered, craning her neck to look up at him. "I don't want to hurt you."

A seductive smile crossed his lips. "My stitches are out, as you well know."

Gwen blushed a delightful shade of crimson, and Reilly's laugh rumbled in his chest.

Days after he'd gotten her in his bed, she'd put a stop to all their bed play after having to give James a story about his having been in the kitchen and reaching for something in a high cabinet for her.

That was most definitely *not* how he tore his stitches.

James reassured a very worried Gwen that such things happened all the time. The moment her attention was diverted, though, James gave Reilly an *are-you-kidding-me?* look. Reilly just shrugged.

If he could have Gwen in his bed every moment for all time, he'd gladly tear his stitches over and over again.

"What happened with your parents?"

Gwen, smart lass, didn't pretend to misunderstand. "The

good news is, they're not upset that I called it off with Anthony. But the bad news is they gave my number out to three men here."

"Did they?" Reilly growled.

She patted his chest as though he was a wild animal in need of comfort. "Yes. But put your hackles down. I set them straight."

"Oh?"

"I told them about us," she replied softly. When he tensed in her arms, she leaned up on her tiptoes and pulled him toward her. She planted a soft kiss on his mouth, and he let her do what she wanted to his lips. She pulled back. "They were surprised and immediately demanded to know the balance of your bank accounts. They promised to find out."

He relaxed fractionally. "'Tis easily given."

"Reilly, no. It's none of their business. It's none of my business."

"They'll want a pre-nup."

She blinked. "Did you overhear us?"

He chuckled. "Nay. But I've known them for years, lass, and all they've ever known is that I'm a simple woodworker."

"You are much more than that," she protested, a small smile playing at her lips.

He gave her a tender smile. "Aye. And they're not to worry. I can provide for you quite comfortably."

She frowned. "I can provide for myself, you know. I've got investments all over the place, and I'm involved with four different venture capitalists who have strong portfolios—"

He leaned into her ear and whispered, "Your money is your money. But my money is ours."

He could almost feel her roll her eyes, and he chuckled.

"I have plenty for us both," she insisted. "You don't have to do that. I don't care that I have more than you, and you better not pull that Neanderthal thought process that the man has to make more—"

He sighed. "Gwen."

"What?"

He stopped dancing and looked her in the eye. "I've thrice your trust fund to my name."

Her mouth dropped open. "Thrice?"

"Thrice."

Her mouth worked for a moment. He took advantage of her silence and began dancing with her again.

"You never told me!" she finally exclaimed.

"Because it doesn't matter. It never has."

She heaved a great sigh, making him smile. He loved that he could surprise her, especially when she thought she knew everything there was to know.

"You're right. But still."

He stopped dancing and stepped back, his hands rubbing circles on her bare arms. "Did you just say I was right?"

She pursed her lips at him in response.

"I'll take that as confirmation," he declared. His eyes softened. "Praise the saints that you had enough sense to never fully let go of me, Gwen. It took me far too long for my brain to accept my own heart's truth."

"Are you being romantic?" she teased, her eyes twinkling. "I mean, keep going. Seriously. Feel free to continue."

He huffed out a laugh. "Cheeky lass."

"Must be the wedding. Weddings make everyone sentimental," she laughed.

He pulled her in close again, relishing the feel of her. He wrapped one arm around her waist and slid his other hand down her arm, then caught her fingers in his. He brought her hand against his chest.

"I love you, Gwendolyn Allen."

She melted into him, and he felt a love so overwhelming, it nearly knocked him to the floor.

"I love you too, Reilly O'Malley." She kept her head against his chest and nuzzled him with her nose. "Now, this might be the wedding talking, or maybe it's just you in this tux-slash-kilt thing you've got going on, but I was wondering if you'd maybe want to make us a permanent thing."

He stumbled, nearly taking her out. "What?"

She righted his bowtie. "Yeah. You and me. We're already bound by destiny and fate and all the rest. You know. Soul mates. So…why not?"

He stood stock-still, stunned. "Are you…"

"Proposing to you?" She nodded, then chewed her lip thoughtfully. "I am, though my original speech had a lot more flowery medieval language."

"Your original speech? You've been planning this?"

He felt winded; he planned a romantic proposal for *her*. He wanted to take her back to Boston, where they met all those years ago. To the hotel, to the bar, where he first realized she was more than just a one-night stand. He wanted to say all the things that he knew then but thought he could never have.

"See, nothing I ever do goes to plan," she explained with a heavy sigh. "So I figured I'd give this one a try. But I don't like the way it sounds, so I'm actually going to go with my original plan."

"Oh?" he managed.

"Yep. Come on."

"I'd hoped to do this for *you!*" he protested. "Gwen, wait—"

"Oh, hush *up*, Reilly," she exclaimed, leading him off the dance floor toward their table. Colin and Ellie sat with Aidan, Emma, and James.

"Do you have it?" she asked without preamble.

The entire table fell absolutely silent. Colin nodded, reaching inside his own jacket. He withdrew a very old, yellowed piece of parchment and handed it to her.

She pushed Reilly into his chair, then got on her knees in between his own.

Reilly folded his arms, a stern look on his face. He didn't like this. He was supposed to ask Gwen. 'Twas *his* privilege to ask for her hand for the rest of his days. "Nay, Gwendolyn, I—"

Gwen halted his words when she flicked her eyes up to his. They were clear and bright, and held such beauty, he was rendered speechless, for her eyes were truly a window to her pure soul.

"I wrote this while James was stitching you up, back at Brianagh's. I left it there, in a paper bag, with instructions for Claire to put it in a loose stone in her chamber, for me to recover in the future." She smiled at Colin. "Colin got it for me, the day I told you how we got to you. Though Claire, bless her, placed it in a stone box so it wouldn't deteriorate."

"Ah. So that's where you hid while Gwen told me of your poor decisions," Reilly intoned to Colin, shooting him a dark look.

Colin flashed him a grin. Gwen looked down at her paper and began to read.

"You are my everything. You are my forever. We're opposites in so many ways, but you make me a better woman, and I want to spend the rest of my life making you smile."

Reilly gaped at her as his brain registered two things simultaneously. She was really, truly proposing to him...and she was doing so in medieval Gaelic.

"I vow, if you accept my hand, that I will sass you and make you grumble. I will go to the bakery instead of burning down your kitchen. And I will give you—" she pointed at a word, and Aidan gave her the pronunciation before she continued, "—bairns to add to our own clan." She slowly folded the paper, and she raised her eyes, raw with vulnerability. In English, she whispered, "Please do me the honor of becoming my husband."

He felt his eyes prick with an unfamiliar sensation. He

nodded, once, and pulled her into his lap. He lightly kissed her jaw, her cheeks, her eyes; finally, he gently kissed her lips.

"Aye, lass. It will always be *aye*."

❧

THE END

*R*eilly stood outside his and Gwen's cottage, the snow falling gently around him. He felt a detached sort of anger, but no cold.

"Why do you disturb me?"

"You have a choice to make," the Maiden replied gently, "as do all Protectors who have claimed their mate."

He leveled the three women in front of him with a hard stare. "I think you know what my choice is."

The Mother sighed. "Aye, we expected so. I believe our decision, then, was a wise one."

"We usually do make wise decisions," the Maiden added mildly.

The Crone hobbled forward. "You've been a good servant, as good as a human can be. And we agree: the time for someone new is upon us."

"Someone new," he repeated, without inflection. "Are warriors so common, then, that 'tis easy enough to pluck another lad from his home and family with a threat to those he loves? Force him to watch all around him die, knowing he can never follow them wherever they go from this earth?"

"*Common* is hardly a word I'd use to describe you. And,

unlike many of your race, we Fates learn from our mistakes," the Crone replied in a lofty tone. "You weren't given much of a choice. You agreed, but under…"

"Duress?" Reilly supplied sardonically.

The Crone slanted him a look. "Different circumstances. You may choose to stay on as a Protector, or you may walk away. The choice is yours, as it is every Protector who's found his mate."

He paused. He'd asked the question thousands of times in his life, but they'd never given him a clear answer. Reilly looked each one in the eye.

"What have I been protecting all this time? The O'Rourkes, of course. But why?"

The Maiden smiled. "Isn't it obvious?"

"Not to me."

"You are protecting us," the Mother said. "We only continue to exist because the legends are kept alive. The O'Rourkes are the keepers of our legend."

He digested that for a moment. "Is that the whole truth?"

"Enough of it."

"If I stop, what will happen to you?"

"We will continue on. But how *well* we continue on will be largely up to you, if you choose to teach."

"Teach what?"

"Your replacement."

Reilly gaped. "You're serious? Did you force him into it?"

The Crone chortled. "Another mistake we have certainly learned from. Our new replacement agreed using naught but your favorite thing…free will. All facets of this have been explained, analyzed, and discussed. The choice was made with all possible knowledge given beforehand, and this time, 'twas not a young child to whom these powers are given."

"I can't wait to see who you've convinced to take my place. I find it difficult to believe that a man could understand everything involved, without experiencing it."

"A *man*," the Crone cackled in amusement. "Have you not been listening, O'Malley? As we've been saying...we learn from our mistakes."

She slammed her staff into the ground, and a fourth figure emerged as the fog cleared.

"Nay," he breathed, icy tendrils of dread snaking down his spine.

"Hello, Cousin." Claire MacWilliam smiled at him confidently. "I think you'll find me a *most* willing student."

~

TO BE CONTINUED...

A NOTE FROM THE AUTHOR

THANK YOU SO MUCH FOR READING AND SUPPORTING AN INDIE AUTHOR!

I hope you enjoyed *Falling Through Time.* If so, please consider writing a quick review wherever you purchased this copy. Every review is important to authors, and helps readers find us so we can continue writing the stories you enjoy.

Please join my mailing list for updates, news, and general good times. (No spamming, ever.)
    www.nancyscanlonbooks.com

Drop me a note — reader email feeds the soul!
    nancy@nancyscanlonbooks.com

FALLING THROUGH TIME

(MISTS OF FATE BOOK FOUR)

Gwendolyn Allen is done waiting.

Reilly O'Malley waited too long.

When the Fates step out, can love step in?

ABOUT THE AUTHOR

Nancy Scanlon is the author of the Mists of Fate series. When she's not writing, she spends her days parenting two kids, playing with her two huge lapdogs, and trying to get her husband to laugh at corny jokes. She adores all things misty, caffeinated, chocolate, and grammatically correct.

Made in United States
Troutdale, OR
11/22/2023